RELENTLESS

RELENTLESS

THE DOMINION TRILOGY: BOOK 1

ROBIN PARRISH

BETHANY HOUSE PUBLISHERS

Minneapolis, Minnesota

Published by Bethany House Publishers
11400 Hampshire Avenue South
Bloomington, Minnesota 55438

Bethany House Publishers is a division of
Baker Publishing Group, Grand Rapids, Michigan.

Printed in the United States of America

ISBN-13: 978-0-7642-0221-6
ISBN-10: 0-7642-0221-9

Library of Congress Cataloging-in-Publication Data

Parrish, Robin.
    Relentless / Robin Parrish.
        p.   cm. — (The Dominion trilogy ; 1)
      ISBN 0-7642-0221-9 (alk. paper)
    1. Doppelgängers—Fiction. 2. Psychic ability—Fiction. 3. Conspiracies—
Fiction. 4. Prophecies—Fiction. 5. Supernatural—Fiction. I. Title. II. Series:
Parrish, Robin. Dominion trilogy ; 1.

    PS3616.A7684R45   2006
    813'.6—dc22   2006011317

**Dedicated to the memory of
Michael Wayland Parrish**

*You would have loved this story, Dad.
I miss you.*

PROLOGUE

Somewhere in the world, an unbearable cry pierced the darkness.

It was the sound of pain.

The sound of birth.

And the sound of death.

It was a sound that would change *everything* . . .

1

Los Angeles, California
Thirty Years Later

Collin Boyd stepped off the Metro bus on his way to work, and across the street he saw *himself* strolling down the sidewalk.

A stubborn but warm February rain was pouring hard across the concrete canyons of downtown. His foot had landed ankle-deep in a drainage puddle, and his half-broken umbrella wasn't extending as it should. But the umbrella, which had rarely seen use, quickly fell out of his hands and he no longer noticed the rain. His eyes were fixed, his head turning slowly to follow the other man down the opposite side of the street.

It wasn't until someone shouted from behind that he finally got his legs moving again.

The man he watched with rapt attention weaved his way casually through the crowd, headed in the direction of Collin's workplace. He wasn't a man who merely *resembled* Collin. He *was* him. The same face, the same body, the same walk. He wore the clothes and raincoat Collin had put on that morning. He carried Collin's briefcase.

It was only then that Collin noticed he no longer *had* his briefcase. When had he seen it last? On the bus? Before that? He'd been so groggy all morning, he couldn't place it.

And what was that on the man's wrist? Collin clenched a hand around his own wrist, feeling for what was missing.

He's wearing Granddad's bracelet . . .

That line of thought was gone once the other man began fussing with the piece of unruly hair up front that Collin could never seem to keep in place.

This impostor wasn't a twin or duplicate. He was *him*, in every way. Every look, every gesture, every expression. And he was walking to work in the rain, under L.A.'s towering skyscrapers, brushing shoulders with countless citizens and tourists.

As if everything were exactly as it should be.

Without ever deciding to, Collin moved his legs. He crossed the bustling downtown street, just aware enough of the cars, buses, and bicycles zipping by to dodge them. But his eyes remained on the man who looked like him, who checked his watch—*No, that's my watch*, he reminded himself—and then picked up his pace, apparently realizing he was about to be late for work.

Late for my work, Collin stupidly thought again, his mind spinning. This was a lie. It had to be a lie.

A twisted joke.

But then, who would play such a prank? He hadn't had any close friends since childhood, and even then he knew that his "friends" had been forced to play with him by the orphanage staff. He couldn't think of a single acquaintance he had now who had anything resembling a sense of humor.

Grant increased his own speed, tailing his doppelganger from about fifteen paces behind. The impossibility of the situation seemed like an absurd thing to think about right now as he spied on himself walking to work in the rain, yet nothing else entered his mind.

It couldn't be impossible if he was looking right at it.

What am I supposed to say if I catch up to him?

Maybe he's my clone. Are they cloning humans yet? Eh, I don't know.

He's living my life. He's walking in my shoes on his way to my job, living my life.

Did he steal my life?

Maybe I'm sitting somewhere in a padded room right now. "Careful there, honey," the kind nurse is saying to my slack-jawed, vacant expression. "You're drooling all over your straitjacket . . ."

Collin's adrenaline surged, and the confusion of the moment was overpowered by a rising agitation.

The other man approached a street corner, and even though the light on the other side was blinking DON'T WALK, he crossed anyway, nearly jogging.

Collin broke into a run and hit the crosswalk full bore. He was half-way across, his eyes still following his quarry, when a blaring horn filled his ears, followed by the metallic screech of brakes. He barely managed to jump backward a few feet before a Metro bus filled the space where he'd just been standing. The angry driver shouted a few choice phrases in Collin's direction, followed by an emphatic hand gesture.

Collin gave a dazed wave. As the bus chugged slowly along, passing within inches of his face, his stunned reflection gazed back at him in the glass windows as they passed by.

He didn't recognize the man in the glass.

Time seemed to shudder. The sounds of vehicles, store owners, tourists, businesspeople, and even planes flying overhead all fell away, until he heard nothing but the rush of blood surging past his ears and pounding in his temples. There was nothing wrong with his eyes, but he couldn't seem to get them to focus. And he felt a sharp pain in his stomach, as if he might vomit.

Somehow he stumbled his way across the street and managed to hold on to his breakfast—*Did I have breakfast?*—and stopped to rest on the sidewalk, the chase erased from his thoughts.

The rain had stopped. He stood under the small canvas awning of a tiny high-end boutique with a floor-to-ceiling storefront window. He looked up, expecting to see mannequins on the other side of the glass, but instead, reflected back at him, was a man he'd never seen before.

Everything about his appearance was unfamiliar. He was taller, appeared to have a rather meaty, athletic build, and he wore high-end clothes much too rugged and in style for Collin's taste. Gone was the tiny, balding spot on top of his head, replaced now by thick brown locks trimmed neatly above his ears. He wasn't wearing his glasses—in fact, he didn't seem to need them. He had a few days' growth of facial hair. Even his flabby midsection was missing.

I've gone mad.

He stared at his reflection for minutes on end, unable to do anything else.

Who am I?

That other man—he's me. And I'm . . . not.

Did we switch?

A stranger looked through his eyes, taking him in.

And not just any stranger, it occurred to him. He was as close to a perfect specimen of manhood as Collin allowed might exist. An absence of creases around the eyes and a naturally pleasant expression indicated a calm, confident, well-adjusted individual. One who was clearly bogged out of his mind at the moment, but still.

Collin admired this man a minute more, unable to remove his eyes from the reflection, barely even remembering to breathe. He never noticed the slender, short brunette standing behind his shoulder, also taking in his reflection, until she whistled in appreciation.

"Well, *some*body got the deluxe package."

He turned at last to face the intruder. She was in her mid-to-late twenties. Wearing a no-muss T-shirt and jeans. She went without makeup, a rarity for L.A., and there was no jewelry either.

And she wore no shoes.

For a second he wondered if she might be homeless. Yet her clothes were too clean. She was pretty and casual, her long brown locks falling off her shoulders in untamed curls, but her expression was a flashing neon billboard that declared her to be sharp and confident. She nodded at the glass window, and he turned once more to peer at his image.

Despite—or perhaps because of—the jumble of thoughts pouring through his mind, a guttural "Huh?" was all he could get out.

My voice is different.

Deeper.

Why is this girl barefoot?

"Oh, I know," she went on. "You have no idea what's going on. Blah-blah-raving-hysteria-blah. I'm just saying . . . You took a shortcut to the top of the food chain, handsome."

"What?"

She placed her hands on his neck, straightening the collar of his brown leather jacket and then examining his reflection once more. "This is the part where I'm probably supposed to say something about . . . 'stepping through the looking glass.' Isn't it? I don't know, maybe that's wrong—I never dug sci-fi. But I *do* love that jacket," she said, nodding at his coat.

"This . . . isn't science fiction," he choked, surprised to find he'd been holding his breath since she started talking.

"You're not wrong," she replied with a cocked eyebrow and a smirk. "Things are about to get *real* complicated and I have an elsewhere to be, so let me cut to the heavy exposition. Put your listening cap on, sport, 'cause I'm about to give you a cheat sheet.

"You've just been dropkicked into the middle of something *so big* you'd never buy it if I tried to explain it now. So here's the big reveal. Are you listening? 'Cause this is the one thing you absolutely *gotta* know: you're being watched, right now, this very minute. Several *groups* of people are keeping tabs on your every snap, crackle, and pop. *Everything you do* from this moment on will blip their radars. So be careful. Though you don't have to fear them *all.*"

"Watching me? How? Why?" he stammered, trying and failing to keep up with the barefoot girl's barrage of information. His heart thudded madly in his chest, his breaths coming in sudden heaves.

She ignored him and continued. "One group is out to help you. They're not the worry. The other group'll kill you the first chance they get. Don't give 'em one."

"*Kill* me?" he asked, his eyes darting about aimlessly, searching for people watching him . . .

All he saw were bored pedestrians going about their business.

His stomach lurched, and he swallowed bile.

The girl nodded. She'd been toying with him at first, but suddenly she turned somber. "Don't bother looking. This particular less-than-philanthropic group has hired one of the best to do their dirty work, and he knows how to stay hidden. His name is Konrad. I'm sure he's watching you with his own two peepers as we speak."

"But . . . but . . . shouldn't I just go to—"

"The cops?" she finished for him, eyebrows raised. "*That* conversation would go well. 'Say, Officer, did you ever see *Invasion of the Body Snatchers?*'"

He opened his mouth, but no words came out.

She knows.

"But what *is* all this? What's going on?" he nearly yelled after collecting himself. "Why is this happening to me? I'm no one! *Why me?*"

She was silent for a moment, studying him. Finally she spoke, looking deep into his eyes. "It has to be you."

"But *why?*"

"Because you're a player now."

"A player?" he faltered. "We're playing? Playing what?"

She was shorter than Collin, yet somehow she managed to look down on him like a lost toddler in a department store. "Don't follow Collin—the old you."

Wait, his name wasn't Collin anymore? He was Collin Boyd. He knew that as certain as he knew he was standing here.

Which, given how nuts he seemed to have gone, wasn't all that reassuring.

But no, of course Collin wouldn't be his name anymore.

New body, new name.

His thoughts were coming too fast now, his eyes still looking into surrounding windows, buildings, cars, pedestrians walking by . . .

"*Listen* to me," she said, grabbing him by the shoulders and forcing him to focus. "*Don't go near* who you used to be. Get out of town and *just keep going*. Don't slow down. Don't stop. Your life is in danger if you do. Every minute you stay in one place brings Konrad that much closer to you. So you should *go*. Right now."

Still he'd didn't move. Just stood there, eyes wide with fear and brow knitted in deep confusion. A small part of him bristled at being given orders by a stranger. None of this made sense and leaving was out of the question until it did.

The barefoot girl let out a deep breath with just a hint of annoyance. When she opened her mouth, she spoke slower, as if enunciating to someone hard of hearing. "I know this is confusing; it will get easier for you. It *will*. But you don't have time to be stubborn right now. And you're *so* not ready to know yet, anyway. Just *go. Now!*"

She stood there watching him, unblinking, unmoving, waiting for him to move. He thought he detected a trace of concern, or perhaps urgency, on her face. Mostly she appeared put out by his refusal to start running.

He glanced over her shoulder in the direction of the office where he worked, and in the distance the old him, the other man—Collin Boyd— was nowhere, probably already inside. The new him had no idea whether or not to trust this strange woman, but there was an urgency in her voice that was hard to ignore. Still, his frustration was palpable as he glanced back at her.

"I'm not ready to know?" he asked. "Know *what?*"

"What's to come," she said without hesitation.

He bored his eyes into hers, but she never blinked. He found it extremely annoying.

She frowned. "Well, I gotta jet. Keep standing here if you want, but don't come crying to me when you're dead."

With that, she turned and flitted off into the busy throng. The rain had stopped just in time for her exit, which he also found annoying.

He started to call after her, but she was long gone. He didn't know what to say anyway.

He didn't even know her name.

With something she said still tugging at his mind, he reached inside his coat pocket in a mechanical, mindless way and pulled out a fine leather wallet he'd never seen before. Opened it.

Inside was a wad of crisp, clean hundred-dollar bills.

There was also a driver's license bearing the name GRANT M. BORROWS. It was the first time he'd seen or heard the name. Whoever this Grant Borrows was, apparently that's who he was now.

The gravity of the situation struck him all at once, and the world began spinning wildly beneath his feet. It was spiraling out of control, and his stomach churned once more.

He caught the eye of a woman who passed him by, entering the clothing store behind him, and as their eyes met, she . . . *smiled* at him.

That was new.

Another brushed his shoulder exiting the store and actually apologized with a sheepish, overly friendly "I'm so sorry!"

Grant began to hyperventilate. No one *ever* looked him in the eye. He'd spent most of his life cultivating the ability *not* to be noticed. Now it felt like everyone was looking him up and down.

Admiring what they saw.

An old Volkswagen van passed by the sidewalk where he stood, and it backfired loudly like a gunshot, snapping him back to the moment.

Somewhere out there—where he would never see—a man named Konrad was watching him. Possibly moving closer. Meaning to kill him. Perhaps he had a gun with Grant in its sights right now.

Grant Borrows ran.

2

Dr. Daniel Cossick had just arrived at his second-floor lab and placed his key into the lock when the door burst open from the inside and a breathless, red-faced brunette stood before him. He sighed. His assistant Lisa always arrived early, and she had a tendency to get excited over little things, so this was nothing new.

"Doctor Cossick! I just registered a spike of *three-point-seven*," she said, eyes wide with excitement.

Every other thought in Daniel's mind vanished into black. He forgot his keys, forgot his briefcase, forgot everything but the three words he'd just heard. *Three-point-seven.*

Three-point-seven!

He dropped everything and ran after her down the dilapidated hall. Lisa flew into the "lab"—a makeshift facility they'd built themselves in an abandoned building in the Warehouse District—with Daniel following and made for the middle of a modest white room overflowing with odd machinery. The atmosphere was alive with mechanical whirrs and beeps, pungent odors, and the occasional fizz of air or fire. Few visitors could stomach being in the room because the odors were so strong and the sounds so constant, but Daniel and Lisa had grown accustomed to it. They both practically lived here, conducting their search.

Always searching.

In the center of the room was the lab's largest piece of equipment, a massive mechanism that looked like half a giant metal sphere had been mounted on top of a collection of circuitry, wires, and semiconductors. It hummed quietly, almost vibrating, but nothing moved because stillness was crucial. It was approximately four feet in diameter and full of a thick, silver liquid that rose almost to the rim.

"My own potion of mercury mixed with a few other potent elements," Daniel would explain to potential investors, though visitors to the lab were increasingly rare. The liquid itself was inconsequential; it was there to provide mass at the correct density that would measure what they were looking for. The mercury mixture usually remained at a flat calm. Daniel had built special dampeners into the undercarriage to prevent shaking of any kind. Even an earthquake could not jar it, unless the whole building was to topple.

But it would shake if there was a *shimmer*.

And a shimmer was what they were searching for.

If Lisa was correct, a three-point-seven would be the largest event Daniel had ever witnessed. By far.

She motioned to the computer station adjacent to the device and pointed at the screen, grinning from ear to ear.

"Look at that!" She chewed on a nail, watching his every move.

He pulled out his glasses and, hands shaking, slipped them on, his eyes never leaving the monitor. There it was. The device had recorded a three-point-seven spike roughly seven minutes ago. His heart fluttered.

"Location?" he asked, without looking up.

"Already on it," she said, still smiling. "Take another ten or twenty minutes to triangulate."

Daniel nodded, studying the dozens of numbers that appeared on the screen. He did some math in his head and then his entire body stiffened, alarmed.

"Close," he said, still staring at the screen. "Less than three miles from here."

He stood, his eyes out of focus, his mind elsewhere. "Downtown," he mumbled to no one, wiping his hands against the sweater he wore.

He seemed to snap to attention, but still didn't look at her. "Get me that location the moment you have it." He began walking away, toward the other end of the hall, to the only other room they'd retrofitted into the building: his office.

"Dr. Cossick?" Lisa called.

He turned around distractedly. "Yes?"

"This is really it, isn't it?" she asked, holding her breath. She was beaming, excited beyond words.

He forced a modest smile for her benefit, but then turned and continued walking.

"I hope not."

Home turned out to be a different neighborhood than Grant had ever known. Instead of his utilitarian apartment, his cab ride steered him into the canyons of downtown amid the shadows of skyscrapers. The Wagner Building was a new high-rise on Wilshire, a few blocks from the famous old Library Tower and L.A.'s Central Library itself where he'd visited once or twice as a child. The key Grant found in his jacket pocket alongside the wallet unlocked the elevator up to the penthouse floor and then slid smoothly into the apartment's front-door lock.

Before opening the door, a twinge of apprehension tingled in his mind, returning his thoughts to the strange barefoot girl he'd met on the street and her warning to get out of town. Which he had completely ignored. Grant *had* hailed a cab, but as soon as he saw the address on the wallet, all thoughts of fleeing were abandoned. He couldn't resist finding out more about this person he'd somehow become.

And a small part of him did it just to spite the girl and her stupid bare feet.

He pushed open the door to the penthouse and saw a shadowy room ahead. His hand felt around on the inside wall until he found the light switch and flipped it on.

Spread out before him was a bachelor's paradise. Black leather furnishings. Spacious surroundings. Giant flatscreen plasma TV. A desk at the far end of the room featured a sleek, stainless steel computer. Speakers from a massive stereo system were situated throughout the room. Chic floor lamps stood at corners like sentries. Modern art adorned the clean, white walls. To the immediate left of the front door was a fully outfitted kitchen with appliances that bore the stainless-steel sheen of restaurant-quality machinery. Beyond the kitchen was a fully-furnished dining room. Somewhere down the long hall beyond the living room was probably a bedroom, a bathroom, and who knew what else.

He stepped inside and continued to gape. But instincts he couldn't explain were telling him something was wrong. It was the middle of the day, and all of the drapes around the room were closed tight. The pillows on the sofa were perfectly arranged. Everything in the kitchen was exactly where it belonged. The apartment looked as if it had never been used. Not one thing was out of place.

Except for the doormat on which he stood, which was crooked by less than an inch.

He put it together a second too late.

The door slammed shut behind him just as someone grabbed his right arm and pressed it into the small of his back. He felt the tip of a knife against his throat.

Without thinking, Grant grabbed the arm holding the knife with his free hand, and twisted it hard. The knife fell to the floor and at the same time, Grant ducked and sent the attacker flying over his left shoulder, where he crashed on the floor in the living room over ten feet away.

Grant couldn't tell which of them was more surprised at what he'd just done—he or the other man, who slumped against the ground. Grant watched the other man fall, but could only stand there numbly, breath caught in his throat. It had all happened so fast.

He had no idea how he'd done it.

His assailant, a short stump of a man clad in a baggy black jumpsuit and shin-high black boots who had to be pushing fifty, lay there for a fraction of a second, stunned at Grant's quick reaction. He looked like he was made of solid brick and frowned in a way that looked as though the expression had been permanently etched into his face.

Konrad, Grant guessed.

What did I ever do to you?

But Konrad's pause lasted only a moment, and he rolled back to his feet and pulled a gun out of a shoulder holster in a simple, fluid motion.

"I wasn't told you could do that," Konrad said. His deep, abrasive voice sounded like a jackhammer pounding into pavement. "I'm a collector; lack of full disclosure means I get something extra. I'm thinking . . . *kneecap.*" He lowered the gun and pointed it at Grant's leg.

Grant had launched into a dead sprint, instincts taking over. He was outside the apartment door before the first shot was fired. He darted down the corridor, unsure where he was headed. He made it to the end of the hall, where he met a full-length window and a sprawling view of the L.A. skyline that should have been breathtaking. But a second shot shattered the glass, and Grant dove around the corner to his right.

A door marked "STAIRS" that he hadn't noticed earlier waited before him. Grant's heart leapt and he dashed through the door. He made it down the first flight before hearing the door slam open behind him, and he rounded to the next floor, just as Konrad fired again.

A pinching pain sliced through his left leg, and he staggered. But the adrenaline was surging now like nothing he'd felt before, and it kept him from stopping. Rounding the next staircase, he caught sight of the adjoining door, which read "ELEVEN."

Come on, come on. Ten flights.

You can do this.

Down he ran, feet flying over each step. It seemed impossible. Just the other night he'd been talking with his landlady about how quiet and lonely and boring his life was. All he had was his job. She wondered if he brought it on himself but he told her that he'd never asked to be alone. Why bother questioning fate? Yet in the dark of the night it had come to him. How pointless it all seemed, this endless stupid pattern, winding around him tighter and tighter.

His job. Being around other people. His whole life.

It felt like a snake twisting around his neck, tightening its grip, and he'd woken many nights in a sweat, gasping for air.

Now *he* was the snake, winding dizzyingly around and around while breathing became harder and harder . . .

Another shot rang out, closer this time, and he instinctively ducked.

"Did you know that dismemberment isn't always fatal?" Konrad said from above. He wasn't shouting, he was growling, quietly. He was keeping up with Grant's frantic pace, but his words had come as casually as if he were riding an elevator.

Halfway down the next flight, Grant grabbed the middle rail and flung himself over, dropping ten feet to the flight below. He landed solidly, but his leg flashed with a stabbing pain, and he kept going down, rolling to the bottom of the stairs. When he stopped, he noticed that his left pant leg was crimson with blood.

But there was no time to think; he jumped to his feet and darted off again, down, down, down.

Come on! This is taking too long!

More shots clanged off of the center railing. Grant moved to the outside edge of the stairs, staying close to the wall. Another flight. Another. More shots.

Keep moving. You can do this.

Maybe I should just stop, let him finish it. Wouldn't it be easier?

The thought of dying wasn't all that bad . . .

"The trick is sealing off the wound," Konrad's voice echoed in the stairwell. "A needle and string will do, but I find that cauterizing the wound works best. With the proper antibiotics, I can take a man apart one inch at a time. It can last for *weeks* before I even *get close* to the vital organs."

And . . . let's keep running, shall we?

The pain in his leg seared now, and he broke into a cold sweat. He may have been more in shape now than before, but he was still human. And his leg screamed in agony.

At last he made it to the door marked "ONE." He had the door open when another idea came to mind. He pushed the door open as far as it would go, so its hydraulic hinge would require several seconds to pull it closed. Then he hopped on one foot, so as to not leave another blood trail, in the direction of the last flight of stairs, which led to the building's mechanical room.

He stopped halfway down the steps and crouched, listening. Konrad's heavy footfalls faded away, and then he heard the open door above him click shut.

Grant wasted no time. Hurtling himself down the remaining steps, he burst through the mechanical room's door. Frantic, he glanced around the warm, dark, dry room, looking for anything that might help. A broomstick he could use as a weapon, something to lodge against the door. But there was nothing. The small room held the building's massive furnace and myriad other equipment, but little else. Even light seemed to be swallowed up by the space.

He felt his way around the furnace to the right, thinking only of how Konrad wouldn't be thrown off the trail long. There on the right side of the room, he came upon a small locked door. He thought about kicking it, but his leg hurt too deeply so he lowered his shoulder and crashed at it with as much force as he could manage.

To his astonishment, it worked, and he let out a triumphant grunt. A narrow flight of stairs beyond the open door led down. He threw himself down them, legs barely working anymore. At the bottom he slammed his body into a second door and dashed through.

Grant couldn't believe his luck. He was standing in the middle of an enormous subway station, bustling with activity. And not just any station—he knew this place, had been here before. It was the Metro Center Station, just across Figueroa Street from the Wagner Building. He remembered the movie-themed artwork adorning the walls. It felt more like a sterile airport than a subterranean tunnel. Its shiny steel fittings mirrored Grant's dilapidated appearance back at him everywhere he looked.

A Blue Line train bulleted by on the tracks nearest him, its engine piercing the roar of the vast crowd.

Grant looked back at the door he'd just passed through. On this side, it read "EMERGENCY EXIT."

He glanced around the subway, his mind racing. About a hundred feet down the corridor, beyond a swell of pedestrians waiting for the next train, he spotted an escalator that led up to sunlight beyond.

He set off again, forcing his way through the crowd, brushing shoulders and nearly shoving others. But once they got a look at his haggard features and bloodied clothes, most were only too happy to get out of his way. He was limping now, blood still dribbling from his leg onto the floor's brick-colored tiles.

He felt light-headed. *Probably from the blood loss*, some part of his mind registered the sensation.

Grant had just placed one foot on the bottom step when he heard another gunshot, followed by hundreds of screams. Konrad was descending the stairs directly above him, and fast.

Grant hobbled in the opposite direction, trying to run, but the other man jumped from near the bottom of the steps, tackling him from behind. The gun went off again as they grappled for it on the floor. A train pulled up and most of the crowd scrambled into it, many of them still screaming.

Grant threw a punch and was surprised to see it connect.

But Konrad stood up, unfazed, and hoisted Grant to his feet as well. Grant's senses were muddled, feeling more of the pain in his leg now. His newfound reflexes seemed to have slowed when the exhaustion had kicked in. His chest heaved and he couldn't catch his breath. He didn't realize what was happening until it was too late to stop it— the other man had shoved him up against the nearest wall and pinned a bulky arm across his chest.

"I still want my kneecap," he growled, his hot breath inches from Grant's face.

3

"You're not going to kill me," Grant announced, surprised at himself.

Konrad punched him in the face. Grant's head thumped against the tiled wall behind him, and he winced at the pain from his nose and mouth.

"You could have shot me in the apartment," he continued, panting, "but you snuck up behind me with a *knife*. On the stairs, you shot me in the *leg*, not the chest," Grant concluded. "You *want* something."

Konrad smiled the ugliest smile Grant had ever seen. He had perfect teeth, but there was a gruesome malevolence in the expression. "Not bad. But if killing you is the only way of getting what I'm here for . . . I've made my peace with it." His hollow eyes slowly moved down Grant's right arm and landed on his hand, which he looked at hungrily. Grant followed his gaze down to the same spot.

And gasped.

A large gold ring, wider on top than underneath, like the shape of a class ring, rested there on his middle finger. The gold was so smooth it might have been liquid. Not a single scratch could be seen. Inset in the widest part of the band was a dark red gemstone. Odd markings were cut as tiny holes into the sides of the band. Grant had never seen the ring before, but he could tell from the sensation that it had been on his finger for a while.

At least since the bus, he guessed.

"You can have it," Grant said, holding out his hand. The chase had worn him out, strength all but gone, breath coming in shooting waves, along with the pounding of his pulse that he could feel in the pain from his leg. His equilibrium was damaged by the blow to the head, and if Konrad hadn't been pinning him against the wall, he might have collapsed.

"Hold it!" a man screamed from twenty feet down the line, in Grant's line of sight and directly behind Konrad. He looked like some kind of Metro security . . .

Without hesitating or even looking, Konrad fired a shot over his shoulder and the security guard went down. The few remaining pedestrians in the station panicked and ran. Konrad holstered the gun and retrieved a knife from his belt—the same one he'd pressed against Grant's throat in the apartment. Letting go with his other arm, he slammed his fist into Grant's face once again. Something cracked this time, but Grant couldn't be sure if it was his head or the ceramic of the wall. He fought the rising bile in his throat as well as the blackness creeping into the edge of his vision.

Konrad clutched Grant's wrist with a powerful, vice-like grip. The blood drained out of it quickly, and soon Grant could no longer feel it. Konrad curled Grant's other fingers into a fist, until only the middle ring finger remained extended.

"Heh," Grant spat deliriously, eyes half-open. "I'm giving you the finger."

Konrad looked into his eyes. "No," he said, "I'm taking it."

His blade touched the side of Grant's finger, just below the ring, where his finger met his hand, and he started to slice.

Grant's head bucked violently and he clenched his eyes closed tight, gritting his teeth. A blinding pain ripped through his head, and his whole body seized.

No!

Grant heard Konrad gasp and then the whistle of something flying through the air. The man's grip relaxed and when Grant opened his eyes, Konrad was staring, neck craned, across the subway station where something glinted on the wall.

The pain faded as quickly as it had come, and Grant saw his one opportunity. He kneed Konrad viciously in the groin with every bit of strength he had left. Konrad doubled over, coughing and wheezing, then collapsed.

Grant staggered away from the wall, towering over the man. Despite his pain, he felt an unmistakable rush of satisfaction.

"*That* was my kneecap!" Grant shouted in a blind rage. "How'd it feel?!"

His eyes shifted to the gun attached to Konrad's belt and lingered there. He couldn't seem to slow his breathing, giving in to a crazed fit of wrath that erupted from him, swelling through his entire being.

Konrad spoke in a wheeze, sensing Grant's next action. "Think carefully . . ." he whispered, "about your next move."

Grant returned his focus, completely incensed, to the man on the ground, who continued speaking while clutching his privates, his face beet red and tears in his eyes. "I know who you really are," he wheezed with a slight bob in his eyebrows. "And if I can't kill *you* . . . I'll settle for those you care about most."

Grant was a bomb ready to explode, his chest swelling equally from the exertion of standing and the outrage he felt. "There *isn't* anyone I care about," he seethed through gritted teeth.

He kicked Konrad across the face, as hard as he could, and the man on the ground was out cold.

Grant braced himself against the wall, winded and stunned that he'd just beaten this man—whom he could only assume was some sort of mercenary or assassin. Despite his pain and fatigue, the fight had felt quite natural, even intuitive. Most of the time, Grant found he hadn't even known what he was doing until it was done.

How could that be?

A handful of people—those who hadn't run at the sight of Konrad's gun—still hovered, watching him. But his attention shifted away from them to a space across the tracks, where a larger group of people were huddled before a round pillar made of solid concrete. A man in a navy blazer shifted to one side, and Grant saw there, sticking out of the pillar, the hilt of his attacker's knife. The blade was buried deep inside the column.

He hesitated, confused. He couldn't recall how the knife had gotten all the way over there. He thought back to the fight . . . Grant had closed his eyes only for a second when the headache struck, and when he opened them, Konrad's hand was empty, his attention drawn elsewhere.

A shot of blinding pain from his leg wrenched him back to the present.

The girl at the storefront—whoever she was . . . She had been right.

He should have bolted when this all started.

Too late now.

He limped in the direction of the stairs leading up and out.

He had to get out of here, find safety.

If such a thing still existed.

"It looks like you're within twenty meters of the convergence," Lisa said into Daniel's earpiece.

"Okay, I'll take it from here," he replied.

She immediately went radio silent. Thankfully.

He liked Lisa. Well, he *tolerated* her, anyway, as much as he tolerated anyone. But if she weren't whip-smart and an astute lab tech, he never would have been able to abide her endless chatter. He hadn't known her for very long before he realized that she lacked a filter between her brain and her mouth—she simply verbalized every thought that entered her mind.

She was good, though—really good. She often caught things that he was too impatient to notice, and she had a way of pushing their research along avenues of thought that he might not otherwise have considered.

But the constant conversation drove him batty, particularly in the mornings. He preferred the silence of his own thoughts.

Daniel stood on the downtown sidewalk under the midday sun, which had finally broken through the clouds, holding his small device in his hand. It was a simple instrument he'd built from pieces of a Pocket PC and some other materials. Its panel lit up whenever a shimmer—or the residual energy given off by a recent shimmer—was nearby. The closer he got, the brighter it glowed. Lisa said it was essentially a high-tech version of the "you're getting warmer" game.

He marched forward another ten paces and glanced at the device. It was brighter here. He looked up. A bus stop faced him across the street.

It had happened right around here, he was sure of it.

But what was he expecting to find? It had taken much longer than he'd hoped for the lab's past-generation systems to narrow down the shimmer's position. As his rumbling stomach reminded him, it was nearing lunchtime. Whatever event had taken place here, it was long over.

Daniel walked forward, crossing the street and nearing the bus stop, when a high-pitched squeal in his earpiece brought him up short.

"Doct—! It hap—a—n!" Lisa was shouting.

He reached up and massaged his ear. "Say again? *Quietly?*"

"It happened again! Another shimmer! Just now!" she replied.

He froze. *Two in one day.*

One was unprecedented. Two was unimaginable.

"How big?" he shouted, not caring about the people on the street who stopped to stare.

"Hang on, it's processing now . . ."

An impossibly long minute passed, and the light changed. A bicyclist squeaked his horn, so Daniel ran out of the street and under the empty glass bus shelter.

"Well?" he asked impatiently.

"Doctor Cossick, . . ." she whispered, "it was a *seven-point-nine.*"

He plopped down on the shelter's plastic bench, aware of nothing around him save his heart pounding madly beneath his chest.

"Where was it?" he finally said.

"Can't tell yet," she mumbled. "It's still triangulating. But *two* of them! *Two shimmers!* Can you *believe* this?"

"Feed me the data," he replied, pulling out a touch-screen device smaller than a laptop. He tapped the screen and looked at the data Lisa was pouring into it by remote. He focused on the numbers and quickly did some preliminary math on the small computer.

When he was finished, he sat back, dropping the pad to his knees.

"I think it's near the Library," he said out loud.

He pulled the smaller device back out of his pocket and turned it on.

Even in the rising midday sun, it glowed ferociously.

4

Grant walked as far as he could before the pain in his leg grew unbearable. It needed dressing, and he had to find someplace safe to hide, get his bearings and consider his options. He'd crossed 110 on West 7th and guessed he was now a mile or so west of the Wagner Building. He'd never been in this part of the city before.

Konrad would wake up soon. Grant wondered if he should have done something more. Perhaps he should have tied Konrad up and thrown him onto one of the moving trains or something. But the people standing around, who'd witnessed the entire fight, had watched him carefully after it was over. Add that weird knife thing to the situation, and he just wanted to get out of there.

He wasn't equipped to deal with what was happening on his own, that much was clear. For that matter, he didn't even know who he was. He'd never heard of this "Grant Borrows." The most likely scenario, he decided, was that somehow, he and this Borrows person had exchanged . . . *lives*.

However impossible that sounded.

He hailed a passing cab and asked the driver—an elderly woman with thin, wiry hair and large horn-rimmed glasses that had lenses set to a high magnification—to take him to the closest drugstore. At the strip mall where she stopped, he handed her three of his crisp hundred-dollar bills, and asked her to please wait. She didn't reply, but her huge eyes got even bigger when he placed the currency into her hand, so he wasn't concerned.

Grant staggered into the store, trying hard not to pass out, and drew expressions from patrons and employees that ranged from puzzled to downright spooked. Most backed away at the sight of him.

Shuffling his way down various aisles, Grant's thoughts lingered bleakly on how he hoped to be waking up any minute now. He picked up a small, brown bottle of peroxide, a roll of gauze, a bottle of Tylenol, and a few snacks. He paid the clerk—whose fearful eyes seemed to silently call for a co-worker to come handle this situation—and asked if they had a restroom.

Once inside the tiny room at the back of the store, he locked the door and rolled his pant leg up to get his first look at the wound on his leg. Or rather, whoever's leg this was. It wasn't a limb he recognized.

It was worse than he'd thought. Much more than a graze. The bullet had torn through one side of his tan, muscular calf and exited straight out the other. He couldn't believe it. There were two holes in his leg. His rear end smacked the floor as he slid down the wall, then he leaned back, took a deep breath, and closed his eyes.

He stayed that way until his breathing slowed.

He eyed the ring on his finger, and timidly touched it with a finger on the other hand. The metal was smooth and warm, and while not exactly store window material, it looked quite old.

Suddenly he tugged at it, alarmed. It wouldn't come off.

He pulled harder.

It wouldn't budge.

At first he thought it was merely stuck, that his finger had swollen. But the ring didn't wiggle *at all*. It was affixed to his finger, as if bonded directly to the skin.

That's why he was going to use a knife, he thought, remembering his struggle in the subway. *Konrad couldn't take the ring off, so he was going to take my whole finger*.

He propped his injured leg up over the open toilet seat, and after a moment's hesitation, poured the peroxide over it. The pain was excruciating, acid bubbling up around the wound and pus pouring out. He turned his leg over and did the same to the other side. He repeated the process several times, until satisfied.

Finally, he stood and popped a few Tylenol in his mouth, then began winding gauze around his leg. Wrap after wrap after wrap.

His mind wandered again, watching the white wrap go round and round. It twisted like the snake in his mind. A pure white snake intent on strangling him . . .

When I woke up this morning, I was Collin Boyd.

Now I'm Grant Borrows.

"My name is Grant Borrows."

"Grant Borrows, nice to meet you."

The white snake spun around its victim again and again. Grant's eyes glazed over, watching it curl and fighting a growing shortness of breath.

I stepped off a bus, found out I was no longer myself, and now I'm cleaning a gunshot wound inside a drugstore bathroom, and there's a ring on my finger that won't come off.

How did I get here?

A few wraps of medical tape would hold the gauze securely in place. He limped painfully to the tiny sink and gazed wearily into the mirror above it.

The handsome man he'd first seen in the store window that morning was still there, looking back at him, but he was a horrible mess now. Bruises on his cheek. Dried blood beneath his nose. His bottom lip was split. Hair disheveled. Eyes dark like a raccoon's. He ran a hand around the back of his head and felt more dried blood, from where it had smacked the concrete wall.

No wonder the store clerk had been terrified. The sudden notion that she might have called the police increased the urgency of his movements.

He poured peroxide over his ring finger where it had been cut, and bandaged it as best he could. He put what remained of his meager supplies in his inside jacket pockets, then washed his hands and face, which provided only a minor improvement. His clothes were still a bloody mess, but he couldn't do anything about it now.

He had to keep moving. He'd stayed in one place too long already.

But where to go?

Grant thought again of the barefoot girl and her warning to keep moving. And he thought about Konrad and the last words he'd uttered.

"If I can't kill you . . . I'll settle for those you care about most."

He gasped, and for once, it wasn't from the pain.

Oh no.

He slammed open the door to the bathroom and ran back out to the cab as best he could, adrenaline surging through him once more as the sun waned on the horizon.

If he knows who I really am, then he knows . . .

About her!

"Where to, honey?" the cab driver's squeaky voice intoned.

"UCLA campus," he replied breathlessly, shoving two more hundred-dollar bills into her hands. "Take Wilshire and run every light you have to!"

Amid the panic it occurred to him that however scared he'd been before . . . it was *nothing* compared to what he was feeling now.

Every hair on Julie Saunders' arms and neck stood on end. It was late as she stopped, all alone in the UCLA faculty offices, to lock her office door, the darkness closing in around her.

She had no idea how or why, but she *knew* she was being watched.

Julie made her way quickly down the hall, breathing fast, eyes darting all around. The only sound came from the keychain jangling in her hand.

The feeling was suffocating, as if the air were made of syrup. She trembled visibly as she exited the building and walked out onto the campus grounds. Once outside, she stopped for a moment and collected herself, taking several deep breaths.

The outside air brought some comfort. The lights in most of the dormitories were still on—but that was no indication of the time, considering how late college students stayed up. The outdoor lamps were also on and she could see the front end of her car peeking at her from its perch atop the adjacent parking garage. The little teal Saturn appeared to be all alone up there.

The sense that she was being watched had not gone away.

Just get me home safe, and I'll never stay at work past sundown again, she thought, her heart pounding. But she knew she'd had little choice besides putting in the extra hours. Recent events had put her behind on everything, most especially grading mid-term papers.

Julie wound the stairs to the top of the garage. Beside her car, she fiddled awkwardly with her keys, hands trembling until she found the right one. Once inside, she locked the doors. Starting the engine made her feel better.

As she quietly backed out of her parking space, her pulse began to calm.

Hundreds of feet away, high atop one of the twin bell towers of the campus's auditorium, Konrad lay on his stomach, cradling a sniper rifle that was propped on the brick ledge. His right eye squinted into the telescopic lens as Julie's car slowly shifted into drive and turned toward the downward exit.

The car turned left, and now the driver's side of the car was facing him. Konrad's mouth stretched into a tight smile. He was going to enjoy this just a little more than usual.

He zeroed in on Julie's head and tightened his grip, waiting patiently. He could make the shot while she was in motion, he knew, but the distance was further than he preferred. So he decided to wait. The hunt was the best part, no doubt. But it failed to provide the divine *thirst* that waiting brought.

A ramp led from the garage to the nearest street; she would have to stop there, before turning out onto the main road. And he would be ready.

Inside the car, Julie glanced at the dashboard clock as she spiraled down the exit ramps. *10:43* P.M.

She sighed. So late, and she still had a long drive ahead on the 405. She was going to need help staying awake that long.

Julie passed through the garage's gated entrance and tapped her brakes until she stopped at her exit onto the main road. She leaned into the passenger's side floorboard to find a CD in her purse. She was only halfway over when the glass in the driver's-side door shattered.

She screamed then unlocked her seatbelt and lay all the way over in the passenger's seat. She looked around, unsure of what to do, when another shot popped loudly, punching a hole in the dashboard just above her.

Still hunched flat in the car, she jammed her foot on the gas, unconcerned about any oncoming traffic she might be turning in to. Once the car had gone a full ninety degrees to the right, she sat up and pushed the pedal as far down as it would go, racing along the college's back roads.

No pain. She glanced down to see if she was hurt. No blood stains. She felt her head and her face, which was moist, but she dabbed it with a finger and saw that the liquid was clear. Only then did she realize that she'd been crying since the first shot was fired.

Julie sped her way south along the campus grounds, wiping her face and dodging students. Her muscles were tensed and she was shivering all over.

She snatched her phone and dialed 911.

An hour later, Konrad was still watching.

Through his sniper scope, he could see the woman sitting in a chair. She was plainly worn out and hadn't regained her composure since his attack. He could see her hands shaking slightly as she accepted a cup of coffee from the duty officer.

She was inside the UCLA Police Department building, near the center of the campus. He watched from an office on the top floor of the Gonda Center, a genetic research building just across the street

A street ran between the Center and the campus police headquarters, with cars passing between very infrequently. A few students could be seen here and there walking and talking, even at this ungodly hour. But Konrad had no fear that he might be discovered. The building was locked down and all the lights were out.

If anyone did somehow intrude on him, he'd simply shoot them in the head with the silenced pistol on his hip.

All of this was part of Konrad's contingency plan, of course, made long before he'd shot holes into the woman's car, just as he'd known she would go straight to the police if he missed. He'd been given a complete file on this woman, which was almost as thick as the file for Borrows. She was a good citizen: she paid her taxes on time, she gave regularly to charities, she often worked late at her office.

She cared. She *loved*. She believed that doing right was what mattered.

Of course she would go straight to the police when someone took a shot at her. She'd be "safe" there.

He was unconcerned about his earlier failure to kill her, but it gnawed at him that he hadn't been able to off Borrows yet. Still, set-backs were inevitable. He was a detail person, and this was a possibility he'd planned for. Besides, the woman's movements would prove even *more* predictable in this state.

Best of all, it prolonged the hunt.

And the hunt was all there was.

So he didn't mind waiting, sipping water from a bottle as he kept an eye on her through the rifle scope. She'd just been handed off to another policeman—a man in a suit sitting behind a desk, concern written all over his face—when a bulky, heavyset man in an overcoat—*Classic detective*, Konrad thought—strode into the office and began speaking to the desk officer with his arms crossed. He looked most displeased.

From what Konrad could tell, the police didn't seem keen on releasing the woman until they were convinced she was out of danger, though it looked like this new policeman might be shaking things up.

Whatever.

Improvising wasn't a problem. Neither was patience.

So he watched, and he waited.

Very patiently.

5

Julie had no idea who this guy in the trench coat was, and she couldn't bring herself to care.

All she could think about was how she should feel perfectly safe right now, and yet she didn't. As the two officers in this small room conferred quietly—some kind of jurisdictional dispute, from the sound of it—she was met with the growing sensation that all of the oxygen was very slowly being vacuumed from the room. It was growing steadily warmer, and her heart beat a little faster with each passing minute.

The young UCLA officer finally cleared his throat before smiling again at Julie, as both officers turned to face her. "This is Detective Drexel, and he's going to be taking care of you and looking into your case, Ms. Saunders."

Julie carefully got to her feet. "I just want this to be over. I still can't believe it. Can I go home?"

Drexel smiled at her reassuringly—though his smile looked an awful lot like the face other people make when they're in pain—as he hefted his considerable weight a step forward in her direction. "Very soon, I promise," he attempted to soothe, but his voice was surprisingly nasal and scratchy for such a barrel-chested man. "I need to get your statement on record at my office downtown, which is between here and your house. I won't delay you any longer than I have to."

Julie thought quietly to herself as Drexel ushered her from the room.

"Could it be gang-related?" she asked.

"I doubt it," he replied casually, his hand steering her shoulder through the all-but-empty outer room and toward the front door. "Any of your students unhappy with their grades lately?"

She offered a halfhearted chuckle. "Students are *always* unhappy with their grades, Detective."

"Stop!" Grant screamed from the back seat of the cab.

They'd reached the street outside of the UCLA Police Department. Standing there on the curb in front of the building was a girl. The girl without shoes.

"Wait right here!" Grant shouted, jumping from the cab.

"Honey, I can't park in the middle of the—" the driver called after him, but he ignored her and ran toward the station house.

Grant had just limped through the building's front door, following the shoeless girl inside, when he stopped cold. The young woman was nowhere to be seen, but Julie was right in front of him, being escorted straight toward him from a hallway on the right. She came closer, into the lobby, and their eyes met from ten feet away. She didn't recognize him, of course, but she held his gaze nonetheless. Perhaps it was Grant's bloodied and battered appearance—which was far worse than hers—but there was a peculiar expression on her face as she gazed at him.

Her long black hair was matted, disheveled, and her face gaunt and weary. Bags drooped under her eyes. If Grant hadn't known who she was, he might not have recognized her. A big man in a blue trench coat had his hand on her shoulder, directing her, but now was shifting his attention to Grant, suspicion unmistakable in his features.

Julie didn't look away as they drew closer together from opposite corners of the lobby. Time slid into slow motion for Grant as they came close enough to touch one another. He couldn't bring himself to speak, couldn't think of what to say, how to explain his situation, his appearance, his fear for her life. What *was* there to say? What could possibly escape from his lips that wouldn't sound like the ramblings of a crazy person?

Grant took a step toward them. The cop yanked Julie out of concern, and at the same moment glass exploded from the window to Grant's immediate right. Julie's bulky escort fell sharply to the ground, but Julie herself stopped cold exactly where she stood.

Grant's breath caught in his throat.

It was as if Julie had been frozen and bolted into place, in mid-stride, her eyes still trained on him. She simply . . . *paused* for a long moment, before her eyes rolled up and her entire body went limp. She collapsed to the floor.

Grant snapped out of his reverie and dove to shield her body with his.

The police department had erupted into chaos, officers screaming and shouting. More shots rang out and some fled for cover and others ran out onto the street. The first officer to attempt an exit had been gunned down, and now his body lay just outside the door.

For the hundredth time that day, Grant's thoughts returned to a single notion: *Why is this happening to me?*

The shooting paused, and Grant knew instinctively that the sniper—Konrad, no doubt—had stopped to reload. Depending on the model, there should be somewhere between five and twelve seconds before the shooting resumed.

Grant blinked.

How do I know that?

No time to figure it out now, Grant labored onto his haunches and threw Julie's limp, unconscious form over his shoulder. With his new body, she felt almost weightless. He took off down the hallway she'd just emerged from, a corridor without windows that paralleled the street outside.

The gunfire and chaos continued behind him, but it faded as he made a left, and then a right. He found himself at another entrance on the far right side of the building. Outside, he gently lay Julie on the grass and felt her pulse.

Alive. He scanned her for wounds, found none. Grant hoisted her up again and carried her toward the front corner of the building.

Peeking cautiously around the brick, he spotted a handful of black-suited officers illuminated by streetlamps aiming, pointing, yelling, running, barking into radios. One of them seemed to have spotted where the gunshots were coming from.

Grant's cab had vanished. He wanted to be angry, after all the money he'd given her, but what could he expect?

No transportation.

Cops everywhere.

And Konrad will start shooting again any second.

Now what?

Come on, you weird new reflexes! Kick in again and tell me what to do!

Grant ducked and pulled Julie farther away from the edge of the building as another shot was fired. He couldn't tell where Konrad had aimed this time, but he felt the need to be even farther away from the target area, all the same. It sounded like he had switched to a semi-automatic.

The policemen preparing to enter the Gondo Center were pinned down. Every time one of the men in black got close to the building, more shots would ring out, sometimes connecting with a leg or an abdomen. One fell and pulled himself to safety. Another fell and did not move. Only a pair of policemen remained able to fight, but they were taking cover behind vehicles.

Running out of time. . . !

Approaching the building was a red Jeep with no side doors and its canvas top missing. The Jeep had stopped at the sight of the drama playing out in front of the police station, and Grant seized the opportunity.

He climbed into the vehicle's passenger side, laid Julie across the backseat, and muttered a "sorry" to the stunned young man in the driver's seat as he kicked him out the other side. The boy rolled on the ground, but Grant didn't wait to see what happened next. He dropped into the driver's seat and gunned the engine.

He'd nearly made a clean getaway when the big cop in the blue trench coat burst through the front door and stopped in front of the car, his gun leveled at Grant's head.

"Let 'er go!" he shouted in a pinched voice, his free hand clutching his opposite shoulder, which was bleeding.

But Konrad chose that moment to start firing again, and the cop turned his attention to the faraway window and fired his pistol in that direction instead.

Grant swerved around the cop and immediately heard a shout of "Hold it!" from behind.

He didn't.

Julie moaned again. She was waking up.

Daniel Cossick had seen some strange things in his life—stranger than most could claim—but there were no words for what he was seeing at this moment.

Midnight had come and gone, and he'd just tracked down the source of the second shimmer at last.

Stepping across fresh yellow police tape, he tentatively touched the knife that was wedged into the subway station column. It had dug all the way into the cement, stopped only by its hilt from going in any further.

The subway was far from empty at this time of night, but no one seemed to care that he was taking a closer look.

He was surprised the police hadn't tried to remove the thing from the wall.

Or maybe they *had*, and couldn't.

"What is it? What do you see?" Lisa squawked eagerly in his ear, making him jump.

When he'd settled, he replied quietly, still examining the knife.

"Exactly what we're looking for. Something impossible."

Daniel took a step forward and leaned in close to the weapon, getting as close an impression of it as he could. It looked rather heavy. Probably at least nine inches in length, handle to razor-sharp tip. The hilt was solid and had a comfortable, form-fitted grip.

This was no pocket toy casually left behind. To whoever owned it, this was something of great value. It would not have been left here by choice.

Daniel knew there was little chance of removing it, but he couldn't resist trying. He gripped it with gloved hands, and after glancing around the station to make sure no one was looking, gave it his best King Arthur tug. It was a pointless exercise.

"What does *that* mean?" Lisa asked.

Daniel turned to see the other roped-off area on the opposite side of the tracks. Spots of dried blood were visible on the ground. He twisted to face the pillar in front of him once more.

"It means the Threshold has been breached," he answered somberly, stepping away from the column but never looking away from the knife. "And all bets are off."

6

Grant drove. For hours, much of the time not realizing where he was going.

He had no destination in mind; he just wanted to get Julie away from danger. Eventually he took the 405 to Rosa Parks and then headed east back to the glow of downtown. Traffic buzzed even this late but never bogged down. He almost took the exit back to his penthouse but dismissed it. It was too dangerous:

The stolen Jeep finally came to a stop almost of its own volition at a small park called Hollenbeck Lake. Sunrise was still an hour or two away and Grant tucked the Jeep as far from streetlamps as possible. His mind should've been whirling, trying to decide what to say to Julie when she fully came to, but exhaustion overtook him and he fell into a fitful sleep.

He roused, chilled, when a glint of dawn peeked off to the east.

Julie made groggy noises from the backseat, and Grant carefully scooped her up into his arms, struggling under the weight on his bad leg. Her pocketbook still drooped over one shoulder. He glanced around frantically and spotted a park bench at the edge of the lake.

Even at daybreak he was unsurprised to find a small handful of runners already there, circling the water. Fitness always came first in L.A.

Grant placed Julie gently upon the bench, just as her eyes began to flutter open. He sat opposite her and steadied her, holding her upright.

She looks so tired . . .

Her eyes focused at last, and she screamed.

"Listen to me, Julie—" he started, letting go of her.

"Who are you! What—"

"Julie, listen! You *know* me! You know who I am!"

She was in danger of hyperventilating, but she said nothing, both terror-filled eyes trained on him, taking in his bloodstained, battered appearance. "I—I do?"

Grant was breathing rapidly, too, his thoughts coming faster than his tongue could handle. "I wish I could do this differently," he spoke hurriedly. "But we don't have time. We won't be safe here for long."

Still she looked at him. He forced himself to breathe more slowly as he gazed into her eyes—those eyes he knew so well, so deep, the skin around them creased by long years of tears and laughter. What a life she'd led . . .

He was suddenly overcome with emotion, sitting next to her for the first time in years. And she looked at him with such intense fear.

He took one last, slow, unsteady breath.

"Julie, I'm Collin. I'm *your brother*."

She stood up from the bench, and began backing away from him. Anguish filled her eyes.

She started to say something, but nothing came out. Instead, she just shook her head, unblinking.

Grant stood. "It's the truth. I know you don't recognize me—*I* don't even recognize me—but I *am* the man you knew as Collin Boyd."

"I'm calling the police right now," she said. She pulled a tiny phone out of her pocketbook. She started to dial and turned and walked away from him.

Grant stood and swallowed. If he couldn't convince her now, then they had no chance. There was no time for this. Konrad would be coming. What could he say that she would believe? One obvious thing came to mind, but he'd been avoiding that conversation for twenty-some years . . .

She was still moving away, nearing the shoreline.

There was no choice.

"The day you left the orphanage," he called out, "was the worst day of my life."

Grant had never spoken aloud these thoughts that had tumbled through his mind so many times. The gravity of the moment struck him just then, and his words came out slowly.

Julie stopped walking. Her fingers paused over the phone, but she didn't face him.

"You held me *so* tight before they took you," he gasped, his throat full. "I was *terrified* when you let go. I tried not to show it. For you. I didn't want to make it worse." A tear built up in one eye, and then tumbled down his face. "I knew you felt bad. Maybe worse than I did. But I was *petrified*, Julie."

She stared off into the increasingly bright sky, blinking back tears of her own.

"I never knew Mom. I barely remember Dad. You were the only family I had left."

"This is cruel," she said, shaking her head, still not looking at him. "You're lying, you *heard* this—!"

"You *begged* your new parents," he went on, barely able to choke back his own tears now. "—*pleaded* with them to take me—adopt me, too. But they live in Seattle and they could only take one of us."

She spun around, tears streaming down her cheeks. "I don't believe you," she shouted. "Collin lives in Glendale; he's probably there right now. You *can't* be him!"

His gaze fell, too pained to meet her eyes. "The next time I saw you, four months had passed. *Four months*, Julie. You said you'd tried to visit sooner, that you asked them about it every day." The tears were falling freely now. "But by then it was too late. You *forgot* about me."

"That's not true! I could *never*—!"

He sniffled and continued, "I know . . . now. I know. But I was lost without you." His breaths came in heaves, and he finally raised his eyes again. "When you left at the end of that first visit—you whispered into my ear. Do you remember what you said?"

She watched him warily, hopefully.

"You told me that when we dream, we go to a special place where anything is possible. You said we would make this our—"

"Our safe house," Julie whispered, finishing for him.

"Where we could meet and play together every single night," Grant concluded. "I went there every night in my sleep, or tried to . . . But even there you never came."

47

Julie's phone fell to the ground.

Crying openly, a hand over her mouth, she walked back to him, staring into his eyes. She stood only inches from him, watching him. Wanting to believe, but dazed and confused. At last her expression softened. "*You* were always there in *my* dreams," she said softly.

They both took choked breaths and then embraced hard, rocking back and forth, holding tight, as morning glowed gold and green all about them.

They never wanted to let go.

"So what do we do about all this?" Julie asked. After he didn't say anything, she prodded. "Collin?"

They were back in the Jeep, and downtown L.A., unusually glossy and clear, beckoned them from dead ahead.

"Grant."

"What?" she asked, distractedly.

"I'm still your brother, but I . . . I'm not Collin anymore. There's too much . . . I can't . . . ." His voice, his entire manner had changed. He was focused and severe, but frustrated and tired, struggling for words. "My name is Grant."

"All right, whatever."

Over the last hour at the park, Grant had filled her in on everything that had happened during the last twenty-four hours. All it had done was open a door to questions he couldn't answer.

Creeping ahead in the morning traffic, Julie finally asked the big question. "How can this be possible?"

"Wish I knew."

"So whoever is after me . . . you think it's the same guy that tried to kill you?" Julie asked.

"Hope so."

"That's an odd thing to hope for."

He massaged his forehead. "It would mean I only have one enemy to worry about. On the other hand, maybe there are dozens of people out there hunting me down. I'm willing to bet that what they're after is *this*." He held up the ring. "Or maybe Konrad is just trying to drive me insane. And maybe it's working."

She took a deep breath and shook her head. None of this made sense to her. How could it? None of it made sense to *him*.

"This guy . . . he's never going to give up, is he?" she asked, fearful. "He'll just keep coming, no matter what we do."

"He won't give up."

"Then . . . what do we do?"

"We have to force his hand."

"And just exactly how do we do that?"

"We go where he'll expect me to go next," he said. "And we *finish* this."

She looked at him, alarmed. He saw her shiver, slightly. "Are you *sure* you're my brother? You don't talk like him. Or *think* like him."

"We can't go back to the police," Grant explained as if it were obvious. "You're obviously not safe there, and they'd never believe my story. They think I kidnapped you."

"Which, technically, you did," she agreed.

"Look, I don't know *how* I'm suddenly able to strategize and make with the big plans, but I need you to trust me. Konrad has the advantage. He can pick us off from anywhere if we slow down long enough to give him the chance. So our only option is to engineer a situation where *we* have the advantage."

She studied him, nonplussed. "You're going to draw him out into the open by being *bait* yourself." It wasn't a question; it was disapproval.

"It'll be all right," said Grant, a deadly glint in his eye. "I'll take care of you. I promise."

"It's not me I'm worried about. And I'm not talking about what this Konrad person is capable of, either. You said *you* nearly killed *him* yesterday afternoon."

Grant made no response.

Julie proceeded with caution. "I know you've had . . . episodes . . . in the past, but you were doing better, weren't you?"

"I was," he said, exasperated. "It was just . . . it felt *natural*. I reacted without thinking. I just knew how to stop him. I knew exactly where and how to hit him to knock him unconscious. I don't know how . . . I just knew."

"And aside from this instinct stuff, you've had an hour of sleep in what, thirty-six hours now?"

"What do you want me to *say!*" shouted Grant. "Am I tired? Yes! Am I on edge? *Yes!* Am I a danger to myself? Maybe. To others? Probably! But this guy's not going to stop to let me get some shut-eye, so unless you have a better idea . . ."

She looked away, out her side window. They inched forward in silence for a few minutes. The morning had already gotten hot and without the Jeep's top, the sun beat down. Grant soon felt badly about his outburst, but anger and frustration were the only sources of energy he had left. He'd apologize later. For now . . .

"Will you kill him?" Julie spoke up in a small voice.

"What?"

She wouldn't look at him; still she stared out her window, squinting into the brightness, though he thought he saw a tear falling down her cheek in her reflection. "Will you kill him?" she repeated. "Can you really do that?"

He didn't answer.

7

Grant insisted they wait until nightfall before making another move. They hid the Jeep and spent the day taking cover in tiny Mestizo restaurants, dark bars, and even a library. Anything to stay out of sight. When night fell, they returned to the Jeep and headed to their destination, pulling up to an old brick apartment building in Glendale, where Grant—*Collin*—had lived for the last seven years. It looked exactly as it always had, though it seemed a little smaller to him now.

Grant stared straight ahead at the apartment, unmoving. The sun was a distant memory now, not to be seen again for hours, and the darkness outside echoed the fear creeping in around them.

"Scared?" Julie prompted.

He nodded, fatigue and anxiety contorting his eyes.

"Me too," Julie admitted. She placed a reassuring hand on his shoulder.

"I, uh, . . . I need to know something," he delicately announced.

"Okay," she replied tentatively.

"Did you ever blame me for what happened to Mom?"

Julie shifted in her seat. "How can you even *ask* that? Of course not!"

A pause. "Then why didn't you ever talk about her? To this day, I hardly know anything about Mom at all."

Julie looked away, paused. "I guess it was too hard."

"And Dad?"

She was silent.

"Did he blame me?"

"*Never*," she answered, without hesitation.

The car became as still as the sleepy neighborhood outside. The question had eaten away at Grant in his waking hours for years. All alone in his most vulnerable moments, he would allow himself to think about it for brief snippets of time, before throwing the usual walls back up in front of his emotions.

Sometimes he even cried.

"Thanks," he replied weakly.

"Dad once told me," Julie said suddenly, thoughtfully, "that you were going to be . . . *different*. He said he thought you might grow up and do *important* things, things different from what most people do."

Grant was taken aback. "Why would he say that?"

She thought for a moment, straining her memory. "I forget why, but he had your mental acuity tested—this was only a few months before he died." Her voice sounded far away, as she thought. "I remember him saying that your test results were 'off the charts.'"

"You're kidding. But I was only three."

"I know," she affirmed.

His mind raced. "Thanks for telling me. I had no idea." He took a deep, shuddering breath and blew it out.

"You can do this, Coll—um, Grant. *Whoever* you are, I know you better than anyone and you're stronger than you think you are."

"Sure," he said, despondent.

Out of the corner of his eye he saw her digging through her purse. She produced a tiny pocket knife attached to a keychain. Before Grant could stop her, she folded out the knife and cut a slash across her wrist.

"Julie!" he cried, grabbing her by the arm.

She used her free arm to take a similar swipe at his wrist. It was then he noticed that the cuts were too shallow to sever a vein; the "knife" was little more than a fingernail clipper attachment. The gashes produced just a tiny inkling of blood, surrounded by angry-looking pink swaths of skin, on both of their wrists.

He watched as she pressed her open wound against his. "There, now we've made a pact."

"Are you crazy?"

"Whatever," Julie replied, undeterred. "It's a pact made in blood, so you can't break it. I'm going to hold you to it."

Grant studied her. "And exactly what are we . . . pact-ing?"

"Never surrender to anger or despair, no matter what. Never give up; never give in."

Grant wanted to laugh at how absurd all of this was, but Julie wouldn't let go. *"Promise* me," she said.

"Fine, okay," he said. "I promise."

At Grant's instructions, Julie was to park the Jeep three blocks down the street, turn off the engine, and wait for him there.

He took a deep breath and limped toward the building's front door. He no longer had the keys to his home, of course—like everything else, that other man, the new "Collin," now had them. So he veered to his left, around the side of the building, and looked in his ground-floor apartment window. One glance inside the darkened space told him that his double wasn't home.

Grant took what was left of the gauze out of his pocket and rolled it around one hand and fingers, like a boxer wrapping his fist.

This will either be very butch, or very bloody.

With a quick snap, he punched straight through the bottom middle window pane. It broke loudly, the shards falling into a crinkled heap on the carpet inside. He waited, watching the building's other windows to see if any lights came on. Nothing.

He snaked a hand inside and unlocked the window, slowly pushing up on the frame. The old window groaned and creaked, resisting his efforts. His thoughts returned to all the times over the years he'd attempted to open this same window from the inside, to get some air, and he could never get it to budge. Now, with his newly muscular frame, he could manage it.

Grant hopped up and crawled into the tiny living room, and then pushed the window closed again. He didn't bother turning on the lights. As small and unremarkable as the apartment was, he knew it well, even in the dark. Once his eyes had adjusted to the darkness, he glanced around and noted that everything was exactly as it had been when he'd left for work yesterday morning.

Creeping down the hall past the door to the bedroom, he made sure his doppelganger wasn't asleep or hiding. No one there. He ventured back into the hall and checked the bathroom. Nothing. The closet across from the front door still held his scarf on a hook, exactly as he'd left it yesterday. The kitchenette around the corner was also clear. Even his coffeepot still held the dregs from his last dose of caffeine.

Grant walked from one end of the apartment to the other, and wound up back in the small living room, where he'd entered. It looked like Collin—this new Collin—hadn't even been home yet.

But Grant's curiosity lasted only moments before he heard someone fumbling with keys outside the door.

The lock spun, the door opened, and Collin stepped inside.

He didn't notice Grant at all. He turned and walked in the opposite direction, into the bedroom. A lamp came on, its light shining into the hallway.

Carefully and quietly, Grant stood. He flinched as the pain in his leg returned with a sharp twinge. He stole down the hall, careful to avoid the places in the floor that creaked. Peering around the open bedroom door, he saw Collin frowning into a large, horizontal mirror that hung on the opposite wall.

Grant quietly walked up behind him and looked at him in the mirror. "How was *your* day?" he asked breezily.

The man tensed, but didn't turn. Instead, he gazed at Grant in the mirror. Grant had expected some kind of reaction, but "Collin" merely sighed and shook his head. He sat down on the edge of the bed, still watching the mirror.

Grant observed him for a moment, puzzled, and then the pain in his leg convinced him to have a seat, too.

It felt abnormal, and yet not, at the same time, as they sat there, side-by-side, watching one another in the mirror.

Grant broke the silence. "Do you want to start, or should I?"

They held eye contact.

"They didn't think you would come back here," Collin said. His voice sounded so odd; Grant wasn't used to hearing it from the outside.

"Sure," Grant replied, nodding slowly.

A pause. Neither of them blinked.

"But I knew you would. I said so. No one listens to me."

"I know the feeling," said Grant.

Another pause.

"Looks like you had difficulty getting here," Collin commented, sizing up Grant's bruises and bloodied leg.

"Yeah."

"Then it's a shame you'll be leaving empty-handed. I can't help you."

"Actually," Grant replied, "you've *already* helped me. Until now, I had no idea if you might be some kind of victim in this, just like me. Or if you were involved. Now I know. Things aren't looking especially good for you."

The thought of beating his former self to a bloody pulp sounded oddly appealing just now. Why not just finish himself off? Do the world a favor . . .

"I didn't do this to you," Collin said.

"Then who did?" Grant's voice gained strength.

The other man just stared at him.

"How did it happen? How can this be real?" Grant cried.

"It shouldn't be," Collin looked away. "But it is."

Grant stood, his pulse rising.

"Who are you?"

"No one."

Grant stepped an inch closer, his pulse rising.

"You're me. Just like that. Does that mean I'm *you*?"

Collin shook his head. "That's not how this works. I'm . . . just a . . . volunteer," Collin replied, and then looked up at Grant. "I'm no one important. You're different."

Grant swallowed. "Someone today told me I was a 'player,'" he paused, brow furrowed, studying the other man's reactions. "What are we playing? Am I a pawn in someone's twisted game?"

"I don't know. Please, Grant, for both our sakes, you've got to leave here and never come back."

Grant snapped.

"What is this?" he roared. He felt like putting the man's head through the mirror. "What is going on?!"

"I don't have any answers for you," Collin replied, speaking slow and calm. "I don't know the extent of your role."

Grant's head sagged. He rubbed his eyes.

"But if I were to guess," Collin suddenly added, and Grant's head popped up, "I'd say you're much more than a pawn. A knight, maybe. Maybe more."

Grant was breathing fast, thoughts and questions shifting through his brain. Tears formed in his eyes, but he angrily fought them back.

"I want my life back!" he said.

Collin rolled his eyes. "*Sure* you do . . ."

Collin's head whipped violently to the side and Grant was surprised to see that he'd just delivered a brutal backhand across Collin's face. He'd never consciously decided to hit the man; it just came out, along with a primal scream of rage.

"Switch us back!" he shouted.

Collin stood, anger rising in his voice. "Look at this place! You live a solitary life in a tiny apartment. No friends. No family. No connections of any kind. You make less money than you deserve. Your entire *existence* is miserable, and *you know it*! I've had it for less than two days, and I'm ready to *let* you finish me off. Why on earth would you want to come back to *this*?"

Grant was stunned.

Only one answer came to mind. "It's who I am."

Collin was unmoved. "Are you sure?" He paused. "Think about it. You've been given a second chance. It's a blank slate. Do you know how many people would *kill* for what's been handed to you? Grant, this is your chance to live the life you *should* have had."

The notion that this could be a desirable situation had never entered Grant's mind. It barely registered now. "I want to know who did this to me. You *must* know."

Collin nodded. "I'm sure you'll run into them, when the time is right."

"Are 'they' the same ones who hired this man to kill me?"

"No, but I heard about him." He cast another glance at Grant's bloodied pant leg. "Konrad is a contract killer. A single-minded mercenary. I don't know who sent him, but his interest in you doesn't extend beyond his payment. And believe me when I say, he *always* gets paid."

Grant held up his hand, and his eyes fell down upon the ring. "Would his payment include this?"

Collin eyed the ring and smiled a humorless smile.

"Just tell me what it is," Grant said imploringly. "*Please*."

Collin cocked his head to one side and gazed at him carefully, as if seeing him for the first time.

"It's the answer—"

Something burst through the bedroom window. It flew straight into the mirror, shattering it into hundreds of shards that flew everywhere.

Collin grabbed Grant and pulled him down to the floor.

Coming to a rest next to them both was a broken liquor bottle with a rag sticking out of its hole. The rag was soaked and on fire. Some part of his brain registered that the crude weapon was called a Molotov cocktail. It was an old but effective and inexpensive trick.

The bottle's contents spilled onto the floor, and with a soft *whoosh* the carpet was ablaze. Before they could react, another bottle sailed through the open window and hit the bed. It too was soon covered with flames.

Grant and Collin ran from the room, more bottles raining in after them. As one, they darted for the apartment door. Collin grabbed his cell phone on the way out and dialed 911, shouting into the phone as they ran through the outer hallway.

At the building's front entrance, Collin burst through the main door first, looking back over his shoulder at Grant.

"It's *him*, come on—!"

They both jumped at the sound of gunfire.

Grant instinctively flung himself down on the floor, just inside the door, covering his head with his hands, as more shots were fired from outside. Collin flew back into the doorway and thudded onto the ground. Grant peered over at him. Collin was lying across the threshold, his chest and arms inside and his legs outside. He made no movement, but his weight kept the old steel door from shutting itself.

Blood pooled beneath him.

8

The gunshots stopped. Grant peeked carefully outside. Konrad stood below the front steps, his gun trained and leveled, waiting for Grant to appear in the open doorway.

It was a silent challenge.

Instead of accepting, Grant pulled on Collin's hands, dragging him out of the doorway. Once Collin's body had cleared the entrance, the door shut itself. It was self-locking.

Grant stood and looked down at Collin's body.

His body.

The blood that had once run through his veins was quietly spilling out onto the floor. It had streaked across the threshold, making a trail where Grant had dragged him.

It should have been me, he thought.

Maybe it is me.

Death had come for him, but it hadn't recognized him.

Grant jumped when the man lying on the ground moaned.

"Grant," he whispered. Grant dropped to his knees and put his ear next to Collin's face. "The ring . . ." he wheezed. "The ring is the answer . . ."

"To what? To my questions?" Grant asked desperately.

Collin shook his head resignedly. "To *the* questions. The only *real* questions that have ever *mattered*."

Konrad resumed his gunfire from outside. There were no holes in the big steel door. But Konrad was undeterred. He began pounding on the door with something heavy.

Grant estimated that he had only a few minutes. Maybe seconds. The man outside was terribly strong. Focused. Determined.

And probably not too happy about that whole subway station thing.

"Grant," Collin whispered.

Grant looked back down at him, as the hammering continued.

"Take this. You should keep something . . . from your life . . ." he said, gesturing vaguely with his wrist. It took Grant a moment to realize that he was talking about the bracelet. The one his grandfather had worn and then passed to Grant's father. Grant inherited it after his father's death. It was handmade, roughly cut from a brass shell casing fired during World War II.

Collin slowly removed the bracelet and dropped it into Grant's inside jacket pocket. Grant felt the weight of it drop into his coat, but made no attempt to put it on.

Not now.

The front door was dented. Grant turned to the hallway leading back to his old apartment and saw the orange glow of flames dancing among shadows. The entire building would soon be burning; he was out of time.

He allowed himself one last glimpse of Collin. The man's chest was no longer rising and falling.

Tears formed behind Grant's eyes again, but he wiped his face furiously. *No no no!* Whoever this man had been, he'd just given his life trying to save Grant's. Blinding anger welled up within him.

He stood to watch the door. The pounding had stopped.

"You can't stay in there, and you know it!" Konrad shouted through the door. From the sound of it, only the steel and a handful of inches separated the two of them. "You'll be burned alive if you do!"

He's not wrong, Grant thought. But what was he supposed to do?

"Come out," Konrad lowered his voice, "and I'll finish it quick."

Grant's face burned red. He was breathing fast now, his mind at full speed.

"Or if you want," the man said, "just open the door, and we can do this where it's *warm*." Konrad chuckled.

Grant leaned down to Collin one last time, and grabbed the cell phone from his hand, which was still clutching it. He put it in his outer jacket pocket and then faced the door, standing tall.

"Then come!" he called.

He turned and walked away, down the burning hallway.

The pounding resumed.

"Wake up!" came a shout in Lisa's cheerful voice.

Daniel started, then rose slowly. He'd been slumped over his desk, asleep. Papers stuck to his arms and face, and he carefully peeled them off.

"Lisa," he said groggily, "I pay you for research, not," he yawned, "arrhythmia."

It was dark and quiet outside. The digital clock on his desk read *5:08* A.M.

"You said you wanted to know when I had the results on the knife tests," she said, with raised eyebrows.

He sat up straight, alert, adjusting his glasses. "Right. What did you find?"

"Come look," she said with an air of mystique.

He stood and followed her down the hall to the large laboratory that housed all of their experiments. She followed the right-side wall until she came to a small device hooked up to a tiny television monitor, which was showing wavy, green lines moving rapidly across its black screen.

"When I input the readings you took of the knife," she said, stopping at the monitor, "this is what I got. I would have told you sooner, but I wanted to make sure it wasn't an equipment malfunction."

Daniel focused on the monitor, brow tightened. He glanced at her and then back at the screen.

"What am I looking at?"

"The knife," she replied matter-of-factly.

He frowned, silent. Then he shook his head.

"I expected matter readings," he said with the air of a college professor, "which look nothing like this. This seems more like—"

"Waves of energy," she finished. "Yeah." She merely stared at him, unflinching.

He was silent a moment.

"You're telling me the knife is *radiating* energy?"

"Not quite. Whether it still is or simply was last night when you took the readings, I couldn't say," she replied, followed by a deep breath. "But these readings were not emanating *from* the knife. They *are* the knife."

He stared at her. "That can't be right."

She nodded slowly, smiling again, eyebrows raised. "I know."

Grant waited for his eyes to adjust to the darkness, but they never did. There was nothing to adjust *to*. Everywhere he looked was black.

The loud pounding against the door continued in the distance, but then suddenly stopped with a crash.

He's in.

Grant listened carefully for the sound of footsteps, for any sound at all. But there was nothing. The stench of smoke filled his nose, and he fought the urge to cough.

He craned his head closer to the door, listening carefully, so carefully. He held his breath so he could hear.

The floor creaked nearby. His muscles stiffened.

But then there was nothing except the soft, distant sounds of flames. He relaxed and took a thick, smoke-filled breath.

The door to the tiny broom closet burst open, and Konrad stood on the other side. His gun was inches from Grant's chest.

Konrad's forefinger wrapped around the trigger and tensed. "It's time I got paid," he said, smirking.

A loud gurgling sound came from around the corner, in the kitchen. Konrad turned, startled for a fraction of a second by the bubbling coffee pot. Which was exactly what Grant was waiting for.

He flung his hand straight into Konrad's face, splashing what remained of the peroxide from the drugstore into the mercenary's eyes. Konrad screamed in pain, both hands covering his eyes, and Grant slugged him as hard as he could in the stomach with his other fist. The short man doubled over, down on his knees, roaring in agony and clawing at his face.

Grant dropped the small brown bottle from his hand and kicked Konrad once more in the gut for good measure. Then he ran.

But he only took a step or two before Konrad's powerful hand wrapped around his ankle—the ankle attached to his wounded leg. Grant yelped in pain and went down face-first onto the floor.

He recovered quickly, kicking backward at the other man with his free leg. But Konrad was crazed, unflinching. His eyes were a mess, and he was bearing down, transferring all of his pain to the powerful grip he had on Grant's leg.

Grant wiggled and kicked with his whole body, but it was like being held in stone. Grant twisted and looked in front of him on the floor. The carpet was in flames, a bonfire only inches from his face.

There was nowhere to go.

Grant looked back at the fire on the floor in front of him again.

Konrad's grip tightened further.

A scream escaped his lips, as if it would help. The apartment door to his left flew open with a wooden *crack*, seemingly of its own accord. How Grant longed to run through it, he was only a few feet away . . .

But it was no good. The liquid fueling the flames rolled closer and the fire came with it, close enough for the heat to burn Grant's face and hair.

The liquid!

Grant snapped his head to the right and saw an unbroken bottle that Konrad had flung through the windows.

Intense heat burning his skin was all he could feel as he strained hard to wrap his fingers around the bottle's neck.

And then he had it. He twisted around sharp and fast, and with all of his remaining strength, he brought the bottle down from over his head to crash against Konrad's skull. Blood and liquid fire snaked down through the unconscious man's dark hair and across his face.

The last thing Grant saw of him was Konrad's blistered, broken scalp in flames. Forcing himself to his feet, he coughed through the smoke as he surveyed the place. There was nothing more to be done here. The flames had spread everywhere. Out in the hall, into the other apartments. Everything that he had ever owned was going up in flames.

He couldn't seem to care.

In the distance, he heard sirens, bringing questions that he had no answers for.

He made his way out of the apartment, delirious and unsteady on his feet, but still careful to avoid the flames. They spread faster now, out into the hall, and then out the building's front door and into the night. Julie brought the Jeep to a screeching halt a few feet away and he fell into the back, utterly spent.

"What happened?" she shouted. "Are you okay?"

"If I ever . . . get my hands on . . . the person who did this to me," he panted, on the brink of unconsciousness, *"I'll kill 'em."*

Two days later, across town at Grandview Cemetery, a closed-casket funeral was held for Collin Boyd—for this man who had become the man Grant once was. It was an outdoor service on a brisk, windy day, with just a handful of white folding chairs containing occupants. Julie attended, tears quietly streaming down her face throughout the entire event, but Grant told her he "just couldn't do it." Watching *himself* be buried . . . It was too much, he said, after everything he'd been through the last few days.

But despite his insistence that he would sit this one out, he'd found his way here anyway. He watched the ceremony from a distance, amid a stand of trees on the east side of the cemetery.

The reverend presiding over the funeral had delivered an unusual message. Grant couldn't quite make it all out—something about "a life that's wasted."

Long after everyone had gone and night had fallen, Grant still stood in his spot by the trees, watching the casket sink into the ground. The loud clacking of the coffin mechanically lowering was the only audible sound in the graveyard.

But he could barely make out the wooden box through his red, bleary eyes.

He was consumed with emotions, thoughts, and regrets. This wasn't just his body that was descending into the ground. It was everything he had been, the life he had known. It was gone, all of it. Forever.

He had always coveted his private life. Being by himself was the only time he found peace. But it was also the source of his greatest turmoil.

He was grateful to have his sister as a part of his life again. But even with her there, even though he was used to relative solitude . . . For the first time since childhood, he felt utterly, terrifyingly *alone*.

Collin Boyd was gone. Dead and buried. Grant Borrows was who he was now.

There was no going back.

Everything he thought he understood about life had changed, in less than an instant. The rules of science and nature and human existence were broken. He couldn't be Collin Boyd anymore, but he had no desire to be Grant Borrows, either.

All he really had to call his own were the questions.

So many questions.

Am I living someone else's life? he thought uselessly. *What right do I have to live a life that isn't my own?*

Shouldn't that be me *going into the ground?*

He studied the coffin as it went lower, lower, lower, until it was beyond his ability to see.

Standing alone in the silent darkness, Grant could keep his feelings in check no longer, and he was tired of trying. He broke down, his battered body collapsing into a shuddering heap on the ground, his shoulders shaking violently.

The sound of his sobs filled the graveyard.

But there was something . . .

What was that?

A faint glow caught his attention between haggard breaths. The ring on his finger had become radiant. It was diffuse, like a light shining deep underwater.

It was shimmering.

Miles away, far outside of town, a middle-aged woman with a serene presence and silver hair stood alone in a darkened room.

All of her attention was focused on the ancient object lying on a table in front of her. She studied it with tremendous mental focus, memorizing its every groove, crevice, and pattern. Her finger ran gently over it, rubbing the scarred, craggy surface.

Something in the room began to glow softly. Her eyes shifted to the source of the light as a smile spread across her features.

"At last," she proclaimed, standing upright, "the Bringer has come."

INTERREGNUM

"PHASE ONE COMPLETE," said a voice hiding behind a pair of slumped shoulders that slouched before a bright computer monitor. The computer and its user were accompanied by dozens of others just like them, lining the outer walls of the shadowy room.

A single reply came from a voice somewhere near the center of the vast room. It was a deep, booming voice, punctuated with unmistakable authority. "Activate Phase Two."

"Yes sir," the computer technician replied without taking his eyes from the screen. "Making the call now."

9

The motorcycle snarled down the murky street through late evening fog, a fog as thick as the motorcycle rider's hot breath. The black, gleaming machine was a bloodthirsty predator, nose to the ground in anticipation of a kill. The two tires chewed asphalt at speeds far above the legal limit, leaving the scent of hot rubber in its wake.

But the man who rode the metallic beast wore an expression of unemotional, intense concentration as he stared without blinking into the onrushing wind. No glasses or helmet visor obstructed his view; he had little use for either. Covered in black from collar to foot, he was completely bald and rather short of stature. He favored the simplistic look primarily for its functionality, but also because of the imposing silhouette it formed.

Fear was a powerful weapon. But it wasn't the most powerful one he carried.

Subterfuge, on the other hand, was pointless. It mattered not whether those he hunted saw his face. If they did, it was the last thing they would see in this life.

To those in the darkest corners of society—those who knew of the terrifying things that happened in the world's underbelly—he was known as the Thresher.

This particular chase had lasted a scant few hours. Another hunter might be disappointed by such a weak prey; the Thresher cared little for how long a hunt lasted. Once begun, he would see it through, regardless of how long it took. As a rule, he refused to stop for food, rest, or sleep until his agreed-upon task was complete.

This one would be over in less than five minutes.

Streetlamps passed overhead as fast as a strobe light. He paid them no attention. His eyes were on the narrow main road ahead, long empty in the deep of night. His senses were alert and his muscles tensed.

Each time a side street appeared to his right, he stole a quick look, briefly searching for signs of his prey. It was on the seventh side street he passed that he caught the faintest glimpse of the other biker before the buildings between them again blocked his view.

He bore no weapons save for the contents of a single scabbard secured to his left hip. From the ornate leather sheath he withdrew a sword, which reverberated on the air like a chime. An intricate pattern was pressed into the blade, which bore all the hallmarks of a Japanese *daito*—thin blade, curved upward at the end. The sword was power-fully sharp with a crystallized edge, made entirely of one of the world's strongest metals—save for its unusually long hilt, which was nearly two feet long by itself. The oversized wooden handle was wrapped in overlapping black leather straps.

The Thresher held the sword out to his side in one hand while guid-ing the motorcycle in the other, eyes still watching the passing streets to the right. His eyes were a glassy void, his breathing slow and cun-ning. As always, once the hunt was nearing its final moments, he relaxed and allowed himself to become an embodiment of undiluted reflex and instinct.

Suddenly he stood on the bike's foot pegs, calling on every last bit of torque the machine had to offer. It roared in protest but obeyed its master, streaking along the twilight pavement at suicidal speeds. Two more side alleys lay ahead, separated by wide blocks of buildings. And though he had no practical idea of how many seconds there would be before he reached the last of the two, he knew precisely when it would occur. He could feel it approaching . . .

The first street passed, and this time he was almost neck-and-neck with the bright red motorcycle he was chasing. He'd gained a second or two on the other man, which was all he needed. He increased his speed to the machine's last ounce of capability, and at the final moment, preparing to strike, he leaned forward as far as the bike's balance would allow.

Milliseconds before clearing the second alleyway, the Thresher flung the sword down the last street with a brutal swing of his right arm. The thin blade reacted as an arrow springing from a bow, darting through the dirty alleyway.

As the red bike came into view, it passed to the immediate left of a large, rusted-out, double-wide Dumpster. The Thresher's sword passed straight in front of his quarry's line of sight and pierced the side of the Dumpster. The sword's oversized hilt stuck out as a blunt instrument— directly in front of the passing motorcyclist's face.

The driver of the red machine didn't have time to realize what was happening until it was too late.

The Thresher watched as his quarry's head collided violently with the sword's protruding hilt, the man's neck wrenching itself sickeningly backward. He fell from the crimson bike with the unmistakable crack of breaking bones, while the bike continued moving out of sight.

In what seemed like only an instant, the Thresher had retrieved his sword from the Dumpster and was on top of the other man, holding his dazed and battered form in a brutal headlock with one arm. His other hand pressed the razor-sharp side edge of the sword against the man's throat with a tight, back-handed grip. He barely seemed to be exerting himself, with practiced, measured movements that applied only the exact amount of energy and force required, and nothing more.

The man flailed and struggled, but his body was still in shock from the blow, and his coordination faltered.

He spat into the bald man's face.

There was a buzzing sound and the Thresher turned loose of the headlock, yet the sword held the other man steadily in place.

"One move, and I'll sever your windpipe," the Thresher said in a calm, gravelly voice that was every bit as frightening as the sword he held with such perfect stillness. The words were marked with a refined British clip.

The hunted man tried to hold his breath as sweat mingled with his own blood, streaming into his eyes and down his face. He felt the edge of the sword prick the skin around his neck, yet he remained as still as he could manage.

The Thresher wiped the spit from his face and fished into one of his pockets, retrieving a tiny phone. He thumbed it open casually. "Yes?" his serious voice intoned.

"Konrad is finished," said the voice on the other end. "You may proceed."

"Parameters?" the Thresher asked, even though he knew the answer. This was no client calling to offer a job. This was *the* call.

The conversation he'd been waiting *years* for. Quite possibly his entire life for.

"You are hereby endowed with authority and purpose beyond that of any law of man," came the emotionless reply. "Do not stop until your task is complete."

The Thresher hesitated for a faint moment, effortlessly maintaining the sword's pressure against his quarry's neck. "The Secretum is confident? This *is* the time?"

"The appointed hour is at hand," was the slightly annoyed reply. "Your destiny has been written, and so shall it be: *the Bringer shall be slain at the hands of the Thresher*. Find him, and perform your function."

The Thresher snapped the phone shut, sliced his target's head from his shoulders in a powerful back-handed chop, wiped the blood off onto the headless torso's shirt, and sheathed the gleaming sword to his side, all in one elegant precise move.

He was gone without another sound.

10

Grant awoke violently, jerking straight up to a sitting position. He was sweating and breathing hard, and every muscle was tensed. It took several quiet minutes before he could remember where he was.

Or *who* he was.

When he'd finally caught his breath, he frowned; his bed sheet was ripped straight down the middle. He was still clutching the two torn halves in his hands. His leg throbbed, bright sunlight streamed in between the cracks in the blinds, and his thoughts drifted back . . .

Three days had passed since his defeat of the mercenary Konrad. And Julie's fussing over him had become more and more pronounced each day.

The morning after Collin and Konrad had died in the fire, Grant and Julie visited an emergency room in Garden Grove, on the south side of L.A.—to avoid any potential connection with the arson. It was more than two hours after they entered the hospital before Grant had finally seen a doctor.

The terse woman at the check-in desk was most unhelpful. When she requested his insurance card and carrier, he asked if she could find his records in the computer based on his name. She appeared rather miffed by the request, but she complied. He was unable to muster any surprise when she called him and Julie back to the desk to pronounce that no "Grant Borrows" had ever been a patient at any hospital on record. Her tone of voice made it clear how satisfied she was upon making this conclusion.

Grant paid the bill in cash.

That afternoon, at his sister's suggestion, they'd both taken up residence in the Wagner Building's high-rise penthouse. Grant still didn't feel like it was really his, but as Julie had put it, they simply had nowhere else to go. He tried to convince her to go back home; with Konrad dead, she should be safe. But she would hear none of it, determined as she was to look after him.

He'd spent each night tossing and turning in bed, snatching only brief moments of unconsciousness—all of which were filled with nightmares about burning buildings and bottles filled with fire and watching his own funeral from inside the coffin. He'd woken up screaming several times, and Julie repeatedly burst into the room and rushed to his side.

Prescription bottles rested on his nightstand, waiting. They were terribly inviting.

That night after the hospital visit, he'd had to physically lean on Julie just to make it inside the condominium, but she never complained. Two brand-new sets of stitches were biting into his leg on either side, where the bullet holes had been. The doctor had also treated him for a mild concussion, along with his other scrapes, and given him a prescription for pain—the very bottles that were currently holding his attention.

And as he'd done several times over the last three days, he quietly opened the nearest pill bottle so Julie wouldn't hear, and ingested more of the contents. He was consuming more than the recommended dosage—Julie had threatened to hide them if he did it again—but he didn't care.

It was late morning when he emerged from the bedroom to find Julie on the computer in the living room. She didn't look up from the screen as he crossed the hall to the bathroom.

"Hey, you ever heard of an 'Inveo Technologies'?" she called out.

"Who?" he replied, shouting through the closed door.

"Could you come out here, Collin? I think I may be on to something."

Grant swung open the bathroom door and crossed the hallway and living room to stand by her side. "Stop calling me Collin," he grumbled.

"Why do you keep saying that?" she demanded. "You *are* Collin on the inside, right?"

"Collin's dead," he said sourly, but then caught her expression. "*I'm me*, yeah. But Collin's gone. You should know, you went to the funeral."

"So what?" she finally turned to look at him. "You're my *brother*. I don't care if you start growing tentacles out of your nose, you're *always* going to be 'Collin' to me."

Grant frowned and turned away. He entered the kitchen and began rooting around in the refrigerator—which, like the apartment, had been fully stocked when they moved in—for something to eat, making quite a racket. Finally he fished out the milk, found a bowl, and poured himself some cereal at the kitchen's bar. He took a seat on a stool, his back stooped low as he leaned over the bowl to eat.

Julie knew that his bending over had less to do with the food than with what was happening inside his head.

"I'm worried about you."

He looked up, spotted her watching him.

"Please stop this," he said, resignedly.

"I can't help it!" she exclaimed, pent-up frustrations erupting. "You internalize *everything*, you always have!"

"How would *you* know what I've 'always' done? Like you were there to see it." He instantly regretted the outburst.

Julie's lips pressed together. "Even *I* can see that everything—all of this *insanity* that's happening to you—it's eating you alive. And it's eating *me* alive that it's eating *you* alive!"

Grant grimaced. *Women . . .*

"I feel . . . *trapped!*" he said. "Like I've been wrapped in unfamiliar skin, and there's no way to escape it. What am I supposed to do? Go *talk* to somebody? There aren't any specialists for this."

"You could talk to me."

Ah. The real problem.

He stepped out from behind the bar and crossed the room to kneel beside her desk chair. "You *know* I've never been much of a talker, Julie. And honestly . . . I haven't even seen you in *years*—"

"That was *your* choice, not mine—"

"I don't want to *talk*. I don't want to get into how I'm feeling. It's too much right now, I can't . . . process . . ."

75

"But," she protested, "you have to get past all of this bitterness and anger and frustration."

"No, I don't," he said plainly.

Julie nearly fell out of her chair.

He pressed the issue. "The pain and the hostility are all that's keeping me going. This drive to find answers is the only reason I have for getting out of bed in the morning."

"No, Collin—" she shook her head vehemently—"You can't give in to that."

"Why not?" he stood, frustrated.

"Because I don't want you to be a person who *hates!*" she howled. Tears began to stream down her cheeks. She crumpled further into her chair. "And neither would Mom and Dad. I want you to be the good man I know you are."

"But I'm *not* a good man!" he exploded at last, his face the color of blood.

She wouldn't face him and he looked away angrily, at a loss for words.

Finally he spoke in a small voice. "I killed him. Konrad. I think I really did it."

Julie stood and lifted his head with one hand. "He *was* trying to kill you."

Grant shook his head, inconsolable.

"When you realized that I was in danger," she said slowly, "what was your first instinct? What did you immediately do?" When he refused to answer, she said, "Think about *that* the next time you decide you're not a good person."

She left him standing there to retrieve something from her desk.

When she returned, Grant saw that it was the brass bracelet that Collin had placed inside his jacket before he died. "You are who you decide to be," she said, placing the bracelet on his wrist. "And *I* have decided that you're a kind, good-hearted man who takes after his father."

Grant embraced her, and she hugged him back. When they let go, she could see on his face that he remained unconvinced, uncertain. But there was hope in his eyes for the first time. That was something.

"You never answered my question, by the way," she re-seated herself at the computer. "Who do you know at Inveo Technologies?"

His face was awash in confusion. "I have no idea what you're talking about."

Julie fingered a small business card from the desktop and handed it to him. "I found this in your jacket. With the bracelet."

What?

He'd checked all of his pockets after his first conversation with that weird barefoot girl, and hadn't noticed any business cards anywhere. His jacket had been empty, at least until Collin had put the—

"It was in the same pocket as Granddad's bracelet?"

Julie nodded.

A clue! At last.

Collin had given him more than he thought. He looked again at the card. It read "Carl MacDugall, CEO, Inveo Technologies."

"Looks like some kind of tech company. They've got a big plant here in California, though it's a ways off, northeast of San Bernardino. Near Apple Valley, I think . . ." Julie was saying. She had pulled up Inveo's website and was clicking rapidly through the pages.

Grant began to pace.

"That man—we'll call him Collin for lack of a real name—he meant for me to find this. This company . . . they're involved, they have to be. It's some kind of conspiracy or something. Maybe they've even got the—I don't know, the *technology* or whatever that did this to me."

Julie watched him from a sideways view but said nothing. He couldn't tell whether she was incredulous at his suggestion that technology was responsible for his brand new life, or if she just didn't like where this line of reasoning was headed.

"Maybe I'm supposed to talk to this Carl MacDugall."

"You *really* think he'd give you an audience?" Julie asked, dubious. "Honey, from the looks of this office complex of his, the man could buy *Bill Gates* if he wanted to. What could possibly make him want to talk to you?"

"He *is* involved," Grant protested. "Or Collin wouldn't have given me that card."

"But what good does it do you?" Julie said, examining the card she held between two fingers. "What did he expect you to do, march into this guy's office and demand answers?"

Grant's eyebrows popped up.

"Don't even think about it," Julie warned, and then turned back to her computer monitor. "The front entrance has three guards, so the rest of the place must be major league."

"I can do this. Don't ask me how, I just know I can. This MacDugall guy and I have got to have a conversation."

Julie's ears were burning red, but Grant ignored her. It felt good to be in forward motion again.

"Are you seriously telling me," Julie remarked slowly, "that you're going to try to get an *appointment* to talk to this person?"

"It'd never work," he concluded after some thought, shaking his head. "It would look too suspicious, and besides, I'd have to make something up—some fake story about why I want to see him—and let's face it, I'm a *terrible* liar."

A hint of a smile played at her lips, accompanying memories of awkward attempts he'd made as a toddler to explain how he'd made a terrible mess or "accidentally" let the dog out of the back yard.

"Then where does that leave us?" she asked.

"Only one option I can think of," he said. "But you're *really* not going to like it."

11

"So that morning, four days ago, did you see anything . . . out of the ordinary?" Daniel asked.

The young man on the other side of the counter had been listening to him very intently, but now he rolled his eyes straight up, vacantly, in what Daniel could only assume was some form of concentration.

"It was the morning of that terrible rainstorm . . ." Daniel prodded.

"Oh right," The boy's eyes lit up. "This one dude came in with, like, *the* most criminal toupee ever," he said, laughing. Daniel didn't respond, so he went on. "I kid you not, it was like *moss* on top of his head, man."

Daniel merely stared at him, eyebrows up.

"Does that help?" the boy asked blankly.

Daniel turned and walked out of the coffee shop into the concrete canyons.

Do I attract *the crazy people? Am I putting something out there that* draws *them to me?*

Dry wind whipping around him, he scratched his head of short-cropped hair while surveying the street from side to side. Were there any other stores on this side of the road he hadn't tried yet? He glanced once again down at the bus stop, a few blocks away. *It began there*, he thought. The further he got away from the shimmers' points of origin, the less likely he was to find out where they were coming from. Or rather, *who* they were coming from, as he suspected.

Why can't I find you, whoever you are?

How did you do it, when so many others have failed?

His cell phone vibrated. He flipped it open as he continued walking down the street.

"What have you got?" He knew it was Lisa. No one else ever called him. He'd sent her to check some of the businesses in the upper floors of the larger buildings while he stuck to the storefront shops on ground level.

"One juicy possibility, though it's sort of a dead issue. So to speak."

"What is it?"

"This snotty secretary at a consulting firm said one of their IT guys was killed a few days ago."

Daniel stopped walking.

"Killed how?" he asked.

"She wouldn't say. Not sure if she just didn't know or if she was holding out on me. But she did mention that the guy lived in Glendale, at the site of that towering inferno from a few days ago. So naturally, I'm wondering if he died in the fire."

He was walking again. "Yeah, yeah. I remember that on the news. Did she give you a name?"

"She didn't want to, but I decided to make myself her new best friend until she felt like opening up."

Daniel found himself sympathizing with the woman at the consulting firm. "What's the name?"

"Collin Boyd," she replied.

"Collin Boyd," he repeated thoughtfully.

"You think he's our shimmer guy?" she asked.

"If he is, then the best lead I've ever had just went up in smoke," he replied.

"Let me see what I can find out about the fire and I'll get back to you," Lisa said. She was always up for a challenge.

The elevator dinged and the doors opened to the Wagner Building's spacious parking deck, which extended four floors below the building. Grant exited, purpose in his stride for the first time in days, and was met by a sea of Mercedes, Cadillacs, Ferraris, and Hummers.

A key chain from a kitchen drawer in his apartment looked an awful lot like car keys. Did the apartment come complete with wheels of some sort? If so, it would be here. He pressed the button on the chain.

A *boop-boop* echoed in the cement garage, and he walked toward it. He made the sound again and, turning to his left, saw where it had come from. A metallic navy blue convertible Corvette seemed to be grinning at him, as if it had just rolled off the assembly line and was hungrily waiting for him to rev the engine. He'd loved Corvettes ever since seeing a picture of his father gripping the wheel of a classic 1960 roadster. It seemed like a good omen to find one waiting for him. For the first time in days, he smiled.

"Nice bracelet," called a familiar voice.

"Mm," his shoulders drooped. "Swell."

He turned.

There she was again, leaning against a concrete pillar a few yards away. *Maybe she has a shoe phobia . . . Wonder if there's a name for that?*

Eh, who am I kidding? I don't care.

"What's the inscription say?" she asked, trying to make it out from where she stood.

"None of your business. What do you want?"

"Well, if what I'm hearing is true, you're setting out on a one-way street to badness. Not only am I *not* the only one who knows what you're planning . . . but only fools rush in to a place like Inveo Technologies. It's not a company; it's a *fortress*. Comes with all the extras, including one of the most state-of-the-art security forces in the world. We're talking *guardapalooza*. Even if you somehow managed to sneak in, the only way out of *that* place is with a tag on your toe."

"And just exactly how do know what I'm planning?" Grant's feathers were ruffling with every word she spoke.

"Fish gotta swim. Birds gotta fly. We all got our purpose."

"And keeping up with my itinerary is yours?" he asked.

"Hey, I'm the one who told you to leave town and not look back."

He frowned.

"But your curiosity got the better of you. Don't suppose I can blame you for that." She cocked her head to one side. "By the way, for what it's worth, it looks like you're out of danger. For the moment. That is, aside from this big 'storm the gates' thing you're working on."

"Who *are* you?"

She just smiled.

"If you can't tell me who you are, then why are you helping me?"

"Oh, you're *so cute*," she said as though she were admiring a friend's baby. "Who said I was here to *help* you?"

He frowned. "You helped me find my sister."

"Did I?" she replied thoughtfully. "You sure of that?"

He *had* seen her outside the UCLA police station, hadn't he? Pointing the way to find his sister? Of course he'd seen her.

Right?

"You're really infuriating." He massaged his forehead.

She nodded, unconcerned. "I get that a lot." She squared her shoulders. "Look, I just stopped by to offer congrats, slugger, and a warning. Instead of this Inveo thing, you really should be looking into the other groups that are keeping an eye on you. There's one in particular that frankly, I expected you to have already found . . .

"But anyway, back to the big victory. That's one down. Burned and buried alive. Juicy." Her eyebrows popped up. "Of course, most of the others watching you have little interest in seeing you *dead*, so hopefully you won't always knee-jerk into violence mode. But I should warn you that *very few* of these folks have your best interests at heart. And just because you defeated Konrad doesn't mean that the ones who hired him won't send somebody else to try again."

His eyes met hers, but she maintained a casual expression. "How many?"

She didn't answer. For a moment, he thought she might not have understood the question.

"How many of these groups *are there*, keeping tabs on me?"

She smiled without humor. "Lot more than you think, bucko. But if what you did to ol' Konrad was just the warm-up . . . Can't *wait* to see how you handle the rest," she said, her eyes dancing.

Grant rolled his eyes and stalked to his car. By the time he checked his rearview mirror, she was gone.

Daniel and Lisa waited two days before visiting the burned-out Glendale apartment building. They figured the police and fire marshals would mostly be done by then and a curious bystander could get a look around easier. Only there wasn't much to look at.

Daniel kept a bandana to his nose as he picked his way through the rubble of the burned down apartment building. He and Lisa had been here for hours and still couldn't make head nor tail of anything they found. It was beyond recognition.

Lisa was wandering around, picking up various things and scanning for traces of a shimmer, but nothing spiked. The one part of the building still standing was the central stairwell, an old brick shaft that reached all three floors. Only the first-floor portion of it remained intact.

"What are you thinking?" Daniel asked her as he continued to sift.

"Well . . . it definitely strikes me as odd that nothing—not one single object—survived this fire."

He nodded. "Someone's covered their tracks."

"Didn't the news say it was a gas main or something?" she said, still looking through the debris.

He eyed her. "Don't believe everything you hear on the news."

She grinned.

"If the police lied to the media about the cause of the fire," Daniel said, "then I'd say there's a good chance this Collin Boyd may not be dead, after all. . . . At any rate, I want to know who he is. Would you go round to the back of the building and jot down the license-plate numbers of the cars back there? We can check them later to see if one of them was his."

She nodded and was off.

He continued sifting for a moment before he noticed that a nearby shadow was moving.

"And how did *you* know Mr. Boyd?" a booming voice said.

He looked up. A man stood to his right with an angry frown on his face. A large man whose bulging midsection protruded from a navy blue trench coat, though only his left arm went through one of the sleeves. His right was under the coat, held in place by what looked like a shoulder sling.

"Old friend from college," Daniel lied. He stuck out his hand to the detective. "Daniel Cossick."

"Matthew Drexel," the cop replied, refusing to take Daniel's hand.

"Do you contaminate the crime scenes of *all* of your college buddies' mishaps?"

"Collin was the first," Daniel said nervously. "My assistant and I— we were just . . . curious . . . about the circumstances surrounding his death. The damage here is just . . . mind-boggling . . ." his voice trailed off as he glanced around.

"That kind of curiosity will land you in jail," said the man, with a dour scowl. He adopted an authoritative swagger as he walked closer.

"You're a police officer, then?" Daniel asked.

The man flipped open a badge. "Detective. I'm investigating the arson/homicide on these premises, which I believe to be connected to . . . another case I'm working on."

"So it *was* just the one death, then?" Daniel probed.

"Just one *body*," Drexel replied slowly, still warily watching Daniel.

The detective narrowed his eyes and took another step closer. They were standing in the sun, but to Daniel it felt like a third-degree heat lamp.

Drexel gestured with his chin toward Lisa. "You want to tell Ms. Moneypenny over there to stop rifling through my evidence?"

"What?" Daniel blustered, then caught on. "Oh! Lisa, this nice officer wants you to quit whatever you're doing back there!"

She appeared from behind the central stairwell wall. "You really a cop?" she shouted.

"You really this guy's assistant?" Drexel replied.

Lisa rolled her eyes at his attempted joke, but then was all business. "You better come see this."

Daniel and Detective Drexel both circled the stairwell until they reached Lisa's vantage point. Sticking out from the other side of the wall was a tiny foot with a black shoe on. As they continued to circle, the full body came into view: an elderly woman with graying purplish hair, her short frame lying facedown, unmoving. Her wrinkled face was turned too far to one side, her eyes closed. She still clenched a large, pearl-white purse with both knobby hands.

Drexel's eyes became tiny slits, and he examined the woman for several minutes without approaching. Then he knelt and seized her hand. It was limp. "Hasn't been dead long. And no burn marks, so she definitely didn't die in the fire." He pushed aside her hair. Dark bruises were visible along her neck. "Her neck is snapped," Drexel concluded.

"Either of you know this woman?" he asked softly.

Daniel exchanged a clueless glance with Lisa, but her eyebrows appeared knitted together.

"I think . . . she's the landlady," she said.

Drexel swore. "You sure about that?"

"No," Lisa answered honestly. The way she effortlessly held the larger man's gaze . . . It occurred to Daniel that Lisa wasn't intimidated by Drexel. Not at all.

While *he* had become unhinged the moment the large man had spoken.

But then, she has no reason to be anxious around a policeman. I, on the other hand . . .

"I'm going to need you both to come with me," Drexel was saying, rising to his feet. "Your knowledge of the victim may be . . . *useful* to my case. And frankly, the fact that you knew him at all means that *you* may not be safe—" The detective's phone rang, interrupting his speech. "Excuse me," he mumbled, and turned away, moving back toward his brown sedan. He was trying to keep Daniel and Lisa from hearing, but it was a quiet Sunday morning in the old neighborhood. They clearly made out the words "cut off his *head*?" as Drexel's voice rose involuntarily as he said it.

Lisa carefully and innocently walked to Daniel's side.

"You're white as a sheet," she whispered. "You all right?"

Daniel wiped sweat from his brow with one hand while whispering back to her. He eyed the cop again, who was now speaking on his car radio, the cord snaking out through the side window.

"I think things just got a lot more complicated."

12

Three days later, Grant sat with Julie in a diner across the street from the Inveo Technologies corporate headquarters, trying not to look nervous. It was one of those tiny truck stops stuck in the middle of desert sprawl like a ship bottomed on a dry lake. They were the only non-regulars in the ramshackle building, which looked like it could collapse in on itself at any moment.

But Grant's attention was elsewhere. The barefoot girl had been right again. This was no simple facility he was looking at. It was a *campus*.

Grant and Julie had spent every waking minute carefully considering his covert entry into Inveo. Hours upon hours they pored over books at the local library, on the computer, digging up old architectural plans from county and district records. It wasn't easy, but they needed every last detail they could find. Of particular interest was the structure's layout and security.

The campus was located well outside of L.A., cozied on the gentle slopes of a mountainside, on a big plot of undeveloped land north of Big Bear Lake. A modest town had sprung up around the Inveo plant, but the town was dwarfed by the scale of the plant itself. The entire Inveo property struck Grant as akin to some kind of modern citadel.

And here he was, about to David his way into this Goliath.

Grant and Julie ate breakfast in silence, both nervous at what waited ahead of them. After leaving cash on their table, they stepped out into the arid wind and squinted across the road at their target. The mammoth complex, dozens of high-rise buildings, sprawled over four square miles of land at a sloping angle, essentially a city unto itself. An enormous manufacturing plant was situated in the middle, with other buildings of all sizes surrounding it. The plant was clearly the oldest of the buildings on the grounds, with metal siding, a flat roof, and add-ons stretched outward in every direction. Many of the other buildings were much newer, with sparkling glass on all sides, or modern brick façades.

Grant's eyes fell upon the tallest of these buildings, which was situated closer than any of the others to the diner, only a few hundred yards across the street and behind a tall perimeter fence. It was the executive building, his target.

Julie sat in the driver's seat of the car and Grant knelt next to her, door open.

"What's your job?" he asked Julie.

"Surveillance. Keep the car ready," she recited, steeling herself.

Grant nodded then retrieved a shopping bag out of the blue convertible's trunk. Carrying the bag, he strolled down the street to an abandoned gas station. It was here that he and Julie had struck gold during their research. Yesterday, while surfing the Net, one of their searches turned up a site on urban legends, which contained an entry about Inveo Technologies and a secret exit built long ago as an executive escape. They were about to write off the legend as a myth when another entry claimed to have proof that it really existed, providing step-by-step details on how to access it from the outside. A few urban explorers even claimed to have snuck into the plant and caused a little mischief. The plant being so big, once you were inside, it wasn't hard to blend in with all of the employees if you could simulate their look, they explained.

Behind the decrepit gas station, Grant hefted open a set of wooden storm doors. A set of stairs inside led down to a cellar, where he tugged on a cord overhead to turn on a lone light bulb. He quickly stripped and put on the gray jumpsuit that was inside the bag, along with a matching pair of gloves. His heart pumping like mad, he stuffed his street clothes into the bag and stowed it under the stairs. A tiny earpiece went into his left ear, completely hidden from sight once inside; Julie had acquired a set of them rush delivery from an online store.

"Okay, I'm set," he said.

"You've got eight minutes until shift change," Julie said.

Grant found the door to the tiny closet on his left, just as the Web site had described. Following the instructions exactly, he stepped inside and shut the door behind him, which left him in the dark. To his right, he felt for and found a set of old wooden shelves attached to the wall. So far the instructions were dead on. Counting down, he grabbed the third one from the top and pulled it straight out. It only gave an inch. He pulled similarly on the top shelf, and then pushed it back in.

Straight ahead, a dim light appeared as the wall suddenly swung open.

"Did it work?" Julie said, her voice clear but a bit tinny in his ear.

"Think so," he replied.

"What do you see?"

"A really long hallway. Dark. What should I expect at the other end?"

She was silent a moment. *"I'm not entirely sure . . ."*

"You can't tell from the floor plans?"

"Collin," Julie deadpanned, *"my expertise in this area is summed up in the number of times I've seen Tom Cruise dangling from that wire in* Mission: Impossible. *Give me a break, okay? Hey, you better hurry— there's less than five minutes."*

Abandoning stealth, Grant sprinted down the narrow corridor. A stench like rotten potatoes filled the hallway, which was lit only by individual light bulbs dangling from the ceiling every thirty feet. A few minutes later, following a couple of turns and some more running, he came upon the next door and opened it. Out of breath, he pulled out a tiny flashlight and turned it on.

Stretched out before him was an enormous basement that looked like a vast warehouse. Wooden crates, cardboard boxes, and assorted shelves stacked floor to ceiling filled with more boxes, consumed the space in every direction.

"What do they make here again?"

"New technologies, according to their website. Whatever that *means."*

He looked to the far left wall and saw his next door. Beyond it, he found a stairwell. So far, so good.

He glanced at his watch again: *5:30.*

Time's up.

He bolted up the stairs.

Opening the door to the first floor, he was met by an enormous, bustling lobby, complete with cherry wood accents, marble and car-peted floors, hand-crafted lounge chairs, and a giant glass façade that stretched from the floor to the vaulted ceiling, over three stories high. A behemoth of a receptionist desk stretched forty feet long, with no less than six employees seated behind it. All of them appeared to be speak-ing into headset telephones. The Inveo logo was emblazoned behind them in a monstrous 3-D art piece that stretched upward the entire three stories; it was a gaudy melting pot of Greek and Roman symbols mixed with high technology, with a stylized "I.T." at the top.

Employees entered and exited the vast atrium, most of those enter-ing making for one of the eight elevators at the far end of the lobby. Grant watched them come and go for a moment, considering how nor-mal their lives were. They were grazing through their day like cows, casual, unconcerned.

Normal.

He'd forgotten what that was like.

This certainly didn't look like the command center for an identity-theft conspiracy.

Grant blended in with the crowd moving toward the elevator, his jumpsuit vaguely resembling that worn by the janitorial staff. As long as no one made a close inspection of his appearance, he'd be fine. The outfit was the least of his worries.

His heart skipped a beat as he approached the crowd inside the concave elevator foyer. This was possibly the riskiest part of his plan. If this didn't work just right, the game was over before it had even begun.

Two sets of elevator doors opened at once and Grant intentionally entered the one that seemed to have more people on board. He squeezed through the tiny, congested space and stood at the back of the elevator.

Craning his neck around those before him, he saw that the panel of buttons was activated by a keycard. As expected. Several of the buttons were already lit up, indicating which floors the car would stop on. But his destination—the floor with Carl MacDugall's office on it—wasn't one of them.

"Um . . ." Grant offering his best embarrassed fumble, "Could you hit sixteen, please?"

The man closest to the panel of buttons turned in surprise. His refined, tailored ensemble stood in stark contrast to Grant's loud coveralls, which he did not fail to notice, offering Grant a quick look up and down. With distaste, he turned back to face the sliding doors.

He pressed the button marked "16" with a pronounced sigh.

Grant breathed a silent sigh of his own, working hard to relax his raging pulse. He ran through his plan once more as the elevator moved up. Julie remained silent in his headpiece, but he could hear her misgivings beneath the dead air.

He knew what she was afraid of. Breaking and entering was one thing. But what if MacDugall refused to talk? Was Grant capable of doing what he must to *make* the man talk?

Guess we'll find out.

The elevator chimed and he exited into a pristine hallway fit for Caesar, complete with ornately-carved Roman pillars. A secretarial pool faced him; most of the desks were empty from the shift change. A few half-glances were cast in his direction from the handful of employees still there, but otherwise no one seemed to take notice of him.

"The hall to your right," Julie said in his ear, though he remembered where to go. A spacious assistant's office at the end of the hall would lead into the vast corner office of Carl MacDugall, chief executive officer.

But he was looking for something else. "Which door is it?" he whispered, then smiled pleasantly at a woman emerging from a rest room on the right.

"Should be the fourth one on your left," Julie answered. *"Assuming they haven't remodeled since the date on these floor plans."*

That's a comforting thought.

The door she directed him to wasn't labeled. There was no way to tell if it was the right one.

But he had no other options. With a deep breath—and a quick glance to both sides to make sure no one was observing him closely—he put his hand on the doorknob and turned it.

To his surprise, it opened. Inside was a lavishly equipped confer- ence room, its centerpiece an oblong mahogany table surrounded by sixteen leather chairs. Doors were situated on either end of the long room, leading sideways into other rooms. He marched to the closest door on his right and opened it.

The next room was a plush office, with more mahogany fixtures, shelves on all of the walls, a flamboyant, hand-carved wooden desk, an old fashioned banker's-style desk lamp, and a burgundy wingback chair. The chair was swiveled in Grant's direction, as if waiting for him. In it sat an elderly fellow who could only be Carl MacDugall.

Streaks of silver defined his perfectly groomed head of hair, along with a navy blue pinstripe suit, manicured nails, and black loafers so shiny Grant found it hard to look directly at them. His brown eyes were sunken deep. He clutched at his pants with one hand yet gave off an appearance of being thoroughly unmoved by Grant's entrance.

"Mr. MacDugall, I hope you'll forgive the unexpected entrance," he began, wasting no time, "but my name is Grant Borrows. Do you know who I am?"

MacDugall looked him in the eye but hesitated, as if trying to decide what to say.

"No," he grunted, his eyes still locked on Grant. He wasn't panick- ing, he was barely even reacting.

This is very, very wrong.

"How about Collin Boyd?" Grant tried again, approaching the desk. "Ever heard that name?"

"I'm afraid not, young man," MacDugall replied, but quickly gave a furtive glance in the direction of his secretary's outer office.

Uh-oh.

"You shouldn't be here," the elder man said suddenly.

Grant ran for the receptionist's door. "You knew I was coming!" he cried. "Who's out there, security?"

He flung the door open, frustration overwhelming all sense of cau- tion.

He froze.

"What do you see?" Julie said breathlessly from his earpiece. *"Who is it?"*

13

San Diego's coolest winds of the year blew hard across the harbor against the Thresher and his motorcycle, tempting it from the road. But he was undeterred. Distractions were pointless.

He had an appointment with an old contact. It had taken days to track her down. In the end, he found her at an art studio that catered to a rather eclectic clientele.

Which was perfectly in keeping with what he knew about her.

"Everyone's buzzin', man," said Lilly, the girl with the paintbrush and palette, adding a flourish of green to her work. "I don't know who started it, but just last night, more'n once I heard, 'Someone's come, someone who can protect us.'"

She looked completely different from the last time he'd seen her. Her hair was pink and purple, her nose and ears were filled with rings, and one arm bore dozens of plastic charm bracelets.

"Us?" he asked her, even though he knew the answer.

"*Us*, man," she said, as if it were obvious. She splashed yellow and orange in furious swings of her brush. In the three minutes since he had found her, Lilly had taken a four-foot-wide canvas and turned it into an impressionist vista of the Santa Ana mountains. It was so breathtakingly beautiful, even he was taken with it.

"Why do you need protecting?" he asked idly, studying her work.

"I gotta *gift*, dude," Lilly gestured toward her canvas. "People hate anyone who's different. *Tell me* you don't know this."

The Thresher watched as she added magnificent, stringlike clouds over the painting's sunset, mixing gorgeous shades of light red, teal, and a deep purplish tone.

"This man who will protect you, who is he?"

"Never said it was a *guy*," she teased, turning to look at him for the first time. "Don't start in with the chauvinist male superiority crap. Because I will *ditch* you right here and now . . ."

He stepped forward and pressed a wad of greenbacks into her hand.

She offered a fake wounded expression for a moment, but then grinned. "They call him Borrows. Friend of mine told me *everyone's* talking 'Borrows this' and 'Borrows that'."

"Fascinating," he said thoughtfully.

"Liar," she jabbed. "You could care less about anything but whoever you're hunting right now."

He eyed her evenly. Watched her sign her initials to the fresh painting and set the used canvas aside for a fresh one.

"Why do you help me, Lilly?" he asked, genuinely curious. "You know who I am and what I do."

"Dude, I may be gifted, but I ain't exactly rollin' in it. I need the bank."

He resigned himself to her answer, satisfied.

"Now when are you going to ask me what you *really* came to ask me?" she cast a quick glance over her shoulder before returning to her canvas.

"What do you know of the Bringer?" he asked.

Lilly stopped painting and turned.

"I've heard the phrase. Whoever or whatever it is, rumor mill says it's in L.A.," Lilly replied, her eyes falling to his hip.

Los Angeles . . . His mind began formulating the fastest route to the big city.

"I see you're still carrying that overgrown knife of yours . . ."

The Thresher didn't reply, looking blandly into her eyes.

"Thought maybe you would've traded up to a gun or something by now. Kill anybody with it lately?" she asked.

He turned to leave.

"It's not for buttering toast, love."

"Okay, you owe me big for this one," Lisa huffed, marching into Daniel's office.

"What? Did you get something?" he replied, glancing up at her. He was shuffling papers, trying to find his desk, which was beneath them . . . somewhere. Probably.

She sighed, frustrated at his lack of attention.

"Well?" he prodded. He clutched another large stack of papers, opened the filing cabinet to his left, and began sorting them in.

"Do you remember Barry?"

"No," he replied without looking up.

"My ex-boyfriend Barry? We went out for a year before he decided he needed a girlfriend who wasn't smarter than him?"

"Still no."

Lisa frowned. "He's got a job as vault security at the bank's main branch downtown. I had to promise the sleazeball that I'd go out with him again sometime, but he tracked down Collin Boyd's last bank statement for me and . . . *get this*. Collin's cell phone bill is still being paid. The most recent payment—four days ago—was paid by automatic debit."

"How can the phone company collect from a dead man's bank account?"

She smiled for the first time. "Because the payment wasn't taken from Collin's account. The billing was changed a week ago to an account belonging to someone else."

The stack of papers fell from Daniel's hands and fluttered across the floor, as he looked up at her.

"Grant Borrows," she grinned, enjoying his growing excitement.

"We've got his name!" he said, breathlessly.

"Um, hello, *I* got his name," she said. "I'll tell you the rest, but first you have to tell me something."

"*Lisa* . . ." Daniel's eyes scanned the ceiling for nothing. "Don't do this now . . ."

It wasn't the first time she'd used her investigative skills to try and bargain her way into his past. Her growing obsession with knowing everything she could about him was something he found not only inappropriate, but annoying to the highest degree.

When she didn't respond, he sighed. "What is it?" he asked resignedly.

"I just want to know why you do this, that's all," she said innocently, clinging tightly to a manila folder she'd just retrieved from her shoulder bag. "Why you study, well . . . what we study."

"Fine," he grimaced, leaning back in his chair and rubbing his eyes. "I guess it goes back to my mother."

Lisa settled into the chair opposite his desk.

"I never knew my dad. He ran out on her before I was born. And having no siblings, it was just me and Mom for my entire childhood. I had an insatiable curiosity about how things work, but it made me accident-prone—constantly sticking my fingers into electrical sockets or trying to open batteries to see the acid inside or . . . well, you get the idea. But no matter what kind of danger I fell into, I always managed to bounce back. Mom said I was just too curious and stubborn to quit learning—I had no time for anything else.

"I was fifteen when the world changed. Mom was crossing the street on her way home—right in front of our house—when a car hit her doing fifty."

Lisa gasped, yet Daniel continued his story as if giving a clinical dissertation.

"She suffered many injuries, but it was the brain damage that proved irreparable. The doctors told me that she still had brain activity, that she was able to see and comprehend, but the part of her brain that allowed her to communicate had been damaged beyond repair. Essentially, she was still my mother 'in there,' in her head, but she was trapped and couldn't express herself, couldn't *be* herself.

"I became obsessed with the human brain. I received my doctorate in neuroscience. Finding alternative ways of allowing my mother's brain to express itself, beyond normal human interaction, became my obsession. But I went beyond the typical fields and embraced extrasensory studies in addition to my continued work on uncovering the deepest mysteries of the human brain. And I subsequently became the laughingstock of my post-graduate studies. Now will you please hand me that file?"

He could tell he'd surprised her. She placed the file on the desk without a word.

He grabbed it and began scanning through it quickly. "Mm, no picture . . ." he muttered.

Lisa snapped back to reality. "I couldn't find records of any kind for anyone with the name 'Grant Borrows' before five days ago. No medical records. No tax history. Not even a Social Security number. It's undoubtedly a fabricated identity."

"What's this medical discharge report? And how on earth do you get this stuff?"

"I know a guy who knows a guy. The Garden Grove Hospital report you have there is our biggest lead. He was treated there for various injuries the same night as the Glendale fire . . ."

"Let me guess," Daniel interjected. "He was treated for, among other things, burns?"

She nodded. "Along with a minor concussion, various cuts and bruises, and a *bullet wound*."

Daniel whistled. What kind of danger was he about to fall into?

14

Grant was thunderstruck. Confused, and a little dizzy.

Staring back at him wasn't a security guard, a policeman, or even a secretary.

It was a woman. And likely the most beautiful woman he'd ever seen. Blond and cherry-lipped. Blue eyes alive with mischief. Dressed in a worker's jumpsuit not that different from his own, though her curves shaped it into something almost trendy. Her mouth was turned up faintly, in seductive amusement.

"I was starting to think you'd *never* get here," she said in a slight Southern drawl.

Her right arm was out, a gloved hand pointed at him as if a gun. But she held no weapon. She gave a *click* as if cocking a trigger, then slinked her way around Grant, eyes still holding his, until she was past him. At the last moment, she winked.

She slowly walked toward MacDugall, her hand leveled at his head the entire time. "Now you be a good boy," she said to the CEO, "and tell this good-lookin' fella the same thing you told me."

Grant was stupefied. It was ridiculous. Yet MacDugall was watching the woman's every move, her every gesture, as if he fully expected her to pull the gun's imaginary trigger any second.

Grant shifted uncomfortably on his feet, almost feeling sorry for MacDugall.

When MacDugall didn't speak up, she placed the tip of her finger next to his temple.

"O-okay, okay!" he said, beads of sweat visible on his forehead. "I, uh . . . I wasn't lying when I said I don't know you, son. But I know what's *happened* to you."

Grant slowly shuffled back toward the desk, his attention suddenly shifting from the beautiful woman. "Did you do this to me?"

MacDugall shook his head quickly, desperately. "No! I just . . ." He blew out a breath. "We research and develop new technologies here. Of all kinds. On a few rare occasions, we've done some—some highly specialized, custom research—"

The blond woman prodded him with her finger. "Get to the good part already." She rolled her eyes impatiently.

Who was this woman? Why was she *helping* him?

"Quite some time ago, when we were a much smaller operation," MacDugall said, eyes shifting like mad, "we conducted some very . . . next generation research and experimentation on behalf of a well-paying client. It was all kept very quiet, completely off the books."

"What kinds of experiments?" Grant immediately demanded.

"Mr. Evers, the client, asked us to develop technologies—mechanical, pharmaceutical, whatever—capable of *enhancing* the functions of the human body."

The blond woman shot Grant a look as if this revelation vindicated her strange actions.

"Evers . . ." Julie said thoughtfully in Grant's ear.

He turned his head and whispered back, "You know that name?"

"No, I don't think so. Evers . . . Evers . . ." she repeated, as if trying to jar it free from her mind.

"And did you succeed in your experiments?" the blond woman prompted.

"No!" MacDugall cried. "Never! That's what I've been trying to *tell*—"

Grant jumped when a blaring siren wailed out, sounding as though it had filled the entire building.

The woman, suddenly furious, turned to MacDugall and said, "BANG!" He recoiled violently, as if the faux gun in her hand had shot him in the head. But before he realized the truth, she backhanded him into unconsciousness. One of his hands fell limp and Grant could see that MacDugall had pressed some kind of alarm button attached to the underside of the arm on his chair.

It occurred to Grant that he was feeling the same way he'd felt on that first day, a week ago, when he'd found out his life had been changed. Nothing made any sense, and things could *not* get any more bizarre . . .

The next thing he knew, the blond woman had grabbed him by the hand and was dragging him through the secretary's office and out into the hall. "Come *on!*" she sighed, thoroughly exasperated.

The last thing Grant saw of MacDugall's office was a security camera over the door, swiveling to follow him.

Swell.

This was just the best plan ever.

The blond woman led Grant to the elevator area—past the secretarial pool, none of whom seemed to care very much about the sirens— and brandished a screwdriver from one of her pockets. The light above the doors indicated that this car was currently on the fifth floor and going down.

She wedged the flat-head between the doors, prying them open. Then she looked back and winked at Grant. "See ya at the bottom," she said merrily. She stepped off the ledge and fell straight down into the empty shaft.

Grant's breath caught in his throat, not believing what he'd just seen. Was this woman *insane?*

An elevator to his right dinged, opened, and spit out a handful of security guards, decked in military body armor.

There was no time to think.

"Hold it!"

Still wearing his jumpsuit and matching gloves, Grant dove into the empty elevator shaft after the woman, grasping desperately at the center bundle of cables that held the elevator. One look down found him fighting the urge to panic.

Two of the guards stood in the doorway above him. A third knelt and tried reaching down far enough to grab Grant with a powerful hand.

One of the standing guards pulled two items from a belt clip: one he barked into, the other he pointed like a pistol. But it didn't quite look like a pistol.

He fired. Grant ducked. Two small darts grazed his left arm, still attached to the guard's device by long wires.

Oh, of course. Taser.

Grant began making his way down the cable, hand-over-hand. Faster and faster he descended, as the guard above shot at him again.

He had started from the sixteenth floor, but he tried not to think about that, or anything else, except that next handful of cable.

Just take one more handhold. One more.

Come on.

One more.

Adrenaline was pumping hard through his veins when his feet finally touched solid ground. His arms were exhausted and he was covered in sweat, panting hard, but he'd made it.

Except he hadn't. This wasn't the bottom; it was only the top of the elevator car. Above him, he could see shadows still moving from the open door he'd come from. He counted the floors as best he could, estimated that he was around the fourth or fifth floor now.

There was a crack in the door in front of him, less than an inch wide.

She went through here.

If she could, so could he.

He squeezed his fingers through the crack, arms still shaky from the exhausting descent. But he managed to force the doors apart with little difficulty. He found himself a few feet below the floor level, so he had to climb up and roll over onto the marble floor. He lay there for a few moments, catching his breath.

When he looked up, a pristinely groomed woman in an immaculate pantsuit stood nearby, waiting for an elevator car.

She was looking down at him as if he were a leper.

His jumpsuit grimy and wet with sweat, Grant stood slowly, still struggling to breathe. Her bug eyes followed him as he strode by her, and he pointed back at the open elevator shaft.

"Don't ride that one," he said.

Her face blanched as she nodded.

He spotted a men's room nearby and ducked inside, locking the door behind him.

"Don't do this often, do ya, big boy?"

He spun around and there she was—the blond woman from the office. She was leaning back against the sink, untying one of her shoelaces. Once done, she wrestled it out of her shoe. She shoved the string into her pants pocket.

"Still . . . points for makin' it this far," she said, smiling. "You might just be worth savin'."

He leaned over on shaky arms, hands on his knees, and tried to catch his breath, while allowing himself a moment to take her in more fully. She had a rosy complexion and strong cheekbones. Her head was tilted to the side as she studied him with deep-set, unconcerned eyes.

"So you *do* do this sort of thing a lot?" he asked between gasps.

"Zip cord makes the trip down easier," she said, holding out a wadded-up, black nylon rope, clipped to her belt on some kind of pulley.

"*That's* what I forgot when I left the house this morning," he wheezed, still panting.

She acknowledged his sarcasm with a smile. Then she grew serious. "The guards know what floor we're on by now. Time for Plan B."

She turned and stepped into one of the bathroom stalls. He staggered after her.

She stood atop the commode, and had her screwdriver out again, unscrewing the grate from a heating duct in the ceiling.

"You're kidding me, right?" he said, the thought of crawling up into the duct remarkably unappealing.

"Y'reckon?" she said absently.

She loosened a second screw and the grate fell open on hinges. She turned to face Grant again. "Give me a boost," she said.

He paused, uncertain. "Why should I trust you?"

"You shouldn't . . ."

The door handle to the bathroom suddenly jiggled from the other side. Then a knock. "Open up!" a deep voice barked.

". . . but it's me or *them*," she finished matter-of-factly.

Grant made a foothold with his hands and lifted her up into the duct. She scrambled nimbly inside as Grant heard keys jangling outside the door.

"You comin' or what?" her voice called from above.

He looked up to see her hand extending down toward him.

He stepped up onto the toilet seat and took the hand as he heard a key slide into the door's lock.

The bathroom door swung open just as he'd pulled the grate closed.

The blond woman pulled the shoestring out of her pocket and tied the grate closed from inside.

15

They crawled. The going was slow through the tight quarters. She was in front, Grant close behind.

The only thought he could manage right now was that this woman must be from one of the "groups of people" the barefoot girl had warned him about. And stunning or not, he needed to be wary around her.

Aside from that, he also found himself wondering if she might be insane.

He broke the silence first, whispering. "Are you a crazy person?"

"No, but you ain't the first to ask."

"Then what's your story? Who are you? And why are you here? Are you *helping* me?"

"Just keep crawlin', big boy," she whispered back, a smile audible in her voice. "There'll be time for questions *after* today's object lesson."

"Hey," Julie broke in, *"I hate to interrupt the rampant and inappropriate flirting but the situation outside has disintegrated."*

"Like what?" Grant stopped crawling. Through another ventilation grate, he saw and heard at least a dozen security guards march below in fast succession.

"Bad time to quit movin'," the blond woman paused and looked back. "Don't make me regret helping you out."

"Police cars, fire trucks, dozens of security vehicles . . ." Julie replied. *"You name it. All blocking the front entrance."*

That was no problem. He had no intention of going *out* the front entrance.

"*And they've barricaded the entire street,*" Julie added. "*The gas station is blocked—I can't reach it.*"

"Perfect."

"You comin' or what?" the blond woman asked in a bored tone of voice.

Grant began crawling again. Something else occurred to him as they moved.

"How did you do that back in the office?" he whispered. "MacDugall wasn't afraid you were going to *scratch* him to death. He really believed you were holding a gun. Didn't he?"

He heard her sigh. "You'd never understand how it works. People trust their eyes too much. It's an easy weakness to exploit."

Grant tried to swallow that. Found that he couldn't.

"So . . . what? You're some kind of—I don't know—illusionist?"

"Sure," she replied, unconvincingly. "Somethin' like that."

They crawled on.

"*She is* so *full of it,*" Julie said.

Something else occurred to Grant.

"Hey, why not use your mojo on the security guards, so we could just *walk* out of here?" he said.

"If it were *that* simple, d'you think we'd be havin' this conversation?" she replied. "Look, you're *way* out of your depth here, sugar. Leave the escape planning to the professionals."

Fifteen minutes later, they dropped through another grate into a tiny office. It was the first one they'd run across that was empty, and it was a long way from the bathroom. They'd watched from above as guards continued to march vigorously throughout the floor, searching everywhere for the intruders. As soon as they disappeared into another area, a new set of guards emerged and searched the same area all over again.

What are they so eager to keep anyone from finding?

As he dropped down into the office behind her, he caught a glimpse of the woman's eyes scanning the entire room. She turned away, trying not to show it, but he could see her inspecting every inch of the office.

Grant stood in place, watching her. She was nearing the door when he whispered again.

"You're a cat burglar!" he said, the same moment he pieced it together.

"*A what?*" Julie cried in his earpiece, so loud the blond woman could hear it.

She turned to face him, raised an eyebrow. "Me. Ow."

His shoulders dropped and he looked down. "I was trying to convince myself you were some kind of government agent . . ."

She walked closer to him, icy cool gaze and platinum smile still intact. "Government jobs are for bland people who look good in a tie. *Real* fieldwork needs imagination, instinct, cunning. And hey, it pays the bills."

"Right. Because who *wouldn't* rather steal to get ahead."

She offered a fake hurt look. "Hey, I don't take nothin' from nobody who can't afford to lose it. Rare art, antiques, fine jewelry, that sort of stuff. And nobody gets hurt. As long as they leave *me* alone, I leave *them* alone."

Grant was unconvinced. "So . . . you're a criminal with a heart of gold. Like Robin Hood—stealing from the rich."

"Mm-hmm," she nodded, then flashed another smile. "Just without that pesky 'giving to the poor' fixation."

Grant rolled his eyes.

"*This woman is* the Devil," Julie said. "*Why are you helping her?*"

"I'm not!" Grant whispered into his earpiece. "She's helping *me*! I mean, I think she is. It's complicated."

"Remind your friend," the blond woman said, "that if it wasn't for me, you'd've never gotten anything out of ol' MacDugall."

"How did you know I would show up in MacDugall's office?" he asked quietly.

"First we make with the escaping," she said. "Answers come later."

Something else clicked in Grant's mind. "Are you the reason the conference room door was unlocked?"

"*Yes,*" she exhaled, annoyed. "Now will you *come on!*"

They made it to the main stairwell without incident and ran down to the first floor. She cracked open the door, and Grant could see through the slit that the gargantuan room was buzzing with activity, even more than before. Dozens of security guards were in the mix now.

He reached over her head and pushed the door shut.

"I know an easier way," he said.

"Oh, really?"

"Oh, really!"

She was dubious, one eyebrow cocked upward. But she had to know the front door was suicide.

"Then impress me, big boy," she said, hands on her hips.

He led the way down the stairs to the basement, along the narrow hall, and into the warehouse-sized room. The main lights were out overhead, but emergency floodlights had been triggered by the alarm. They made their way through crates and boxes until they reached the furthest wall. Grant had to feel around for a few minutes under her wilting gaze before he finally found the hidden doorway. A small pedal on the floor, hidden under a nearby shelf, triggered it open.

Grant walked in and she followed, gazing around the narrow corridor that led back to the gas station. She pushed the door shut behind them.

They walked in silence.

Suddenly Grant jumped and shouted.

She did the same. "What's wrong?"

"My cell phone vibrated. Hasn't happened in a long while."

She turned and walked on.

He pulled the phone open and kept walking, pressing it to his face. "Yeah?"

"Hello. I'm trying to find information about a man named Collin Boyd," a voice on the other end said. A male voice.

Grant's mind froze; that was the last thing he'd expected to hear. Still, this *was* his old cell phone; he'd pulled it off Collin's body in the burning hallway.

He swallowed and rubbed his thumb against the ring again. It was a nervous habit he'd fast developed.

"Collin is dead," he said softly, where the woman couldn't hear.

"Yes, I know," the voice said. "But this phone is registered in his name, is it not?"

"Yes, this is Collin's phone, but—"

"Well, there we are then," the man said, sounding pleased with himself. "There are no coincidences."

"Look, this isn't a good time—"

"Have you, by any chance, seen inanimate objects moving by themselves lately?"

Grant stopped cold. The blonde up ahead of him noticed and turned around to see what he was doing.

"Could you say that again?" Grant said.

"You've seen some strange things happen lately, haven't you? Things you can't explain. Like a hunting knife burying itself deep inside a column made of solid concrete."

Grant was too stunned to answer.

The woman approached him in the corridor. "Come *on*," she whispered. "I can see the exit. We're nearly there!"

Grant ignored her, listening to the phone.

"Fine. Get caught." She turned and walked off without him.

"Whoever you are," the voice on the phone said, "we need to talk. My name is Daniel Cossick. I'm a scientist, and I think I can help you. But know this: you're not just witnessing these strange events—I believe you're *causing* them. Call me back at this number when you're ready to talk."

Grant pulled the phone away from his face and beeped it off, too stunned to think or move.

"Who was that, Collin?" Julie asked.

He heard a door open in the distance and looked up. The woman was already at the gas station cellar, going in.

He walked after her.

Grant soon reached the cellar, passed through the broom closet, grabbed his bag under the stairs, and ran up and out. Night had fallen, and it was growing cold out.

He had just reached the top of the steps when he saw her lying facedown on the ground, near the corner edge of the building.

He ran to her, kneeling down and feeling her pulse. She was alive.

"She's all right, just had a bit of a shock," said a voice above him.

Grant looked up, but it was too late. Torrents of electricity flowed through him and he felt his entire body clench, folding itself into a fetal position until all he knew was darkness.

16

Grant awoke to the sound of screaming.

He noticed he couldn't move before his droopy eyes opened. He was handcuffed to a chair, his ankles shackled around the chair's legs. His chair was near the corner of a vast, dark room with no windows. Two dozen security guards stood around him in a semicircle. Beyond them, he could see security monitors, desks, and gear of all kinds. Enormous digital screens were on every wall, showing scenes from all around the Inveo campus.

This was no security office. It was a full-fledged operations center. *They could coordinate a war from in here if they wanted to,* Grant thought. *What is a new technologies developer doing with this kind of firepower?*

He glanced up at the guards. They were watching him. No, they were watching the blond woman, who was five feet away to his right, also cuffed to a chair. Most of the guards were expressionless, others appeared to be enjoying this.

Her entire body convulsed.

One of the guards had pulled a chair up right in front of her and was using a Taser gun to shock her. *It must be on a lower setting. She's still conscious.*

The two darts from the gun were attached to her stomach and the guard was zapping her over and over. She braced herself, trying not to react, but she couldn't help it. The electricity surged through her, and she shook violently. But she refused to make a sound.

"Aw, come on, I want to hear that girly scream again," the guard with the Taser said, grinning, holding down the switch.

She bit down on her lip, hot tears burning her cheeks, refusing to give in. But he didn't stop until she screamed.

"That wasn't so hard, was it?"

"Hey," Grant said with a slur, "I'm awake . . . My turn now."

The guard barely glanced over. "Sorry," the man grunted. "We're under orders not to harm you."

"What? Why?"

The guard looked back at the woman. "You know, honey," he said, inching closer to her, "you'd probably think this is a high-stress job. It's really not. Sure, big place like this, people are always doing things they shouldn't. Activating emergency exits by going out the *wrong door*—" he tapped the Taser for a second and she jumped—"lighting one up in the bathroom and setting off the *sprinklers*—" another jolt—"parking in the boss's *spot*—" again—"and guess who has to deal with it all?" He glanced around at the other guards in the room. "*We* do."

He sighed. "Now, big, strapping fellas that we are, we signed on to run with a high-risk security task force. But *look* at this place. So much technology, what do they need us for? Instead of keeping this place secure, we end up helping old Mrs. Greenburg to the ladies' room. Do we look like Boy Scouts to you?"

She opened her eyes, panting; sweat was dripping off of her, and her hair was soaked. Grant knew she must've been dying to tell these "boy scouts" *exactly* what they looked like but, to her credit, she was holding her tongue.

"So as you might imagine," the guard continued when she didn't say anything, "when we get our hands on a pair of real-life criminals, caught in a real-life criminal act. . . . well, that's a red-letter day." He smiled and shocked her again. She screamed.

"You call holding and torturing us *legal*?" Grant asked.

"We'd be working in law enforcement if any of us cared about what's 'legal,'" the guard said with a bored expression. His empty eyes stayed on Grant as he Tasered the woman again, calmly holding the button down. A few of the other men in the room chuckled as she shook so hard Grant thought she might break the chair.

He was becoming increasingly frantic each time the woman

received another jolt. She wouldn't be able to withstand this forever. But what could he do? He couldn't even *move*.

His thoughts returned to that strange phone call, and what the man had said.

Was it possible? Was he responsible for the knife in the subway wall? Could he have somehow caused the knife to leave Konrad's hand?

It was bizarre, but he had no other explanation.

He strained his memory, trying to remember how it had felt, in the moment. He'd been hit by a wave of panic. It had washed over him accompanied by a cold sweat, and then there had been that mind-splitting headache that lasted for just a second. He remembered closing his eyes with the pain, and when he'd opened them, it was over.

There are no coincidences. That's what the man on the phone had said.

Grant took a long, deep breath.

He closed his eyes and focused on trying to recreate that feeling of overwhelming panic. He thought about being captured, trapped by security guards who were clearly sadistic, and probably had no intention of releasing him.

The panic began to build and he breathed faster.

He thought of the woman seated next to him. The Taser darts embedded into her stomach. The pain she was experiencing. Her waning stamina. Whoever she was, whatever she had done—no one deserved this kind of cold-blooded cruelty. And he was responsible. *He* had led her out that secret exit.

He began to sweat, his chest rising and falling harder. Faster and faster he breathed, the cold panic mounting, until—

A violent pain stabbed through his brain. Someone shouted.

And just as fast as it had happened, the headache was gone.

He opened his eyes to see the guard no longer holding his Taser— he wasn't even in the *chair*. Instead, he had curled up on the floor, clenching his stomach with both hands. Blood was visible between his fingers.

"Holy . . ." one of the other guards muttered. "Get some help! *Go!*" the man shouted. Two of the guards left the room. The one who'd shouted for help knelt down beside the man on the ground. The others had frozen in shock, but now they moved in for a closer look, eyes wide.

Grant looked over at the woman. A hole had been ripped in the side of her jumpsuit, where the pocket was, but otherwise she looked okay, although she was barely conscious and her breathing shallow.

"Forget it," one of the guards said. "We'll take him to medical." The kneeling guard nodded and three others moved in to help pick up the man on the ground.

They hefted him, and he grunted in pain. As they marched toward the door, they passed Grant, and he looked between them at the injured man. He gasped.

The familiar black handle of the blond woman's screwdriver was sticking out of the guard's stomach.

He'd never consciously thought about the man with the Taser gun *or* the screwdriver. He'd just forced himself to panic, and the rest had somehow happened.

"Watch them!" the guard who had knelt down shouted back at the others in the room, as they carried the injured man out.

The remaining dozen or so guards became all business, dispersing throughout the room, some taking up positions at various monitors, one standing in front of Grant and the woman.

Grant began breathing faster.

Could he do it twice? They *had* to get out of here.

Now.

He shut his eyes tight and bore down, clenching every muscle he could. He started to shudder, sweating again. He thought about the man with the screwdriver in his gut and that *he* had somehow caused it . . .

The panic hit again.

His brain seized, much harder this time.

He nearly blacked out.

When Grant opened his eyes, he was lying against the corner wall, on the floor. The cuffs were still around his wrists and ankles, but the chains were broken. He was free!

The pungent odor of burning metal awakened him to the chaos filling the room. The metal chair he had been sitting in was sticking straight out of one of the enormous digital screens across the room, smoke and sparks pouring from the gaping hole. One of the guards reached for a fire extinguisher, the others looked like they were too stunned to react.

That was when Grant noticed they were one short. The guard that had been standing right in front of him was gone. Grant looked across the room at the chair again and saw that the spot where the guard had been standing was directly between the chair and where Grant now lay.

He didn't move for a long moment, looking harder at the broken screen and the chair sticking out of it, as he swallowed the obvious implication.

Finally, he hopped up and moved toward the woman. One of the guards noticed and ran over to him. The guard threw a wide punch and Grant ducked it, bringing his fist up into the guard's stomach. It knocked the wind out of him, and he doubled over. Grant saw a key-chain on the guard's belt loop and he swiftly reached in and grabbed it. Then punched him again in the stomach. The guard toppled over.

The few guards that were left were still attending to the electrical fire or shouting into radios. They seemed to have forgotten about their prisoners in the corner.

Grant found his earpiece on the ground and put it back on.

"You still there?" he whispered.

"What happened? Are you okay?!"

"Tell you later. I'm in a humongous room inside some kind of security bunker. Need a way out."

"All right, hold on." Grant knew she must be checking the floor plans. *"Is there a door at the far corner of the room?"*

"Looks like it."

"Take it."

With a glance at the still-distracted guards, Grant uncuffed the woman and scooped her up in his arms. She was shaking all over, unable to stand. But the look on her face was completely changed. Gone was the playful grin, the seductive eyes. She was aghast, drained of color.

She took in the chair in the screen and then turned back to Grant.

Whatever had happened, Grant realized she'd seen the whole thing.

Grant ran out the door and into a long, dark corridor. He couldn't see to the hallway's end, and the only exit from the hall that was visible was the door he'd just come from.

"What am I looking for?" he asked Julie.

"A door," she replied, as if it were obvious. *"Other end of the hall."*

Grant ran as fast as he could until the end of the hall became visible. There were *two* doors, one to the left, one to the right.

He chose left.

When he opened the door, he nearly dropped the girl.

A small, wide foyer gave way to a massive, O-shaped metal structure.

Grant stepped inside. Neither he nor the blond woman could take their eyes off of the three-story-high mechanism. It looked like a massive bank vault but was probably much thicker and had to weigh over a ton. And just like a vault, there were hinges on one side . . .

A quiet hum filled the room.

Grant was certain this wouldn't appear on Julie's floor plans. Which only made him all the more curious as to what was behind it.

A security panel waited patiently on the right side of the room, for what looked like a keycard, retinal scan, and vocal identification. There was nothing else in the room.

The door itself was flat and smooth.

Grant glanced at the woman in his arms; she was still staring at the big metal door, her eyes wide and taking in the entire thing.

This . . . this was breathtaking. Massive and beyond comprehension.

"What's going on?" Julie cried in his ear. *"Did you find the door?"*

"Uh-huh," he replied, dumbstruck. "We found the door."

17

The blond woman in Grant's arms was gaping at the door as well, but finally she croaked, "We can't stay—they're comin'."

"But . . ." he protested, "we've got to find out what's behind this thing. It could explain *everything* that's happened to me!"

"Then we'll come back for it *later*," she implored. "If they find us, they'll *kill* us. We gotta go!"

"No! We'll never make it this far again! All the answers I'm looking for could be behind this thing!" Something about the size of it was . . . captivating.

"You'll find a way," the woman said slowly.

He didn't hear her.

"Hey." She put her hand on his cheek. "I'll help you find a way. I promise."

For the first time, he transferred his attention away from the door and really looked the blond woman in the eyes. A bright shade of blue, her eyes were soft, round, and absolutely stunning, yet dark and pained from her ordeal. For the first time all evening, he felt like he was seeing the real her.

Finally he nodded, taking one last look at the door. He turned and exited the room, opening the opposite door on the right of the hall. It led to a stairwell, going only up.

They were underground. *Deep* underground, from the look of these stairs.

Grant charged up the steps, adrenaline surging again, flight after flight.

After several minutes, they emerged from a nondescript door into a garage full of minivans, sedans, and golf carts, all marked "Inveo SECURITY." The guards themselves were nowhere to be seen.

"We're in some kind of security garage," Grant reported to Julie.

"Good. If you go out the back door, there's a smaller side entrance to the campus. I can meet you there."

Grant turned; the back garage entrance was open. But no, that wouldn't work. He was sweating, fatigued, and his mind was reeling from the day's events; he couldn't carry his new friend any farther. Besides, the side entrance would no doubt be shut tight, so how was he supposed to . . .

An idea sparked, and Grant dumped the blond woman in the passenger seat of the nearest security van. He found a corkboard hanging from a nearby wall where dozens of key rings, all numbered, waited. A sticker on the rear bumper of the security van said "08." He snatched the corresponding key from the board.

"Julie, change of plan. You start heading back toward L.A. We'll meet up with you shortly."

Grant cranked the van's engine to life and jammed the pedal to the floor. A few guards lurked just outside the exit, and they began screaming at him, but he never slowed, nearly ran them over.

The tires squealed loudly as the van took the corner at full speed, bearing down on the side entrance. It was gated, a barbed wire fence blocking the way along with an enormous metal arm.

"Seatbelt on and head down!" Grant shouted. Still shaking, she fiddled with her seatbelt until it locked; then she leaned over all the way, covering her head with her arms.

A guard emerged from the gatehouse when he saw the van approaching at high speed, but he was far too late.

Grant covered his face with one arm and kept the other on the wheel as the van exploded through the gate with a horrible screeching. Metal grinded and clashed against metal, but it only lasted a moment, and then they were out.

Grant never let up from the gas pedal, the van careening down the road. But the woman was still leaning over in her seat.

He wiped his sweat-soaked face with a dirty sleeve.

"It's okay, we made it," he said, panting.

She slowly sat back up and looked around, rubbing her arms and shivering.

"No we didn't," she said softly.

She was looking behind. He checked the rear-view and saw flashing red-and-blue lights.

He punched the steering wheel in frustration, and the horn blared.

Checking his surroundings, he saw that they were on what had to have been the local main street. It was late, so most of the stores and streets were deserted, save for cruising teenagers and joyriders.

"Are you able to get up on your own?" Grant asked the woman beside him, a plan rapidly formulating.

"I think so," she said uneasily.

"Julie, how far out are you?" *She* should *be on the same road we are . . .*

"Few miles outside of downtown, why?"

"Anywhere nearby where you can pull off the road inconspicuously?"

"Um . . . Yeah, I see a car dealership a few blocks ahead."

"Turn in," Grant commanded, "and shut off the car and all the lights. Wait there."

"Okay . . ." Julie replied, clearly wanting to know more, but not asking.

Grant glanced quickly over each shoulder. "Good, sliding doors on both sides . . ." he mumbled.

"You're not thinkin' what I think you're thinkin' . . ." said the blond woman.

Grant nodded, assuming she was already on the same page with him. "We need something to aim for, something that'll cover our tracks but won't hurt anybody."

"You're crazy," she commented wearily, but quickly joined him in scanning the road for an appropriate target.

The chasing vehicles behind them had crept closer, the leader less than three car's lengths away. Grant couldn't see how many cars there were, but from the noise of all the sirens, it had to be a lot.

They know what we saw underground . . . Grant surmised.

A sign for a car dealership was visible in the distance, on the right side of the road.

"Julie, can you hear sirens?"

"I'll say," she replied. *"Sounds like a fleet."*

"We're in a yellow security van. We're about to pass you," he said. Then he turned to his passenger. "Open the doors."

She nodded and carefully got to her feet in the speeding van, holding tight to seats, the ceiling—whatever she could find.

Just as the second door slid open, the van shot past the car lot like a bullet, police cars and more security vehicles right behind.

"Stand by, Julie . . . *There.*"

A rock face on the side of the mountain was ahead on the left, at least a hundred feet from the nearest buildings.

"You ready?!" Grant shouted.

"No," the blond woman replied, "but go on and do it anyway!"

Grant jammed the pedal all the way down and swerved the car just enough so that it would aim for the rock face. When they were three hundred feet away, he turned off the car's headlights, jumped out of his seat, and shouted, "Now!"

She jumped out of the van's right side, and he followed suit on the left, hitting the ground with a hard crack and rolling at an impossible speed. He came to a rest against a wooden road barrier.

Grant looked up just in time to watch the van ram straight into the mountain, generating sparks, fire, and the loudest crash he had ever heard.

Twenty minutes later, Grant was driving the Corvette, the barely conscious blond woman riding shotgun and Julie in the backseat. Grant and his companion were scraped and bruised, but they'd both managed to escape with no broken bones.

"You're insane," Julie huffed. "If I had known what you were going to do—"

"Why do you think I didn't tell you?" he cut her off.

She pouted in the backseat.

His blond companion stirred awake and watched him drive for a very long time before speaking up.

"So what's your name?" she asked in a tired, raspy voice.

"Grant," he replied. "Grant Borrows."

"Well, Grant Borrows," she replied slowly. "I'm Hannah." She held her hand out to him. "And I am very pleased to meet you."

He took her hand and held it. She seemed to take strength from it. She sat up taller in the seat.

They let go and she studied her hand for a moment, lost in thought.

"Grant, I need to ask you something . . . And it might sound a little odd."

She sat back in her seat, relaxing, and began peeling off her gloves.

"Okay . . ." he said, curious, but still watching the road, nervously checking the rear-view for signs of the Inveo security or the police.

Hannah looked down for a moment, and then back up at him.

"You used to be someone else, didn't you?"

His head snapped around. "How do you know that?"

She pulled the glove off from her right hand and lifted it for him to see. Resting there was a gold ring with an inset burgundy gemstone.

"Because *I* used to be someone else."

The Corvette's tires screeched to a halt in the middle of the road.

He took her hand and pulled it closer, biting off his own glove with his teeth. Julie leaned forward from the backseat. Grant compared the two rings. Hers was slightly smaller, and it had none of the etchings or markings on the sides that his had. Otherwise, the two rings were identical.

Grant let go and sat back in the driver's seat, his mind spinning. Hannah and Julie both watched him silently.

"I'm not the only one," Hannah broke the silence. "There're others."

He looked her in the eye and tried to speak, but found himself breathless.

"How many?" he got out.

"I don't know. I know a place where some of them live, or *hide* . . . It's a sort of a . . . commune. People like us, who live . . . *away*. From the rest of the world. A friend of mine runs the place; the same friend who sent me to Inveo to help you. They're the only ones that I know of myself. But I'm told there are many more . . . out there." She gazed out the front window.

Grant put a hand to his forehead and rubbed it. His eyes darted all around, lost in thought.

Suddenly he sat upright and focused his eyes on the road ahead.

He began driving.

"Where?"

"I don't know—"

"No, this group—the commune or whatever. Where are *they*?"

Hannah nodded, exhaling slowly. "Right, I'll let 'em know you'd like to meet—"

"No, *now*. How do I get there?"

"Grant," she hesitated, "these people live in total seclusion from the outside world. And they don't like visitors . . ."

"I don't care!" he shouted. "If this friend of yours knows about me, he might have answers. If he can tell me *anything* about what's happened to me and why . . . And just knowing that I'm not alone, I'm not the only one . . ."

He shook his head.

"*No!*" he cried. His gaze was set dead ahead. "We're going there *now*."

18

An old road snaking deep into a canyon miles outside of Thousand Oaks led Grant, Julie, and Hannah to a paved driveway. Cracked and broken cement made the way tough for the Corvette, but eventually they pulled up to a sturdy-looking gate and a ten-foot-high electric fence. In the distance stood a large, single-story brick complex.

Being this close to answers raised goosebumps on Grant's arms. Would this bleak, uninviting place reveal to him all that he longed to know?

At the edge of the gate nearest the driveway, a surprisingly modern keycard entry system was mostly obscured from external view by over-hanging brush. Grant hadn't noticed the high-tech machine until they were right beside it.

But he was more interested in the building that had just emerged into sight.

"Is that . . . what I think it is?"

"It used to be a . . . *facility*," Hannah replied uneasily, still sporting reddened skin and fatigue from her ordeal. "Government abandoned it and sold the property after the 'deinstitutionalization' of the early '60s. 'Community care' became all the rage afterwards, as I've been told. Many times."

"What kind of facility?"

"I believe the preferred term is 'mental health institution'," she replied.

"So it's an insane asylum," he concluded.

"Pretty much. They thought the foliage would soothe the patients."

It was so different than what he was expecting. Grant's eyes searched the front of the edifice for any signs of life, any evidence that this was a place to be excited about visiting. But the doors were solid and what few windows there were, were high off the ground, with iron bars over them. The brick walls were chipping away slowly, entire bricks missing from a few spots.

"You said this friend of yours would be expecting us," Grant prodded.

"Yep," Hannah replied.

"I didn't see you make any calls. How does he know we're coming?"

"Been expecting you, from what I understand, for a long while now. Before you ask, I don't know how that's possible. And by the by—my friend's a 'she', not a 'he'."

"Duly noted."

He parked the Corvette in front of the decaying facility and helped Hannah out of the car. She kept telling him she was fine, but he practically had to carry her up the five or six steps that led to the front door. Julie pulled up the rear, watching both of them warily.

"Dr. Cossick?"

"Yeah," Daniel said absentmindedly, poring over computations on his laptop.

"Detective Drexel is here to see you," Lisa said formally. Then, lowering her voice and scrunching her face, she added, "Guess we didn't pacify him enough the last time?"

Daniel grimaced. *Great.* He quickly shut his laptop.

Lisa showed their guest into Daniel's office, and Daniel rose to shake the man's hand.

Drexel removed his fedora while offering half a haggard smile. The heavyset man had a few days' worth of stubble, and his clothes and trench coat looked like they hadn't seen the inside of a washing machine in years.

Daniel took in all of this in less than a second but decided to politely ignore it.

"How can I help you today, Detective?"

"Well, I'm not sure you can," Drexel began, forcing a cordial smile, "but I hope so." He noticed the business card holder on Daniel's desk and picked one up, pocketing it. "I have this problem."

Daniel returned to his chair, listening. "Related to the Boyd case?"

Drexel nodded. "Boyd's sister was kidnapped not long before the arson on his apartment, you see. And I believe the kidnapper may be the same man who started the fire."

Whoa.

"As you can imagine," the detective continued, "I've been trying to find out who this man is, but I haven't been having much luck."

"I'm sorry to hear that, Detective, but I'm not sure how I can help."

"The name 'Grant Borrows' ring a bell with you?"

Daniel blinked. "No."

"Hmm," Drexel said slowly, showing an exaggerated confusion on his face. "Now that's very odd." He reached inside his coat pocket and pulled out a piece of paper. Unfolding it, his eyes moved back and forth, skimming the document as he continued to speak.

"See, I followed the trail from Mr. Boyd's most recent bank statement to a mobile phone, which is now being paid for by this 'Grant Borrows'. Then I talked to his wireless provider, and a gentleman there was kind enough to run a trace on all of Borrows' recent calls on that phone."

A trickle of sweat formed on the back of Daniel's neck and wiggled its way south.

"Now here's my favorite part," Drexel said, relishing his tale. "The phone has only been used one time since the kidnapping. It was an *incoming* call, and it took place just about three hours ago, much to my surprise."

Daniel tried not to react, but he could feel the blood draining from his face.

"Would you like to know who called him?" Drexel said with complete sincerity.

Daniel sat back in his chair and did his best to stare blankly at the detective.

But instead of reading from the document, Drexel folded the paper and put it back inside his coat. "I think we both know the answer to that question."

Daniel cleared his throat, squared his shoulders. "Detective, are you accusing me of doing something unlawful?"

Drexel smiled. "Right now, I'd say it qualifies as circumstantial. But I *know* you know who this man is. And based on what I've seen of your 'scientific research facility' out there"—he nodded his head in the direction of the lab—"I suspect you're just as interested in finding him as I am. What I can't figure out is *why*."

"And if I *am* looking for this 'Grant Borrows'?"

"Then you and I are destined to be best friends."

"Detective, I don't know this man. I can assure you I have absolutely no information on him, whoever he is." Daniel sat up straight in his chair. "*If* we dialed his phone from the lab, then it must've been an accident."

"Well," Drexel said, still smiling, "you might want to take some time to give that statement some careful consideration, Doctor. You see, you may not know Borrows, and you may not know me, but I know *you*. I checked you out. And I found out about some very interesting things you've been involved with in the past—downright *appalling* things, if you want to know the truth—that I'm sure you wouldn't want anyone else to know. Like maybe that pretty young assistant of yours."

An exaggerated gagging sound resembling a cat with a hairball was heard coming from the outer office.

"I don't have anything to hide, Detective," he said. "We all do things in life we're not proud of. I'm not ashamed of my past. Are you?"

Drexel stood, his wide frame casting a shadow over the entire wall behind him. "You may not be ashamed of your past, but I *know* you're hiding from it. Or maybe someone in it." He put his hat back on his head and moved to go. "Think it over, Doc. That lab o' yours down the hall has a lot of specialized equipment in it. Pretty delicate stuff from the look of it. Nothing you'd want anyone else messing with, I'm guessing. You know, we got a *whole* bunch of science geeks in our forensics unit who'd just *love* to get in there and take all that stuff apart to find out what it does."

Drexel opened the office door. "I'll be in touch," he said, pulling out Daniel's business card and waving it at him.

Daniel stood. "You won't be allowed back in here without a search warrant."

"Don't tempt me," Drexel said, the smug grin still on his face, as he turned and walked out.

Lisa gave Drexel the evil eye as he strolled out of the outer office and down the hall to the exit. When he was safely gone, she wheeled around and burst into Daniel's office.

"He's dirty," she said. Daniel was still standing exactly where Drexel had left him, fuming.

"Oh, I got the feeling he wasn't threatening us for the common good," he replied.

"No," she said, crinkling her nose, "didn't you smell him? He's *dirty*."

"He's got nothing and he knows it. We're not doing anything even *remotely* illegal here. How were *we* supposed to know the man we're investigating is involved in a kidnapping?" He sat back down, mind racing, and then looked back up at her. "We'd better double-check our permits, make sure they're all up-to-date."

She nodded.

"And that file you started on Borrows? Get rid of it."

After Hannah inserted her keycard in the scanner beside the main entrance, Grant pushed open the double doors and was greeted by the dry, musty smell of books. A long hallway stretched before them, but instead of white-painted walls, the hall was crammed floor to ceiling with books. Every shape, every size. Some thick, some as narrow and flimsy as magazines. One stack after another after another, completely covering the walls, as if the building were being supported by the numerous volumes. So many of them . . . Thousands, tens of thousands, that he could see and far more than he could count.

A few of the stacks leaned precariously inward toward the long hallway he now traversed, and Grant was struck by an odd sense of claustrophobia. He couldn't shake the feeling that the walls had sprouted long fingers made of hardbacks and paperbacks that were trying to reach out and touch him.

He was struck by how quiet it was. Nestled deep in the woods, the facility was far away from civilization, but even those who lived here seemed to make very little noise.

The long, dimly lit corridor led the three of them to another set of double doors. These doors were glass on top, with criss-crossed wire inside. They opened suddenly with a flourish as Grant, Julie, and Hannah approached them. A nondescript man and woman stood on either side and motioned for them to enter.

Grant glanced at Hannah, who offered him a reassuring, if weak, nod.

Inside was a large, rectangular room which they had entered near one corner. Lush and soothing with an "old fashioned charm," this room showed the most evidence of renovation of anything Grant had seen so far.

And here too, the walls were stuffed, packed, and jammed with books of every size, shape, and color. Wooden fixtures and a low ceiling added to the "cozy" feel. The area nearest to them appeared to be a lounge of sorts: a pool table, a sofa and bean bags, a few small desks with reading lamps, a handful of laptop computers, and a modest television set.

In the middle of the room was a fireplace made of grayish red bricks, surrounded by wingback chairs and small end tables. A dark crimson rug ran underneath this furniture; it was at least two inches thick, made of long, furry tendrils of string.

There were people everywhere. Dozens of them. The residents, Grant assumed. They looked disarmingly normal, and closer inspection revealed individuals from all walks of life, all social classes, and various races and ages. But he saw no children. And each and every one of them wore a golden ring on their right-hand middle finger.

On the far end of the room, in relative seclusion, sat an ancient-looking desk piled high with dozens—perhaps hundreds—more books. Barely visible behind the mountains of books was the top of a simple desk chair. If one looked hard enough, a small grayish-white mop of hair could be seen leaning against the chair's headrest.

Every person in the room had stopped whatever they were doing as soon as Grant had entered, and now they watched him with great interest. Whispers buzzed like a swarm of bees throughout the room, as the men and women leaned in to one another, all eyes unwavering from Grant.

He absent mindedly rubbed his thumb against the ring.

The woman who had helped open the double doors quickly walked to the desk and stepped behind it, whispering something to the person who sat there.

"Brilliant!" a female voice announced in an impeccable British accent.

A woman emerged from behind the desk. She couldn't have been more than forty-five and was short in stature, yet her nearly all-white hair made her look older. She stood tall—as tall as she could, anyway—as though a metal rod was holding her back straight. Large eyes peered down a pudgy nose over the rims of bifocal glasses to land on Grant, and she walked forward calmly but purposefully, and outstretched her hand.

"Welcome, Mr. Borrows," she said with a gleam in her eyes. "Welcome to the Common Room. My name is Morgan."

The Thresher shoved his motorcycle's kickstand down, and stepped off into dirt.

Ahead he saw a honky-tonk bar that couldn't have been any more stereotypical if it tried. Rust and mold covered the building's exterior in a sort of patchwork of disgusting colors. A bright red neon light flashed the word "BEER" over the door, which was solid, looked rather thick, and had no window to see inside.

He opened the door. A wall of cigarette and cigar smoke, sweat, and stale alcohol rushed at him but did not slow him down.

The interior was even less appealing than the outside. Dingy lights hung low from overhead, illuminating a handful of pool tables, a jukebox, a bar and stools, and a few tables.

The dozen or so patrons turned as he entered, surveying the newcomer who dared intrude on their private haunt. They looked like feral dogs, sniffing to see who had invaded their territory. And not one of them failed to notice the scabbard hanging from his hip.

"I'm looking for Mr. Odell," the Thresher said, to everyone.

"Don't know nobody by that name, son," called a filthy man in a white apron, standing behind the bar. "But weapons ain't allowed in here."

The Thresher scanned the crowd. Nearly every man had the telling bulge of a shoulder gun holster under their jackets. The few who didn't had large knives attached to their hips.

He locked eyes again with the bartender. "I know Mr. Odell is here." He took a menacing step forward, but still spoke calmly. "And I don't like repeating myself."

"What d'ya want with 'im?" someone called out from a murky corner of the room.

"A conversation," the Thresher replied.

"And if he don't feel like talkin'?" another man shouted.

The Thresher slowly and carefully reached for the handle of his sword.

"Then very soon, he will feel differently."

Grant was still speechless from his surroundings. It was a moment before he replied to Morgan. "Um, is 'Morgan' your first name or last?"

"Neither," she replied, offering him a knowing smile. "May I call you Grant?"

"Okay." He gestured. "My sister, Julie."

Morgan acknowledged Julie with a polite nod. "We have a great deal to discuss, Grant, yet I feel as though I know you already," she said in her quick British clip. "Please, please have a seat."

But Grant found himself once again staring at the innumerable volumes covering the walls.

"All these books . . ." he began, taking in his surroundings in wonder.

She gestured to a chair in front of the crackling fireplace. "Oh yes, they are mine. But we'll get to that. Right now, we have more important matters to discuss."

Morgan joined him at the fire in a tall armchair that seemed to recognize her shape and weight. Julie and Hannah took seats not far from the fireplace as well, but it was clear that this conversation was meant for Grant and Morgan. The elder woman watched him intently, waiting for him to speak.

"Who are you people?"

"We are those who must withdraw from society in order to survive it," replied Morgan. "Like you, we have all undergone a drastic change to everything we know. For many of us, secluding ourselves was the only remaining option if we wished to conduct normal lives. The world does not welcome us anymore, so we have *made* a place where we can belong, here, together. In this place, far from the cares of civilization, we are safe."

"Sounds pretty good to me," Grant said, attempting a lighthearted chuckle. "Where do I sign up?"

But Morgan was somber. "That luxury is not available to you."

"Why not?"

"Because . . ." she hesitated, savoring this moment, as though she had waited a lifetime for it . . .

"Because you are the Bringer."

"The what?" Grant asked dumbly.

"Your entire world has changed," Morgan said in her polite diction, the smile gone from her face, replaced by a furrowed brow of concentration. She was concentrating on him, studying his every response and facial tic.

Her statement wasn't a question.

Grant looked down at his feet. He'd liked this woman instantly, and yet . . . there was a lingering sense of perception about her that made him crumple under her gaze.

"Yes, it has," he said.

"You feel like a doormat in a world of boots, I imagine. It began with this," she said, producing her right hand. A sparkling gold ring rested on her middle finger, with an inset burgundy gemstone.

He nodded, then glanced briefly around the room. The others watched with rapt attention, some of them nervously stroking their own rings.

Morgan stared at his ring for a long moment, then shook her head in . . . was that wonder?

"I know you have millions of questions. Or quite possibly more." Her soft eyes twinkled as her face became round and welcoming again. "I am afraid I do not have quite that many answers, but I will tell you all that I can. First, I wonder if you would tell *me* something."

"Okay," he replied tentatively.

"How have you been sleeping of late?"

"I haven't."

"Quite," she nodded thoughtfully. "'And thereby hangs a tale.' You tell yourself the nightmares come from the *trauma* you have endured."

It wasn't a question, but he answered anyway. "Yeah."

Her round eyes were stern, but he detected a hint of compassion in them. "When the truth is that you've learned very quickly how to keep yourself busy, running headlong from one task to the next. No time for sitting idle and putting genuine thought into how you feel. Oh no, can't have that. Because *that* is more frightening than anything in your nightmarish dreams."

Grant wanted to argue with this logic but found that he couldn't.

"Yes, I understand you all too well, Grant," she said with a gentle smile, as if reading his mind. "We've never met, of course. I simply recognize a familiar pattern."

"So you have trouble sleeping, too?"

Morgan smiled again. "As Hamlet said, 'There's the rub.' I *do not* sleep. Ever. Grant, *all* of us here have been through precisely what you're facing now. We know every feeling, every fear, every ridiculous notion that has crossed your mind since this began. *Nothing* makes sense to you right now, does it?"

He shook his head.

She took a deep breath and never moved her eyes away from his. "I like to begin by telling my own story. It seems to help those who come here to know that their experience was not as uncommon as they think."

She leaned back in the chair and collected her thoughts. "It happened rather inconspicuously, really. In my former life, I was a librarian working at the London Library, near St. James Park. As I was leaving work one day, I stopped in the rest room. I caught my reflection in the mirror while washing my hands . . . and I screamed. The reflection I saw was not my own. And a foreign voice was screaming. I had a different face, different clothes. My purse was gone, and had been replaced by a different one, sitting in the same spot on the counter where I'd left mine. No one else entered nor left the rest room while I was inside, so I opened the purse. Within, I found a photo I.D. that matched the woman in the mirror, and a set of keys I didn't recognize."

He nodded. This sounded very familiar.

"After a great deal of study and investigation, I eventually came upon a few others who had also experienced 'the Shift,' as we call it. Most of us had nowhere to go, and many were so traumatized by the shaking of the foundations of their very existence that they lived in mortal fear of what might happen to them next. After all, if one's identity is so malleable, so vulnerable, that it can be taken away in a heartbeat . . . then *anything* is possible. So I decided to create a haven where those like us could gather and be safe. Eventually . . . we found this place."

She grew silent, allowing Grant time to process this.

"How many are here?"

Morgan's shoulders rose in a small shrug. "Perhaps fifty or sixty at any given time. It varies. This building was constructed to hold more than two hundred, but we've never reached even half that capacity. Still most who find their way here never leave."

"But why?"

"You *know* why. They want a place to bury their heads and hope the world will not fall apart on them again. You remember that feeling? That cold ache in the pit of your stomach when you first realized that everything you know had irrevocably changed, forever?"

"I remember," he replied. "But I can't imagine just deciding to run away and hide—not even *trying* to find out what happened and why."

"Of course you can, dear boy," she replied calmly. "You considered it yourself in those first few moments after the Shift. We all do. It's *terrifying* to see everything you are and everything you know, stripped away in a single moment. Your very flesh and blood has been replaced, and some find it very easy to lose their entire identity to that. When the world caves in, you contemplate throwing in the towel. That is the first reaction we all share."

He thought back to his own experience that first day.

"Do not kid yourself, Grant," she said with sad, compassionate eyes. "All that separates you from my friends here is a thin line spread across a scant few seconds. Each of us decides in those first moments: run and hide, or press on. But we all began at the same intersection."

He looked down at the tiny scar on his wrist that Julie had made, then raised his head to meet her eyes. An entire conversation passed silently between them in that look.

Never give up. Never give in. Never surrender to anger or despair.

"As I was saying," Morgan continued, "most, once they come here, decide to stay. Some, like your friend Hannah, come and go as they wish. Our door is always open to those like us, who have nowhere else to go. Often, many of them will gather their intellects together—which are considerable, given the fact that everyone here is a *genius* of one type or another—and spend their time quite literally deliberating and sorting out the vast mysteries of the universe. They call themselves the Loci."

"An asylum full of geniuses," Grant mused. "Genius Loci, I get it. And have they turned up *answers* to any of life's big mysteries?"

"They have."

"Then why not share their answers with the world?"

Morgan gave a sad smile. "It is easier to *learn* about the world than try to save it, is it not?"

Then she sat forward on her chair, bowing her head. He thought she was praying or concentrating at first, but then saw the muscles on her neck were clenched tight. And she was squeezing her eyelids together.

"Morgan!" Hannah cried.

"I'm all right, Hannah," Morgan whispered. "Don't make a fuss." She massaged her temples for a few moments as Hannah edged out of her chair, prepared to jump to the rescue. Morgan finally opened her eyes and sat back in the chair. She looked sideways at Hannah, who was still standing. "But *you* are *not* all right. You have been electrocuted. Severely, from the looks of it. You should see a doctor."

"I'm *fine*," Hannah said forcefully, still watching Morgan with concern. She returned to her chair. "Never better."

Grant watched them both with concern and curiosity, then settled on Morgan.

"I get headaches," she told him quietly.

"She gets *migraines*," Hannah corrected her, loudly.

Morgan's lips curled into a frown. "Migraines, then." She shot a look at Hannah, who held her gaze without flinching. Eventually she looked back to Grant.

"You are overwhelmed," she consoled. "This is a great deal of information to absorb."

"None of it seems to bother *you*," he said abruptly.

"That's because I've been doing this longer than you. Longer than anyone, in point of fact."

He blinked. "You mean—"

Morgan nodded. "To the best of my knowledge, I was the first to undergo the Shift. It was over fourteen years ago that I found someone new in that mirror at the London Library. And I have never encountered another who predates me. I was the very first to have *this*." She held up her ring hand again.

Fourteen years! There were people in this world who had lived for almost fifteen years with what had just happened to him only weeks ago. It was mind-boggling.

His eyes fell upon her ring.

"Tell me about the rings." he said, sitting up straight in his chair now. "Why won't they come off?"

She glanced around the room and then leaned in closer to him. "They *do* come off," she whispered. "But only after the wearer dies."

Grant thought of the contract killer, Konrad, who had wanted his ring. *He knew. He either had to kill me or cut off my finger altogether. Both of which he tried . . .*

"Do the rings trigger the . . . the Shift?" he asked.

"The two *do* always seem to coincide. But all I can tell you with certainty is that, despite their appearance, the rings are *not* made of gold, nor any other precious metal that I can identify. It appears they're comprised of some kind of alloy that's stronger—its molecules packed together more densely—than any metal that exists in nature. They're *so* strong, in fact, that I haven't even been able to chip off any residue for study."

"Are you a scientist?" Grant asked.

Morgan offered a bemused smile. "Hardly. I was born a lover of books and shall die one. I'd rather be spending my time with Dickens and Steinbeck, but in the years after the Shift, I spent much of my time searching the world and researching our civilization's entire wellspring of knowledge to find out all I could about these rings. Unfortunately, I've learned precious little with regard to their origin. But as for what they are . . ." she paused in thought, "I need to *show* you what I've learned, rather than try to explain it. But before we get to that, though, I would ask you to fill in some gaps for me. Tell me how all this began for *you*."

He launched into his story, beginning with the morning he spotted himself, Collin, walking down the sidewalk, and ending with his daring escape from the Inveo plant with Hannah, only hours before.

Morgan watched him with a soft gaze throughout the entire story. She was patient and allowed him to tell it in his own time. When he finished, she looked away for a few minutes.

Finally she looked at him again. "May I see your ring, please?"

He held out his hand.

She adjusted her bifocals until they rested on the very tip of her nose. Gently turning his hand to the side, her eyes narrowed as she studied the ring.

While she was looking at his ring, he glanced at hers. It was just like Hannah's—nearly identical to his own, only slightly smaller and with no markings on the sides.

Morgan let go of him and sat back in her chair, her eyes focusing on him even more intently than before.

"There can be no doubt; you *are* the Bringer. Does anyone else know of what's happened to you, besides your sister?" He caught a trace of urgency in her voice.

He thought for a moment. "There's this weird girl who keeps following me around."

One eyebrow went up. "A girl?"

"She won't tell me who she is. She just keeps popping up and telling me—well, I guess you could call it advice. She's . . . younger than me. Not much I can say about her appearance. Nothing sticks out. Well, except that she's always barefoot."

Morgan's spine straightened as she sat up in her chair. "Barefoot?" She stared at him over the rims of her bifocals once again. "This girl— she had long brown hair? No makeup or jewelry?"

"Sounds right," Grant nodded. "You know her?"

"We have never met," Morgan shook her head, gazing off in thought. "I thought she was something of an urban myth. Someone fitting that description has been spotted a few times in the past, watching those like us, scrutinizing our movements. But the glimpses of her have been so fleeting I ascribed the whole affair to group imagination."

She focused on Grant again. "She actually *spoke* to you?"

He nodded.

"What did she talk about?"

"Odd things . . . I don't know . . . The conversations are always so short. But it seemed like, in some way . . . I think she's trying to help me."

"Hmm," Morgan replied. She leaned back in her chair, lost in thought again.

"You mentioned wanting to show me something . . ." Grant prompted her.

Her attention snapped back to him. "Ah, yes, quite so." Her expression changed and she formed her words slowly and carefully. "I hesitate to say this, Grant, because I realize full well how it will sound to you. But please trust that I would not ask anything of you if it were not of the greatest importance. In this case, I do not see any alternative."

Grant leaned back in his seat, wary. "All right."

"In order to show you what I want to show you," she began, "I need a favor. A very important item was due to be delivered to me, but it was intercepted before I received it. And I need it back. I want *you* to retrieve it for me."

Dread flooded Grant's heart. "What?"

"Morgan, he's no thief!" Hannah said, rising precariously from her chair. "If there's somethin' you need, *I'll* go get it for you."

"Dear, you can't even *walk*," was Morgan's reply. "We haven't time to wait for your recovery."

Morgan spoke to Grant with utmost sincerity. "I promise you, Grant, this won't involve committing any sort of crime. In point of fact, you'll be *resolving* a crime. The object I'm asking you to retrieve belongs to me. I merely need you to it get back."

"What do you know of the Bringer?" the Thresher demanded.

The short, scrawny man he held off of the floor by the lapels of his jacket seemed to balk at this question.

But there was no one around to save him. The bar's remaining patrons were unconscious, resting peacefully on the floor. Apparently this crowd lived for a good brawl, but the Thresher had overpowered the entire room in under two minutes, before rounding on the man he had come here for.

The drunken man dangling in the air drooled beer down his shirt, his eyes over-wide and his expressions exaggerated.

In a flash, the Thresher's sword was out and upheld, ready to strike, as he held the man with one hand.

"I won't ask a second time," his brogue accent intoned, menacingly.

The drunken man stared all-too-obviously at the gold ring upon his own finger. "I heard the phrase before, but that's all, man, I swear," he slurred.

Why must they always resist? the Thresher thought, bored.

"I couldn't help noticing," he observed gently, "that during our entire conversation, you haven't been able to take your eyes off of that golden bauble on your right hand. Which means that to get your *full* attention, I will have to eliminate the offending hand from your field of vision."

The Thresher prepared to swing, but the drunken man shouted, "Wait, wait!"

But the Thresher refused to return his arm to its former position; he held the sword up in striking position, waiting for the other man to continue.

"This guy I know . . ." the drunken man slurred, "he runs with this crowd that squats in some kind of super-secret location. I dunno where they are, man, but he told me they've all been talking about this 'Bringer', and how he's . . . 'on his way' or something."

When the man stopped speaking, the Thresher prompted, "Continue."

"I don't know no more than that, man! Honest!"

The Thresher studied the drunken man, discerning the truth from his features. "If you've lied to me—"

"I'm not that stupid!" the other man bellowed. "You got a *rep*, man! Nobody's gonna disrespect *you*, you're the Thresh—" He broke off suddenly, realizing he'd said more than he'd meant to.

The Thresher brought the sword to rest against the drunken man's throat, and lowered the man far enough that his mouth was right next to the man's ear.

"*How*," he breathed hot air, "do you know *that name*?"

"I-I-I uh, I heard it—" the man blustered.

The Thresher dropped the man to the floor. "From *whom?*" he asked, raising the blade and preparing to strike. Fire had suddenly come to his listless eyes.

But he never got the opportunity to find out more. Something struck the back of his head forcefully, and he collapsed to the floor, unconscious.

20

In the end, Grant hadn't agreed or disagreed. Morning approached and since the job had to be completed under night's cloak everybody decided to discuss again after some rest. Grant and Julie accepted rooms for the evening and soon said farewell. After their departure, Morgan ventured deeper into the asylum, winding her way into a distant back corner to the only occupied room in the wing.

Approaching the door carefully, she knocked on it.

"*Sí?*" a tired, low-pitched Latin voice called out from behind the door.

Morgan entered.

Sitting on the bed was a bronze-skinned woman with a wrinkled face and a serious expression. She was knitting.

They called her Marta, though Morgan had no idea what her original name might have been. She was the oldest of all the Loci at seventy-nine years of age—the oldest Morgan had ever met who had experienced the Shift.

Marta preferred solitude, so she lived alone in this abandoned section of the facility and rarely left her room. Morgan thought back to their first meeting, only a few years ago, when she had asked Marta to come live here. Having nowhere else to go, the old woman had agreed, on one condition: she had no desire to be around others. The Shift had been so traumatic for her at her age that she simply wanted to be left alone.

But occasionally, she would tolerate visits from Morgan, at those times when she had important information.

Marta did not look up as Morgan walked in.

"This man you have brought here. He will learn the truth very soon," the old woman said without greeting or preamble. She spoke in Spanish, as she knew not a single word of English and didn't care to. But Morgan understood her.

Morgan took a seat at a small desk opposite the bed, turning the chair to face Marta.

"What truth is that?" Morgan asked.

"His truth. Who and what he is," Marta said matter-of-factly. *"When that happens, he may become . . . unpredictable."*

"He's *already* unpredictable. Are you saying I should take some kind of precautions?" asked Morgan.

"He will become what he will become. Your actions will change nothing," Marta answered evenly.

"And is he becoming what I believe he is?"

Marta stopped knitting and looked up into Morgan's eyes for the first time. She studied Morgan for a long moment before speaking. *"This man is part of something greater than all of us. Vast and powerful, it reaches back through the fabric of history to the very beginning of time. Those like him have been with us since it all began, in one form or another."*

Morgan frowned. "I need more, dear. If you want me to be on guard, I'm going to need more from you than vague notions about who he's turning into . . ."

"No," Marta said flatly. *"He has* always *been* who *he is now. But* what *he is becoming is . . . something else. And it is unavoidable."*

"I don't understand," said Morgan.

Marta sighed. *"There are some storms that even* you *cannot quell."*

The two women stared at each other for a moment, Morgan wondering, as always, if Marta's intuition could be false. But she'd certainly been proven right many times in the past.

"And if I were you," Marta suddenly said, *"I would discourage him from keeping company with that burglar woman."*

Hannah.

"Why?"

"A friendship forged between them will not end well."

By evening, Grant was gone and Julie paced the Common Room. Hannah had recovered enough to drive Grant to his destination, so here Julie was, all alone in this loony bin with these weird people who just stood around and stared at her.

"I don't like this," Julie finally said, to no one in particular.

"Then we share something in common, dear," Morgan replied from her chair at the fireplace, her eyes glued to the latest hardback to grab her attention. "But I promise you, I would not have asked this of him if it weren't absolutely vital."

"You keep saying that," Julie retorted. "Feeling guilty?"

"Quite so," Morgan answered, without hesitation, looking up from her book for the first time.

Julie frowned, regretful. She shivered, her hand shaking from nerves as she took the seat opposite Morgan in front of the fire.

"You seem nervous," Morgan said, eying Julie with a studious expression.

"Of course I am."

"You wish that you could be with him, to help him," Morgan stated.

"Yeah!" Julie cried, realizing it herself for the first time.

"But this is not the reason you tremble."

Julie blinked, staring wide-eyed at Morgan.

"Tell me," Morgan went on, lowering her voice yet full of compassion, "how long has it been since you were diagnosed?"

Julie was taken aback, though she regrouped fast. "I don't know what you're—"

"My dear, you've been demonstrating minor uncontrollable shakes since you and your brother arrived. I'm no diagnostician, but I *am* well-read, and I recognize the symptoms of Parkinson's when I see them."

Julie was flabbergasted. Tears stung her eyes, but she blinked them back.

"It was about a month ago," she whispered in reply, struggling to keep her composure. "Only a few weeks before my brother and I reunited."

Morgan sighed in sympathy. "Grant doesn't know?"

Julie shook her head, tears spilling out. "*Please* don't tell him. He has enough to worry about, and he *needs* me . . . Frankly, I'm afraid for him. *All the time.* He's been through so much. I feel like I'm desperately holding on to him, trying to pull him back all by myself . . ."

Morgan smiled sensitively. "I won't tell him, dear, you have my word. But if I may offer an unsolicited word of advice: show *confidence* in him. Make him *see* that you have faith he will overcome his obstacles. *That's* what he needs from you now."

"I just don't know what to think about any of this," Julie replied, sniffling. "All this stuff about him and you and the others and those rings. . . . I just don't believe it."

Morgan tilted her head, the faintest hint of a smile forming at the edge of her lips. "Sometimes *belief* is all you really need."

"What am I supposed to believe *in?*" Julie asked, flustered, looking away. She turned back to face Morgan when she felt the elder woman's hand rest on top of hers, quieting its trembling with a gentle, steady grip.

Morgan leaned forward in her chair just slightly. Her eyes twinkled in the firelight.

"Believe," she said softly, "that all that is happening to your brother—*and* to you—is not random."

21

Hannah stopped the convertible three blocks from their destination. All she and Grant could see in every direction were darkened homes in a modest residential development. It was after one; the entire neighborhood should be asleep.

Grant glanced at Hannah, who was behind the wheel.

This is the part where I'm supposed to get out . . .

Hannah took his hand in hers. "It's gonna be okay. You're *way* more capable than ya think you are."

He smiled weakly, insincerely.

"And I don't care *what* Morgan says," Hannah added, "I ain't leaving you here, big boy. I'll be waiting—and *watching*—right here, in case anything goes wrong."

Grant nodded appreciatively and took a deep breath. Hannah handed him a large flashlight, and he got out of the car.

He imagined—or rather *hoped*—that he looked catlike as he crept up the dark sidewalk. The black shirt and pants he'd put on at the asylum helped him blend in with the night—even though the shirt was two sizes too big—but he still felt like he had no idea what he was doing.

How am I supposed to do this? I'm no good at this stuff.

Who is Morgan, anyway?

His thoughts drifted back to that afternoon, when he'd finally emerged from his "cell" at the asylum. Sleep had come only because he was wholly exhausted, but even so, the nightmares remained. After a shower and a little food, he'd found Morgan in the Common Room, chatting with a dozen of the others. Hannah was there, scowling, as was Julie, sitting in one corner alone and fidgeting.

Morgan had spotted him first as he walked in and motioned him forward.

Before she could speak, he blurted out, "Let's just get this over with."

"Of course," she replied. "The task is a simple one. Go to this address"—she handed him a folded-up piece of paper—"and retrieve a small, brown cardboard box, wrapped in brown packing paper and tied with twine. You'll know it when you see it. It will be fairly heavy for its size. Its 'owner' will be occupied this evening."

Grant frowned. "What's in the box?"

"A fragment," she replied. When he was unimpressed, she continued, "You want to know what all of this is about? Why we experienced the Shift and what these rings are doing on our fingers? This little brown box holds the key to answering every one of your questions."

"And this address? What's there?"

"It's a residence out in Van Nuys," she replied calmly, "Beyond that. . . ."

He was nonplussed. "So that's it," he motioned wide with his hands, in desperation. "Go to this mystery address and pick up some nondescript brown box. It'll be that simple?"

"Of course it won't," Morgan said casually. "Nothing ever is. But I need you to understand something, Grant, and it's very important that you hear me clearly on this: What I want to show you is something I have never shown *anyone*. I hate the idea of testing you as much as you do, but I can't show you what I have to show you until I *know* you are indeed the one meant to see it. And if you can't complete this task, then you are not that person."

Grant swallowed. "That your idea of a pep talk?"

"As a matter of fact, it is," Morgan replied.

Grant opened the paper and read the address; he didn't recognize it. Morgan said it was near the Van Nuys airport.

Grant's head dropped and shook back and forth, his mind swimming.

"Why can't anything ever be simple? Why does everything have to be complicated?" he muttered.

"I think you know why," she replied, unmoved. "And if you don't, you soon will."

He turned to go.

"You can do this, Grant," Morgan said. "I believe in you."

She sounded completely convinced.

Now, in the dead of night, he ducked behind a patch of bushes near the street after spotting the address in question. There was nothing remarkable about it. It was a simple two-story house. A garage on the far end of the house was closed, which meant he couldn't tell if anybody was home. The place wasn't especially large. White siding with charcoal shudders and highlights. Windows all around, on both floors.

It was no different from the many other homes in the neighborhood.

Grant's new instincts offered nothing about break-in techniques, so he focused on the windows. The solid front door didn't look like it would budge anyway.

He tiptoed to the right side of the house, feeling a bit silly, and pushed up on the first window he came to.

Locked.

He tried the next one.

Also locked.

He stole a few quick looks around to make sure there was no activity, and prayed for silence as he punched a fist through the windowpane. The gloves Hannah had given him during their drive protected his skin.

The glass tinkled loudly, and he crouched under the window, waiting a full minute to make sure no one reacted. No lights came on inside the house. No activity from any of the neighboring homes. No alarm went off.

Grant took a deep breath and stood. Reaching in, he unlocked the window, pushed up, and climbed through.

He pulled out the flashlight and flicked it on, sweeping the downstairs area with the tiny light. He was in the dining room. He scanned the table in the middle of the room and then moved on.

The next room looked like it should have been the living room or den, but whoever lived here was using it as some sort of personal space. A large oak desk sat against the far wall, with various disheveled items on top, including a computer buried underneath some of the others. A punching bag hung from the ceiling in the corner to his right. To his left were several bookcases full of books.

He walked to the desk and quietly opened each drawer, shifting things aside and looking for the small cardboard box. Nothing.

He surveyed the floor, the walls. No sign of a safe. The shelves next to the door held dozens of books. One book on the top shelf was enormous, over a foot tall and easily five inches thick.

Grant walked closer. It appeared to be some sort of exhaustive dictionary, but . . .

No one would be that obvious, would they?

He pulled down the oversized book. It was lighter than he'd expected. He opened it.

The book was hollow. A small, brown box tied with twine rested in its cavity, and Grant pulled it out. He held his flashlight up to the box; it was about five inches square, and about an inch thick.

Click.

Grant froze.

He felt the pistol's cool steel on his right ear.

"You don't belong here," a voice growled. The man with the gun reached to the wall beside him with his free hand and turned on the light.

Grant glanced sideways and the two of them locked eyes.

"But then," the man said, "you must hear that a lot."

It was Detective Drexel.

Grant's memory rushed back to Julie's description of him from her encounter at UCLA. Grant had only seen the man once, staring down the barrel of a gun. And here they were again, history repeating itself.

Drexel stepped back and motioned for Grant to turn around fully. Grant complied and they faced one another.

Grant felt the panic begin to rise in his throat, but he closed his eyes and forced himself to be calm. After what had happened at the Inveo security office, he was determined not to let it out again until he could find a way to control it.

"Mr. Borrows," Drexel began with a smug grin, the gun still trained on Grant. "You wouldn't *believe* all the trouble I've gone through to find you. And where do you turn up? Right in my own home."

Grant's thoughts were elsewhere. Having nothing to lose, he held up the box between them. "Did *you* steal this?"

"I'm a *policeman*," Drexel snarled, snatching the box out of Grant's hand. "I don't steal, I *recover evidence*. Who sent you after this?"

Drexel's eyes focused on the box for a split second, and in that second, Grant reacted. He darted left through the open doorway that he'd come in.

Drexel fired but missed.

Grant tore through the house in a straight line for the front door, but just as he reached it, Drexel fired another shot, and this one punched a hole in the front door only inches above Grant's shoulder. He stopped.

"Move and I'll kill you," Drexel's intimidating voice called. "Hands up."

Grant complied. Drexel approached him from behind, taking the box and setting it on a small lamp stand in the hall.

"Breaking and entering is a misdemeanor," he said as he stopped a few feet away. "That'll do for a start." He pulled a pair of handcuffs out of his pants pocket with his free hand. He snapped one cuff into place, and then brought that arm down behind Grant. He grabbed the other arm.

Grant brought a leg up to kick Drexel between the legs; Drexel cried out in pain, and Grant turned and opened the front door, reaching for the latch to the glass outer door.

But before he touched it, an alarm sounded. Floodlights flashed on, both inside and out.

"Don't go," Drexel said lightly. "We're about to have company."

Grant turned to see Drexel holding some kind of panic button in his free hand. The gun was still extended in his other. He had tears in his eyes from the pain, but he was smiling again.

Grant wanted to cover his ears because of the loud blaring of the security sirens, but he was afraid to move. Drexel's entire appearance had suddenly become crazed.

"On your knees, hands behind your head!" he screamed.

Grant dropped to the floor and couldn't keep his hands from

shaking as he laced them behind his neck. Instincts he couldn't control were flooding his mind with techniques to take Drexel down, how to sweep the other man's feet out from under him and pin him to the ground, or how to quickly snatch the gun away. But Drexel had a tight grip on the pistol and his finger was steady on the trigger.

Grant watched as Drexel snatched a radio off of his belt clip and began whispering into it.

"This is Detective Drexel—there's somebody in my house and I think he's armed! I need *backup!*" He threw the radio aside and stepped forward, grinning. "No need to bother with an arrest now. It was only self-defense."

Drexel extended the gun and touched it to the top of Grant's down-turned head.

And Grant panicked.

The entire neighborhood awoke to the sound of a concussive blast, as every window in Drexel's house exploded outward.

NO! STOP!!

Grant came to moments later, curled up on the ground in agony. The pain this time was more intense than anything he'd ever imagined possible, and it had lasted longer.

His eyes gaped wide, his heart racing again. His eyes burned as he blinked them back and stumbled to his feet, taking in the impossible sight before him.

It looked as if a bomb had gone off, only nothing was charred. Every object around him had been overturned or broken. The house still stood, but all of the windows and doors had exploded.

Grant took a few unsteady steps and heard breathing.

He found Drexel lying on his back, over ten feet away down the hall. The gun was nowhere in sight. Drexel was awake, breathing fast, an entirely new look on his face. One Grant hadn't seen on him before.

Terror.

He saw Grant coming and his breathing rate increased. The man had a few cuts on his face but didn't look seriously injured.

Grant wasn't faring much better. He was in shock, cold and wobbly, his eyes darting everywhere. It was all he could do not to panic again at the sight of what he had somehow just done.

"I left the-the box on the table . . . r-right there!" the other man stammered, raising an arm to point. "Just take it and get out!"

Grant swallowed as he spotted the box under a pile of rubble that used to be the small end table. He braced himself on the wall as he leaned over to recover it.

Rising again, he stared at the fallen detective for another moment before turning and walking drunkenly down the hall and out the empty doorway.

Drexel raised his head enough to watch Grant go. When Grant was out of sight, he craned to the left and saw his radio on the ground, under a smashed picture frame.

He fished it out with a shaking hand, but didn't get up.

"This is Drexel," he spoke into the radio, out of breath. "Disregard previous call. Repeat: cancel backup. False alarm."

Then something smoldered behind his eyes and he slowly sat upright. He keyed the radio again and his mouth twisted into an angry snarl.

"But get me a forensics unit down here right away. And put an unmarked car at the laboratory of Daniel Cossick. If he *burps*, I want a full report."

22

An hour later, Grant flung the box at Morgan. His fists were balled and shaking, his entire body barely containing his fury.

She caught the box in her hand and examined it. "Nicely done," she said.

"*Nice?*" he nearly spat the word.

Julie had dozed off in her chair in the far corner but jerked awake at Grant's raised voice. She leaped from her chair and began running for Grant, but she stopped when she saw how he looked. He felt the blood in his face, and he knew his stance and expression must have looked threatening.

Hannah stood a safe distance behind Grant, watching closely, but staying out of it.

Morgan was unruffled, examining him. He knew he looked terrible—clothes ripped, hair askew, bruises and dirt all over. Fear and anger writhed through him, and he was barely keeping it contained.

Grant was terrified of what he was capable of, and outraged that she'd forced him to do it.

"You got the job done," she said, appraising him.

"You owe me answers," he said shakily, but he stood up taller. "And they had *better* be worth it."

"Indeed." She looked down, gathering her thoughts. A crowd of residents gathered behind her. "Pose your questions, Grant. And I shall answer."

"*What am I?*"

"You are the Bringer. The fulcrum on which all of our fates will turn."

He didn't blink. "You're going to have to do better than that."

She looked around at the gathered crowd, her expression becoming resolute. She joined her hands in front and then turned back to him, leveling her gaze.

"As it was with each of us, the Shift affected you in ways more than physical. It was mental as well."

"Meaning what? I'm not me anymore?"

"No, you're still you . . . more or less." She paused. "Have you ever heard the statistic that says that humans only use a small percentage of their brains?"

His impatience was boiling over. "I heard it was a *myth* . . ."

She nodded. "The theories posited that anywhere from seventy to ninety percent of the human brain is unused. Those same theories stated that if we were ever to tap into the idle parts of our minds, we might gain enhanced mental skills. Abilities like a photographic memory might become attainable by *everyone*."

Grant's expression was unchanged.

"Most modern scientists," she continued, "have discounted this as nonsense, and they're probably right. But modern science ignores most of what it refuses to understand. These theories have validity and we're the proof. Each of us. Our mental amplifications are as unique as our fingerprints."

Now she had his attention.

"I know how this sounds. And I honestly have no idea *how* it works. I only know that it *does*. However it happens, *something* extra—maybe that extra seventy percent of brain power, maybe something else altogether—is switched 'on' in us when the Shift occurs."

Grant had difficulty swallowing this. "All of them?" he said.

"I have met over one hundred people over the years who wear rings like ours, and the resulting enhancements are different in each and every one of them."

"Different how?"

"A rare few, like Hannah, have stronger, more overt skills. I cannot conceive of how she does it, but through some sort of profound mental persuasion, she's able to convince others that they're seeing things that aren't there."

Grant's mind raced back to everything he'd seen Hannah do at the Inveo plant . . .

"Most of us, however," Morgan went on, "have more mundane skills."

"Like what?"

Beside Morgan stood an elderly man. She smiled at him and placed a hand on his shoulder. "Nigel, what's four hundred thirty-two thousand, six hundred ninety-one *squared*?"

"One hundred eighty-seven billion, two hundred twenty-one million, five hundred one thousand, four hundred eighty-one," he replied without hesitation.

Grant's eyebrows popped up.

"The majority of us have these kinds of talents—unique intuitions or expanded mental capacities based on very normal human functions. Like our human calculator here."

"What about you?" Grant asked, beginning to calm. "What can you do?"

"I can remember everything that happens within my perception with *perfect, absolute clarity*."

"You really *do* have a photographic memory?"

"It's far more than that," she said, speaking plainly and directly. "Every conversation I've heard since the day of the Shift, I can repeat to you *verbatim*. And it goes beyond words. Every smell I've breathed in, I can recall with the precision of a bloodhound. Every surface I've touched, every taste I've sampled. Every sound I've heard. Everything I see. Every word of every book I've read. I remember it all, without error . . . and without effort."

"That's why you have migraines."

She nodded. "And why I don't sleep. My brain simply never stops retaining, working, filing away information. I can catch brief snippets of unconscious rest every now and again, but my mind rarely lets that happen, and I can't explain how, but my body is somehow able to manage with a lack of cognitive rest. I've theorized that perhaps since the body is *regulated* by the mind . . ."

"So the books that line the halls," Grant interjected. "You've read them *all*?"

Morgan smiled a humorless smile. "Are you familiar with the saying, 'The more you eat, the more you *want* to eat'?"

Grant nodded.

"I'm afraid the same axiom applies to knowledge. I have read and memorized every word of every volume you see in this building—save the stack atop my desk. When I say that I am the most well-read person on this planet, it is a statement of fact, and nothing more."

Grant was reeling, trying to process all of this.

Morgan took a deep breath. "I've told you all this, Grant, because it's important that you know what the rest of us can do. I need you to understand *us* before I can explain *you*."

His heart fluttered. "Okay."

"Each of us can do something extraordinary. But of all of the unusual skills that we possess, *none* of us—not one—is as powerful as you."

"I'm different?"

"We're *all* different," she said. "You're *special*."

He swallowed.

"Grant, it's my belief that whatever has happened to us all . . . *We*"—she motioned to herself and the others—"are just the warm-up. *You* are the main event."

"Why?"

"Because *no one* has ever manifested abilities like yours, with genuine, physical power. And more importantly, I base it on that ring on your finger."

He held it up, glanced at it. "It's just like yours. Like *all* of yours."

"It's *similar*," she corrected him. "But the markings etched into the sides are tremendously significant. None of ours have those symbols."

"So? Why does that make *me* Mr. Special?"

Morgan broke away from the others and they parted as she moved toward the fireplace. "Because of *this*," she said. With one foot, she stepped on a brick just in front of the fire, which gave way like a large button.

Grant heard a *click*. The entire fireplace—mantel, bricks, and all—swiveled slowly open, like a door.

"Follow me, please," Morgan said. "Your sister may join us, as well." She retrieved a long wooden match from a box by the fire and stuck it into the fire. When it lit, she entered the dark opening in the wall.

Grant didn't snap out of his astonishment until he felt Julie's hand clasp his. He couldn't see anything at all in the space Morgan had just confidently entered, but he and Julie followed nonetheless. Morgan touched something on the wall—he couldn't see what—and the fireplace behind them swiveled shut again, sealing them into the darkness.

"Don't be frightened," Morgan said gently, as her tiny, flickering light led the way. "No one has ever been down here except me. There are stairs ahead, so watch your step."

Grant found his eyes adjusting to the dark quickly, as he carefully and cautiously got his footing on each new step before placing his weight on it. He also tried to help Julie, who seemed even more unsteady than he was.

As they neared the bottom of the steps, a new question popped into his head.

"Why didn't you invite Hannah to come down with us?"

"She can't be trusted." Immediately she stopped descending the steps and turned, a frown on her face flickering in the candlelight. "I apologize, that was a poor choice of words. I *do* trust her. She's a good friend, she's one of *us*, and she is indebted to me because of a matter that occurred between us several years ago."

"Then—?"

"She's a *thief*. By definition, she does not hold to the same codes and principles inherent in some others. And I make no exaggeration when I say that she is capable of *anything*. You've seen her in action; I'm sure you can attest to this."

Memories of Hannah's exploits again swam inside Grant's mind as they reached the bottom of the stairs and came into what seemed to be some kind of underground laboratory. Only without cement or bricks or even wood. It was more like a cave, carved right out of the earth. The walls around them weren't even perfectly vertical; it looked like huge chunks of the ground had been scooped away, and this small room beneath the asylum was the result.

Candles lined the perimeter of the room. Some of them were

already burning, and she lit a few more.

"This room was here already when we moved in," she said as an aside, "but I had the entrance upstairs specially made. I'm not sure what they might have done in here related to mental patient care, and frankly I don't *care* to know. But I have found it to be an effective vault, even though no electricity runs into here."

A small table almost like a flat podium stood in the middle of the room, and she approached it. The table was covered with a large piece of sandy brown burlap.

"Grant, you are special because your ring is different from all the others. And I know that makes you special, because of *this*." She held up the small box he'd given her, still tied with twine.

He and Julie walked closer as she untied the box. She pulled out the small object inside and held it next to a tall candle on the edge of the center table. They looked closer.

Candlelight danced over a small piece of brown stone, full of tiny, intricate symbols.

"Do you understand now?"

He never moved his eyes from the piece of stone, but whatever she was seeing, he didn't.

"Not really," he said, though Julie was squeezing his hand awfully hard.

"Then I'll bring it into focus for you," she said.

She unwrapped the cloth on the table to reveal a much larger, flat slab of brown stone that matched the one in her hand. It was about eighteen inches across and twelve inches high, with an obvious chunk missing, broken off at an angle in one corner. It too was filled with markings just like the piece in her hand. It was writing of some sort, though Grant had no idea where it might have come from.

Cracks ran through the slab, and he realized that this wasn't merely one piece—it was several small pieces fit together, like a jigsaw puzzle.

Morgan placed the small stone Grant had taken from Drexel's home on the table and slid it into the missing spot in the bottom corner. It fit perfectly. The stone—whatever it was—was now whole, complete.

"Over the last decade, I have studied every resource I can get my hands on—ancient texts, historical records, forgotten libraries—to find out all I can about the rings we wear. Where do they come from? What do they do? How did we get them? And do you know what I found? *Nothing*. No record of what they are or where they came from exists, anywhere in the world.

"Or so I believed," Morgan continued, "until I came upon this artifact, many years ago. It was broken, its pieces scattered across the globe. Collecting and assembling it has been my life's work since the Shift. I have been unable to determine where it came from, but it's *thousands* of years old. Perhaps older. Do you recall what I said earlier, about how the rings have a molecular density greater than any known substance in nature? I've tested the chemical structure of the stone, and its molecular cohesion shows the same density as the rings."

"But it was shattered."

"Yes. Which worries me greatly. The power that could break this stone . . ."

Grant was still confused. "But what does any of this prove?"

"Do you not see it? The symbols on the tablet—look closely. Here," Morgan pointed, "the piece you just retrieved is the final one, and there are more of the symbols there. Grant, a section of the symbols on this tablet match the etchings on your ring *precisely*."

He pulled away from the table, suddenly not liking where this conversation was going. "But . . . if the tablet talks about this ring, and it's as ancient as you say it is, why do you assume that it has anything to do with me? Couldn't *anyone* have worn this ring in all that time?"

A hesitant look shadowed her face. "There's more. I've never quite come up with a complete word-for-word translation, but I've been able to decipher many of the *meanings* behind these symbols. One key area I've decoded is numbers.

"I've discovered a date on the tablet, Grant," she said portentously, taking a step closer to him as he continued to slowly creep backward. "The date refers to you."

"How do you know that?"

"Because it matches the date you experienced the Shift."

Grant moved backward until his back hit the wall. He caused a few of the candles to tumble to the ground, but Morgan ignored them. Julie, meanwhile, was speechless, her eyes bouncing hopelessly between Morgan and Grant.

The date on this ancient hunk of rock matches the date I spotted myself walking down the sidewalk downtown? The day all of this began?

"That's preposterous," he blurted out, but the shock and concern never left his features.

"Whatever is happening to all of us," Morgan said with conviction, "it hinges on you. The Shift. The rings. This tablet. Our enhanced abilities. You are the *key* to it all, Grant."

Grant swallowed and fought the urge to pass out. This wasn't happening, it couldn't be true . . . He shook his head. There were no words, no other response.

She moved closer to him, her eyes piercing his soul.

"The bits of the stone tablet I've been able to translate speak of a 'miracle man' called 'the Bringer,' whose destiny it is to 'shape the future.' That man . . . is *you*."

23

Morning came, and once again Grant had been up all night. Only this time, he had been talking with Morgan. Julie had fallen asleep somewhere along the way. Morgan had no more details or speculation to offer him, but she helped him sort through the stone tablet's implications, and gave him her word that she would always help him with all of the resources at her disposal. She also promised that she would keep working to translate the entire tablet, encouraged now that it was completed and a full translation was possible.

When they finally emerged from the hidden room, the Common Room was louder than usual. There seemed to be a buzz about the room, which for the first time featured no one who stopped to stare at him for long periods of time. Instead, the Loci were coming and going, to and fro, busy little workers. They had purpose in their movements, and Grant realized that all of this commotion was because of him.

They knew, and they understood.

Julie walked away, lost in her own thoughts.

Grant noticed that Hannah was still around, helping with chores and other tasks. He was a little surprised to find himself *encouraged* to see her friendly face, considering Morgan's earlier warning, though he couldn't quite put his finger on when it was he'd begun thinking of her face as "friendly."

Grant was about to break away from Morgan and approach Hannah when Morgan touched his arm and pulled him aside.

"May I ask you one last personal question before you go?" she said quietly.

"Sure."

"Who were you, before all this? Before the Shift?"

"My name was—"

"No no no. I'm not asking for a *name*. Who *were* you? What was your *identity*, your purpose, your path? What was your existence like?"

He looked into her gaze until he could look no more. Finally, he spoke again. "I was . . . alone."

Morgan examined him thoughtfully for a moment. "I thought as much. What would you say was your greatest weakness?"

He looked away, stunned at her forthright manner regarding his deepest, most hidden feelings. "I had some problems, growing up. At the orphanage . . . sometimes I would pick fights with other kids. On purpose. And I almost always *lost*. When I finally got out of that place, I told myself it was all over, and now was my chance to make a clean break, to start again. But there were a few times, in public places . . . when I lashed out. My anger would just build and build . . . until it exploded."

"So you isolated yourself to ward off the temptation," she summed up. "Very noble, in a way. But in all this time, you had no friends?"

"No."

"No family?"

"Just Julie. But I stayed away."

"Acquaintances, co-workers? Not even a pet?"

Grant shook his head.

"My, my," she breathed in deeply, examining him with new eyes. "You embraced it. You allowed it to change the very foundations of who you are."

He breathed faster, old feelings rushing to the surface. "I never *asked* for everyone in my life to run out on me," he huffed. "Why are you asking me about this?"

"Grant, my fate and that of those around us is about to be decided at your hands. I'd like to know if you're more Jekyll or Hyde."

"Morgan!" someone shouted.

They both turned as a tall, thin, black man Grant hadn't yet met stormed through the Common Room doors and marched straight up to

Morgan. He appeared to be ignoring Grant.

"It was *too soon!*" he cried, his eyes twitching wildly behind his oval, wire-rimmed glasses. "How *could* you?!"

The man had short, braided hair and was clearly agitated, gesturing wildly with his arms. He was impossibly thin and couldn't have been more than twenty-three.

Morgan was untroubled by his actions. She merely stared at him.

"Grant, I don't believe you've met Fletcher," Morgan said without taking her eyes off of the newcomer. "You'll have to forgive his . . . *zeal*. He's made it his self-appointed mission to guard the safety of this place and the Loci who live here. His enthusiasm sometimes gets the best of him. But I keep him around because he's a genius."

"I thought you were *all* geniuses, of one kind or another."

"Well, yes. But he's different. Fletcher is capable of multiple thoughts at the same time. He's quite brilliant, capable of seeing patterns and connections that others physically cannot."

Finally Fletcher turned his twitchy frame in Grant's direction, though he barely acknowledged him at all. "I provide the intuition that her vast knowledge of cold facts utterly lacks." He returned his attention to Morgan. "This man could be anyone. How could you take him to see the stone so soon? You don't know *anything* about him!"

"Enough," Morgan said forcefully, her face calm but her volume matching his. "I know *enough*."

"You're jeopardizing our safety by trusting him." His eyes darted back and forth quickly between Grant and Morgan. "He's killed at least one person—*that we know of*—and injured several others. Morgan, he blew up a house, for crying out loud!"

Morgan's lips stretched into a thin frown as Fletcher continued talking for another minute. Her head slowly turned to look in his direction.

"Young man, are you aware that your lips are still moving?" she said, interrupting him.

He fell silent, registering an appalled expression.

"You should look after that," she said, her eyebrows slightly raised.

He glared at her. Then stormed off.

"Don't mind him. You are *always* welcome here, Grant. Though when you stop by, I would thank you to bring me a new book or two, if you can." She offered a knowing smile. "Preferably something rare."

He nodded, and Morgan excused herself.

Hannah noticed the opening and approached. She must have guessed the meaning of the stare Grant couldn't hide because she smiled.

"Sleep makes all things better," she quipped. She grabbed his hand and gave it a little squeeze, and he found himself squeezing back, overwhelmed and grateful to have sympathetic human contact. "You should try it."

"No, I'm glad to be headed home. Though to be honest, I am a little worried," he said sheepishly.

"What, because of those Inveo people?" she replied.

"They can identify us."

"We don't know that anybody other than the security guards ever actually saw our faces, and they were a bunch of psychos, anyway," she replied. "I'm thinkin' the question they have to ask themselves is, do they know more about us, or do we know more about them? We saw their entire operation. Their 'war room' or whatever. Not to mention that enormous door, which leads to God only knows what. I'm guessin' that's not the kinda info they'd want the police or the media to find out about."

"But that's all the more reason for them to come after us," he said.

She sighed, rolled her eyes. "They won't try anything, they'll be too afraid after what you did to them. You certainly struck fear into that detective's heart tonight, too. And if they *do* come after us, I'll just put tarantulas in their dreams." He thought she might be joking, but reconsidered at her expression.

"You can do that?" he said.

"Tip of the iceberg, big boy," she said, breaking into that thousand-dollar smile, with those gorgeous ruby lips and radiant white teeth . . .

Her cell phone rang. She pulled it out and looked at the display.

"Sorry, I've been waiting to hear from a client," she said, and started walking away.

"Remind me to have a talk with you about your line of work sometime," Grant called out.

Still walking, she craned her head around and stuck her tongue out at him, before flashing that big smile again.

The smile that he was finding increasingly pleasant.

On the front doorstep, Hannah opened her ringing phone.
"Yeah?"

She walked lightly down the front steps and glanced at her watch. Then she walked away from the building, along the broken driveway until she was as far away as she dared.

"No, I was just talkin' to him before you called," she said, her voice low.

The voice on the other end responded.

"Yes . . . I understand."

She listened to the phone.

"Trust me . . ." she said, turning back to gaze at the asylum. "He has no idea."

24

"You're not going to get anything out of him," said a man with the name "Hanson" on his nametag. He seemed like a competent kid, but a bit young for a lieutenant. And the way he kept sizing up Drexel's bruises and scrapes was starting to grate. "He hasn't said a word since we brought him in after that 911 call."

"He hasn't met *me*," Drexel replied.

Drexel put his hand on the doorknob to the interrogation room and opened it.

"So . . . the legendary Thresher, caught with his guard down," Drexel said. He began circling the small metal chair in the interrogation room. The bald man sitting within it tensed briefly but said nothing. A bright spotlight shone from above—the only light in the room—and the Thresher's hands were cuffed in plastic restraints behind him.

"Oh, I know all about you," Drexel continued, noting the other man's edge. "It would seem your skills are surpassed only by your legendary status in your line of work. Did you know you're creeping up the FBI's Most Wanted list? Though they never had a picture to go with the profile till now."

The Thresher squared his shoulders, sat upright.

Drexel leaned forward and lowered his voice, so only his captive could hear him speak. "I know what you're looking for. You want the Bringer."

The Thresher turned to face him for the first time. "For your sake, I hope you're going to tell me where to find him."

"Ah, he speaks!" Drexel triumphed. "Idiots here were just telling me how they couldn't get a single word out of you. Now that we're friends, why don't you tell me your real name. To go along with your portrait."

"I have none."

Drexel shrugged. "Never hurts to ask. So how *did* they capture you, anyway?"

"They cheated," the Thresher replied.

"Cheated!" Drexel laughed out loud. "Let me guess, *everyone* who defeats you cheats."

"No one has *ever* defeated me. Your men scored no victory," the Thresher spat. "Where is triumph when you lack the spine to look your opponent in the eye? Those adolescents with guns and nightsticks knew they had no chance of besting me. Just as *you* do. So you seek to intimidate me." He paused then continued with a note of amusement in his voice. "Intimidate . . . *me*."

Drexel slapped him hard across the back of his bald head. "Men in handcuffs shouldn't mock."

He didn't say anything else for a moment, just circled the man for a minute or two. Finally he asked, "Are the rumors true? Do you really get a million per hit, in cash?"

The Thresher made no response.

"What a stash you must have!" Drexel continued. "A man might wonder what you spend that kind of money on."

Still there was no response.

"They say you're real selective about the jobs you'll take," Drexel continued, still walking in a circle around the chair. "But no one's ever been able to figure out what your method of selection is."

The Thresher did not even move in his chair, he simply continued staring straight ahead.

"Ah, well," Drexel resolved. "Back to business at hand, I guess. Let's start with this, my new favorite piece of evidence." Drexel produced the sword from somewhere beyond the room's darkness and continued to circle until he was standing in front of the seated man. He hefted the sword with his good right arm—the other was still in a shoulder brace from his episode at the UCLA office. "Don't suppose you'd care to tell me what these markings on the blade signify?"

The Thresher looked up at Drexel.

He kicked out sharply with his foot, knocking the sword out of Drexel's hand. It arced into the air until the tip was pointing down; soaring downward, the mighty blade sliced through the plastic cuffs and as his hands became free, he caught the sword in one hand at the last second.

The Thresher stood and the sword became a blur of movement. Drexel's belt disappeared from his pants, flying off into the air behind the Thresher. His pants instantly fell around his ankles and he felt a sharp sting across his rear end that could only have come from the flat of the sword's blade. The pain thrust him suddenly forward, but his feet were tangled in the fallen trousers and there was nothing nearby to grab.

As he toppled over, the Thresher caught him by the forehead with a single hand. The arm attached to that hand was outstretched far enough to keep Drexel out of his reach; the Thresher sat on a nearby table calmly, his arm keeping Drexel from falling over without breaking a sweat.

It had all happened much too fast for Drexel to react to. Now he found himself leaning over far, arms flailing madly to get his balance back. He panicked as his bulbous belly touched the sword's edge, which the Thresher held in position by sitting on the hilt, wedging it between himself and the tabletop.

Yet he sat there staring at Drexel with utmost calm.

The Thresher leaned in to whisper a response to Drexel's last question. "You wanted to know what the markings on the blade signify? More than a right waste like you could *ever* comprehend."

Drexel awoke minutes later, surrounded by fellow policemen.

"What happened? Where'd he go?" he stammered.

"Long gone," one of the cops replied. "Looks like he knocked you out somehow."

Drexel came to his feet, not entirely steady, and pulled his pants back up with an angry jolt.

Blood surged through him and pounded against his temples.

That's it, then.

Enough was enough. The department wanted results, and he was going to get them.

No matter what.

He flipped open his phone from one of his pockets and stormed out the door.

"We're moving to Plan B," he said when the ringing stopped. "Do it *now*."

He hung up, withdrew a business card from his pocket, and dialed the number printed on it.

"I've told you already, Detective. I don't know anything about this man you mentioned," Daniel said into his phone, as he walked down the second-floor steps. Drexel had called just as Daniel was leaving the lab; Lisa had gone home hours ago.

"I had no idea," Drexel replied, "ethical scientist types like yourself were so skilled at lying."

Daniel walked out the front door into the cool night air in the warehouse district. It was unusually cold, yet he began to sweat at Drexel's implication. "Detective, I've contacted my lawyer, and I *know* you have no right to search or seize anything on my property without just cause."

Silence met him on the phone line, as he turned around to lock the outside door of the old brick warehouse building.

With a deep snarl, Drexel said, "We'll have to find one then."

Daniel stared at his phone, wondering if that had been a smart move. He'd meant to stave off the other man, but instead he'd somehow challenged him to up his game.

He wondered what else Drexel might have up his sleeve. Anything was possible.

It occurred to him just then how remarkably silent it was, there on the usually busy street behind him. Even the wind had momentarily stopped, holding its breath.

His phone rang again and he jumped.

Lisa . . .

Before he could answer it, he heard a loud crack.

The phone fell out of his hand and he slumped to the ground.

His mind was reacting too slowly, he realized—the crack had been something hitting the back of his head. On his hands and knees, he grabbed the door handle in front of him to steady himself and stand back up. He had a firm grip on it, and he gradually, carefully got to his feet. He turned around.

Something hard swung sideways into him, and he heard another sickening *pop*. He fell again, backward this time, as the wind was knocked out of him and a sharp pain shot through his chest.

Coughing, Daniel looked up through bleary eyes at the three obscure figures that towered over him. He couldn't make out their features. He saw only dark silhouettes. Perhaps they were men wearing hooded sweatshirts. Or perhaps they were wolves, tenderizing their next meal. The nearest one was holding a large metal bat. But as he lay there, none of them moved a muscle.

They watched him.

Daniel raised a hand straight up into the air. "Please, don't . . ." he gasped.

The bat came down again in a flash, this time into his stomach, and it was all he could manage to swallow the rising nausea.

"No—" he tried to say, but it didn't sound right, and he couldn't catch his breath.

One of them grabbed him by his straight brown hair and lifted, forcing him to stand. Daniel flailed his arms about, trying to get the man to let go, but he was facing the wall now and couldn't see what they were doing.

He gasped hard, eyes filled with blood and pain as the bat collided with his legs from behind. He fell yet again, fast and hard, the strength in his legs leaving as violent pain coursed through them.

Somewhere nearby, something was ringing.

What is that. . . ? I know that sound . . .

He fought to remain conscious as he realized it was his phone, still ringing from before. If only he could get his fingers around it . . . He threw an arm out in the direction the sound was coming from, but his eyes were bleary and bloodshot, and suddenly the sound stopped.

And then fists, feet, knees, and the heavy baseball bat descended upon him, all at once. Blows came from all sides, and he knew only pain. It was happening too fast. There was no time to react. One of the men stomped hard on his upturned foot and it twisted to the side with a sharp *snap*.

He couldn't get angry, couldn't be sad. Couldn't be afraid. Couldn't even cry.

He could only *feel*.

Barely holding to consciousness, he was outstretched on his chest now, though he didn't remember turning over. He opened his swollen eyes as much as possible, barely able to see through the haze of agony.

One fierce kick to the face ended that, as he finally, gratefully slipped into nothingness.

25

An accident on the 101 turned the trip back from Las Virgenes Canyon into a wasted afternoon. The winding canyon roads suited the Corvette perfectly while the stalled traffic surrounding them now was like making a Thoroughbred pull a plow. Eventually they growled their way back to the Wagner Building and into the parking garage. Finding a space and setting the brake, Grant said, "I need a plan."

"Agreed," Julie replied. She'd been brooding silently in the passenger seat since leaving the asylum. He thought she might yell on the drive back but she'd sat quiet and serious. It was like it was almost too much and the weight of everything had found her shoulders. The sun had waned in the horizon and vanished once they arrived at home, yet this was the first word she'd uttered during the drive.

"Think I might jot some things down, gather my thoughts, maybe see if I can come up with some idea of what I should do next," he continued. "Want to help?"

"I was wondering if I could borrow the car, actually," she replied. In response to his unspoken question, she said, "I haven't been home in a while. Thought I should check the mail, make sure my bills are caught up. Won't take long."

Something was wrong with this scenario, and Grant didn't have to be her brother to see it. But she was so distant, so withdrawn . . . and his mind was running in a hundred different directions. He didn't press the matter.

"Sure," he tossed her the keys and got out of the vehicle. "See you after a while."

Julie nodded in reply as she scooted over to the driver's seat and started the engine again. She backed out of the parking space and was out of sight in a moment.

Grant shook his head. *What's eating her? Probably everything.*

He'd just reached the door to the parking garage's elevator, glad to be exiting the nighttime shadows, when a voice said, "Nice to see you with some forward momentum."

Terrific. Her again.

His barefoot friend sauntered into view from an open stairwell beside the elevator. Her hands were clasped behind her back and she was typically smug.

"Admit it," she said playfully, "you missed me."

"Between escaping death within inches of my life—*twice*—and learning that I may be the culmination of some kind of ancient prophecy . . . no, sorry, you never once crossed my mind."

"Might want to spit that bitter pill back out before you choke on it," she remarked sourly. "So it's true. You had a little meet-'n'-greet with the one and only Morgan herself."

"Why didn't you tell me there were other people out there like me? Why did you let me think I was the only one?"

"You weren't ready to know," she said, dismissing him. "So how are the genius Loci?"

Grant said nothing.

"Morgan and her 'flock' definitely fall into the 'good guy' camp," the girl replied. "I'm sure she seemed eager to help you. But Morgan has her own agenda, just like everybody else. She sees a lot more potential in you than you do. And she may not be wrong."

Grant snorted. "All of this advice. So which camp do *you* fall into? Are you one of the good guys?"

"There are more colors in the crayon box than black and white, hot-shot," she countered. "Everyone's got their own agenda, and I do mean *everyone*. And it's rarely the one they let you see. But I would have *thought* you would've pieced together by now that I'm risking my own life and limb every time I stick my neck out far enough to speak to you."

"Then why *do* you talk to me? Are you manipulating me too?" He sighed, irritated and tired. "Everyone I've met since this began has pulled and prodded and wanted a piece of me."

"But you keep bouncing back, sweetie." She smiled. "That's why I like you. I'm here to watch you. I'm to observe your actions and file reports on your progress. I do the same for the others—the ones I can keep track of, anyway, before they disappear off to Morgan's little hide-away."

"So if you're trying to help me," Grant said, piecing the story together, "which is a violation of your 'orders,' then why not give me anything more to go on? Why all the vague clues?"

"You want something solid? Okay, how about this. Drexel intercepted that fragment of the stone tablet—not to learn anything from it himself, not to foil Morgan's plans—but to lure *you* to his apartment. A plan your new pal Morgan unwittingly accommodated."

"What? But . . ." Grant faltered, "how could he know Morgan would send me to get it?"

"Drexel may be little more than a cop who knows more than he should, but he knows *enough* about Morgan to know that she'd pay *any* price to get that fragment back. Sweetie, seriously, you're starting to worry me. In case you hadn't noticed—and clearly you *haven't*—this entire 'game' you're playing is completely rigged. Has been from the start. The things that have happened to you over the last few weeks may feel random to you, but it's all connected."

Grant's brow furrowed, anger rising once more at the layers upon layers of manipulation he'd been subjected to. He rubbed at the ring's underside.

"If you're going to play to win," the girl said, conviction in her voice, "then you have to go off script. And you've *got* to learn not to take 'no' for an answer. Do you even know what you're capable of?"

"I'm starting to."

"You could probably stand to learn a thing or two from your new girlfriend. Mayhem and anarchy—that's right up her alley, isn't it?"

"Who's swallowing the bitter pill now?"

"The point is, you need to start putting your handy-dandy new skills to work and break down some doors, pal. It's time to stop playing by everyone else's rules."

"Sounds like you're applying to be my coach," Grant joked, but she made no response, positive or negative. He found he was fast warming to the idea of coloring outside the lines. "Okay, then. I want to know your name. And I'm not taking 'no' for an answer."

A smile played at the corner of her lips, and her eyes became narrow openings. But he could tell her annoyance wasn't sincere.

"Fine," she said, pursing her lips. "My name is Alex."

Much to her relief, Julie found her apartment exactly as she'd left it.

But truth be told, she had little interest in checking the mail *or* paying her bills. She bypassed both on her way to the spare room she used for storage.

Boxes, unused and broken appliances, and a multitude of college textbooks crammed the room. So much had been taken from her early in life that now she had a hard time parting with anything. Julie had difficulty finding her footing, as very little of the carpet was visible. Goose-stepping around the poorly organized room was the best she could manage.

"Where is it. . . ?" she mumbled, rifling through box after box.

One hour and thirteen boxes later, she had a eureka moment. *This is it.*

Now she could show Grant some cold, hard facts about this conspiracy he was caught up in. She had evidence in her hand that proved that none of what Grant was experiencing would be solved via lunatic prophecies. She'd heard quite enough of Morgan filling her brother's head with bizarre theories for one lifetime, thank you very much.

Julie could handle the "enhanced mental abilities" thing. She could deal with the "Shift." She could even swallow the notion that Morgan had somehow read every single one of the thousands of books lining the walls at the asylum.

But this "Bringer" nonsense was going too far.

Grant had enough on his mind trying to sort out the truth, his anger issues, and even his very identity, without complicating matters with ideas better suited to the realm of mythology.

Leaving the room, she seized three spare college textbooks on her way out.

Morgan would probably enjoy reading these. Just because she's misguided doesn't mean I can't be nice to her.

This is not happening.

Lisa glanced down at the LCD clock on the dashboard of her Honda Civic, which read *3:42* A.M. She looked up, saw that the light had turned green, and jammed her foot down on the gas pedal.

She flew through traffic, swerving around the few cars on the road at this hour with her blinkers flashing like mad. Eyes wide, she gripped the wheel with both hands as the next light turned red, and slammed on the brakes. Her tires squealed as she barely avoided colliding with the car that had already stopped in front of her.

Lisa swallowed, her eyes frantically searching for nothing. It was still dark out, but the streetlights cast an eerie orange glow onto the streets.

Who would do something like this? Her mind raced, recalling the few things Daniel had told her about his past. From what she had been able to glean, she knew that he had once been the golden boy at a megacorporation—though she didn't know which one—working on something revolutionary. It didn't end well, but she knew whatever he had worked on there was somehow related to what the two of them were studying now.

The light turned green and she slammed her foot onto the gas pedal once again, swerving around a massive black SUV.

Her thoughts went back to the phone call she'd received only minutes ago. The woman on the phone, with all the sweetness in the world, evaded Lisa's questions and simply told her, "It would be good if a friend or family member could get here quickly."

They don't usually say that about people who are alive, do they?

Her heart jumped into her throat and soon tears were spilling out of her eyes.

Another light turned red and she stopped once again, now barely able to see through the haze of tears, and she broke down, no longer caring about the light.

The car jarred as something bumped it from behind, and she looked into her rear mirror. The black Expedition had caught up to her, and now the light had turned green.

She was bumped again, a little harder this time.

All right, all right . . .

Lisa hit the gas, but quickly realized she wasn't moving under her own power. The monstrous SUV behind her was *pushing* her down the road, literally bumper to bumper. Bright light poured in from the Expedition's headlamps blinding Lisa off her rearview mirror and she was so taken by surprise that for a second she could do nothing. The two vehicles plowed ahead, gaining frightening speed, as cars passing the other way blared their warning.

A red light ahead finally roused Lisa from her stupor. She didn't know what intersection waited for her, but it was a busy one, and the SUV was pushing her toward it at fifteen, now twenty miles an hour. Cars poured across from either direction and she was headed straight for them.

She had seconds to react. Maybe less.

With too many cars ahead of her in the right-hand lane, Lisa saw her only hope.

Foot off the gas, she waited for two cars to pass headed the other way, and then simultaneously swung the wheel hard to the left and jammed on her brakes.

Squealing tires and the horrendous sound of something tearing at the back of her car filled the air, and the Civic swung into a devastating arc, crossing the double-lines then corkscrewing across the two oncoming lanes before slamming into parked cars outside an Asian grocer.

It was over. It was now 3:45 A.M. and yet Lisa felt like the last few minutes had taken hours.

The SUV!

She whirled to see what had become of the vehicle but it was gone. The light was green at the intersection and now early morning L.A. traffic rolled toward her, slowed to gape, and then headed off. Sirens blared somewhere in the distance. Headed to help her.

She glanced at herself in the mirror. A thin line of blood snaked down her face and both her head and right shoulder ached—she must have banged them sometime but couldn't remember—yet otherwise she felt okay. Daniel was the one who needed help. Daniel was the one in the hospital.

Lisa let up on the brake, which she'd still held slammed to the floor, and offered the Civic some gas. It groaned but moved. The sound of sirens grew closer, but she didn't look back. She pointed her car back toward the hospital and drove, but it was only Daniel's battered, torn face that she could picture in her mind as the car lumbered its way toward him.

26

"Wake up," a voice called out of the darkness. "Collin?"

"Hannah?" Grant mumbled. "Alex?"

"Sorry to disappoint you," Julie replied, sitting on the edge of his bed. "And who's Alex?"

"What time is it?" Grant mumbled, sitting up. He saw that the clock by his bed read *4:22* A.M. "What's going on?"

"I found something I need to show you," she replied, plopping the three heavy college textbooks she'd retrieved onto the bed, where they bounced.

He picked up the first book. *A History of Modern Sociology.*

"Not the books themselves," she said, retrieving a handful of small envelopes from inside. *"These."*

He opened one of the envelopes and unfolded its contents. "Looks like a love letter from Dad to Mom."

She nodded. "About half of what I found are those little love notes, but the rest are formal letters written by Dad to a friend of his, another officer. I think the guy was his superior, but from the letters it sounds like the two of them were close friends. Collin, this man—this friend of Dad's—his name was Harlan *Evers.*"

"Evers?" he replied, groggy. "Where do I know that name?"

"From that guy MacDugall at the Inveo plant. Didn't he say his big, secret customer from years ago was named Evers? I know it's not an uncommon name, but there could be a link."

"Right, right . . ." he began to catch on, but was still too sleepy to catch the implications of what she was saying.

"Here," Julie pulled something small out of her purse and handed it to him, "take a look at this."

It was a small, round piece of engraved metal with an ornate ribbon attached.

"I found that among some of Dad's old things, along with the letters. You remember Dad was an Army tactician, right?"

"Barely."

"Well, he was," she continued, gaining steam. "I looked through his entire service record—the parts that are unclassified, anyway—and Dad was never awarded any medals."

He was examining the medal but stopped at this revelation, catching her eye.

"But Mom was."

Grant sat up straighter. "Mom was in the Army? You never told me that."

"I didn't know," she replied. "Dad never mentioned it. She must have been discharged before we were born. But I read through all of these letters, and it sounds like their mutual Army affiliation was how they met. I'm guessing that when she got out, Dad chose to stay in. I don't know, maybe they decided one of them had to stay home with the kids."

Grant leaned back against the bed's headboard, and looked far away. "Okay . . . So you're thinking that this Harlan Evers man probably knew Mom *and* Dad."

"Right," she nodded. "And I keep thinking about that story I told you, about how Dad had your mental acuity tested when you were very young. If this Evers guy is still alive, maybe he can explain that. At the very least, his connection to Inveo Technologies seems way too coincidental."

It took him a moment to put it together.

"You think he might be able to explain what's happening to me," he concluded.

"At the very least, it would be worth looking into, just to find out if he's still alive."

Everyone in the waiting area gawked as Lisa rushed into the emergency room at full tilt. She came to a sudden stop in the middle of the room, trying to find the admitting desk.

"Daniel Cossick!" she yelled, sprinting to the desk. "Where is he? Is he alive?"

The nurse looked up, and her eyes widened in alarm. Lisa knew. Blood had dried on her face and more than just her shoulder ached now. Her right eye had already started to swell a bit and her entire right leg throbbed. It didn't matter. Only Daniel did.

"Are you the woman I spoke with on the phone?"

"Yes!" Lisa shouted. "I'm Lisa Hazelton! I'm his assistant! Is he all right?!"

"He's in surgery, Ms. Hazelton."—She motioned toward the waiting room—"Please have a seat."

Lisa didn't budge. "What happened? Did they find whoever did this to him?" Her voice was loud enough for the entire emergency room to hear.

"Please sit, before you fall over."

Lisa stared at her for a moment but finally caved and collapsed anxiously into one of the waiting room chairs.

The woman took a seat beside her, sitting on the edge of the couch.

"My name is Evelyn," she said gently. "Does Mr. Cossick have any family that should be notified?"

Lisa shook her head. "His mother lives in a nursing home upstate, but she's not coherent," she said quickly, still staring at the woman.

"As near as we can tell," Evelyn said, "Mr. Cossick—"

"*Doctor* Cossick."

"—was attacked outside a parking garage in the warehouse district."

Lisa nodded impatiently, prodding her to speed up. "Yeah, his lab is on the second floor, it's where we work. Did they take anything?"

"They never entered the building," Evelyn continued, "and we found Dr. Cossick's wallet still in his pants when they brought him in. The police said it looked as if he was leaving for the night, locking up, when several individuals snuck up from behind—we believe there was more than one of them because of the extent of his injuries. A homeless man found him lying on the ground outside the building and believed he was dead. He found your boss's phone on the ground and dialed 911.

But while on the phone, he noticed that Dr. Cossick was still breathing."

"Will he make it?" Lisa asked, quieter.

Evelyn was silent for a moment, as if trying to decide how to say it. She reached out to put a steadying hand on top of Lisa's, but Lisa jerked away.

"His injuries were *extensive*, Ms. Hazelton," she said tentatively. "He's in critical condition."

"*Just tell me* if he's going to live."

Evelyn hesitated, but finally spoke. "He has three broken ribs and a punctured lung. He has a fractured wrist, both of his legs are broken, and his right ankle has been shattered in three places. There are some broken fingers; he's covered in bruises. And he has a severe concussion. The doctor believes there could be brain damage. They've gone to surgery because the doctor feared there could be internal trauma. Normally, we would never risk keeping a patient unconscious this long after a concussion, but the doctor felt there was no—"

"What are his chances?" Lisa whispered. The tears had appeared out of nowhere as the elder woman had listed Daniel's injuries, and were now pouring openly down her face. She made no attempt to wipe them away.

Evelyn spoke slowly. "We won't know until the doctor can assess his internal injuries. If that assessment goes well, then our biggest concern is the concussion and the potential brain damage. He should be out of surgery soon. If he wakes up within a few hours . . . then that's a good sign. But the longer he remains unconscious . . ."

Lisa choked back her tears and sat back in her seat.

"Ms. Hazelton, why don't you come on back and I'll have the attending take a look at your injuries," Evelyn said.

Slowly and carefully, Lisa rose to her feet. She didn't follow Evelyn, however, just crossed the lobby to a restroom on wobbly legs and found an empty stall.

Stepping inside, Lisa locked the door behind her.

She turned around and threw up.

"The General is not available at this time, sir."

"General?" Grant said, then moved the phone's receiver away from his mouth. "He's a *general?*"

Julie shrugged but watched with tremendous interest.

"Perhaps you could tell the General that the son of Frank Boyd, his best friend, would very much like to talk with him."

A pause. "Hold, please, sir."

Grant smirked at his sister as he waited. She rose from the sofa and opened the window blinds. They were high enough that she could see the sun struggling to cut through the morning's haze over the sprawl of the L.A. valley.

There was a knock at the apartment door. Grant and Julie eyed one another quizzically; no one had ever visited them here before.

Julie opened the door.

"Hannah!" Grant called out in surprise. "Um, come on in."

She slipped through the room, dropping a tiny purse on the kitchen counter and seating herself across from Grant in the living room without preamble.

"Thought I'd pop by and see if you needed any help," she said, flashing that gorgeous smile and crossing her legs. "Figured you'd be planning your big re-infiltration of Inveo Technologies about now."

Grant couldn't form a coherent thought in response. He'd never in his life met anyone who flirted as casually as most people breathe.

"How'd you know where we live?" Julie asked accusingly, still standing at the front door but now her arms were crossed.

"I'm a *thief*, cupcake. And I know your names," Hannah paused, tossing her long blond locks out of her face. "Work it out."

Julie opened her mouth, a sarcastic retort prepped and ready, but Grant waved a hand when the gentleman at the military base returned to the phone.

"Sir, I'm sorry, but General Evers says he has no memory of a Frank Boyd."

"That's impossible," Grant replied, his heart rate rising.

"I'm sorry, sir."

"Tell him," Grant said, "he's *going* to help me whether he wants to or not." He hung up.

"That probably wasn't smart," Julie said, warningly.

Grant placed the phone onto its cradle. "He's stonewalling me," his disappointed voice intoned.

"Who is?" Hannah asked.

"Evers. Harlan Evers. We found out who he is. You up for a little cloak-and-dagger?"

She smiled. "Always."

27

Lisa rubbed her eyes, fighting fatigue. She was in the middle of filling out her *fourth* form of the morning—or was it afternoon now? or evening?—having been questioned by the police at length about the car wreck and then patched up by a P.A.

"Dr. Cossick's been taken down to Intensive Care," Evelyn called out softly.

Lisa sprung from her seat and hurried to the counter where the admittance clerk stood. "Can I see him?"

"Follow me."

Evelyn led her down a long, white hall to the left, through a set of locked doors that buzzed before she could open them. Down another hall and inside a door to the right, they came upon eight neat rooms, cloistered about a busy nurses' station. Evelyn led her inside the first one on the right, where a short, squat nurse stood fussing over a gurney.

Lisa's hand flew up to cover her mouth and she felt weak in the knees. The tears came again, but she blinked them back.

"This is Grace," Evelyn said. "She'll be watching over Dr. Cossick until he's moved to his own room." And with that, she swept silently back down the hall.

"How is he?" Lisa stammered, carefully lowering herself into a chair beside the bed. "Will he make it?"

Grace smiled. "He's a fighter. Most folks in his state wouldn't have made it down here at all."

Despite herself, Lisa let out a small, quick laugh. She wiped her eyes and looked at him again. If she hadn't had assurance this was Daniel, she would never have known. There were bandages wrapped around his forehead and his entire face looked like one big, grayish-blue swollen egg. Casts had been applied to his left wrist and both lower legs. A cylindrical metal contraption with needle-like pins sticking out of it enclosed his right ankle. White tape was strapped all across his chest. And everywhere skin was visible, she saw discolorations and scabs.

It was so quiet here. She thought she detected the sound of rain outside, though there were no windows nearby to see out.

"What's that?" she said, pointing. Red stains were seeping through the tape over his chest.

The nurse frowned, knowing the answer would only upset Lisa more. "It's okay, the blood's dried. It's from his incision. They had to explore to make sure everything was okay," she said gently. "They were able to repair the lung, but I'm afraid they had to remove his spleen."

"But he's going to make it, right?"

Grace looked back at Daniel and adjusted his breathing tube. "He'll tell us the answer to that when he's ready."

Rain soaked through Grant's clothes in the night's heavy darkness as his feet pounded the muddy earth and his concentration was focused on only one thing:

Keep going.

Have to keep going.

Grant had never run this hard in his life. Even trying to escape Konrad was nothing like this. He'd been running as fast as his leg would allow for fifteen minutes and even with his new and improved physique, he was nearing exhaustion. It was all he could do not to trip over his own feet.

He tasted dirt when he stumbled and landed face-first while rounding a corner. Staggering back up, he made his way around another building and stopped for a second, leaning over, gasping for air.

There he listened.

The dogs were still barking but it sounded like they'd stopped moving. Then he saw the glow of flashlights from around the corner, and he realized they were closing fast.

That got him moving again.

"Hannah?" he whispered into his earpiece. "Need a little help here!"

"There!" a voice from behind shouted, and Grant ducked into a supply bunker. He heard his pursuer's footfalls come and then go. He breathed a sigh of relief.

The door to the bunker was ratcheted open and his heart skipped a beat.

Hannah stood there, grinning. "Sent those boys an image of you runnin' the other way. That'll keep them for a bit. I think I found the headquarters building, but it ain't gonna be easy to reach. You ready to let loose with the big whammy?"

"The only way I know to unleash it," he replied, "is to panic. I don't think I'll have too hard a time with that tonight."

For an army base that bordered on dilapidated and was rumored to be in danger of closing down, its military police had proven surprisingly severe. The three that were chasing him had brought along two very angry-sounding attack dogs. Grant and Hannah had been forced to split up once inside the compound.

"Here we go," Hannah said, eagerly opening the door.

They dashed.

Rounding a corner, Hannah pointed out a three-story building about five hundred yards away.

A vivid white floodlight blinked into existence from somewhere high above, illuminating their movements like dancers on stage. They ducked around another building just as they heard shouts of "Hold it!"

Grant yelped when a loud gunshot went off and chunks of the corner behind him chipped away.

"Warnin' shot!" Hannah shouted.

Which meant only one thing: he wouldn't be so lucky next time.

Already his legs were weary again, but he poured on the speed, doing his best to keep up with Hannah, who barely seemed to be breaking a sweat.

Another gunshot was fired and he instinctively ducked. The action made him lose his balance and slip in the mud, toppling onto his back. Something hot and wet was running down his right arm, but there was no time to examine it; Hannah was already pulling him to his feet.

"No time to rest, big boy," she said.

I've been shot, he thought, struggling to stand. *Again.*

The headquarters building was only a few hundred meters away now, but more troops were pouring out upon them from all directions. Hannah dragged him further, though he felt like giving up. Their pursuers were close enough that he could hear the dogs breathing.

Have I lost my mind? Trying to storm a military base? I'm not Rambo.

Ahead, dozens of troops were massing in front of the headquarters building, forming a line they would never be able to cross. Still they didn't stop running. More gunshots went off from behind as they approached the ranks of the soldiers ahead, all with automatic weapons trained on them . . .

"DON'T MOVE!" one of them shouted. "Stop or be killed!!"

"You're up," Hannah remarked.

He thought of the building ahead, wondering which window might be Evers' office . . .

Panic flooded his heart just as another shot went off and he let out a primal, terrified scream . . .

Blinding pain shot through his head . . .

He stumbled again . . .

When he opened his eyes, the soldiers had vanished.

No, they weren't gone. They were slumped on the ground, backs against the headquarters building. Unconscious.

"What happened?" he whispered.

"I think ya *swatted* 'em," Hannah replied.

A dozen more MPs appeared and surrounded them in a circle, fingers hair-triggered on their rifles. They were screaming at the intruders to get their hands up and get down on the ground.

"That'll do, boys," said a new player, approaching from the front of the building. He was broad-shouldered and hard-nosed. Though he must've been in his midsixties, he looked as though he could eat a box of cigars for breakfast. "Return to your posts," he barked.

The men lowered their weapons and turned away, some stopping to help the unconscious soldiers at the foot of the building.

"You're Frank's boy?" Evers asked, throwing Grant a stern look.

"I am."

"You *better* be," Evers growled. "Because if you're not, then that means you *stole* that bracelet you're wearing, and I'll have to kill you myself."

Grant glanced down at the bracelet on his wrist.

"*You* come with me," Evers ordered. "Your girlfriend'll have to wait out here."

"She's not—"

"It's all right," Hannah spoke up, and he got the distinct impression she'd interrupted what he was about to say on purpose. "Go on. I'll be fine."

28

Evers led the way up two flights of stairs to his office. It was smaller than Grant would've thought and smelled stale.

"Find a seat, if you can," Evers said, rounding on his desk. Wrinkles around his eyes and mouth spoke of his long years of service to his country. He had a gruff and menacing manner, but there was a look in his eyes that was almost . . . resigned.

Grant looked about and saw the problem. Files, papers, manuals, and other assorted trinkets were filling most of the spaces throughout the room.

"D.C.'s putting me out to pasture as soon as they close us down here," Evers muttered. "Assuming I make it till then."

What does that mean?

Grant moved aside a large stack of folders and sat in the chair they had been occupying. "So you recognize my granddad's bracelet?"

"'Course. Your dad treasured it. I don't remember Frank without it. It wasn't military protocol of course, but he was the best at what he did, so I let him get away with it. His father had made it by hand during *double-u double-u two.*"

"So you were his superior officer?" Grant probed.

"That's right. For oh . . . about sixteen years or so. I considered him my protégé. I was grooming him to take my place one day, but that didn't happen."

"Did you know my mother too?"

Evers nodded, his beady eyes trained calmly on Grant. "I was best

195

man at their wedding. Your father was very laid-back; I didn't think he was capable of getting nervous. He proved me wrong that day."

"Were they colleagues? Was my mother in the Army, too? Is that how they met?"

Evers studied him, a trace of a scowl on his lips. "Quit beating around the bush, Grant." Grant's eyes grew as Evers emphasized a name he'd never told him. "Yes, I know what's happened to you, and I know you didn't Battle-of-Normandy your way in here just to get a play-by-play on your parents' courtship. Ask me what you came here for."

But Grant was too stunned to go forward just yet. "How do you know that name? How could you *possibly* know what's happened to me?"

"It was my business at one time to keep tabs on these things. You can't tell from looking around this place, but I've spent most of my life keeping secrets. Trust me when I say I've gotten good at it."

"Tell me about Inveo Technologies."

Evers hesitated, visibly surprised. "Inveo is a dead end. That's not what you really came here for."

Grant was undeterred. "Did you or did you not hire a man named Carl MacDugall at Inveo Technologies to research ways of enhancing the capabilities of the human body?"

Evers sighed. "I did."

"Why?"

"Did MacDugall bother telling you *when* I placed that order?"

"No . . . What difference does it make?"

"All the difference in the world, son. It was right about the same time your father tested your mental acuity." Evers leaned forward. "You see, the bioengineering research at Inveo—I placed the order, yes. But it was done at your *father's* request."

Nine hours passed after Daniel was admitted to the ICU before he stirred.

Lisa let out an enormous sigh of relief when he started twitching his head. She shot out of her seat to stand right next to him.

He tried licking his lips, but the breathing tube was in the way. "Mmm-mm," he moaned.

"It's about time, sleepyhead," she said. She was trying to be cheerful but couldn't quite pull it off. Seeing him this way was overwhelming.

Daniel tried to open his eyes, but they were swollen too badly and he found he couldn't.

Grace, the nurse, left to find the doctor and a few moments later rushed back in, Daniel's surgeon right behind.

"Go ahead," the doctor nodded to Grace.

"Take a deep breath in . . ." she grabbed the tube as Daniel complied, "and blow it out." As he did, she pulled out the tube.

He coughed and gagged then settled.

For a moment, Lisa thought he might have fallen back to sleep. She carefully pushed his mussed hair out of his face.

"Amehgunnaliff?" Daniel mumbled.

The doctor turned to Lisa quizzically.

"Is he going to live?" she whispered.

The doctor smiled. "Yes," he said, carefully checking Grant's vitals, "we think you'll recover just fine. You have a long road ahead, I'm afraid. And you may never get full use of that ankle back. We're going to take good care of you."

"Imalife?" Daniel asked deliriously, as though he hadn't understood the doctor's report.

The doctor smiled. "Yes, you're alive. And we're going to keep you that way." He turned to Lisa and said quietly, "We've asked that a patrolman be posted outside your door, just to be safe."

"Thanks," Lisa said quietly. Then, turning to Daniel, "You hear that? You're going to be okay," she said, a little louder than necessary.

Daniel managed a weak nod.

The doctor told Lisa he'd be back to check in another hour. She returned to her chair beside the bed.

"Do you remember what happened?" she said softly into his ear.

He nodded weakly, and his breath suddenly caught in his throat, before he released it and breathed normally again. Lisa detected a trace of clear fluid around his puffed-up eyes.

"Good thing you're too stubborn and curious to give in to this sort of thing," she tried joking. But she quickly bit her lip as she watched his battered, unrecognizable body inhale and exhale with difficulty. She stretched out a hand to grasp his, but then thought better of it and rested her hand very gently on top of his instead.

She started when his hand came to life and grabbed hers. She had thought he had no strength left in his body, but he was holding frightfully tight.

Lisa looked at his face, and his eyes were still unable to open, but his lips moved. She leaned in closer to hear.

"Don' leaf me," he whispered. "Don' go anywhere, okay?"

Lisa couldn't hold back the flood of emotions pouring into and out of her heart. How often had she wanted to take his hand in hers?

But never like this . . .

Her tears came, and she was glad he couldn't see them or her own injuries.

"Didn't you hear what the doctor said?" She placed her other hand on top of his, smiling sweetly. "We're going to take good care of you."

Grant felt sick to his stomach.

"My *father*? *He* wanted to find ways of enhancing the human body?" It made no sense.

"I don't know exactly *what* he was after," Evers replied. "I headed up a tactical analysis unit that had been granted a wide berth by the Pentagon. One of the projects your father worked on led him to these experiments at Inveo Technologies. And in the years after his death, I came to suspect a number of things about him. One was that maybe he had you tested for the *same project* that he contracted Inveo for."

"I don't understand," Grant shook his head, suddenly full of more questions than he'd come here with. If that was possible.

"Let me back up," Evers said, still eying Grant. "Bet you didn't know I'm your godfather."

Grant's eyebrows popped up.

"I am. Your parents were remarkable people. Your mother, Cynthia, was just a beautiful, beautiful person. And smart as a tack—I actually thought she was smarter than your dad, and that's saying something. I assume you know how she died?"

Grant swallowed. "There were . . ." His throat constricted and he cleared it. "There were complications when I was born."

Evers nodded, examining him. "Most men would have shut down after losing someone that way. Not Frank. He had *such* a strong sense of purpose. He grieved for your mom in his own way, but he kept going. He refused to take any time off, and I saw the pain in his eyes nearly every day, but he continued to serve. And he loved his children very much. He spoke of you constantly."

Evers sighed. Grant said nothing, waiting for the elder man to continue.

"Grant, has it never struck you as *odd* that both of your parents died within a few years of each other?"

"No . . ." Grant replied, disbelieving what he'd just heard. "It didn't strike me as *odd*, it struck me as terrifying."

"Son," Evers said, a trace of compassion in his voice for the first time, "we *all* have that moment in life when something terrible happens for the first time. Something so unexpected, so awful, that it . . . it takes the magic out of the world. Life becomes harder, colder. And everything we do in our lives, from that day on, is our way of coping with that one moment. We stop living and we merely exist. We either choose to move on from that, or we let it consume us."

"I don't believe that," Grant replied, but in truth, his mind was racing, trying to piece together what Evers was insinuating.

"My best friend's death has consumed *me* for much of my life," Evers said. "I couldn't ever get past the odd timing of it all."

"Timing?" Grant said, trying to hold his growing worry inside. "He got clipped by a drunk driver. People die all the time." Grant stared hard at the man. "I'm not sure I understand where you're going with this."

"I was *there* the day your father ordered your mental acuity tested, Grant," Evers replied. "I thought it strange for a three-year-old, but at the time, I figured maybe he was hoping you would turn out to be as smart as your mom. I remember when the results came back so high— I had hoped he'd be ecstatic. But instead he became distant, somber.

"Two months later he died in that horrific car accident. Body wrecked beyond recognition. And now, you have yourself a whole new life and the ability to *think* things into happening. That's an ability that—*I* believe—only someone with as high a mental acuity as yours could ever hope to control."

The room was dead silent. Grant was having trouble remembering to breathe.

"You're not suggesting—"

"I've gone over it in my mind so many times, over the years," Evers replied. "Then when I heard about what happened to you recently . . . it has to be linked. And it can't be an accident."

"You think he was *killed*? Because of me?" Grant exhaled.

Evers let out a humorless laugh. "I'm not nearly as clever as I once was, but I am good at my job. I've been trained to take distinct variables and place them into a cohesive explanation. It's what I do. And when I put the pieces of this puzzle together, *this* is one of the two explanations that I come up with."

"But . . . why? Who would want him dead? And what would it accomplish?"

"Think about it. With your mother dead from childbirth and your father subsequently removed from the equation, what was the result? You. Isolated. Alone. No one to teach you about your future, no one to groom you for your destiny."

"But that would mean my father . . ." Grant slowly realized as he said it, "He knew. He knew what I was going to become."

Evers avoided Grant's eyes. "At the very least, I think he suspected."

Grant sat stunned. "And what was the other explanation?" He could hardly imagine.

Evers' face look concerned. "I don't put much stock in that one."

Grant waited.

"Well, given the timing and the terrible circumstances of the accident. There's the slim chance . . . that the whole thing may have been arranged. To just make it *look* like. . . ."

29

"What aren't you telling me?" Grant said.

"I've already told you too much," Evers replied. It struck Grant that suddenly Evers looked very old. "It won't be long now," he said quietly.

Grant's mind was racing too fast to catch the remark, but once he did, he came crashing to a stop.

"Not long until what?"

"There's more," Evers said, urgency rising into his voice, "*much* more you need to know; I'm sorry I won't get a chance to tell you. But you don't last as long as I have in this business without planning for every possible contingency, and trust me, I have. So did your father."

"I don't understand," said Grant.

"How long has it been, son?" Evers asked, wistful. "How long since you were there? Your parents' old house?"

Grant blinked. "I don't know. More than twenty-five years, I guess."

"Go back."

"What? Why?" The first home he'd ever known—where his father and sister lived with him, before the orphanage—was military housing on an old Army base north of Monterey. Only vague images remained as his memory of the place. "Would the house even still be there?"

"The base is closed, of course," Evers said, undeterred. "It's a museum now. But the houses stand. Empty and rotting, but they stand."

"But why should I go back there?" That old house was the last place Grant wanted to be.

"You're looking for a safe. Your *father's* safe. He kept one, hidden somewhere in the attic. I don't think he ever knew I knew about it. It contained all of his old records and personal files. There's information in those files that—well, it's not exactly what you're searching for, but you need to see it."

A siren began to wail loudly, throughout the entire base. Grant saw flashing lights outside the building and all of the base's floodlights came on.

It hit Grant like a truck. "The sirens are for *you*! This is why you didn't want to talk to me!"

He was on his feet in an instant, but Evers grabbed him by the shoulders and spun him around.

"If you go and find your father's files," Evers said sternly, as if the sirens weren't sounding, "you're going to learn things that will be hard to accept. Things about your parents *and* about yourself. Take it from an old man—sometimes ignorance truly *is* bliss, son. Do you understand what I'm telling you? Think long and hard about whether or not you want to do this. Because once you turn this corner, once you know this truth, there will be no going back. Not ever."

Too much was happening too fast . . .

Evers squared his shoulders and sat back down at his desk. "You should go now," he said quietly. "Looks like the base is closing down a bit earlier than expected . . ."

In a daze, Grant made for the door.

His father could be alive.

His heart surged at the thought, yet all he could feel was sad and lost at the very idea. How could this possibly be true?

Evers shouted, rousing Grant. "Not that way!" He pointed toward the window. "Use the slide. Quickly, now."

Grant had no idea what was happening, but he went to the window as instructed. A large metal box marked "Fire Slide" rested beneath the windowsill. He opened it and found a large bundle of fabric wrapped around dozens of wide metallic rings.

Grant slid the window up and threw the bundle in his arms outward as far as he could. It stretched into a fabric tube that glided to the ground, extending over thirty feet away from the building.

"Good luck, son," Evers said as Grant climbed into the tube, feet first.

Grant merely nodded, unable to form words. He heard footsteps approaching in the hallway outside Evers' office.

Go. Move!

Just as he let go and began his rapid descent through the slide, he heard the door to the office burst open.

Evers' voice matter-of-factly said, "End of the line, eh, boys?"

As Grant's feet landed on terra firma, he heard a gunshot.

Run!

He spotted Hannah hiding behind some bushes not far away. He grabbed her and ran.

It was late afternoon when Lisa exited a cab to step onto the sidewalk in front of the building that housed Daniel's lab. Her next-door neighbor had been kind enough to sit with Daniel at the hospital (he was asleep, or she never would have left his side), while she made a quick trip back to the lab to pick up some of his personal items.

She was still so dazed by the previous day's events that she didn't notice the big black van parked in front of the building. She only snapped out of her reverie when she saw that the front door to the lab was cracked open.

Her heart leapt into her throat. She pushed the door open carefully and looked up the stairs. She could hear loud voices talking and a variety of clanging sounds, like in the kitchen of a big restaurant.

Desperate now at the terrible possibilities of that noise, she ran up the stairs, down the hall, and into the lab. A cacophony of activity met her there, as white-clad men and women were everywhere, examining the lab's equipment, taking the machines apart, putting pieces into plastic bags and cardboard boxes, and carrying them out the door behind her.

There were over a dozen of them there, all in white jumpsuits with the word "FORENSICS" emblazoned across their shoulders.

Lisa ran to the nearest one and grabbed his arm. "What do you people think you're doing? This is delicate equipment! You can't just come in here and do this!"

The short man with a detached expression pushed his black-rimmed glasses up on his nose and tried his best to look down on her. "Are you Mr. Cossick's assistant?"

There was a loud crash in the middle of the room, and she looked up to see two men bickering over who'd dropped a computer server that now lay shattered at their feet.

"*Doctor* Cossick, and yes, I am," she replied, turning back to him with a furious gaze. "Who are *you* supposed to be?"

He lifted his chin slightly. "We're with the LAPD. Your employer was attacked on these premises, ma'am, and we're here with a court order to find out what the attackers were looking for."

She knew exactly whose orders this had come from. She felt as though steam was rushing out of her ears. "That *vile*, no-good, wretched, *spiteful*, corrupt, bottom-dwelling *crook*!!" she screamed in outrage.

Two patrolmen rushed up and grabbed her by each arm, dragging her out of the building. "If Drexel thinks he can get away with this—!" she yelled.

The short man she'd shouted at was unperturbed. "Wait, before you remove her . . ." He turned back to the countertop he had been working at, and held up a small metallic device for her to see.

"Could you tell me what this is for?" he asked.

"*You* . . . sleazy. . . !" Lisa started between clenched teeth. But she was out of the lab before she could finish. The men in blue escorted her down the stairs and back to her car, then stationed themselves on either side of the building's door to ensure she wouldn't come back.

Ten minutes later, she continued to pace on the opposite side of the street. It had taken several minutes of breathing exercises to cool off.

The lab was a total loss.

Daniel would be *so* devastated.

She sat up straight as another thought struck her. She pulled out her phone and hit one of the speed-dial numbers.

"Gordon," she said when Daniel's lawyer answered. "It's Lisa Hazelton. Have you heard what's happened?"

He hadn't. She told him. Then she told him about the lab.

"If they have a court order," he told her, "then there's nothing you can do but stay out of their way."

Lisa sighed, frustrated.

"Do you believe they're genuinely looking for evidence about Daniel's attack?" the lawyer asked.

She glanced back at the building and the two officers standing outside, watching her.

"Not for one minute," she replied.

Half an hour later, Grant and Hannah were speeding back toward downtown. Grant was too lost in thought, rubbing his thumb against his ring, so Hannah was driving, listening to him tell of his encounter with Harlan Evers, while keeping both eyes on the dark road ahead.

After his story had ended and she had allowed him some time to think, she spoke.

"So you're thinkin' the same thing I am, right?"

"Morgan."

"Oh yeah," she nodded. "You *gotta* go to Morgan with this."

"Agreed," he looked away. "But it's late . . . Let's make it tomorrow."

Hannah tossed her hair. "Meet ya there for lunch."

30

Finch Bailey didn't seem to appreciate it when Collin tripped him at the lunch table.

All of the other kids laughed heartily as the larger boy's food went flying and Finch landed in a mound of mashed potatoes. But Finch wasn't laughing.

Just as Collin expected.

When asked later by one of the orphanage workers why he did it, he looked the woman straight in the eye and said, "Just seemed like the thing to do."

Three hours later on the playground, Collin was alone on the swing set, when Finch shoved him from behind in midswing, making Collin dive out of it. As he rose, sand clinging to his face, he snatched a handful of sand and flung it straight into Finch's laughing face.

A caretaker broke in before it went any further but as she led Finch away he turned and mouthed, "Just you wait."

Later that night, Collin was only pretending to be asleep on the bottom of the bunk bed, when he heard footsteps approaching. More than one pair of footsteps.

Hands grabbed all four of his limbs and dragged him out of bed. He struggled against them, but only halfheartedly. Duct tape was placed over his eyes and mouth and the other three or four boys—Collin couldn't tell how many there were, exactly—dragged him roughly out of the building, intentionally banging his head into various solid objects along the way.

Half an hour later, he was lying in the poison oak patch deep in the woods behind the orphanage. The other boys had stripped him to his boxers on the cool spring evening, and used more of the duct tape to strap his feet together and his hands in back.

Then they began hitting. But he only pretended to flinch, to fight back.

Light at first, the impacts grew harder and harder until fists were involved. A hardness coursed through his body with each blow. He willed himself to take it. Soon Collin felt hot, sticky blood running out of his nose. But they stopped long enough to rub ivy leaves across his bare chest, arms, and legs.

It was late the next morning before the frantic orphanage workers found him; he was shivering and wet with the morning dew, with so many dark red rashes covering his body, they'd rushed him to the emergency room.

He'd never bothered to try and free himself or crawl out of the woods because he wanted to see the other boys pay for doing this to him. Almost as much as he yearned for the ordeal to last as long as it possibly could . . .

"NO STOP!!"

Grant bucked straight up in bed, panting, covered in sweat.

He slowly eased himself back down onto his pillow and glanced at his bedside clock. Through the window blinds, he could make out a soft glow as the sun began to greet the horizon. The world was at peace.

But he was not.

He used the bed's sheets to wipe sweat from his forehead as he lay there with his eyes wide open.

Where did that *come from?*

He hadn't thought of that particular episode from his childhood in years.

He decided to leave early for the asylum; he needed advice, and not on anything he'd learned from Harlan Evers . . .

The Thresher was looking straight down at the ground, over twenty-five feet below, when his phone vibrated.

His arms and legs were completely outstretched, bracing his position in the narrow space between two neighboring downtown hotels. The confines of the tight outdoor corridor were far too small to hold a car or truck; instead, it merely allowed for rear entrance to both hotels.

The Thresher carefully released his right hand from the brick wall, shifting his balance to accommodate three limbs, and thumbed open his cell phone.

"Yes?" he whispered.

"Your presence is required."

"Devlin," the Thresher replied in recognition, still whispering. "Been a long time."

"Too long. I've been made aware of your recent movements. You must meet with me, at once."

"If you know what I'm doing, then you know I'm at a critical stage. I've no time for . . . guidance."

"The Secretum disagrees," Devlin replied without emotion.

Below, a door opened and a man carrying a large bag exited.

"Very well," the Thresher said, snapping the phone shut.

He let go of the walls and plummeted to the ground.

Landing without a sound, he rolled to absorb the impact. While on his back in midroll, he kicked the man with the bag.

The man landed sprawled out on all fours a few feet away. He immediately looked up to find the Thresher towering over him from a few feet away, his sword out and pointed right in the man's face. But the blade was turned sideways, and the bag of food hung from it, unspoiled.

"This is the third consecutive Friday morning you've made this delivery," the Thresher said in his soft inflection, holding the sword perfectly motionless.

The young man on the ground was in complete shock, trying to reason out what had just happened. And more importantly, how.

"*Where* are you taking it?" the Thresher asked.

When Lisa walked into Daniel's hospital room bright and early that morning, she was surprised to see him sitting up in his bed. He'd slept the entire previous day, and the rest seemed to have done him well. The swelling around his eyes had gone down, and he could finally see her again.

A nurse was feeding him.

"Lisa!" he nearly shouted, spewing Jell-O everywhere. "There you are!"

"I can't believe you're up!" she exclaimed. "Are you okay?"

"Better now that you're here," he replied weakly.

Her heart did a back flip.

"I went by the office to pick up some things for you, and then I had to call Gordon. May I?" Lisa asked the nurse. The nurse smiled in reply and handed her the tray of food. In a moment, she was gone.

Daniel was rooting around inside his mouth with his tongue. "Huh. I think I'm missing a couple of fillings . . . and the teeth they filled," he said, lost in thought. When she sat next to him, he snapped to attention. "Why'd you meet with Gordon?" he asked evenly. "And why do you have bruises all over you?"

She'd hoped to wait a while before telling him everything, but he seemed much more coherent now and clearly wouldn't accept a postponement to this conversation.

"You weren't the only one that was attacked," she said.

His face registered horror.

"I'm okay. No permanent damage. My car is a thing of the past, but I'm good."

He winced and put an arm over his chest, where the cracked ribs were. "Gordon?" he asked again through the pain.

Lisa sighed. "The lab's been ransacked by the police. A forensics unit pretty much tore the whole thing apart, piece by piece. Gordon said there's nothing we can do—they had a court order, and they've declared the entire premises a crime scene. It's gone, Daniel. I'm sorry."

He looked down, unable to meet her gaze. But instead of despondent and inconsolable, he seemed rather resigned.

"What?" she asked.

Daniel hesitated, then offered something that might have resembled a smile. "Doesn't seem all that bad, compared to being nearly beaten to death."

She winced. Thinking about the attack and how it must have felt was something she couldn't bear to dwell on.

"And the other thing is," he said softly, "this terrible thing meant to harm us might be for the best, all things considered."

"How can you say that?" Lisa nearly came out of her chair.

"I don't believe in coincidences. *Everything* is traceable to cause and effect." He sounded for a moment like his old self.

She threw a quick glance outside the room's door. He nodded.

"Drexel," he concluded. "This was about Drexel trying to get to Borrows. All of it."

"I think so, too," she nodded. "We could probably never prove it, but I think he paid some thugs to attack you, to give him a legal excuse to search our office. He wants Grant's file."

Alarm flashed across his face. "Did you get rid of it?"

"I burned it," she said and then held up a blank CD. "Encrypted, too."

"Good girl," he patted her hand, and leaned back, resting his eyes. He let out a long, painful breath, concerns and troubles fading into pain and exhaustion.

She wished she could simply let him rest, but he needed to know. "Daniel, the police have stationed a cop outside your door at all times. For *protection*."

Daniel looked up at the door sharply. Then he looked back at her, and what was left of his complexion under all of the scratches and blotches turned completely white. "He wouldn't . . ." he whispered.

She turned and looked back out the door again. "I don't think you can stay here."

Daniel started breathing faster, which caused him pain in his chest again. "But I can't even *move!*" he gasped. "The doctor just told me that I'm going to have to relearn how to walk! He said it'll take months of physical therapy. My ankle may even need another surgery."

He looked at her and then back at the door, fear and desperation all over his face. "What are we going to do?"

Butterflies fluttered in her stomach, as everything rested on her shoulders for a change. She wasn't used to being in this position and was in no way convinced she was capable of doing something like this alone.

"We've got no choice. We have to get you out of here."

31

Grant had just started the Corvette's engine, Julie in the passenger seat, and begun to back out, when he hit the brakes.

"What?" Julie asked, hurling forward into her seatbelt.

"It's *her*," Grant said, staring into his rear-view.

Julie's head spun around. All she could see was a denim jacket and simple black T-shirt, standing right behind the car.

He got out of the car; Julie followed suit.

"There's this guy who's in danger and could use your help. In a to-the-rescue kind of way."

"So?"

"So, that's what people with abilities like yours do, buster," Alex replied, mildly annoyed. "Or at least, what you *should* be doing."

Grant rolled his eyes. "I don't have time for this . . ."

"Neither does the guy who needs your help. I know you're all consumed with this 'quest for answers,' but don't you think it's about time you started putting this awesome new ability of yours to good use?"

Grant just stared. He couldn't believe he was getting a lecture on who to be from this woman.

"There," she said, letting out a long breath. "Any of that get through? It was, like, my civic duty or whatever."

"A for effort, C for delivery."

"All right, then let me try a different approach," she said, crossing her arms. "Go see this guy who needs your help . . . and I'll tell you who was responsible for your Shift."

"You *know* who did this to me?"

"Of course she does," Julie jumped in. On Grant's look of astonishment, she added, "It's obvious, isn't it? She *works* for him."

Grant paused. "Is that true?"

Alex surveyed Julie. "Home run for the rookie. Look, there's not much time. Go do whatever it is you've got to do, but meet me at St. Frances Hospital by sundown. And watch your back."

"That's *my* job," Julie retorted.

When Grant and Julie emerged from the long hallway full of books and into the Common Room, he spotted Morgan and Fletcher sitting in the lounge area, on opposite sides of a chess board. He couldn't hear their conversation, but given how heated Fletcher looked, it wasn't hard to guess.

Grant took his sister by the hand and led her across the floor. Many of the Loci customarily stopped to stare as he entered the room.

"Ah, Grant," Morgan smiled warmly. "Good to see—"

"Wonderful," Fletcher groused. "He's back."

Grant wasted no time. "These are for you." He handed her Julie's college textbooks. "Can we talk in private?"

"Certainly," she replied, rising from her seat. Fletcher was about to protest but Morgan just held up a hand.

Grant followed Morgan through the Common Room. Eyes followed him and the room buzzed.

"Do they have to do that?"

Morgan looked up. The Loci were still standing about the room, watching them as they exited out into the hallway. "They intend to be witnesses."

"Witnesses?"

"To what you are going to do. They mean not to miss it."

The small white room she led him to contained a countertop, cabinets, an examination table, and a couple of tiny, uncomfortable-looking chairs. She sat in one and invited him to sit in the other. As before, she waited for him to speak first.

Grant gathered his thoughts before opening his mouth.

"I need some advice," he began. "I think I'm developing . . . feelings . . . for Hannah."

A hint of a smile played at the corner of Morgan's mouth. "I see," she said in an unsurprised tone of voice.

"Am I nuts to want to pursue something like this now? With everything that's going on?"

Morgan allowed herself one full breath. "Attraction, passion, love . . . these aren't my area of expertise. But if I may be so bold . . . your entire world has fallen apart and rebuilt itself into something unfamiliar, Grant. It's only natural that one of your most fundamental human needs—to be cared for—is going unmet, and that you should attempt to fill that hole. My advice would be to be careful that you genuinely feel for her as you think you do."

Grant considered this, something piquing his curiosity. "Sounds like solid advice. So, uh . . . what makes you think you're not good at this sort of thing?"

"Experience," she replied. "I don't seem cut out for romance myself. My last relationship was . . . well, it was devastating. Goodness, it's been *ages* since I've talked about it."

The hesitancy in her voice made Grant wonder if she always played this role of advice-giver, but rarely had anyone to open up to herself. He felt for her in this position, everyone looking up to her, depending on her. It was a notion he was beginning to identify with.

"What was his name?"

She smiled. "Payton. I met him after the Shift. He was another like us—another Loci. Payton went through the Shift about two years after I did. He was the very first person I met who had undergone the Shift as well. The joy of finally meeting someone else who knows what this feels like! Well, it's overwhelming, isn't it?"

Grant settled back in his chair, listening quietly.

"We fell in love very quickly," Morgan went on. "Perhaps too quickly. It was around the same time that I first discovered the existence of the stone tablet—or rather, the fragments that make up the tablet. Collecting them became my passion, and Payton picked it up quickly as well. He and I spent years flying all over the world—Argentina, Malaysia, Tibet, Zaire, and dozens of other countries—following any leads we got our hands on that could lead us to more of the fragments. We turned up quite a few of them—most of what I have now, what I showed you— came from that trip." She looked away, tears forming in her eyes.

"Something went wrong?" Grant offered.

She nodded. "Payton and I had found evidence of another fragment buried in a cave in France. The French government refused to allow us to dig in the caves—the location is a historical landmark—but we did it anyway. I suppose we dug too deep. There was a cave-in. Payton pushed me clear, but I had to watch as he was buried under a pile of enormous rocks, only inches from where I lay. I tried with all my might to dig him out, but the boulders were too heavy. I tried to find help, but there was no one in the area. So I went back in and found his hand protruding clear of the rubble. It wasn't moving, but I held it until I felt it go cold. And then . . ."

She trailed off and he watched her.

"I *ran*. I just panicked. We had no permission to be there and too many questions would uncover our plans. I loved Payton with all my heart, truly I did. But I'd always led a quiet, uneventful life until the Shift. And I never would have had the nerve to go on these globe-trotting adventures alone. Payton had a vibrant, infectious personality. And when he died and suddenly I was completely alone . . . I didn't know what to do.

"Leaving him there was the hardest and worst thing I've ever done in my life. I couldn't bring myself to go home to London, so I ran away here, to the States. And I entered a deep depression that lasted for years."

Grant could hear the bitterness, the brokenness in her voice, and he realized this was something she'd held inside for a very long time.

"After I reached the States," she said quietly, "I didn't have it in me to continue the search for the tablets myself. The weight of what I'd done bore down on me, and I just wanted to hide. That's when I first began thinking of a place where I and others like me could live in seclusion, safe from the cares of the world."

"Hiding from the world doesn't make it go away," Grant said softly. "I'm beginning to realize that."

She nodded. "I know it as well. Yet I hide anyway. Part of me really *is* afraid to step out into the world, fearful of who else might get hurt or what I might cause. Mostly, I'm just too ashamed to leave this place. The pain that was born in that cave stays with me every moment of every day. My 'miraculous' perfect memory won't let the pain fade. The thunder of the rocks as they fell. Payton's screams. The jagged rock edges my fingers scraped as I tried to dig him out. The dust that burned my eyes. The warmth—and then the cold—of his hand, as the life ebbed . . . I still remember every detail."

"I'm sorry," Grant said. There was nothing else to say.

She wiped the tears from her eyes and smiled. "Thank you for listening."

There was really nothing else for her to say, either.

32

Grant was eating lunch with his sister in the asylum's dining room when Hannah entered the room. She sauntered her way in their direction and helped herself to a seat.

"So . . . I'm not your girlfriend, huh?"

"Huh?" he asked.

"Back at the military base. Evers thought I was your girlfriend, and you were about to tell him I wasn't." She flashed those beautiful teeth before stealing one of his french fries.

He backpedaled. "That's not what I . . . I mean, I'm not *opposed* . . . I just didn't know what to—"

"Relax, darlin'. I just like watchin' you squirm."

Grant didn't laugh, though she was clearly enjoying herself. Instead, he turned to his sister, growing serious. "Could you give us a minute?"

Julie nodded and walked away.

"What's up?" Hannah asked, leaning on top of the table, as if waiting to be filled in on the latest gossip.

"Why are you so determined to help me?" he asked quietly. "I need to know the truth."

Her eyes narrowed. "You saved my life. That ain't reason enough?"

"It *is*, it's just . . ." he grappled for the words. "I have to know why a cat burglar would want to help a total stranger? I mean, say it out loud and doesn't it strike you as strange? Tell me *why*."

"I got no big noble explanation."

He considered this. "Then tell me who you really are. Inside."

Hannah sat back in her chair, uncertainty written across her face. But she seemed to be determined to indulge him. "I'm still tryin' to figure that out. Growing up, I was a brat. Spoiled little rich girl and the apple of my daddy's eye."

She looked away, collecting her thoughts.

She cleared her throat. "Mom passed when I was seven, and I was all he had left, so he showered me with attention and gifts and love. It ruined me, of course, but not a day or an hour goes by when I don't think of him. He was bright and funny. And very brave. He was everything I wanted to be."

"Was?" Grant said.

"He was killed when I was sixteen. Assassinated, in fact. He was a senator, believe it or not. He led the fight on some kind of bill about . . . actually, I can't remember what it was about. It don't matter now. Someone out there didn't like what he had to say," she said, with a far-off look in her eyes.

"So how does a straight-laced politician's daughter turn to a life of crime?"

"Took the scenic route," she offered a wry smile. "And I never said I was straight-laced."

"The scenic route?"

"I went into foster care at sixteen. Ran away a few months later. Fell in love at nineteen. Found out the guy I was in love with was a drug dealer when I saw him get his head blown off by a competing dealer. Went to the police, helped them track down the killer. Testified in court, the whole nine yards. Guy got off, not guilty, 'cause the testimony of a destitute runaway couldn't stack up against his mega-lawyer squad. It was after that, that I started seein' the world in all its splendid shades of gray. If there was no justice in the world, if people you love could get killed right in front of you and no one cared if they got away with it . . . then what did anything matter?"

Grant sat up straighter, engrossed in her story now. Her walls were falling away as Grant watched in fascination. This wasn't easy for her.

"After the trial, I started stealin'. I needed the money but I also wanted to strike back at the world that'd taken everyone away from me. Turns out I was pretty good at it. I'm a little older and wiser now, so I know a lot of the stuff going on in my head that got me here was unjustified. I *know* I shouldn't be doing what I'm doing. But at least now I do it for high-enders; I won't work for criminals. Mostly I get a lot of corporate warfare, that sort of thing. No one gets hurt, and no one suffers. Guess I do it 'cause it's the one thing I'm good for."

"You do it for the rush," Grant clarified.

"I do it for kicks, capitalist rivalry, and the American way."

Grant folded his arms and sat back. "Then why do you help me?" he repeated again.

She sighed, and when she spoke again, her words came out slowly. "I can't put it into words. Maybe I'm seein' something I ain't seen since before my father passed. Maybe I feel the connection of another orphan. We both know nobody should ever feel that kind of alone. Maybe . . ." she hesitated, "I just like you."

Grant felt an urge to reach out and take her hand, but he resisted . . .

"The one thing I can tell you for sure," she concluded, "is that bein' around you makes me want to be *better*."

She sat back now, keeping her gaze fixed on him. "Even Morgan doesn't know all that," she said softly.

Grant was silent for a long time. Hannah waited patiently.

"I, uh . . . I'm not . . ." he fumbled for words when his mouth finally opened. "If you need me as some sort of bridge to your past, to recon- nect with your old life, then I'm okay with that. But I don't think you can build a relationship on that. If you want more, then it's time to—"

The sound of a throat clearing came from nearby. Grant turned to see Fletcher peering down on the two of them as if he'd just changed the channel to a soap opera, and couldn't be more disgusted by it.

Hannah, meanwhile, was doing everything in her power to main- tain her composure, painting a false grin on her face and blinking hard.

"Morgan wants to see you right away," Fletcher intoned.

"Can it wait?" Grant asked. "We're talking . . ." he explained, grasp- ing at an easy explanation for what he was feeling.

"It's urgent," Fletcher replied, indifferent to Grant's concerns. "Marta wants to meet you."

Morgan massaged her temples as today's migraine—which was actually *yesterday's* migraine refusing to die—slowed her thinking as well as her pace. Grant walked alongside as she led him through the labyrinthine asylum.

"I don't suppose you speak Spanish?" she asked, as they navigated the book-lined halls.

"No," Grant replied, wondering what it must've been like for the patients who once called this place home.

If they hadn't lost their minds before, this place would certainly do it . . .

"No matter," Morgan replied. "I'll translate."

He glanced at her, thoughtful. "How many languages do you speak?"

"Three thousand, eight hundred fifty-seven. But many are dialects."

Grant nearly tripped over his feet.

"What I do is not merely about remembering the facts that I'm exposed to," she reminded him. "I have razor-sharp clarity. I *memorize* every single fact I encounter. Without even having to try."

"So . . . all you'd have to do is read a foreign dictionary once, and you'll become fluent in the entire language?" He began catching on.

"It takes some time to learn syntax and grammar. And idioms, local colloquialisms, and pop culture references are often lost on me, so I don't know how I'd fare if I ever visited any of those countries in person. But I can get by."

Grant dwelled on that a moment. "So what does this Marta do? What's her mental thing?"

"The most peculiar I've ever encountered," Morgan replied. "Think of the most *analytical* person you've ever known. Such a person would be capable of looking at a situation, weighing the possibilities quickly, and determining potential outcomes to various actions they might take."

Grant thought of Evers. "Sure, okay."

"Imagine that kind of analytical mind magnified times ten," Morgan said. "Times *twenty*. Possibly even one hundred."

"So . . . what? She can predict what's going to happen in my future?"

"Not as such," Morgan replied. "She sees . . . potentialities. If she fully grasps the dynamics of a situation—and she always does, very quickly—she can determine all eventual outcomes of that situation. With remarkable accuracy."

Grant absorbed this. "So if meeting her is this important, why didn't you bring me to see her before?"

"It took some . . . convincing . . . for her to agree to meet you."

Morgan approached the lonely door at the far end of one corner of the building. With a gentle knock, she opened it and ushered Grant inside.

"This is Marta," she said.

"Hello," Grant offered, but the elder woman did not react.

"This," Morgan addressed Marta, switching to Spanish, *"is my friend . . ."*

Marta immediately lifted her eyes and focused on Grant. Her pupils contracted at the sight of him, and through her lips suddenly passed the words, *"El Traerador."*

Grant didn't have to speak the language to know what phrase she'd just uttered. He exchanged a glance with Morgan, already frowning at the mention of the Bringer.

"Sí," Morgan replied. "He's come to meet you."

The old woman studied Grant like a dead insect on a microscope slide. She didn't strike him as unkind, yet he was never comfortable with this kind of scrutiny.

"Is she going to talk, or what?" his eyes swiveled to Morgan.

Before she could answer, Marta made what sounded like an off-hand remark to Morgan. Morgan nodded.

"What'd she just say?" Grant asked accusingly.

"She said your impatience will be your downfall."

He scowled.

Marta's tone changed when she began speaking again. She sounded like a storyteller, revealing ancient wisdom with the greatest of passion.

"The winds of change are blowing through these old bones," Morgan translated as Marta seemed to be choosing her words carefully. "And if you have ears to hear, you will know and understand what they are trying to tell you. The very earth feels . . . *different*."

Grant swallowed. "Different how?"

Marta continued before Morgan could relay the question. "Danger surrounds you from all sides. Yet the truth eludes you, though it has been within your grasp from the beginning. Soon you will find it impossible to ignore."

She said something else, which Morgan didn't translate right away.

"Are you certain?" Morgan asked, and Marta repeated her words precisely, the same vocal inflections.

Grant watched.

"She says," Morgan said, facing Grant at last, "that the choices you make will decide the fates of all."

Grant hesitated. "'All' of you here at the asylum?" he clarified.

Morgan conferred with Marta.

"She will only say 'all'," said Morgan.

Marta spoke again.

"Something . . ." Morgan translated slowly, "something *unbelievable* . . . is about to happen."

Outside the asylum, Hannah leaned back against Grant's car. Anyone who saw her there might have assumed she was waiting for Grant to come out.

But instead, she was angrily wiping at her eyes, which were burning red. She gazed upward, searching the afternoon sky. She wiped them again, fighting the overwhelming feeling that was surging up within her.

Finally she stood up, away from the car, and retrieved her phone. She keyed in speed dial.

"I'm out," she said, when the person on the other end answered. "You better think *long and hard* before you threaten me! I did what you wanted. But my part is *over*. I'm out!"

33

"I don't actually know his name . . ." Alex said.

Grant towered over her, angrily staring her down in front of the hospital's main entrance. As agreed, he had met her just as the sun was descending. Her chosen hiding place was behind a grouping of shrubs.

"You said you work for him!" Grant shouted.

"Yeah," Alex replied. "I didn't say the two of us are best pals. I've never even met the guy. Or maybe the gal. I don't really know which. My orders always come by carrier."

Grant sighed, stifling his frustrations once again. His thoughts turned back to Morgan's subtle warning about running headlong into avoidance of how he felt. Once again, he'd been confronted by huge revelations—his father's possible faked death, Morgan's surprising confiding in him, Hannah's admissions, Marta's predictions—and yet here he was, turning to another enormous task.

But what does she expect me to do? Sit around and mope?

And stopping long enough to consider how all of this seemed to center on him, the sheer improbability of it all . . .

It was unbearable.

"So . . . is this boss of yours interested in helping me as much as you are?"

"What makes you think he hasn't already?" she said knowingly. "Be careful who you trust, sweetie, but be *more* careful who you assume your enemy is. Things are never that cut and dried."

"Why is he manipulating all of us? What's he after, in the end?"

"He wants to rig the game, no mistaking that. But as to what the game is exactly . . . you'd have to ask him."

"I don't believe you," he said suspiciously. "You can't tell me you've worked for him—or her—for *this long* and don't know *anything* about him. Is he the good guy or the bad guy?"

She nodded. "All I can give you is his title. I've heard it a few times, though don't ask me how—I'm not supposed to know it. And whatever you do, don't repeat it to anyone."

He waited impatiently as she took a dramatic breath.

"He's called the *Keeper*."

He almost laughed.

The Bringer. And the Keeper.

Doesn't that sound like a happy combination?

"Yeah," she replied. "Now I held up my end of the bargain . . ."

"Fine," he said resignedly. "Tell me where to find this person who needs my help so desperately."

"There you go again, always assuming the worst," Alex sighed, hands on hips. "Just because this guy needs your help doesn't mean you're going home empty-handed in this. This guy's in seriously bad condition, but he's in worse danger the longer he stays here. *You're* going to have to find a way to get him out. And he's going to need supplies and equipment to recover—"

"What do you mean, I'm not going home empty-handed?"

"Mosey up to Room 458 and find out."

Lisa stirred when she heard a nurse come in to check Daniel's vitals. It was dusk outside, yet she was surprised to see Daniel awake again so soon. His swelling had gone down considerably in the last few days, and it was nice to see him looking more like his old self again, even *with* all the bandages.

She smiled at him and he offered something resembling a smile in return. But she knew that half-smile better than he realized. His mind was preoccupied.

Lisa waited until the nurse left to speak. "What are you thinking?"

"About how I asked you not to leave me here alone. But it's been days now, and really, if something was going to happen, I think it would have by now. Please go home and get some rest. That chair can't possibly be comfortable."

"What are you talking about?" Lisa replied with a smile. "Me and this chair have bonded. We've been through some experiences together. I'm not going *anywhere*."

He smiled wearily at her. "Lisa, everything you've done for me has been wonderful. I've been through traumatic things before; I've pulled through things—well, maybe not worse than this, but still pretty bad. Now I think it's time to be honest. I'm not escaping from here. What comes, comes."

"Quitter," she replied, in a voice that almost made him smile.

Daniel sighed. "You know . . . even if you *could* get me out of here, where would you even take me? The lab has been destroyed, my home and your apartment probably aren't secure . . ."

"I know a place," she replied. When he eyed her curiously, she said defensively, "I *have* thought this through, you know."

He smiled. "You always have been the brains of the operation."

"I can't believe you finally figured that out!" She laughed out loud.

He laughed as well, but then started gasping when the laughter triggered his cracked ribs. He brought both hands up to brace his chest as he tried to catch his breath. Lisa jumped up and helped, placing his oxygen mask back over his mouth and nose until the pain subsided.

It was a while before he removed the mask and lay back on his inclined bed.

Lisa returned to her chair and shook her head at him. "This Grant Borrows person . . . What makes you so sure that he's worth all this? Worth everything you've been through?"

"I have my reasons," Daniel croaked. When she wouldn't release his gaze, he added, "There are plenty of things about me you still don't know."

She was about to respond when everything went black.

The power went off all over the entire hospital, but the emergency generators immediately kicked in. It wasn't enough electricity to power everything in the building, only the essential systems. The medical equipment Daniel was hooked up to continued unabated, but the only light came from the emergency beams out in the hall.

They heard panicked screams erupt from other rooms on the floor, and nurses running around, trying to keep patients calm and making sure everyone was okay.

Once her eyes had adjusted, Lisa finally saw Daniel again. Terror had returned to his eyes, and she looked away before he saw her notice it. Instead, she took his hand in a reassuring way.

"Must be a storm coming up or something," she tried.

"This is it, isn't it?" Daniel whispered. "They're coming for me."

She tried to show him a reassuring smile, but the screams were closer now. They both turned to look through the open door.

The patrolman outside was already on his feet, and he peeked inside the doorway. "Don't leave this room," he growled. "Lock the door."

Lisa did as commanded and then rejoined Daniel and took his hand again.

"It's okay, it's probably nothing. Maybe a car hit a power line . . ." she was saying. The room was almost pitch dark, the only light now coming from the city lights outside the window.

"Lisa, I ought to tell you something," Daniel said gently.

Her heart pounded madly in her chest, but before he could say anymore, there was a loud crash against the door from the other side. She screamed.

They clutched each other's hands even tighter.

Strange sounds came from outside, and they continued to watch as something else crashed into the door, and then there were grunts and kicks and blows.

A loud pop like a small explosion went off somewhere out there, and there was one last violent crash against the door, before everything went silent. They heard jangling, the sound of keys.

Lisa looked at the man beside her and whispered. "Daniel, I—"

He turned and looked at her. "You've never called me 'Daniel' before."

The door crashed open, and they both gasped.

The policeman slumped to the floor just inside the doorway, his body propped up against it from the outside.

Standing behind him in the doorway was a tall silhouette. A man. He produced an empty gurney and steered it into the room.

"I . . . I'm here to, uh . . . rescue you," the man stated. "Apparently."

"Sorry, *who* are you again?" Lisa asked skeptically as she ran along beside their mysterious savior, dragging Daniel's I.V. stand.

"It's not important," Grant replied, maneuvering Daniel's gurney through the dark corridors and toward an elevator.

"Power's still out," Lisa breathed. "How's an elevator supposed to help?"

"They operate on a back-up grid, in case of emergencies," Grant explained, turning around to drag the gurney onto the elevator car. Daniel looked horrid with both legs outstretched in full casts, his right ankle still sporting the complex metallic contraption. He seemed to be worn out already from all of the excitement, but he startled when Grant pulled him over the doorsill and the gurney bumped.

"Easy!" Lisa screeched. "He's not a sack of potatoes!"

Grant sighed.

"How do you intend to get us out of here?" Daniel whispered.

"No worries," Grant replied. "I've been in tighter spots than this."

"I feel better already," Lisa muttered.

The elevator arrived and Grant allowed the adrenaline to flow, to begin to build up . . .

The lights were coming back up on the bottom floor, where there was a great deal of commotion. It was almost shoulder-to-shoulder as hospital workers kept coming out of their offices to find out what was going on.

"Hannah, are we ready?" Grant whispered into his earpiece.

"Stand by," was the terse reply. She'd been acting funny since their last conversation, but there wasn't time to reflect now.

A moment later, the building's fire alarm went off. Grant wrapped his fingers tightly around the gurney's handle and walked, Lisa working hard to keep up. But instead of heading for the exit, he turned and went deeper into the hospital.

"What are you *doing?*" Lisa cried.

Grant ignored her and kept running. Down a series of winding hallways, he made for a doorway marked "Surgery."

"Get the door," he instructed.

Lisa was exasperated, but she complied, watching Grant with eyes of fire.

He pushed Daniel through, into the abandoned department.

"Third door on the right," Hannah instructed in his earpiece.

"I see it," he answered.

"Who are you talking to?" Lisa exclaimed. Then she noticed the heavy, wide, metal door he was aiming for. It looked like some kind of special exit used only for delivery of organs brought in for emergency transplant procedures. "We'll never get that open!"

"I know," Grant replied, turning inward. He allowed the panic to build and build, until his body convulsed, his brain seized, and he nearly fell to the ground. When he opened his eyes, the metal door was gone, resting on the cement ground outside in two crumpled pieces.

Lisa was gaping at him in shock, but managed to gather her wits as he wheeled Daniel through the open doorway. An ambulance came out of nowhere and screeched to a halt directly in front of them, blocking their path, Hannah at the wheel.

"This thing should have enough supplies to last him a while," she reported quietly. "I'll drop you off, gut it, and ditch it someplace."

Grant and Lisa hitched the gurney into its lowest position and lifted it into the ambulance floor, sliding it inside as though they were paramedics who'd done it all their lives. Once it was secure, and they'd climbed in after, Grant pounded on the front panel and shouted "Go!" to Hannah.

After they were out on the road, Grant climbed up front.

"Are you sure about this?" Hannah asked. "I mean, he's gonna need some heavy-duty medical know-how."

"Let me worry about that, would you?" he snapped.

"Sorry. Just figured you'd want to make sure he gets better."

"Got a lot of people asking me for that these days," Grant muttered loud enough for her to hear it.

A stop light turned red and she was forced to halt the vehicle. "Maybe I shouldn't have come. You're so good at everything, you probably could have handled this just fine without me."

"I probably could!" he shouted louder than he'd intended.

Why am I angry at her? he instantly thought.

Their eyes met—tears in hers and exhaustion in his—and their features softened. An unspoken apology was expressed on her face. Her beautiful face and those round eyes, full of longing . . .

In that moment, Grant knew *exactly* how he felt about her. It was undeniable.

His hand found its way across the space between them and pushed hair out of her eyes, behind one ear, and held its place there, cradling her jaw. She made no move to pull away . . .

"How did you do that thing with the door?" Lisa shouted from the back, after Grant's arm had returned to his seat and a comfortable silence had passed.

"I don't have time to explain," he said, turning around. "My name is—"

"Borrows," Daniel croaked. "You're Grant Borrows, aren't you?"

Grant nodded in shock.

"Then you and I have a great deal to talk about."

34

Thankfully, Grant's keycard operated the service elevator in the Wagner Building or they wouldn't have been able to get Daniel upstairs. Night cloaked their movements and as soon as they had him comfortable and the medical supplies from the ambulance stowed, Hannah left to dump the vehicle.

When she left, Lisa cornered Grant. "You listen to me," she said quietly. "What's happened to Daniel—I mean, *Dr. Cossick* . . . All those broken bones and bruises and internal bleeding? It's because of *you*. He lost everything—"

Grant watched as she stopped to collect herself, pools forming beneath her eyes.

He wondered just how close these two were.

"So I'm telling you *right now*," Lisa said, a fierceness appearing behind her vulnerability. "If I find out that you weren't worth what he's done for you . . . I will make you live to regret it."

Grant blinked, thumbing his ring nervously from underneath. "Um, yeah . . . You got it."

Julie appeared from her bedroom, ignored the visitors and turned straight to Grant.

"What did you do now? And why did you steal an ambulance?" she asked, sleepy.

"How do you know about that?" he asked.

"It's all over the news. Or rather, you are. They've got police sketches of you and everything that they're showing on television.

Saying you were involved in another kidnapping—after *my* abduction—this time of a local research scientist." She saw Daniel for the first time on his gurney near the window and stopped for a long second. "Okay," she said, testy, "explanation. *Now*."

"Well—" Grant replied but Lisa interrupted.

"I tried to get him to take a rest, recover his strength, but he's determined to talk to you. So come on."

Grant and Julie followed Lisa back into the living room. Daniel's head was turned to the window and the shimmering sea of lights that filled the dark as sure as stars filled the sky. He appeared lost in thought at the sight of it all.

As if sensing Grant approach, he let out a shuddering breath.

"I have a question," Daniel said, wringing his hands together again and again, turning his eyes to Grant. "If your entire identity is stripped away from you . . . what remains? What's still there? Who *are* you, really?"

Julie hung back toward the couch, but Grant stood in place. "So you know, then," he said.

"I suspected."

Grant sat on the arm of the couch where Daniel could see him.

"Forgive me," Daniel tentatively began. "This is Lisa. My assistant. Do you prefer Grant or Collin?"

"Grant. My sister, Julie."

"Of course," Daniel nodded nervously. "Please call me Daniel."

Lisa retrieved a clear bag of fluid from a handful of supplies she'd brought from the ambulance—Hannah was due back in an hour or so with more—and hung it from a metallic rod sticking out of the top of Daniel's wheelchair. She plugged the line from the saline I.V. bag into the matching line still sticking out of his forearm.

Daniel nodded a quick thanks to her and then turned his attention back to Grant. Lisa walked to the countertop that separated the kitchen from the living room and leaned back against it. She merely stood there, watching and listening.

"I don't know how to answer your question," Grant said, standing and approaching the gurney. "I'm still trying to figure that out. A few weeks ago, everything was normal. Now, I have a different name, a different face, and a different life. And I can do things that no one should be able to do . . ."

"Yes, I know," Daniel's eyes danced with a twitchy energy that was disproportionate to his damaged body. "And to have come so far in only a handful of days . . ." he echoed thoughtfully. "I, on the other hand, have been waiting for this moment for *much* longer than two weeks."

Daniel swallowed and groaned as he shifted on his makeshift bed. "I have so much I need to tell you, and I hope you'll allow me a bit of patience as I sort all this out. As you can see, it hasn't been an easy road getting here."

"What's happened to you?" asked Grant, unable to hold the question back any longer. "And why were you in danger at the hospital?"

"I had a run-in with a detective named Drexel."

"We've met," Grant grimaced. "*He* did this to you? Why?"

Daniel averted his eyes and dabbed at his forehead again. "I think he was growing desperate. Drexel's one aim of late seems to have been to track you down," he said meekly. "But before you let yourself feel too badly about your part in this, you should probably know that I'm not exactly guiltless, in the grand scheme."

"Meaning?"

"We'll get to that," Daniel said, casting a glance at Lisa. "First, would you mind filling in the blanks for me on what's happened to you? I mean, I know some of it, but I need to piece the details together. All of them."

Grant studied the other man. Daniel already knew what he could do, and he appeared to know the truth about who he used to be. Giving him the remaining particulars posed little risk.

So Grant told him.

He told him about that first day, about his sudden, inexplicable Shift and his encounter with the other man—Collin, the man who'd taken on the identity of his former self. He showed Daniel the ring he wore, and explained what little he understood about his strange new mental ability. He told him about saving Julie from the hit man, Konrad, and their struggle in his old apartment.

Grant continued the story with his adventure at Inveo Technologies and what he found out there about Harlan Evers. He told him about meeting Hannah, and Morgan, and her unusual home and the others who lived there, the Loci. He told him about his encounter at Drexel's home, and what he did to the place. He told him about meeting Harlan Evers at the military base, and the bombshell the old man had dropped on him about his father—before the general was murdered by his own troops.

And lastly, he told Daniel about Alex, and what she claimed her role was in all of this. He ended by mentioning the person Alex said she worked for—the Keeper, the presumed mastermind who had some-how engineered Grant's Shift.

He didn't leave out a single detail that he could recall. It was the first time he had told the entire story to one person, and it was the first time Julie had heard some of the most recent information.

And all the while, Daniel listened with rapt attention, barely moving and hardly blinking at all.

Finally, Grant finished his story and fell silent.

He watched as Daniel processed this new data. It was a while before he attempted to speak.

"That's . . . something," Daniel mumbled. "Under normal circumstances, I would find it all too incredible and coincidental to believe. That is, if I didn't know what I came here to tell you. You see . . . where you see a sequence of random events, random manipulations . . . I see intent at work. I see *purpose*."

Alex was home asleep in her bed when a hand was placed over her mouth to prevent her from screaming.

"My dear little girl . . ."

She froze, her eyes darting about. She knew that voice.

"Don't be afraid," said the man who had forced entry into her home.

Yet she nearly hyperventilated. This was impossible; her home was one hundred percent secure from outside influence.

"I'm not going to kill you. I'm not even going to arrest you," he continued.

Drexel.

"You're much too valuable for that. I have bigger plans."

The Thresher's sword clanged loudly against Devlin's, the regal white-haired man *tsk*-ing and shifting his eyes unfavorably, as his feet danced lightly across the mat.

"I see you still cling to your sword's grip too tightly," the older man frowned, disapprovingly.

The Thresher lunged. "I see you still talk too much during a match."

But Devlin spun away, surprisingly fast for a man of his age, and sliced into the Thresher's left shoulder, leaving a red streak. The Thresher moved like lightning and cut a shallow gash into his mentor's right leg.

They had been at this for hours in a solitary sparring room at a local gym, having told the building's owners that they were merely sparring with rubber-tipped weapons. But they were all too real, and the Thresher had learned long ago not to rush the elder man's speeches. He would make his point when he was ready, and no sooner.

Devlin slashed into the Thresher's arm again, a cut deep enough this time to leave blood on his blade. The old man seemed more put-out by this success than his pupil.

"Is *this* what you consider fast these days?" he spat, taking a closer look at the red streak on his sword.

Which accent was it this time? Australian? Kiwi? The Thresher couldn't tell and had long ago given up trying to guess them all. Devlin had always been shifting between dozens of accents and dialects for as long as the Thresher had known him. It was a way of becoming invisible when the elder gentleman was forced to venture out into public. Yet he kept up the practice daily, whether public or private.

Man of a thousand pretenses, the Thresher thought. It was just one of the many reasons he had come to despise the man.

For his part, the Thresher had no time nor use for deception. He found it pointless.

The Thresher watched him through vicious eyes. "I could take you with ease," he replied, his weapon held low and threatening.

"Yes I know. As do you," Devlin said, lunging sharply to the right. The Thresher dodged the blow with a swift twist to his left and a parry. "Your skills have never been uncertain." The Thresher swung low and Devlin jumped. "You were beaten and taken captive by men with no proficiency of any kind. Because you knew there was no one who could defeat you."

The Thresher stopped. "I've grown overconfident." It was very nearly a question.

But not quite.

"You have no room for exploitable weaknesses. Your task is too critical. You know what is at stake, what now depends on you."

The Thresher swished and disarmed his opponent with a cunning flick. Devlin's sword went flying through the air.

"I do."

"And you know *why* all of this falls to you?" Devlin asked though he certainly knew the answer.

"I know why *you* believe it is my task. And I have agreed to take it on. But I do not share your convictions."

Devlin shook his head. "To know all that you know, and still not worship as the Secretum does. I shall never understand it."

The Thresher met his gaze coldly, uncaring what the other man thought of his beliefs.

Devlin squared his shoulders and placed his hands behind him. Back to business. "You have his location?" he asked calmly.

"I'm close."

"Then return to your duty."

Lisa insisted they stop so Daniel could rest, but the man shrugged her off. He couldn't sleep at this point anyway. It was better to push through. The time to rest would come. Lisa agreed, but without success, and finally sulked away.

Daniel asked Grant, "Have you ever heard the term 'psychokinesis' before?"

"Moving things with your mind?" Grant asked.

Daniel nodded. "Right. It's a fringe-science subset of parapsychology. Most 'rational' scientists completely discredit it without bothering to give it any genuine study, even though there are hundreds of documented, proven cases where no other explanation is available to rationalize how an unusual phenomenon occurred. Parapsychology is far more legitimate than it's given credit for.

"In recent years, it's become a central field of study in the science of war. Imagine the balance of power shifting in a fight because all of the enemy's guns have been removed from their hands, or their missiles are triggered to explode in the launch tube. The problem is, in almost every documented case where psychokinesis occurs, it's a random, sub-conscious act. The by-product of a strong emotion or a violent deed. If it isn't controllable, it's of no use."

"So *this* is what I've been doing? Moving things with my mind?"

"Not exactly," Daniel paused, taking a drink to quench his parched lips. "Your thoughts affect material around you. It's something much stronger than simply forcing your will onto an inanimate object. We found the knife that was embedded in the column in the subway. The results of tests we ran were . . . not at all what I was expecting."

"Keep talking."

"Well, there are pressurized weapons in the world capable of push-ing solid metal deep into hardened concrete, but we *know* nothing like that was present in the subway. Which means only a powerful blast of energy or a projected force could have done it. So I was hoping to find a latent energy signature—an after-effect 'fingerprint' of whatever did this to the knife. But instead of showing an energy fingerprint, the readings we got indicated that the knife itself somehow had become energy."

Grant rubbed his forehead, glanced at Julie. "I'm sorry, I'm not fol-lowing this."

"My theory," said Daniel, "is that somehow, your mind is able to transform its thoughts directly into energy. You didn't move the knife by thinking about it, because I don't think you were in control of what happened that way. When you panicked, your mind released some kind of energy that forced the knife as far away from you as it could go. Your brain produced this blast that was fairly random, but it accom-plished its purpose: your life was saved. Now you're learning to control it, aren't you? That's how you got us out of the hospital."

Grant nodded.

"I can help you with this; it's the reason I've been searching for you. If you *do* gain control over it, it's possible that you could even overcome the coinciding headaches you mentioned."

If he was making a sales pitch, Grant was already sold. But some-thing still felt off.

"What's the catch?" Grant said.

"The catch," replied Daniel, looking away, "is that you're going to have to trust me. Despite what I've been involved with."

Grant's eyes narrowed. "Why don't I like the sound of that?"

"For all the right reasons," Daniel said wistfully.

35

"Lisa?" Daniel called. She immediately sprung to attention and ran to him, fearing he was in some sort of pain. When she came near, he said, "I need you to go get something for me."

She looked at him suspiciously. "You want me to leave? *Now?*"

"I need something from the lab."

"There's nothing left at the lab," she said automatically, watching him closely.

"*This* will be," he said, not meeting her gaze. He directed her to move aside the desk in his office if it was still there and pry loose the floor tile directly beneath the left rear leg of the desk. Inside, she would find a box.

"I need that box," he said quietly.

She hesitated.

"I'll be safe here," he said. "Please."

"All right, but I'll be back quick." She turned to go.

"Be careful," he called out. "The police could still be watching the building."

When Lisa came to the door, she stopped short. She turned back to look at Grant, a quizzical expression written across her face.

Grant answered her unspoken question by reaching inside a pocket and pulling out his keys. He tossed them to her, and she caught them in one hand.

"The blue Corvette convertible," he said.

Daniel listened for her to be completely gone before he spoke again.

"Lisa's done most of our fact-finding on you. She's even been here to your apartment, but you weren't at home." His voice trailed off as he became lost in thought again.

Grant said nothing.

"She's a good person," Daniel said, looking back up. "She's treated me like family—closer, like . . ." he swallowed as his eyes moistened. "But she can't know what I'm about to tell you. Not ever. It . . . it would destroy her."

Grant sat up straight, glanced quickly at Julie. Daniel had his attention now.

"Despite what my detractors might tell you," he began, looking back up at Grant, "I *am* a very serious scientist. So please believe me when I say: what I'm about to tell you has taken a long time for me to accept." He took a deep breath and let it out slowly.

"Five years ago, I was working as a research technician at a major lab funded by a megacorporation."

"Let me guess," Grant interjected. "Inveo Technologies?"

"It was a company called Paragenics Group," Daniel replied. "But I understand Inveo has become one of their largest competitors over the years. Anyway, I wasn't working on anything terribly special. There were dozens of us working on the same kinds of things, although we were each allowed to have free rein and try our own methods. I was mapping brain responses to various stimuli.

"I had been there for nine months, happily working at proving various theories I had about the capabilities of the human brain and extrasensory perception. I was experiencing more success than most of my colleagues, and scuttlebutt said that my work had not gone without notice from the higher-ups, that I would soon surpass my colleagues.

"Then, one day everything at the lab changed. A full staff meeting was called, and we were told that a private investor had purchased controlling interest in the company, and that we might notice a number of unfamiliar faces around the building. We were to think nothing of it."

"Who was the investor?" Grant asked.

"I never found out. But just as they said, soon there were dozens of new workers combing the facility—and not just scientists. Men and women in gray camouflage jumpsuits constantly made the rounds. We were never told who they were, but we suspected they were some kind of independent security force. Our building had security already, but these guys . . . they wore no insignia, no emblem, nothing to identify them. Nothing changed in regard to our work, though, so after a while, we just got used to seeing them.

"But slowly, more and more new security measures were put into place all around our building. None of us knew what it was about, but you can imagine the rumors. Some of the scientists even resigned in protest.

"One morning, one of the gray-clad men came to my lab and said I was to report to a sub-level of the facility only available to those with the highest level of clearance. He escorted me through a number of checkpoints and inspections, but it seemed some sort of emergency was taking place, so they couldn't afford to detain me very long.

"When I reached the secured area, it was a large, white underground hallway, enormous in size, and it ended in the distance with a heavily secured vault door made of steel. Two security guards stood to the left and right of the door."

Grant glanced at Julie. This sounded an awful lot like what they'd found beneath Inveo Technologies.

"My escort handed me off to one of the company's senior staff members—a scientist herself—who met me there in the hall. She made me sign a nondisclosure form on the spot, and warned me that if I were ever to tell anyone what I was about to see, they would be within their rights to bring the full legal weight of the company down upon me.

"To my disappointment, we didn't go through the vaulted door. Instead, she ushered me into a small side room, where a group of about half a dozen scientists in lab coats—none of whom I recognized—surrounded a man sitting in a chair in the middle of the room. There was nothing in the room but the scientists and their subject, who wore a standard hospital gown." He gestured at his own gown. "My companion introduced me to the other scientists, and they acknowledged me with guarded expressions. One or two of them shook my hand.

"They asked me to run some of the specialized tests I'd developed on the man in the chair. I still have no idea who he was. He had the most blank expression on his face I had ever seen, and he never moved or spoke except while I ran the test. I had done these tests dozens of times before, so even though I was uneasy with such an attentive audience, I did as I was told.

"I ran my tests for hours. I was used to getting maybe one right answer out of every twenty or so, if I was lucky. That was considered a 'good' score, and I'd never gotten anything higher out of the college students and others who volunteered for my tests. So you'll understand that it was one of the most profound moments of my scientific career when I watched this guy *nail* every test I threw at him. He was certifiably gifted; it was the most potent case of genuine ESP I have ever seen. Over the course of the afternoon, I tried every test I knew, and he defeated them all, even though he appeared barely cogent. I believe the scientists would have allowed me to keep going indefinitely, but after a few hours, I simply had nothing else left to try. It was the most thrilling, most astounding thing I'd ever witnessed.

"Finally, the scientists thanked me for my time and told me I could go. I suddenly remembered the nondisclosure agreement and was so disappointed that the vindication for all of my work had finally been discovered, yet I couldn't tell anyone about it. I couldn't imagine any reason they wouldn't want everyone in the world to know about this man and what he could do.

"But just as I was about to leave, the man fell to the floor. I was horrified, afraid that one of my tests had somehow triggered this. But the other scientists did little to help him—it was almost as if they'd been expecting this. I watched as blood oozed from his ears onto the floor.

"He was dead in minutes. Some kind of seizure, they told me. I must've looked panicked, because as soon as they'd determined the man was dead, they all turned to focus their attention on me. The woman who led me into the room grabbed me by the arm and led me back out. As we walked, she assured me that the proper authorities would be contacted and that I had nothing to worry about since I had been conducting perfectly legal, harmless scientific tests.

"I was so stunned, I simply wandered back upstairs to my office. But as the hours passed, the more my suspicions stirred. No ambulance or police cars arrived at the facility that day. No one ever came to question me as a witness. And as far as anyone else in the building proper knew, it was just another typical day at work.

"At quitting time, instead of leaving, I went back downstairs to the underground hallway. I still had my clearance from earlier in the day, and the guards stared at me, but they let me through, probably assuming I had been called back down. I went back to the room where we had conducted the tests, and to my surprise, I could hear from outside all of the scientists from earlier, still in the room. I put my ear to the door and listened.

"I couldn't make out everything they said, but I heard them repeatedly mention something called 'Project Threshold.' From the way they talked about it, succeeding with this project was the focus of whatever they were doing. As these thoughts went through my mind, something hit my head and I blacked out."

Daniel took an awkward pause, his eyes closed tight.

"When I awoke," he continued, "I couldn't move. I remember it was so cold, and so *quiet*. I was lying on my back, and I could turn my head to either side, but beyond that, I was completely immobilized. When my eyes adjusted to the brightness of the room, I found myself in this vast space—to call it a 'room' would be an injustice. It was what was on the other side of that enormous vault door. Lying all around me, filling the entire space were flat, cold, stainless steel tables just like the one I was on, and they were occupied.

"Men and women, all young adults, were lying on every table. And none of them could move, either, even though none of us were strapped down. I came to realize later that some kind of paralytic toxin had been used on us. Do you have any idea how that feels? To be completely unfettered, yet unable to move. It was . . . horrifying."

Daniel closed his eyes again, seeing it in his mind. "Some of the others were awake, some were unconscious. All of them wore hospital gowns like the dead man, and it was then I realized I was wearing one, too."

Grant watched as Daniel paused, closed his eyes, and shook his head.

"I watched as well as I could manage for over three hours as the people on the tables around me were subjected to every stimulus you can imagine. Electroshock, chemicals, gases, even direct neurological surgery. It was grotesque, dehumanizing. I wanted to cry out for help but was afraid to draw attention to myself. I tried to get my body to move, but it wouldn't obey. It was no use.

"The woman who had met me earlier appeared at the head of my table and looked down at me. I could see her upside down if I craned my head back. I asked her what all this was and what they were going to do to me.

"She said that curiosity may have killed the cat, but here, they had much better uses for the curious. The long and short of it is that my suspicions were essentially true. I had become one of the subjects of Project Threshold, which was dedicated to finding individuals with latent mental abilities, and activating those abilities. This was the 'threshold' they were trying to cross and access. What I was proving the existence of upstairs through legitimate testing, these people were trying to *force* into being through any means possible.

"They ran test after test on their subjects' mental outputs; anyone who registered a spike in output they referred to as a 'shimmer.' It was a shorthand code used to indicate a promising subject. But not one of their subjects survived the radical procedures long enough to be considered a success, just like the man I had tested for them earlier. I asked her why they were doing this, but she wouldn't say.

"They hooked me up to an artery line, and another scientist appeared with a syringe containing some kind of ugly, brown liquid. I was more scared than I'd ever been in my life, and all I could think about was that man who had collapsed on the floor, bleeding from his ears. I despised them for what they were doing, but I was . . . I was petrified . . ."

Daniel stopped speaking and suddenly he looked very pale. Tired. Like a feeble, elderly man. Grant wondered how the man lying prone before him could ever have escaped the predicament he described.

"God forgive me . . . I made a deal."

"You *what!*" Grant exclaimed. "How—?"

"I know, I know," Daniel said, dejectedly. "But when you're just lying there, at someone else's mercy, staring death in the face and you're absolutely, unequivocally powerless to stop it . . . the ethical questions just . . . go away. There *are* no options, no alternatives. If you've never been in that situation, you can't know. The human capacity for self-preservation forces all other choices out of the equation."

"*Of course* you had other choices!" Grant thundered. "Listen to you, trying to methodically justify your involvement in this . . . this *conspiracy*! You've actually lived with this long enough to make it into something okay, in your mind, haven't you? How long did it take you to come up with that bit about self-preservation?"

"Easy words when you're sitting in the comfort of home," Daniel replied dolefully. "Remember that if I hadn't made a deal with them, I wouldn't be here now, telling you what I know."

"That doesn't make it right!" Grant spat.

"Don't you think I know that?" Daniel shouted back at him. "Don't you think I lie awake every night, thinking of all those other test subjects, consumed with guilt?" He began coughing, clutching his chest with his good hand.

"Good! You *should* feel guilty!" Grant raged.

"Calm down . . ." Julie said quietly. She grabbed his arm and guided him back to his seat, though he had no memory of having stood. Then she went to the kitchen and got Daniel a glass of water. He received it gratefully.

"To finish my story," Daniel continued doggedly after recovering, "I reminded the Paragenics people of my success rate and managed to convince them that my skills were too valuable to be wasted this way. I suggested that I could help—not with their attempts to create mentally advanced humans, but in finding those who were born with mental gifts. They agreed, and since I had long proven that I work best in solitude, they left me to my own methods. I would function independently, outside of the company. But all of the work I did was for them, and they kept a *very* close eye on my activities.

"They implanted a tracer device into a filling in one of my back teeth. They offered me a strict budget from which to operate, and I was instructed to report back to them weekly on whatever findings I had, or the deal was off. If I missed a week reporting in, if I refused to continue my research, or if I told anyone what they were up to, they would use the tracer to track me down and I would be brought back to the vault. All they required was that I continue my research, attempting to find people with 'potent, enhanced mental skills' like they were looking for. They didn't care what methods I used to do it."

He leaned his head back, spent. "There, that's it . . . That's the secret I've been holding on to for five years, the thing that no one knows. Not even Lisa. I made a deal with the devil to save my skin. I'm a—"

"A *coward*," Grant said bitterly, but without raising his voice this time.

"Yes," Daniel replied. "And now I've got the rest of my life to try to make up for it."

Grant wanted to say more, but he was still angry and didn't trust himself.

When Grant remained silent, Daniel picked up his story. "I created methods of detection that were noninvasive," he said. "If I had to do this, I was determined that no would be hurt because of me. Most of the people I tested never even knew they were being studied. And every day I hoped and prayed that I would never find what I was looking for. But I had to at least *try*, or I was dead."

Daniel shook his head and then offered the tiniest hint of a smile. "When those thugs attacked me and my lab was destroyed . . . a part of me was *relieved*. It meant no more working for Paragenics, no more research. The tracer filling is gone from my tooth; it was knocked loose during the attack. I can finally, legitimately, get out from under their thumb."

Grant was still frowning angrily at Daniel, yet as his temper cooled, he tried to keep telling himself that Daniel had only done what most people would do in the same situation. And the poor guy was certainly broken and defeated enough as it was, without needing anyone else's judgment.

As Grant processed these things, along with Daniel's story, one question rose to the surface.

"You said you made regular reports to them. You called me on the phone over a week ago, so you've known about me and what I can do for at least that long. Did you tell your superiors about me?"

"Of course not!" Daniel looked startled, almost offended.

Grant was unabashedly suspicious.

"Grant, you wouldn't even be sitting here if they knew about you!"

"All right," Grant conceded. But another thought was buzzing in his head—one that had been building for a while as he'd listened to Daniel's tale. "What if I'm one of those people Paragenics experimented on? Or maybe I'm the product of one of their competitors, like Inveo Technologies. Could I be one of their successes?"

Daniel sat up straight, his eyes suddenly brighter.

"That's just the thing," Daniel said, his eyes wider now than Grant had yet seen them. *"That's* what I came here to tell you. Despite the millions of dollars Paragenics poured into its experiments . . . despite everyone that died at their hands . . . they *never* had a success. At least, not one that survived more than a few hours. They even abandoned Project Threshold about a year ago and filled in their underground labs with concrete, to make sure no one would follow their work. The company still exists, and they told me to continue my clandestine research on the off chance that I might succeed. But the 'Threshold' was never crossed. They never succeeded at all.

"Somehow, entirely on your own . . . *you did.*"

36

"Drop it, Fletcher."

"Why won't you tell me what she said?" he replied, watching her with those magnified eyeglasses of his.

"I've told you before, what Marta and I talk about stays between the two of us," Morgan told him, massaging her forehead.

"But something's different this time, I can tell," he whined. "She told you something about Grant, didn't she? Something big. Something you didn't want to hear."

Morgan cut her eyes away from him, mildly irritated. It was then that she noticed how full the Common Room was today. Quite a few visitors staying this week.

Every one of them were Loci, of course.

"I'm not answering your questions, Fletcher."

"You just did."

"Will you leave it alone?" she said, louder. A few others in the room turned and looked.

"Why are you so intent on trusting this guy?" Fletcher said, his volume rising to match hers.

"Why are you so intent on *not* trusting him?" she shouted.

Fletcher frowned and leaned back in his seat. Everyone in the room was watching now. Morgan *never* shouted.

"I'll say it again. His ring may be different than everyone else's," Fletcher said. "But it can't possibly be *that* important."

"And yet," Morgan said, leveling her gaze on him, "it *is*."

"How do you know?" Fletcher challenged.

"Because his coming was predicted over seven *thousand* years ago," she replied, to audible gasps throughout the room. Not one of the Loci knew of the existence of the stone tablet, aside from herself and Grant. "*Believe it*, all of you. In fact, let everyone know," she said, turning to address the entire room. "The magnitude of this cannot be overstated. He is *the Bringer*. And his time is near."

"*You* breached the Threshold, Grant," Daniel said. "This is the reason I've been trying so hard to find you. I couldn't care less about what Paragenics might want with you—I just want to *help* you. Because you've succeeded where no one else *ever* could."

"But I *didn't*!" Grant protested. "At least, I never *chose* to. Everything that's happened to me has been completely outside of my control."

"Which is the unavoidable point we keep coming back to . . ." Daniel thought aloud, nodding. He looked away, considering this for a few moments, following this thought to its conclusion . . .

And then a dawn of comprehension passed over his face and his mouth opened as he looked up at Grant, locking eyes with him.

"All these years," he said urgently, "I've known *what* Paragenics and their rivals were up to, but I never knew *why*. Why was it so important for them to cross this threshold? *Why* were they willing to risk illegal experimentation with such a high body count? What could *possibly* be so important? And now that I know your story . . . I think I'm finally beginning to understand.

"I assumed," Daniel continued, "that Paragenics was doing what they were doing for military applications. Power. Money. I figured they were trying to create a new breed of soldier—and probably for the highest bidder. But they failed miserably, and their work was abandoned.

"From what you've told me, though, it looks like the results they were after are appearing in hundreds of people—if not more—entirely at random. From a spectator's point-of-view, there's *nothing* connecting all of you to one another, except for these strange rings on your fingers. But what if there *is* something that connects all of you?"

Grant took Julie's hand in his and leaned forward in his chair, desperate to understand. "What, then?"

"The Loci you mention—*all* of their abilities could have strategic defensive or offensive applications, if used correctly. They make you unique—or more *advanced* than your average human. So *if* advanced human beings are popping up all over the world *now*, then the logical conclusion is that there must be a reason for it. I told you I saw a purpose, a design in all of this. What if that purpose isn't one that science can explain?"

"Then what could explain it?" Grant shoved his hand close to Daniel's face. "I mean, look at this thing. There's no way it just landed there on its own."

"If it's not a natural occurrence," Daniel said quietly, "then it must be a *super*natural one."

Grant leaned back, looking at Daniel anew. "I don't believe in the supernatural."

". . . Said the man who was placed inside a new body."

"But you're a scientist! How can you possibly believe in some hocus-pocus explanation for all this?"

"Grant, you have to understand . . ." Daniel said, taking on his best scholarly tone. "Scientists study the order of nature. But one thing science has *never* been able to explain is *why* that order exists. Why are there scientific laws that hold the universe together? Why doesn't everything spiral out of control, into chaos? As much as we try to reason our way around it, some parts of our existence simply can't be explained with formulas or proofs.

"The human brain's complexity, for example. Our ability to be self-aware and have consciousness and reasoning and imagination. The fact that as vast as the solar system is, our planet rests in the one orbit—the one *precise* position around our sun that's capable of supporting life. There are a million examples all around us."

Grant sighed, shaking his head bitterly. "You're sounding less and less like a scientist, Doc. Here I thought you were going to explain to me how all of this is even possible. Instead, you want me to believe that 'fate' magically intervened. Even if that were true, *why*? Why did I have to go through the Shift? Why couldn't I have been given this ring as Collin Boyd?"

"Listen to yourself, Grant," Daniel said urgently. "Don't you see? You're answering your own question. If all this is happening *now*, to *you* . . . then it's happening to you now *for a reason*. A reason outside human understanding," he said with a note of finality.

A reason outside human understanding?

What kind of answer was that?

What possible reason could there be?

Grant froze.

Julie watched him fearfully, not understanding.

A chill crept down Grant's spine as a single thought went off in his head like a flash bomb.

"I'm going to be *needed* . . ." he said, facing Daniel, face stricken with alarm.

Grant looked down, lost in his thoughts. But Daniel studied him intently. Grant followed the line of reasoning through to the same conclusion that the doctor had apparently perceived only moments ago.

Grant's head snapped back up to look Daniel in the eye.

In that instant, he *had it*.

At long last, he *knew*.

All of the questions he had about why this had happened to him. All of his fears. His doubts. His confusion. Everything he had learned about himself, about what he could do. The rings. The stone tablet. The others that had been Shifted.

It all came crashing together in one perfect moment of crystallization.

For the first time in a very long time, *everything* made sense.

"*Something's coming* . . ." he breathed, his eyes enormous.

Daniel nodded gravely. Julie gasped, hand flying up to cover her mouth.

Grant leaned back in his seat, his mind swimming, his heart pounding visibly beneath his shirt.

"Something bigger than *anything* that has ever been," Daniel was saying slowly, with great emphasis. "Something the rest of humanity is not equipped to deal with. I can't even *guess* what shape it might take, or when it will happen, but the logical conclusion here is that you, and possibly the others, are meant to stop it."

Grant sat back in his chair, trying to suppress the feeling of weakness that had overcome him. A cold sweat broke out across his brow and he closed his eyes, trying to get a handle on what all this meant.

He finally understood. Not *how*. But definitely *why*.

Something was coming. Something only he would be able to stop.

It was preposterous!

Who was *he* to save the world? And who would be foolish enough to choose him for it?

He was no one.

And the others? What of them?

As he thought of Morgan and Hannah and all of the others that had been Shifted, an odd sensation encompassed him, as if every part of his body had been hit with a mild electric shock, right down to his marrow.

He opened his eyes to see Daniel gaping at him.

"Grant, what—?" Daniel was saying.

Grant looked down.

His ring was glowing.

It had only glowed one time before—the night it shimmered in the graveyard after Collin had been buried.

But something was different. This wasn't the same as before.

Instead of shimmering evenly, the light was growing.

"Daniel . . ." Grant said in alarm as he watched the light become brighter.

And then the blinding pain returned, jolting him with such intensity that he fell off the sofa. It was worse than ever before. He clutched his head with both hands, as if he could somehow stop the unbearable pain by squeezing his skull.

NO NO NO!!

"Collin!" Julie screamed, kneeling at his side, trying to keep him from convulsing.

The pain spread the brighter the light became. From Grant's head down through every part of his body—chest, arms, hands, legs, feet—it was everywhere. Searing, ripping, shredding through him with an intensity beyond anything he'd ever imagined possible.

He writhed on the floor, screaming, twitching as if his flesh was being wrenched off of his bones.

Morgan had just stood from her chair when a prickling

sensation at the back of her neck told her something was wrong.

All around the Common Room, everything was growing brighter. And the light was still rising.

But it wasn't a natural light; outside it was the dead of night.

Everywhere the Loci sat, stood, talked, played, watched television, read, or slept—throughout the entire facility, all of their rings had begun to glow.

The collective glow grew brighter and brighter until it became impossible to see anything other than white.

Hannah grabbed her keys. She'd dumped the ambulance at LAX, wiped it of prints, and had taken a cab back to her apartment to shower and change. The doctor they rescued probably was asleep which meant she might get Grant to herself.

Before she could open her door, though, a warmth grew at her hand and she watched amazed as the ring on her finger glowed white hot until she melted into it.

Daniel strained to see through the blinding, shimmering light, which continued to grow brighter and brighter, until closing his eyes no longer impeded it.

He tried blocking his eyes with an arm, but still it seemed that he could *feel* the light penetrating every pore of his body. Grant was thrashing about on the floor, and Julie was now screaming as well. Soon, he joined them, until the only sound in the apartment was desperate, anguished wailing.

And then, as unexpectedly as it had began, the light flashed out of existence, as though its power had been cut.

When Daniel opened his eyes, his vision was gone.

"Grant?" he called out repeatedly.

There was no answer, though he could hear Julie weeping.

Several minutes passed before his sight finally returned. When it did, Daniel strained to see the spot where he'd last looked at Grant.

Grant was still lying there on the floor.

But he was unconscious, curled into a fetal ball.

Frozen in a repose of infinite pain.

Julie was cradling him, weeping uncontrollably. Daniel asked no questions of Julie. There were none necessary.

His lips looked blue.

He wasn't moving.

And his chest was still.

All through Morgan's asylum, every person—Morgan, Fletcher, Marta, and the more than fifty other Loci currently in residence or visiting—all of them spontaneously crumpled to the floor, unconscious.

Hannah collapsed by herself next to her apartment door.

All of the others who had experienced the Shift, all around the world—including those who had never been accounted for—all of them, everywhere, slid into oblivion at the precise moment that their rings stopped glowing.

Not a single one of them moved.

Not one of them breathed.

INTERREGNUM

THE KEEPER *knew*.

Knew that Grant had met with Daniel. Knew what the two of them had figured out. Knew who Hannah had been working for, until recently. And that Alex was helping Grant, blatantly against orders, but had just been removed from the playing board.

The Keeper knew exactly what had just happened to all of those who wore the rings, and what it would mean.

Most of all, the Keeper knew of the threat that was coming.

The Keeper smiled at the thought of so much meticulous preparation coming together like a perfectly strategized game of chess.

It was only a matter of time.

History, after all, could not be avoided.

The Bringer was close now.

Very close.

37

A cloud.

No, a mist.

A misty cloud.

That's what it was.

That's what he saw.

That's what he was *inside of*.

It was beautiful, swirling in lovely, soothing hues of purple and pink and blue. It caressed his skin, and he decided he'd never felt a more peaceful sensation.

Some barely conscious part of him knew that nothing like this place existed anywhere in the world. Yet it felt remarkably comforting. Its soothing essence poured through him, saturating him with happiness.

A noise.

He heard something.

Grant looked ahead. A distortion of some kind was visible in the distance. It was an odd mixture of light and darkness, of sound and silence, that seemed to be coming closer. After a moment it resolved into a blurred outline Grant recognized as a person coming toward him.

The figure drew closer, and the sound grew louder.

Soon, he thought he heard words among the sound.

It was a voice.

A person.

Someone spoke. Or was it singing?

Whatever it was, it was drawing nearer in the tranquil, unruffled clouds. Despite his curiosity, and an elusive sense in the pit of his stomach that something wasn't right, Grant couldn't help reveling at the thought of staying here forever.

He only had a mild curiosity about the figure as it drew nearer—near enough for him to make out a humanlike shape. But everything was so peaceful here; there were no concerns, no fears.

"Grant," the voice said.

It came closer now, close enough to reach out and touch, and yet still all he saw was a milky outline.

"Hello, sweetheart," it said, the clouds rippling and shifting colors with every inflection.

He could think of no one who'd ever called him "sweetheart."

"It is an eternity in a moment, given to us," the voice replied.

What's happening to me?

Where did that pain come from?

What is this place? he thought.

"It is the Forging," the shape continued in a remarkably smooth, dignified voice. A hue of yellow formed at the edge of the rippling mist as the shape spoke. "It began the first time the pain took hold of you, but you resist."

It hurts. It's too much. I can't take it.

"I know," it said soothingly. "But this is your portion. Everything has been leading to this moment, and it *must* be done. The others will not last without you."

They wouldn't want me to suffer.

"Suffering is not what this is about," it said sympathetically, the clouds' colors turning to soft pink. "Today is a new step in your journey; it is not the last. You must ask yourself what you are willing to go through, to reach the journey's end. Are you willing to sacrifice? Are you willing to absorb your greatest fear, and make it part of your very being? Are you willing to follow the path that has been set before you?"

No! I don't want this! I don't want any part of it.

"No flesh ever does. That isn't the point." The clouds were growing redder now . . .

I just want to stay here, Grant thought. And then another thought came to mind, something he intuitively knew was true, yet had not explanation for. *I want to stay with you.*

The form began to coalesce into a more distinctive shape. A shape he recognized as female.

"I want that, too, my love. But we are not asked what we want. Only what we are willing to *do*." The clouds reverted to their original blue and purple . . .

But why? *Why must I do this? What is all this about?*

"It's about living."

This is life? *Is this how life is supposed to be? Full of pain and injustice and grief and selfishness? Is this fair? Or right? Or just?*

"One day you will have the answers to every question. Stay true to yourself. *Nothing* is as it seems. Today, you must go back."

Her form took on the properties of skin and hair and clothing, and he saw her face for the first time.

She looked strikingly familiar.

"This is not the path I would have chosen for you, my beautiful boy. But it is what *is*, and there is no other who can traverse it. Go back now. Go back to the ones who need you."

Her face glowed the most beautiful, radiant, white light he had ever seen. It grew brighter and brighter . . .

"Mom!" Grant screamed.

His breathing came too fast; he was going to hyperventilate. But he couldn't slow himself.

Was that really her? Had he just seen his mother?

He looked around. He was in his bedroom. Sitting up in bed. He couldn't remember how he got here.

He felt a staggering soreness all over, as if every muscle in his body had been stretched and pulled and exercised beyond failure. Every movement brought a world of aches.

Before the dream—if it *was* a dream—the last thing he remembered was watching his ring glow brighter than bright. And then the pain, pain beyond imagining that had waged war on his entire system. No wonder he was sore.

But that place . . . that . . . *dreamscape* . . . it was familiar. He had seen it before . . . somewhere . . .

"You're awake!" a voice exclaimed. His sister. "*He's awake!!*" Julie called out, louder.

She ran and threw her arms around him, squeezing him tight. "Are you all right? What happened? How do you feel?"

Grant shook his head, not ready to share his dream yet.

The Forging, she called it . . .

Lisa appeared at the bedroom door. Daniel, too. She was pushing him in a wheelchair.

"Does anything hurt?" Daniel asked, inspecting him like a used car.

"Everything I own hurts," Grant moaned, wincing with each breath, each tilt of his head. Coupled with this was a crushing exhaustion. He barely had the energy to raise a finger.

"You looked like you were . . ." Daniel commented, "I've never seen anything like it."

"I don't—I . . . I can't explain it," Grant whispered, his mind charging full speed ahead though his breathing at last was slowing.

He remembered the pain that had encompassed him and how it felt. It was horrific. And then he had seen the mist and then . . . *her*.

"Did I die?" he whispered, his eyes still closed.

"No!" Julie cried.

Daniel hesitated. Grant couldn't believe the man was in a wheelchair. "I . . . don't know. Your breathing was almost nonexistent. Julie said you were cold to the touch. My best guess: you were in some kind of catatonia."

Grant looked down at his left arm and noticed the line sticking out of it for the first time. He carefully pulled it out, fighting the urge to wince with each new movement.

"We hooked you up to an I.V.," Julie explained, "to make sure you didn't dehydrate."

"I feel okay . . . Aside from the soreness. It's like a truck ran over me . . . and then a tank." He glanced outside his bedroom window, and the midday sun startled him. Plus it finally fully registered that Daniel was in a wheelchair. "Wait—how long was I out?" he asked.

Daniel looked at the watch wrapped around the cast on his broken wrist. "About thirty-six hours now."

Grant just looked at him. "I've been asleep for a day and a half?"

The three of them nodded in unison.

"But it feels like I haven't slept in *days!*"

The only response the others could give was to watch him with concern.

For a day and a half, I've been in a coma. Or . . . something.

What's happening to me?

What is the Forging?

And the woman?

She couldn't have been . . .

Could she?

He looked down at his ring. It had returned to normal. No glowing, no shimmering.

But as Grant settled uncomfortably into this skin again, he realized for the first time that he felt something else, something new that he couldn't explain. It was a very odd sensation.

"Have you talked to Hannah?" he asked. "Or Morgan, or any of the others?"

"No, we haven't heard from anyone," Julie replied.

Thirty-six hours and no word from Hannah or Morgan. Or even Alex.

He looked up again and saw them watching—*scrutinizing*—his every tick and movement.

"I'm going to need a little while to sort this out," Grant said, holding Julie's hands tighter than before. His thoughts were coming faster than he could keep up with—his blackout, his dream, Daniel's revelation about why he had been Shifted, his friends, his father, his mother.

Grant stopped and gazed at Daniel and Lisa. "Thanks for staying to help."

Daniel shook his head, looked down, unable to meet Grant's eyes. "Didn't think it would be a good idea to leave, under the circumstances."

"Thanks," Grant mumbled.

"Hope you don't mind," Lisa offhandedly remarked, "but we helped ourselves to one of your unused apartments. We didn't have anywhere else to go, and this building's got decent security tech . . ."

Grant stopped, midthought. Again. "What do you mean, *my* apartments?"

"This building was anonymously purchased two months ago. It took some digging but we finally found a trail that names you as primary owner," Daniel said. "According to the paperwork, you own the whole thing."

Grant laid back down. "Somebody wake me when the world stops being crazy."

But as soon as he'd closed his eyes, the strange new feeling asserted itself again. It was as though he'd forgotten something, something so significant that it was making him edgy and fretful. And it was becoming more pronounced with each moment that passed.

He sat back up with effort, and gazed out the bright window at the Los Angeles skyline beyond. "Something's wrong."

"I thought we established *that* with our *last* conversation," Daniel retorted.

"Not with . . . the world. It's something else," Grant replied, concentrating. "Something . . . closer, more personal."

"Like what?" Julie asked, watching him closely.

"I don't know, something's just . . . *off*," Grant replied, frustrated. He closed his eyes again. "I feel it."

"Do you feel it yet?" Drexel's voice whispered into her ear. "Has it started taking effect?"

Alex craned her neck to look into his eyes, only inches away from her own. "I really, really wish you were dead," she said drunkenly.

"Mmm," he muttered, backing away from the chair she was tied to. "You wouldn't have lied about that, anyway."

He grabbed another chair and sat directly in front of her. He glanced at his watch, calculating if enough time had yet passed for the truth serum to take effect. Her demeanor had changed in the last few minutes. She looked a little loopy and doe-eyed. But she could simply be trying to throw him off.

"What's your name?" he barked.

"Alex," she replied immediately.

The drug had taken effect.

"Okay, what's your last name?"

"Don't have one," she smiled, and giggled dreamily.

Drexel backhanded her across the face.

"Ow-w-w!" she yelled. "You are a mean, stupid, ugly man. And you're . . . *mean*."

"*Stop* wasting my time, little girl. Tell me everything you know about Grant Borrows."

"Can't," she said.

Drexel was taken aback and nearly struck her again, but stopped himself. She *couldn't* lie or withhold information while under the influence. The drug he'd used was far too powerful, even for someone with conditioning.

"Why not?" he asked.

"He doesn't exist."

"Grant Borrows does not exist?" Drexel repeated.

"*Duh*," she rolled her eyes in an exaggerated, childlike way.

He followed her eyeline to the ceiling far above, where a dimming skylight was letting in the first effects of dusk. The empty warehouse where they sat was musty and dirty and dark, but it suited his purposes. They had been here for hours, days even. The truth serum was his last resort.

He tried a different tactic.

"A military base was raided about a week ago. Sources say they saw Grant Borrows there. *Was* he there?"

"Yep," she replied.

"Why did he go there?"

"To talk to Harlan Evers."

"Who is Harlan Evers?"

"Used to be Frank Boyd's best friend, before he died."

"And who was Frank Boyd?"

"Grant's father," she replied, exasperated, as if it were painfully obvious.

Boyd . . . I know that name.

He took a few minutes to word his next question carefully.

"Does Frank Boyd have any surviving relatives?"

"His kids. Collin and Julie," she said.

Collin Boyd. That was it. The man who died in the arson in Glendale. The UCLA professor's brother . . . Of course.

Drexel let out a slow breath as comprehension spread across his face.

Got you now, he smiled.

"Now, my dear," he said, settling into his seat, "we're going to head back to the station and run a background check on Mr. Boyd . . . But first, why don't you tell me everything you know about our good friend Collin."

38

Daniel watched from his wheelchair as Grant paced the living room. It was late at night, and Julie and Lisa had both given up long ago and gone to sleep.

Daniel didn't know Grant very well yet, but he could tell that this was not normal behavior. Despite the dark circles that were now a permanent fixture around his eyes, every step, every gesture, every word screamed agitation.

Grant had decided to try walking around, moving his joints and muscles, which from the way he was walking were incredibly stiff. He'd been at it for hours and had been forced to stop several times, but he seemed determined to push through the pain and exhaustion. Daniel envied him. It'd be weeks before he could pace like that.

"I know something's wrong . . ." Grant said for the umpteenth time. Daniel had heard him say these words so many times now, he'd decided Grant wasn't actually saying it to him. Daniel wished for a way to help, but he was exhausted. A glance at his wristwatch showed "1:57 A.M."

"Why don't we try a mental focusing exercise then?" he suggested, pulling the small electronic device Lisa had retrieved for him the other day from a bag at his side. Grant continued to walk back and forth. "It might help you relax, and it could be a first step toward harnessing your abilities."

"Sure, sure," Grant said, distractedly, plopping down on the sofa. He saw the device.

Daniel noticed his glance and said, "It measures your pyschokinetic output."

"You're going to . . . *clock* my brain power?"

"Something like that. Just ignore it, you won't ever know it's on. Lean back and let your eyes go out of focus," Daniel instructed. Then he began speaking in a soft monotone. "Relax your body, let go of your tension. Ignore the sounds of the world around you. Let everything fade away. Make your mind a blank canvas, with no distractions, no thoughts. No doubts. No worries. Slow your breathing. In . . . and out. In . . . and out. That's good."

He watched as Grant seemed to be following his instructions to the letter, and he suddenly wondered if this might be a bad idea—surely Grant would fall asleep if they kept this up for long. "Very good. Keep your eyes closed, and keep breathing slowly," he said, looking all around, trying to find . . . "Let's see, here we are." He spotted a magazine on the coffee table.

"There's something directly in front of you, Grant, on the table. A magazine. Keep breathing in and out slowly, there you go. Now when I give the word, I want you to open your eyes and focus on that magazine. Don't look at anything else, don't let yourself *see* anything else. Just focus on the magazine, and don't let go of it."

Daniel waited, watching Grant inhale and exhale repeatedly.

"Open your eyes," he instructed.

Grant's eyelids opened leisurely and immediately focused on the magazine atop the table, about four feet away from him.

"Relax, keep breathing slowly, that's good," Daniel was saying. "Focus your attention *only* on the object. Now I want you to picture an imaginary hand, reaching out from your own body and picking up the magazine. Really *see* it in your mind. Use your imagination to stretch out and grab it. Let me know when you have a firm grip on it."

Sweat formed across Grant's forehead as he focused with tremendous intensity on the paper object resting on the table. "I can't . . . I can't see it . . ."

Daniel watched him patiently. "If it helps, reach out with your real hand as far as you can. Use it as a focal point."

Grant extended his arm, which was still a foot and a half shy of touching the magazine. But he found it a little easier to concentrate on holding the paper booklet this way. When at last he felt comfortable with his focus, he whispered, "Okay, think I got it."

Daniel turned to the magazine. "Lift it," he said.

Ever-so-slowly, as Grant's arm inched upward, the magazine did as well. It hung there in midair, suspended by nothing.

Daniel watched in astonishment.

After a second more, Grant let the magazine fall. He seemed dazed. After a moment he asked, "Do you really believe all that stuff you told me the other day, about me and . . . what I'm meant to do?"

"Absolutely!" Daniel answered. "Look at what you just did! Grant, you might as well get used to it: you are a bona fide he—"

"*Don't* say the 'H' word!" Grant bellowed, releasing some of his pent-up energy. "Don't even *think* it! I am *not* . . . one of those, and I never *will* be."

"Yes you are. You're not like *me,*" he added. "You're better. Whether you like it or not, you have a responsibility to use this power of yours to help other people."

"I don't *care* about other people!" Grant exploded, the confines of the apartment seeming much too small for him. Daniel thought he almost felt the room shake in time with Grant's tirade. "What have people ever done for me?" Grant fumed. "Walked out on me, that's what! Betrayed me! Manipulated me! I never *wanted* this power, I never *chose* it, and if I could undo it, I *would!*" He thrust a hand out at the magazine and this time it flew apart with a loud *pop*, becoming a fireworks display of confetti. The tiny, shredded pieces fluttered silently to the ground.

Daniel watched the last of the paper bits fall to the table. Silence permeated the air but when he glanced at Grant, the man was far away again.

Farther than ever.

"I see them," Grant whispered. "Oh no . . ." He gasped, and then stood to his feet.

"Who? What's wrong?" Daniel stammered.

"They're not *moving* . . . *That's* what I've been feeling—this strange sensation. I was feeling *them!*" Grant shouted and ran to the front door. "They're still. All of them!"

Then he burst from the door and Daniel was left only with the echo of the man's horror at something Daniel couldn't fathom.

39

What if they're all dead?

The question burrowed its way through Grant's gut like a worm during the impossibly long drive to Morgan's facility. He went far above the speed limit whenever he felt he could get away with it, but had to slow down at the busier intersections. When he finally hit the suburb roads, he floored it.

At last, the cement driveway came into view, and he never slowed as he screeched his tires into a full-on turn onto the long, ruined path. When he came to a stop in front of the asylum, he hopped out of the car and ran to the front steps.

Grant slid the I.D. card Morgan had given him through the reader and was met by a cold stillness when he opened the door. He couldn't claim surprise at what he saw, because he had already *felt* it. But his jaw fell anyway, and the blood drained out of his face.

This can't be real.

Inside, he carefully stepped around the bodies sprawled on the floor. Each one of them looked as if they had been in the middle of something—walking to another room, carrying a tray full of something to eat, writing in a notebook, or looking for a book to read—when they had simply *dropped* to the ground, unconscious.

Grant crept down the long hallway, his eyes lingering on a younger resident sprawled on the ground. A basketball lay nearby.

Just a kid . . . Couldn't be more than seventeen . . .

Tears welled up as he stared at the young man, and for once he was unable to hold them back. A sharp pain began boring into his temples.

Dead . . . They're all dead . . .

A sob suddenly escaped his lips and he couldn't hold it back. It was the only audible sound in the building.

He stumbled over an older man's outstretched arm as he walked past the boy, and then he cried out again.

With great effort, Grant made his way to the Common Room. There he found over two dozen others in similar condition. On the couch. Slumped over the pool table. Lying on the ground.

He found Morgan on the ground near her favorite chair by the fireplace. She was lying chest-down on the ground, her head turned sickeningly to one side.

Tears poured openly down Grant's cheeks and he made no effort to wipe them away. This couldn't be real. He couldn't be seeing what he was seeing . . .

Another headache pain stabbed at his temples, but still he ignored it.

As he glanced around at all of the dead bodies, the enormity of the scene set in. He was the only living person in a building full of dead people.

The room began to spin . . .

He plopped down hard onto the ground, near Morgan, and began weeping openly into his hands. He barely knew most of these people. But somehow, in a way that defied words or reasoning, he just *knew* . . . This was his fault.

His phone chirped in his inside pocket but he let it ring. It stopped after a minute or two but then started again. Aggravated now, he yanked it out and opened it, but couldn't think of anything to say.

"Grant? Hello, are you there?" It was Daniel.

"Yeah," Grant managed to get out. Talking was the last thing he wanted to do. Words were pointless now.

"What happened? Where are you?"

"They're dead," Grant whispered, choking on another sob.

"Are you sure?" Daniel replied. "Have you checked them? We thought *you* were dead at first, too."

Grant felt the headache in his temple again and tried blinking it away. It subsided, and he reached out a hand to feel Morgan's body.

"Morgan's cold. I can't find a pulse."

"Hmm," Daniel said with a clinical tone. "You were cold too, but we eventually found a faint pulse on you. Maybe hers is too faint to detect. What else can you see?"

"Hang on . . ." he mumbled. He stood up on his haunches and carefully rolled Morgan over onto her back. "She's got a nasty bruise on her forehead. She must've hit the corner of the table as she fell."

Daniel's words escaped quickly. "Grant, *dead people don't bruise.*"

Grant gasped slightly, a glimmer of hope flickering to life. "Are you sure?" he asked, examining the egg-shaped bruise up-close.

"It's impossible," Daniel said, still talking fast. "When a body dies, blood stops flowing. Without blood flow, a corpse can't develop a new bruise, no matter what you do to it."

Grant's mind spun, and his eyes landed on the ring on her right hand, middle finger.

A ring can be removed after its wearer dies. He remembered her speaking those words to him.

He cradled the phone between his neck and shoulder, and grabbed Morgan's ring and tugged at it. It didn't budge.

His heart skipped a beat and he swallowed. "I think you're right," he said into the phone, his voice growing stronger now. "I think they're still alive!"

Daniel said nothing.

"But how do—what do I *do?*" Grant said.

Daniel's reply was excruciatingly slow in coming. "I've never heard of anything like this before. If they're not dead, then they must be in some kind of catatonia, like you were. If we only knew what it was that woke you up . . ." Daniel said, thinking aloud.

Grant's thoughts shot back to his dream and lingered there.

"You still have no idea what roused you?" Daniel asked when Grant didn't reply.

"Not . . . exactly," he said quietly.

"Well, there's obviously a connection between what happened to you and what happened to them," Daniel began reasoning again. "You're all on parallel paths of some kind . . ."

Grant sat up straight. "What did you say?"

"I said you're all on . . ." he began, but Grant was no longer listening. Something had just triggered in his mind.

275

How did the woman in his dream say it?

"You must ask yourself what you are willing to endure to reach the journey's end. Are you willing to sacrifice? Are you willing to absorb your greatest fear and make it part of your very being?"

He closed his eyes and remembered the look on her face.

Are you willing? she had said.

I don't want to hurt, he thought. *But I am willing.*

"Grant, are you still there?" Daniel's voice was saying into the phone.

Grant's demeanor had changed, a new resolve now set deep into his bones.

"I'll call you back," he said, and hung up the phone.

He knelt down beside Morgan on the floor, and with a deep, long breath . . . he let go. Let go of his fear, his doubt. His questions and frustrations. His desires and needs. His anger at life for doing this to him.

He released it all.

His heart fluttered, and immediately the pain returned and seized him once more.

But this time, instead of fighting, he disappeared into it.

Its ferocity was beyond imagining, but he didn't struggle. He relaxed and let it overtake him.

Grant managed to force his eyes open as the pain surged through him and he saw that the light had returned. His ring was glowing again, as were all of the others around him, growing and shimmering.

The pain increased again. Scorching and fierce. Every inch of his skin felt as though it was being ripped apart, his bones being crushed into powder. His nerve endings sizzled like cattle prods. His blood raced through his veins like scalding hot oil, burning him from the inside out. And his heart was pumping much too fast . . .

He was sure he would pass out any moment now, and he would welcome it when it came. No one could withstand this kind of pain and remain conscious. It had to be scientifically impossible, as Daniel would probably tell him.

Yet the pain grew larger still, and he remained awake and aware. It became so potent that he could no longer tell one part of his body from another. It melted together and burst outward as though every molecule in his body was being rent and torn from every other.

And for one, brief glimpse of a moment, his senses extended far beyond himself and he touched them . . . *all* the Loci, everywhere.

Then he felt his lungs gasp in a deep breath of air. Slowly—very slowly—he became aware that the pain was subsiding. Feeling returned to his limbs, and his breathing began to slow. His heart decelerated as well, and his blood no longer burned like acid. It dwindled farther and farther until he felt a tingling sensation all over, and his familiar headache, now a dull echo of a whisper.

Grant opened his eyes and massaged his temples as he looked around the facility. He'd never felt so tired in his life.

The light from the rings was gone.

And silence was no longer the only sound he heard.

Morgan's chest was rising and falling in normal rhythm. The others were breathing as well, and some of them were beginning to stir.

Grant couldn't remember when he'd begun to cry, but his cheeks were soaking wet now, and more tears soon joined them. He could barely move, the after-effects of the pain too crippling.

Yet despite this, he couldn't stop an enormous smile from spreading across his face.

Grant hung up the phone and returned it to his pocket, dwelling on how eager he was to get back home and talk to Hannah, see with his own eyes that she was okay.

As he slowly waddled back into the Common Room, which was now bustling with activity, he drew a number of wide-eyed stares. None of the Loci had any idea what had happened; they knew only that they were alive thanks to him.

Grant made a careful beeline for Morgan, who was watching him from her chair across the room, as Fletcher, per usual, was murmuring in her ear. Meanwhile, another resident—a young girl—was rubbing some kind of ointment on Morgan's forehead with a small cloth.

Grant eased slowly into the chair opposite Morgan, cautious not to overextend his aching muscles.

"Can you tell us what happened?" she asked.

"I think I *understand* what happened, but I don't think I can explain it," he replied, still smiling for no apparent reason. He was beyond tired, yet his body surged with excitement.

"Think about *trying*," Fletcher said, his mouth a thin, tight line.

Morgan turned away from the girl who was nursing her bruise and threw a nasty gaze at Fletcher.

He shivered, despite himself.

Morgan spoke. "I know the rings glowed before we all lost consciousness—all of them. And that's something that's . . . rare, at best."

"But it has happened before?" Grant asked.

"I'm not certain what triggers it, but it always seems to be a precursor to something significant. I've witnessed 'multiple glows' when someone new is given a ring, for example, but I don't believe that to be the only time it happens."

A moment passed in silence.

"I think *I* did it. Whatever happened to you all, I believe I'm responsible for it," Grant said. "But it was something that *had* to happen. I don't know why, I just know it did."

"How do you know?" Morgan said, creasing her brow.

"Because everything's changed," Grant said. "I can feel it."

"Feel what?" Fletcher said.

"*You*," Grant replied. "I have this . . . *sense* of all of you. Not like I can read your minds or feel your feelings. I just have a very strong impression of you. Like I can close my eyes and still see you."

Neither Morgan nor Fletcher spoke as they considered this and studied him. For once, Grant found he didn't mind their stares, nor that of the other Loci. He was still smiling, though he was so drained his eyes were trying to close by themselves.

"So you're saying," Morgan spoke up, "some type of connection has been . . . switched 'on' . . . or forged between you and the rest of us?"

The Forging.

"Yeah," he replied, looking far away. "That's probably a good word for it . . . And none of you experienced the pain that I did?"

Morgan shook her head. "We should be thirsty and starved, but we're fine."

He didn't reply, as she continued watching him.

"What do you think it means?" Grant said at last, ending with a yawn.

She shook her head again, her eyebrows raised. "This is new territory for all of us."

40

Despite his profound fatigue, Grant lay awake most of the night, staring at the ceiling and trying to sort out the Forging. Things were becoming clearer, and he'd made up his mind that it was now time to chase down Evers' clue. He needed to return to his boyhood home. But even with that concluded, other concerns nagged him.

His conflicted feelings for Hannah, for one. They had plans to meet up late afternoon at the asylum.

And then there was the Keeper . . .

Who are you? Grant thought.

Finally well before dawn, he gave up pretending. Sleep would not come. Bleary-eyed and depleted, he roused himself and began preparing for the day, particularly for the inevitable conversation with Julie. How would she handle the idea that their father could still be alive and in hiding somewhere? That during all these years, he'd never bothered to contact them?

How would she feel about returning to their childhood home?

Will she dread it as much as I do?

Then again, she might want *to go . . .*

Grant dressed and left the apartment before his sister was awake.

He descended in the elevator to the parking garage and the door chimed, then it opened.

Some small part of him expected to see Alex. It seemed like time for one of their encounters, but he was greeted only by the silence of the garage.

Grant took a tired step toward his car when there was a flash of movement before his eyes and somehow, he was flying through the air. He crashed into the side of a nearby car and slumped to the ground, rattled. His instincts were telling him to roll, to get to his feet, to look up. But the sleepiness and soreness were too pronounced, his reflexes too sluggish.

Grant struggled to his feet and looked around through bleary eyes. No one. He was all alone in the hollow surroundings of the garage. He shook the cobwebs out of his brain. He may have been tired, but not *that* tired. Whatever just happened—he didn't imagine it.

But he hadn't seen anyone there and couldn't see anyone now.

With a start, he heard a sound from behind and turned to look, yet saw nothing.

But wait, there *was* . . . Something itching at the edge of his awareness. He was too drained to concentrate on it fully, but it was a familiar sensation. He could feel the presence of another.

Grant listened in silence but only heard the sounds of the elevator descending. Finally, he walked toward the car again.

He made it halfway across the garage, when there was another glimpse of movement out of the corner of his eye. Then Grant found himself lying on the ground, a throbbing pain in his stomach, where it seemed he'd been kicked.

"All right!" he shouted. "Who—"

A flash of movement later, and there was a figure standing above him, holding a very long, thin sword that curved slightly along the far end of the blade. It had an unusually long handle, and its tip was only inches from Grant's left eye.

He froze.

Out of his other eye, he made out the shape of the man holding the sword, standing over him. He was shorter than Grant, thin with bulging muscles. He wore a simple black jumpsuit. He was bald.

The man's hands were covered by tight leather gloves, but Grant knew—he could *feel*—a ring hiding under one of those gloves.

"What's wrong with you?" asked the man, his deep-throated British accent neither offering an accusation nor sarcasm; he was genuinely curious. "It should not be this easy." He had a gruff manner and spoke in an all-business tone.

Grant said nothing. The man's sword was so close to his eye, he was afraid to move or provoke him. And Grant's mind was too tired to try anything just now . . .

The man pulled the sword back a few inches. "Up."

Grant complied slowly, and as he rose, so did the sword. When Grant was upright, the man was gone, reappearing at his left side. He brought the sword around and up in a quick slice with one hand. He stopped cold when its tip made contact with the underside of Grant's head, just below his chin. He made a small nick there, enough to bring forth a drop of blood that oozed down Grant's neck.

The attacker held his sword in position with a stillness carved out of stone.

Grant tried to be calm, his chin angled upward to keep from making the incision worse. He held his breath, afraid any movement would project his head downward into the razor-sharp blade.

The man looked him up and down. Finally he shook his head.

"You're a pathetic child," he said, incredulous. "Lost and barely conscious."

The man walked slowly in a semicircle around Grant, ending when they were face to face. Still he held the sword so that its tip never lost contact with Grant's neck.

Grant dared to speak, causing his throat to vibrate against the tip of the sword. "What do you want?" He could barely get the words out, his voice quivering.

"You don't even know who you are," the man decided, disgust evident in his voice.

Finally, he pulled the sword back a few inches—enough for Grant to stand at ease. "I'll not kill a pitiful, untrained fool. Go and rest. Prepare yourself. *Then* we shall begin again."

As far as the other man was concerned, that seemed to be that. He held out the sword, but only in a defensive posture. Grant assumed he was free to go.

He let out a shaky breath and glanced down at the sword again. It was then that he saw there was a row of symbols etched along the length of the blade. The symbols looked familiar.

"What do you want with me?" he said, stalling for time as he stared at the symbols, memorizing them.

The man stood unmoving, the sword still pointed at Grant. "I have no interest in *you*," he replied. "My quarrel is with the *abomination*." His voice full of menace, he made a swift slice through the air, after which Grant felt a stinging pain on the top of his hand. He flinched and withdrew the hand. A bleeding gash extended from Grant's wrist in a straight line down his hand, forming a red line that was unmistakably pointing at his ring.

"I will not show mercy twice," the man replied calmly, straightening himself up and sheathing the sword. "*Go. I'm allowing you this one chance to ready yourself. Use it.*"

There was a blur, and Grant was suddenly alone, cradling his bleeding hand in silence.

One heartbeat later, he blacked out.

As the sun was rising, Morgan and Fletcher made their way from room to room throughout the asylum, on his suggestion that they check to make sure everyone "really *did* wake up."

They knocked on doors and carefully peeked inside. Everyone they encountered was perfectly fine—most of them still sleeping soundly.

After a while of this, Fletcher closed another door and continued their private conversation.

"And you don't think there's any chance he did this on purpose?" he asked.

Their feet clicked in unison as they walked down a lonely hallway in the back of the building.

"It's obvious he didn't," Morgan replied, her matter-of-fact tone leaving no room for argument. "He was in tremendous pain."

Fletcher was quiet as they walked along.

"What?" she finally said, noticing his look of frustration.

"If he didn't do it on purpose, then that's even worse!" he cried as they walked.

Morgan stopped, near another door. It was Marta's room.

"How is it worse?" she asked.

"If Grant didn't do . . . whatever he did . . . on purpose," he cried, exasperated, "then that means he has no control over what he's capable of. Who knows what he might do next!"

She turned away from him and knocked on Marta's door. When

there was no reply, she assumed Marta was asleep and opened it.

"Look, I know you trust him, and you probably feel like this was all part of some grand scheme," Fletcher was saying. "But personally, I just feel lucky that we all survived."

"We didn't," she whispered. .

He followed her gaze inside the room to the old woman lying on the bed.

Marta's eyes were open, staring at nothing. Her jaw was slack. Her body stiff.

She was dead.

Lisa was lost in thought as she boarded the elevator. She punched in the number for the penthouse, knowing that she could find Daniel there.

He was *always* there.

Lisa and Daniel had become "roommates" in a spare apartment on the floor beneath Grant's place, where she was supposed to be helping him recuperate. But upstairs was where she continuously found him.

She couldn't really blame him for it. Grant's home was certainly where all the action was.

Still, they had that nice, cushy apartment all to themselves . . . and Daniel was only a handful of days out from the attempt on his life. He had a lot of mending to do. She couldn't help wishing, as long as they had to be cooped up in this place, that they might use this time to become better . . . *friends*.

At least, to start with.

It didn't *all* have to be about Grant, did it?

Lisa put her key in the door to Grant's apartment. She half-expected to find Daniel napping in his wheelchair. She'd put a stop to that, it was time to get started with his physical therapy . . .

Instead, she found him at Grant's computer, leaning, squinting into the screen.

"Hey!" she called.

Daniel jumped, and turned off the monitor, knocking the mouse off of the desk in the process.

"Hi," he said distractedly.

"What are you doing?" she asked.

"Just . . . keeping up with the latest science journals," he said, glancing quickly back at the now-dark monitor. "Seeing if there's anything new in parapsychology. Figured it might help the cause."

"Well," she said, "there's plenty of time for research later. Right now, it's time to start working on retraining those muscles of yours."

His shoulders sank. Physical therapy was at the very bottom of his priority list. "All right."

Lisa had him successfully using power bands on his broken arm in under ten minutes. Considering Lisa had no training for this, other than some homework she'd done on the Internet, she felt this was a good beginning. And Grant had offered to help as well . . .

Where was Grant, anyway?

Daniel was beginning to complain that the work was hurting too much when the front door to the apartment burst open.

Grant stood in the doorway. His eyes were drooping, his hair a tangled mess, his clothes rumpled—and his hand was bleeding.

"Grant!" Daniel shouted, losing his concentration on his work and accidentally firing the power band across the room like a slingshot.

"He knew . . ." Grant mumbled, disjointed. "He knew who I am . . ." He staggered inside, ignoring the open door behind him, and threw his keys onto the kitchen counter. He seemed to be having trouble keeping his legs steady.

"What's wrong?" Daniel shouted. "What happened to your hand?"

Grant looked up, noticing them for the first time.

"How did . . . how did he know?" Grant said, barely intelligible.

He collapsed.

41

As he so often did—as he had done nearly every night since the Shift—Grant startled himself awake, screaming.

"Easy!" cried a female voice. It was Julie. She had been sitting across the room, leaning back in a chair, her nose buried in a book, but now she was on her feet and at his side. "Take it easy, honey."

"How long—"

"Ten hours," she replied. "How do you feel?"

"Man, are *you* a snoozer," came a voice from the door. Lisa stood there, hands on her hips.

Grant rose from the bed and walked to the bedroom's picture window, looking out at the late afternoon sun covering the city below.

"Ten hours . . . he'll be coming soon . . ." he mumbled to himself. *What do I do?*

Daniel wheeled himself into the room on his own, complaining about how sadistic Lisa was for refusing to help him get around for "at least two hours," while Grant was sleeping.

Grant walked to Julie's chair, grabbed the book out of it, and flipped to an empty page in the back. He found a pen on his nightstand and made a quick sketch, and then handed the book to Daniel.

"You ever seen symbols like that before?" Grant asked.

"No . . ." Daniel studied it carefully. "Never. They're suggestive of the markings on your ring, though."

"Yeah . . . they really are . . ." Grant said, turning to look out the window again, lost in thought.

285

"Collin, what's going on?" Julie asked. "How'd you get that gash on your hand?"

Grant glanced down at the bandages they'd applied to the cut. "A man attacked me as I was leaving this morning. I couldn't even touch him. He used this sword . . . And those symbols were on it."

"A *sword*. Really?" Lisa mused.

The others turned to look at her.

"If you want to kill somebody, there are easier ways," she said into their stares. "If he chose a sword over a gun, he must've had a reason for it."

"He's good at it," Grant summed it up. "That's reason enough."

Grant looked back at Daniel. "The way this guy talked, he was . . . formal. He *let* me go because I was too tired to fight. It was like an 'honor' thing. But he's coming back, and he expects me to be 'prepared' when he gets here."

"You have to run," Julie said, as if it was obvious and she couldn't believe she was the only one saying it. "Collin, you have to get out of here, leave town, and don't look back. I'll come with you, we'll go somewhere he can't find us—"

"No," Grant said, stern but resigned. "Running won't help. This guy . . . he's not like Konrad. He's different."

Daniel nodded. "Well," he said, eyes darting back and forth in thought, "I'll help you practice your skills until he shows up. But being prepared also means knowing all you can about your opponent. And the only real clue we have to his identity is the sword."

"That's not the *only* clue we have," Grant said, taking a moment to look each of them in the eye, in turn. "He was wearing a ring. He's one of the Loci."

Daniel whistled. "So that means—"

"He has some sort of mental power, yeah. Thing is . . . he moved fast. Like, *impossibly* fast. I don't see how something like that could be a *mental* power."

"You think maybe he works for this 'Keeper' person Alex told you about?" Julie offered.

"The sword is the key," Daniel repeated. "We need to find out everything we can about it."

"Research girl to the rescue," Lisa chimed in, turning to leave.

"Wait," Grant said. He took the book from Daniel's hands and ripped out the page he'd drawn on. "Could you get a copy of this to Morgan? She might know something about these symbols."

"Okay." She left.

Daniel held up the small device he'd used the day before to test Grant's brainpower. "I can adapt this to alert us if anyone else with mental powers enters the building."

Grant nodded. "Good. That's good."

"You should rest," Julie said, trying to maneuver him back to the bed.

"No, I can't, there's no time—"

"There's *never* time! Morgan was right! You need to slow down. You're running headlong from one thing to the next, when you need to stop and deal with what's happened to you."

Grant fixed her with a stare. "Tell that to the maniac with the sword who wants to run me through."

Daniel watched the two of them in silence for a moment, before gesturing with his good arm toward the living room. "If everything else is settled, we'd better get started."

Three hours later, Grant and Daniel paused for dinner. Daniel was pleased at how quick a study Grant had proven to be. Yet he was his own worst critic as well, never feeling that his efforts were powerful enough to beat this new foe.

They started with simple things—books, matchsticks, CDs, picture frames. Before they'd stopped, Grant was stretching out his arm to "grab" larger, more complex objects. Tables, bookcases, even the sofa.

At the very least, Grant relished that no panicking was required in his efforts, and those mind-blistering headaches vanished as well.

Julie watched the news as the two of them practiced, and was pleased to report that most of the media had pushed him back to brief "still at large" mentions over halfway into the evening broadcasts. At this rate, she suggested, he'd be forgotten by the weekend.

As they sat eating, discussing Grant's progress and theories on who the mysterious man with the sword could be, Grant's phone rang. Morgan's name appeared in the display.

"Hello, Grant. How are you holding up?"

"Morgan, hi. Did Lisa find you okay?"

"Yes, she left here to return to your place some time ago," Morgan replied. She took a deep breath. "We've turned up a few answers about this man with the sword, but there's very little that's definitive."

Grant put the phone on speaker, so Julie and Daniel could hear. "Tell me."

"Well, to start with, I compared the stone tablet with these symbols you sent me—the ones you saw on the sword."

"And?"

"The symbols from the sword are on the tablet as well. If I could translate the rest of the tablet, we may find out more about both of you, but I feel like I'm hitting a brick wall here. You're *positive* this man was one of the Loci?"

"Yeah. I could feel him."

"Hmm. The fact that these particular symbols are on the tablet means that whoever this man is . . . he has a part to play in all of this." She paused, silence lingering in the air. "I heard a story once—I rather thought it was embellished—from one of the private detectives I hired to find the stone tablet fragments. He said he saw a man carrying a sword, dressed in black, who *exterminated* an entire police squadron in Chile. They called him 'the Thresher.'"

"The Thresher . . ."

"Grant, there's something else. Over the years, during my travels and then here at the asylum, I've heard whispers of a group—a *society*—that exists. They are rumored to know everything about our rings: where they come from, how they work, and why they exist. But we have no understanding of their agenda."

"Why didn't you mention this before?"

"Because I had no reason to believe it was true before," replied Morgan.

It was only a second before Grant caught on. "You think Mr. Slice-and-Dice is a member of this secret society? That what—he's acting on their orders to kill me?"

"I don't even know if they exist. But the symbols from the tablet appearing on his sword clearly suggest that there's a much larger plot at work. I wanted you to be aware."

"All right," he said with a sigh.

There was a knock at the door.

"She's back," Daniel said, breathing a sigh of relief.

"What about the name?" Grant asked, walking to the door. "What's a 'thresher'?"

"There's a species of shark called the thresher, of the genus *Alopias*," Morgan said in a schoolteacher tone. "They keep mostly to themselves, though they *are* predators. The thresher has an exceptionally long, thin tail that it uses as a weapon.

He turned the knob to let Lisa in.

Wait, Lisa wouldn't knock, I gave her a key . . .

And suddenly he was standing toe-to-toe with the Thresher.

They both froze.

"You look rested," the bald man said, sizing him up. "Thank you."

The sword appeared in a flash. Grant took a swing at his opponent, but the man vanished. Then when he jerked his head to the left he found the man with the sword standing right beside him.

42

Daniel looked up as he heard a sharp bang from a few feet away. The front door had been blown off its hinges and the Thresher was lying out in the hall.

"Better," said a voice at the door. The Thresher stood there, but none of them had seen him rise from the floor.

At his side stood Grant, breathing fast with a panicked look on his face. Julie crouched behind Daniel's chair and helped him right it.

He's losing control again . . . Daniel thought.

The Thresher made a counterclockwise twist, sword extended. The blade made a deep gash in Grant's left shoulder.

No, not just one gash. There were three of them, like bloody military stripes down Grant's arm.

How is he doing this? Daniel wondered.

Grant gestured toward the coffee table with an outstretched hand and it flew up off of the floor toward his attacker, but the Thresher pivoted in place and sliced it down the middle. He ducked to avoid the two halves, and Daniel used the opportunity to move.

"No!" Julie screamed.

"RUN!" Daniel yelled, crashing his wheelchair into the Thresher from behind, knocking him over.

Grant hesitated only a second. Then he propelled Julie forward with his mind, grabbed her by the hand when she was close enough, and the two of them were gone, out the door and down the hall. They jumped into the elevator just as the doors were closing.

The Thresher was on his feet and spun in the air, sword in hand once again . . . when he stopped, the blade was less than an inch from Daniel's neck.

But he held it there, examining Daniel in his wheelchair for the first time.

He brought the sword up above his head and then swung it down hard against the gasket bolt attached to the chair's left wheel. The wheel immediately fell off of the axle and the chair collapsed.

He turned and stalked out the door after Grant, leaving Daniel helpless and immobilized, all his injuries crying again in agony.

Grant swung into the driver's seat as Julie was already buckling herself into the passenger's side. She flicked the switch that mechanically extended the top until it was up, covering the cab, as Grant brought the engine to life.

"Um," Julie said, her eyes growing as she stared straight ahead, across the parking aisle to the next row, "now would be a good time to go."

Grant followed her gaze just in time to see a man on a high-powered motorcycle racing down the row parallel to them at dangerous speeds. The man on the bike had a sword hanging from his hip.

Grant put the car in reverse and jammed the pedal, swinging out in a right-reverse turn. He threw the Corvette into drive while they were still moving backward, causing the tires' rubber to spin against the pavement. They began moving forward just as the motorcycle turned down their aisle and raced toward them from behind.

The two vehicles remained only a few feet apart as they drove in circles, spiraling down through the parking garage until they came to the street level. Grant was immediately reminded of the snake strangling him in his dreams but there was no time to dwell on it. The electronic gate ahead allowed only residents to enter or exit the garage via a keycard.

Grant floored it, racing toward the gate at fifty miles an hour.

"You *do* see that, right?" a nervous Julie said, leaning back in her seat.

"Down!" Grant yelled.

She ducked and they crashed through the gate and kept going.

Julie turned around to look. "Well, you own the building, so I guess it's okay."

Grant swerved into the left-hand lane, which was unusually empty, and the man on the motorcycle broke out from behind them and came around to the right lane, appearing at the car's passenger side.

"Down!" Grant screamed again.

Her head ducked just as the sword came slashing across the side window, shattering it. Grant swerved right to slam into the motorcycle, which veered away.

Julie sat back up to see them racing ahead of the motorcycle, which was falling behind in the midday traffic.

"Who *is* this guy?" she breathed.

Grant poured on more speed as they entered a busier downtown street, darting dangerously around other cars, trucks, and buses. He glanced into the rearview mirror and saw that the motorcycle was further back now, but keeping pace.

"I thought the rings only give you enhanced *mental* abilities," Julie went on, bracing herself against the side of the car as Grant turned again, ignoring a red light. "Why would extra brainpower let him move super-fast?"

"I don't know!" Grant replied, jerking the steering wheel to the right and narrowly missing the rear fender of a pickup truck that was slowing down to turn. "Maybe he can manipulate time or something."

Julie looked back. "His motorcycle isn't going any faster than the regular variety."

Grant turned left, running a red light and flying through a narrow gap in the oncoming traffic. Julie screamed as the oncoming cars swerved and fishtailed into one another. Straight ahead was the ramp for the 110. The motorcycle quickly appeared and closed the gap between them.

"He's catching up," Julie warned, watching behind again and clutching the door handle with white knuckles.

The Corvette rocketed up the on-ramp and hurtled onto the freeway, finding just enough of a gap between cars to race to an open lane. Grant swerved wildly in and out of the traffic, and immediately the man on the motorcycle shifted lanes to the left to come up beside Grant.

"Hold on!" Grant shouted.

He jerked the car to the right, out onto the shoulder, and slammed the gas. The Corvette growled in appreciation and blasted forward. Soon the other cars on the highway were little more than blurry colors speeding by as the Corvette raced down the edge of the road at well over one hundred miles an hour.

Julie clung to her seat as they edged dangerously close to the cement barrier on her side. "Where did you learn to drive like this?" she shouted.

"I *didn't*! Is he still behind us?" Grant said, not daring to look anywhere but straight ahead.

She turned in her seat. "Yes, but he's further back than before."

"How *far* back?"

"Maybe three hundred feet. And getting further away."

Grant let up on the gas, slightly, and they began to slow.

"What are you doing!" Julie shouted as if he were crazy.

"Make sure your belt is tight," Grant replied, glancing into the rear mirror.

The black motorcycle inched closer and closer, but Grant waited. Waited until he knew the other man would be ready to make his move to try and come up beside them again.

The motorcycle was less than thirty feet behind them now, with nothing between the two vehicles.

"What are you going to do?" Julie cried, watching the motorcycle and shivering with the wild motions of the car.

"Stop turning around!" Grant shouted. "And brace yourself!"

She faced forward, clenching the armrests again.

Grant never took his eyes off of the mirror. The motorcycle drew closer, and Grant watched the handlebars, waiting to see them begin to turn.

They turned.

Grant slammed on the car's brakes with both feet, rising up from his seat, and a violent squeal came from the tire assembly that drowned out all other noise on the busy highway.

The motorcycle had just begun to turn left, and now swung around to slam sideways into the rear of the car. The man in the mask flew forward, landing on top of the car.

When the car finally came to a halt several hundred feet away, smoke was rising from all four tires, and the smell of hot rubber permeated the air. Cars, trucks, and SUVs continued speeding by, mere inches from them.

Grant returned to his seat, out of breath, and Julie was trying to catch hers as well. They both looked up, slowly, at the same time, to see the edge of the other man's head, visible at the very top of the windshield. He looked rattled, but he was alive. His eyes blinked open and he shook his head, trying to clear it. Then he stopped, and his eyes focused on the two of them inside the car.

"Um," Julie said a little louder than usual, "he looks *angry*."

Grant punched the gas pedal again, and in the rear-view, he watched as the man rolled off of the car and continued rolling until he came to a stop on the ground far behind them.

Grant merged back into traffic, and picked up speed. Julie, meanwhile, tore a strip off of her shirt around the bottom.

"Put this around your arm before you bleed to death," she said.

His phone rang in his pocket. He reached inside and tossed it to Julie, while he clumsily worked at tying off the cloth around the three gashes in his arm with one hand and his teeth.

"Hello?" she answered the ringing phone, leaning back in her chair, worn out. She closed her eyes.

"It's Morgan," she said, handing him the phone back. Grant took it, his thoughts still focused on putting as much distance as possible between them and the Thresher.

"Grant, are you all right?" Morgan said. "Daniel just telephoned."

"How is he?"

"Lisa's there with him now. They're okay. Listen, I think you should make for the asylum," Morgan said.

"What?! I'm not leading a dangerous sociopath to your front door!"

"He's one of *us*," she replied. "Perhaps we can find a way to reason with him."

"Forget it," Grant said, his voice leaving no room for argument.

"Very well," Morgan said. "But there's one other thing you should keep in mind: This man is mentioned on the tablet, just as you are. This man is connected to your destiny, Grant. Your friend Daniel told you something was coming, and that whatever it is, you would be all that stands between it and humanity. This Thresher may very well be a precursor to whatever it is. He could even be the *thing* that's coming, himself."

Grant's head began to hurt. "Okay . . . one step at a time. Why don't you take a picture of the tablet and email it to Daniel? It would probably be a good idea to put your heads together—"

"Something's happening!" Morgan suddenly shouted. Grant could hear screaming through the phone, distant, and then a boom that thundered so loud that he pulled the phone away from his ear in pain. Even Julie reacted to the sound.

"Morgan?" Grant yelled into the phone.

No one replied but he could hear breathing. Quick, panting breaths.

Another thundering boom echoed into the phone, followed by crashing of what sounded like glass and plywood.

"Morgan, talk to me!" Grant cried.

"They're here!" Morgan whispered, "Grant, come quickly! Here they come, I have to—"

As the line disconnected, the horror of comprehension hit Grant square in the face. In his mind's eye, he could see all of it.

All of *them*. And what was happening to them.

No . . .

NO!!

43

Morgan huddled quietly with the others she'd grabbed on her way into the underground cave. She pressed an ear to the door.

The hidden basement room, where the tablet fragments were stored, was thankfully still hidden. They were using it as a refuge. But the asylum itself was a different story.

Outside, the world had gone insane.

Some residents were screaming as they ran. A few had refused to run and tried going toe-to-toe with the invaders. Sounds of struggle— grunting, striking, yelling—were soon replaced with silence. Heavy footfalls could be heard all around, along with the crash of windows being destroyed and furniture being overturned.

She forced herself to suppress the urge to open the door and try to gather more inside. They would only be surrendering all of their lives.

Grant . . . we need you.

Come quickly!

She had no idea if Grant could hear her or not—if his newfound "feeling" of them, as he called it, would alert him to their danger.

But she knew he was their only hope.

Morgan had her suspicions about who was behind this raid, but she had no doubts whatsoever about what they were after. They wanted the tablet.

Or rather, *he* did.

Almost in answer to her thoughts, a voice rang out.

"Oh, Morga-a-an! Come out and pla-a-ay!" a squeaky, male voice shouted from some distance away.

"Quiet!" she whispered to the few others that had entered the room with her, and were now cowering at the bottom of the stairs.

She pushed the swiveling door open a hair's breadth, and looked out. The Common Room was clear, aside from a few unconscious residents scattered about. *He* wasn't out there—he was somewhere further away.

The asylum couldn't have been easy to break into, she knew. The few windows there were had bars, and she herself had seen to the installation of a fairly advanced security system. Still, if it was who she thought it was, she knew it was only a matter of time before the secret room would be found.

Her people had probably put up a good struggle, she knew. There were no fighters here, but some of the Loci had more esoteric abilities that could come in handy to keep them hidden or help them elude an attacker. They would be scattered throughout the building, panicked, alone.

The assault had come so fast. Out of nowhere.

Another scream rang out, much closer, and the people inside the hidden room had to stifle screams of their own. Morgan listened closely through the door and thought she heard crying. Whoever it was, they were close.

She risked cracking the door open a little more. Across the Common Room stretched over the double-doorway's threshold, she could see a boy—the seventeen-year-old, Thomas, she thought it was—on his hands and knees. He sniffled, tears in his eyes, but those eyes were angry and bloodshot. Someone from behind put a foot into the small of his back, forcing him facedown onto the ground. Morgan couldn't see who it was; they were on the other side of the door.

She didn't need to see who it was. She already knew.

"Morgan! If you're not standing in front of me in ten seconds, this one gets to eat from a straw for the rest of his life!"

Without hesitating, Morgan opened the door just far enough to squeeze out, closed it, and snuck across the outer wall of the Common Room, so the hidden chamber would remain hidden.

When she was far enough away to consider it safe, she stepped in and leveled a gaze at their attacker.

There he stood. Dirty trench coat in place, too-wide tie lying lopsided across his ample belly. And he was grinning. As usual.

"What do you want, Drexel?"

"Do you really have to ask?"

Drexel stepped off of the boy's back and grabbed the back of his T-shirt, pulling him up off the ground. He turned the corner and took a few steps into the Common Room, facing Morgan and holding Thomas around the neck, gun pointed at his head.

Morgan matched his steps, backing away carefully, but not too far.

The boy beneath Drexel's arm was squirming but trying not to, as he was leaning back painfully under Drexel's powerful grip, off-balance and unsure how to stay upright. His cheeks were wet.

"How did you find us?" Morgan asked calmly.

"Got me a stool pigeon," he gamely replied, then called behind him. "C'mon in here, Judas!"

A young woman wearing handcuffs in front walked into the room and looked at Drexel like he was the most revolting thing she'd ever seen.

It's that barefoot girl . . .

Alex.

Morgan stared at her in open shock. "You sold us out?"

"Oh yeah, she was only too eager to give up her secrets." Drexel grinned.

The barefoot girl looked at him angrily and opened her mouth to respond, but Drexel reached out and whacked her in the back of the head with the side of his pistol.

"Now, now," he said. "Remember our agreement, little girl. Every word you say equals one bullet I put in one of the freaks here."

Alex clamped her lips shut, refusing to look at Morgan. Instead, she took a seat near Drexel. Her eyes darted back and forth, looking at nothing, as if she was trying to reason her way through something.

"Didn't you know?" Drexel went on, turning back to Morgan. "She spends all of her time watching you people. If you need to find out something about any of you, there's only one person you need to see."

He winked at Alex, then he gestured to Morgan in mock courtesy. "Let's talk. Take a seat, *please*."

She sat on a couch facing him, and he stepped closer, still clutching the boy under his grip.

"Here's the deal," Drexel began. "We both know why I'm here. I'm not going to bother threatening *you*, because we both know you'd sooner let me shoot you in the face than tell me anything about where to find the stone tablet. So I'm going to kill *them*, instead." He nodded at the unconscious people lying around the room. Some were bleeding. All were bruised.

Morgan's mind raced, sifting through the trillions of pieces of information she could call up at will, trying to think of something, anything she could do to stall. Thomas' ability—a highly advanced aptitude for physics—would be of no use in this situation.

"I'm guessing," Drexel continued, "that seeing your precious followers lined up and killed, one by one, would be the strongest possible motivator for you. So we'll start with this one." He looked down at Thomas, whom he had in a powerful vice around the neck. The boy began turning red.

"You wouldn't know how to read it," Morgan said quietly. "You couldn't possibly have any idea—"

"*Don't* try distracting me with that all that extra gray matter of yours," Drexel interjected. "This really couldn't be simpler. Give me what I want, or this one gets a bullet in the head. Three seconds."

Morgan stood from the couch and took a step closer to him. She looked at Thomas struggling to breathe under Drexel's powerful arm. He wouldn't last.

She looked Drexel in the eye. He was awaiting her response.

"Time's up," he said, smiling again. He cocked the safety back and pressed the pistol so hard into Thomas' temple she thought he might break the boy's skin.

So young . . . Thomas had barely begun living.

He had so much yet to experience . . .

Morgan glanced at Thomas and then looked back up at Drexel. "Shoot him," she said.

Infuriated, Drexel backhanded her across the face with the pistol, and she fell to the floor. But she turned over quickly, resting on her elbows, ignoring the blood oozing from her forehead, and looked at him again.

"I will never help you," Morgan said with icy steel. "You can kill every last one of us—my people know what's at stake. But you will *never* get the tablet!"

A roar of rage escaped Drexel's lips and he threw Thomas to the ground next to her. He leveled the gun on Morgan and pulled the trigger.

Working his horn as heavily as his gas pedal, Grant sped up as he exited the highway and turned onto the surface road where Morgan's facility was located, a few miles outside of just about everything. Neither he nor Julie bothered to speak; their mutual sweat and heart rates were enough to indicate that they were both thinking the exact same thing.

Grant's eyes shifted to the rearview mirror just in time to see something impossible.

The black motorcycle was right behind them again, but the rider wasn't sitting on the seat. He was *standing* on it.

And just as Grant looked up, the man leaped from the seat and flew forward in the air toward them.

There was no time. No time to react, no time to shout a warning, to swerve or duck . . .

The Corvette's fabric top was shredded as the sword slashed vertically down through it.

The sword kept going until it met Grant's right shoulder and pierced his flesh down to the bone.

Grant screamed.

Julie screamed.

He slammed on the brakes, but this time the attacker was ready, bracing himself on his perch atop the car.

Julie wasn't so lucky, her body slamming hard into her seatbelt. The impact and the sudden appearance of the sword were too much of a shock, and she passed out.

Clutching his shoulder, Grant opened the door and let himself spill out onto the empty road. He backed away on his hands and knees.

The attacker jumped from the roof of the car and landed before him on the ground, perfectly balanced. Grant stopped as the sword was pointed at him again. His shoulder ached agonizingly, but he tried to ignore it.

The masked man walked forward until the sword was inches from Grant's face.

"Good chase," he said. "Not good enough."

Grant's hand came up lightning fast and clutched the end of the blade. He focused all his thoughts on the sword. In that split second, the weapon jumped out of the Thresher's hand high into the air and stuck itself in the grassy soil at the edge of the road.

And for that one, brief, glorious second, Grant saw the other man's eyes go wide. Grant didn't know if it was wonder or fear that he saw, and he didn't care. Even if it was only momentary, he'd scored a point.

He didn't waste it. In that same moment, Grant wrapped his legs around the Thresher's, and then straightened them, scissoring the man violently to the ground.

He lunged onto the Thresher, delivering a powerful blow to the head, but his attacker recovered fast and in less than an instant, everything was reversed, and *he* was on top of Grant. It had happened so fast that Grant couldn't stop it.

Punches fell upon Grant's head and stomach, each one coming faster and faster than the one before. Too fast to block. His head turned to the side and he caught sight of a loosely hanging tree limb, on one of the many trees surrounding them aside the lonely road.

As the Thresher continued to strike at him, he focused with all his might on that limb. It broke free and speared through the air, impaling his attacker's arm.

Grant brought both feet up and kicked hard against the man, sending him flying backward.

But he hadn't realized what direction he was facing when he kicked, and he sent the other man sailing toward his sword, still stuck into the ground on the side of the road.

Both men got to their feet at the same time, but the Thresher had his hand around the hilt of his sword before Grant could reach him. By the time Grant was fully standing, he felt a stinging sensation in his stomach and looked down to see a long, straight line of blood stretching across his gut. It wasn't a deep cut, but it stung, and he'd never even seen the swing of the blade.

In the next moment, he was on the ground, his head aching from a strong blow to his jaw.

As the world came into focus around him, he was barely aware of the blade that was once again resting against his throat. Only this time, his attacker stood over him, triumphant.

"I was almost impressed."

He lifted the sword.

"Almost."

44

Gunfire.

Someone was shooting.

Grant's attacker heard it as well, pausing his final strike.

And then, to Grant's great astonishment, the Thresher pulled away, mounted his bike, and roared away. Grant could only lay there in shock, wondering why this man would simply *leave* on the cusp of victory. He was obviously no coward.

"*Collin!*" Julie screamed, exiting the car at last. She bolted to his side and helped him to his feet. Every part of his body ached, his mind bordering on delusion. It was the most brutal attack he'd ever suffered, which, given his history, was saying a lot. The fact that he'd made it out in one piece was as surprising as it was confusing.

Julie practically had to drag him as she gently placed him in the passenger's side of the car. When she was safely in the driver's seat, Grant mumbled through split, bleeding lips, his eyes only half open.

"Where'd he go?"

Julie followed the Thresher's line of exit and it finally hit her. "Wait, isn't the asylum that way?"

Grant would have thought he was out of adrenaline, but somehow it spiked once more.

"GOOO!" he bellowed.

Drexel's bullet only grazed Morgan, though his aim had been true. Something threw him off balance, slamming into him from the side.

On the floor now, Drexel turned to see that Alex was on top of him, kicking and tearing with everything she had. It was a feeble effort; she was unable to cause the big man any pain. He plucked her off of him with one arm and flung her across the room to join Morgan and the boy on the ground.

Morgan was unconscious, bleeding from the graze just above her left ear.

The gun had fallen out of Drexel's hand when Alex pushed him, so he freed the baton that was dangling from the other side of his belt.

"*Big* mistake, girly-girl," he growled, returning to his feet, spinning the stick threateningly in his hands. He advanced on them.

"Not as big as yours," said a quiet, gravelly voice from behind.

Drexel spun but was too late.

The Thresher was on him in a burst of furious motion, the stick flying free of Drexel's hand along with the belt it had been attached to. The gun was nowhere in sight as the Thresher stood atop him, eyes flaring.

"Do you know what your mistake was?" the Thresher said calmly. "It was getting in my way."

"*You*," Drexel breathed, recognizing the other man. Then he laughed. "This is a pretty bold move, don't you think? Crashing a party where you're severely outnumbered?"

"The only person outnumbered here," said Grant's weary voice from the front door, "is *you*, Detective. Your keystone cops ran when they saw *him* coming," Grant nodded toward the Thresher. "I'm getting the feeling that you two have already met."

Drexel threw the Thresher off of him, toward the hallway, and surprised everyone with the fluidity of his massive frame lumbering in the Thresher's direction. The other man was already on his feet, but Drexel crashed into him like a linebacker, plowing him through the double doors.

The Thresher didn't stop to think. He gave in to instinct, springing straight up and driving his fist into the air. It collided with Drexel's chin and knocked him backward onto his rear end.

Drexel had barely hit the ground when he swung his meaty arm into the Thresher's head. Drexel was on top of the other man now, but the Thresher kicked him backward over his head—an astonishing feat for his lithe frame. Drexel swept the Thresher's feet out from under him and the bald man landed with a heavy thud. Drexel jumped to his feet and ran for the front door.

Grant stepped aside, out of his path, but the double doors sprung to life, crashing together in Drexel's face as he reached them. Then he was flying through the air, and landed roughly on the cracked cement at the bottom of the front steps.

Drexel regrouped fast and threw himself onto Grant, pinning him to the ground. He pressed both hands against Grant's larynx, and Grant fought the sudden weariness rising within him.

Sleep was a tangible thing that he could reach out and touch . . . and he *wanted* it . . .

Instead he turned his head to the side and focused on the Thresher, who was approaching.

But he couldn't focus. The world was too dark.

Drexel spoke.

"You probably think I'm just a dirty cop who dabbles in profiteering, making shady choices to get ahead. You may even think I'm redeemable. But I want you to know the *truth* about the man who defeated you, Grant: *I crave the shadow.* The thought of breaking all two hundred and six bones in your body, one by one, *slowly* . . . before I let you die . . . It gives me cold chills."

Grant could barely keep his eyes open as the darkness took hold of him.

But instead of passing out, the pressure on his throat eased up and he could see again.

Alex stood above the both of them, holding Drexel's gun in both hands. But she held it steady, unwaveringly trained on him.

The detective twisted to look up. "You wouldn't . . ." he said.

The Thresher appeared over Alex's shoulder and inspected the situation, the fury evident in Alex's eyes. "I rather think she would," he said simply.

But before Alex got the chance, the Thresher's sword was out again and Drexel's weight atop Grant was gone. He sat up gingerly and saw the Thresher holding Drexel at knifepoint. Drexel was seated on the ground, back up against the driver's side of Grant's car.

Grant gasped angrily for air. Not knowing where the strength within him came from, he stood and wrenched the gun from Alex's hands, joining the Thresher to look down at Drexel in victory. He leveled the gun on Drexel's head.

"Shall I finish it," the Thresher whispered, "or will you?"

The pain and the rage were fueling his movements now, yet Grant's finger hesitated on the trigger. It would be so quick, so easy, to pull that trigger. He didn't even need the gun in his hand. He could just *think* it, and Drexel's head would pop like a grape.

"No, Grant! You *can't*!" Julie shouted, emerging from the other side of the car. "Never give in, never surrender! Remember?"

She rounded the car slowly, watching the fire in Grant's eyes blaze.

Her hand grasped the top of his right wrist, and held to the bracelet there. "Don't forget who you really are," she said softly. "Don't throw away the goodness inside of you—not for *him*."

Grant watched Drexel, saw the fear in his eyes. And suddenly, he stepped back, breathing slower. He turned to Julie with tears in his eyes and embraced her.

"You called me Grant," he whispered in her ear.

She pulled away and smiled.

The Thresher watched all of this dispassionately. "If that's your decision . . ." He brought the sword up and was about to strike . . .

"Payton?" asked a voice from the asylum doorway. A disbelieving voice.

Grant knew that voice.

In the reflection of the blade, he saw her approaching. White hair . . . Middle aged . . .

It was Morgan.

But no, it couldn't be Morgan.

Morgan never goes outside the asylum.

Not for anything.

But there she was, standing on the front steps. She moved slowly forward, daringly stepping within striking distance of the Thresher, but she wasn't looking at his sword.

She was looking into his eyes.

The sword came away from Drexel's neck, and everyone there watched in stunned silence as the blade fell to the ground.

No, that wasn't quite right.

The Thresher had *thrown* it down.

Morgan stared at the man before her, dumbfounded.

"*Payton?*" she cried. "Is it really you?"

"No, love," his soft British accent intoned. "Payton is *dead.*"

The blood drained from Morgan's face.

"You left him to die," Payton said. "Remember?"

45

Morgan and Payton stood five feet apart, faces grim, staring at one another. This run-down courtyard, continents away from where they'd last been together seemed hardly the place for a reunion.

Yet here they were.

Morgan looked into Payton's eyes. The eyes she remembered so well. The eyes she could get lost in and feel safer than anyplace else in the world.

But she barely recognized them. Their warmth had been replaced by a steely coldness that chilled her to the bone.

A small crowd began to gather, pouring from the front door. And Alex stood by, watching with tremendous interest. But Morgan and Payton noticed none of this. The world was empty to them, aside from one another.

They heard nothing else, saw nothing else. Refused to blink.

Neither of them spoke. Morgan was still flushed with shock, but Payton faced her calmly, hands clasped behind his back. Birds and crickets chirped in the surrounding trees, but otherwise not a sound was heard.

Grant watched, waiting for someone to speak. Considered speaking himself to break the tension but decided against it.

This man who stood before them—this warrior with a sword who had attacked and nearly killed him, and moved faster than anyone could see—this couldn't *possibly* be the man Morgan had once been in love with.

Could he?

She had certainly never mentioned that he knew how to fight. The way Morgan had described him, he sounded more like a hopeless romantic.

Payton extended his right arm to point at Grant.

"If you lot knew who this man really is," Payton seethed, "you wouldn't be helping him. You would *beg* me to kill him."

Morgan didn't flinch, though a trickle of blood from her head wound dripped onto her shirt. "I *do* know who he is. It's *you* that concerns me. You look like Payton . . ."

Payton took a step closer to her, a mixture of emotions broiling just beneath his surface. "Oh, it's me. No parlor trick. But I am not the man you remember with that flawless memory of yours."

"Certainly not," Morgan stood her ground. "The man I knew was a man of peace. He would *never* have taken another life."

"Nine years is a long time, love."

Morgan tried to keep up a composed appearance, but her breathing had changed, her eyes were shifting around, and her entire body had become tense. "I don't understand. Any of this. What's happened to you?"

"*You* happened. That day in France, when I pushed you out of the way of the cave-in, only to have you leave me for dead while you saved yourself. Everything that happened to both of us after that was a direct result of *your* decision. You could say it was a defining moment."

"You can't possibly think I left you in that cave, knowing you had *any* chance of living. I held your hand until it went cold, I can still remember—"

"Did you have any idea how much I *lived* for you?" he spat, taking a step closer to her. "Did you know that if it had been you buried beneath the earth, I would *still* be there, holding your hand? I would have found a way to get you out. I would have done *something* . . . After I was Shifted, you were the one bright spot in an existence turned upside-down, the one source of hope I had. I would have done *any-thing*—" He broke off, looking away. Then his gaze pierced hers again. "If it had been you, I wouldn't have been able to live. Do you get that? Did you have any clue how *deep* my feelings ran?"

Morgan went pale, then she whispered, "I don't think I did."

"You want to know what's happened to me?" Payton said, his voice rising. He took another step closer until mere inches separated them. "I did what I had to do, to live without you."

She looked down.

"*Forget* the man who loved you," Payton went on, right in her face. "I am not that raving mad, lovesick child who held to the notion that love could make anything better. That man *died* nine years ago. You won't be seeing him again."

A few tears escaped Morgan's eyes as she whispered, still looking down, "Who has taken his place?"

"Someone you don't want to know."

Morgan, Grant could tell, was using every measure at her disposal to keep her composure. He had always known her to be so calm and wise, that even in the short time he'd gotten to know her, he could see that now she was in a turmoil that was unprecedented. She closed her eyes and squeezed out a few more tears while Payton stared her down, daring her to respond.

She took several deep breaths and then forced herself to look at Payton once more.

"What do you want with *him*?" Morgan quietly asked, nodding to Grant.

Payton answered slowly, over-pronouncing his words as if he were speaking to a child. "I want him to die."

"Grant is not your enemy."

Payton blinked for the first time since spotting Morgan. His eyes shifted over to Grant and then back to Morgan. His body weight shifted back a bit, the slightest hint of confusion creeping across his features.

"His name is Grant?" Payton asked suspiciously. "Grant *Borrows*? This man is the great 'savior of the Loci'?"

Morgan nodded, noting his sudden change.

Payton took a full step back and stared at Grant, a dazed sort of doubt overtaking his features. No one spoke. Grant looked back at him in confusion.

"But he wears the *Seal*," Payton said in clench-jawed protest.

Morgan studied him. "The what?"

"This can't be." Payton looked all around, at the ground, at the sky, at everyone present. "Unless . . . unless I have been misdirected."

"Hey, Drexel's gone!" Alex shouted.

Everyone turned to look, and the detective was nowhere to be seen. The woods closed in thickly around the asylum, and he'd slipped off when Morgan appeared. Grant knew he was out there, but they'd never find him now.

Still Morgan was undeterred from her conversation with Payton. "Does that mean you won't harm Grant?" she asked.

Payton turned sharply as he kicked his sword off of the ground, caught the handle, and swished it until the tip was poking Grant in the chest, all in one movement. Julie cried in protest but Grant pulled her behind him with one hand.

"Even if he *is* this man 'Borrows,' he is still wearing *that*," Payton nodded at Grant's ring. "And the time of the Seal is nearly upon us. I have sworn by blood to prevent his coming, and I will fulfill that vow. But this matter of identity must be resolved."

Grant opened his mouth to explain, but he couldn't think of anything. He was too exhausted. And Payton was already walking away anyway, sheathing his sword.

As he mounted his motorcycle, Grant called out, "Hey!"

Payton turned his head.

"Where'd you get that sword?" Grant asked.

Payton roared the bike's engine to life.

"It was constructed centuries ago for a singular purpose," he replied. "To slay the Bringer."

46

"He always had quick reflexes," Morgan explained an hour later to Grant from behind her desk in the Common Room. Fletcher had joined them, and Julie sat beside Grant, applying bandages to his cuts. "I never made the connection until today that his reflexes could *be* his mental gift . . ."

She was silent for so long that even Julie stopped what she was doing—applying a large bandage around Grant's stomach—to look up.

The stillness of the room caught up with her finally, and Morgan snapped out of her reverie.

"I'm sorry," she said. "I can't reconcile the man I knew with the man we just met. And I can't help suspecting that it's all my fault . . ."

Grant allowed her a moment before he spoke again. "I don't understand how extra brain power enables his *body* to move faster."

Alex approached from behind. "Your physical body is regulated by your mental processes," she said. "It's basic physics, sweetie. The neurons that send commands from his brain to the rest of his body move at an accelerated rate—*that's* his mental gift. It's all connected, so his muscles are able to react equally fast. But it only gives him a quick burst of speed. He couldn't maintain it."

"Oh good, it's the turncoat," Fletcher mumbled.

"So, he can't *run* that fast?" Grant asked.

"He could for a few seconds. Enough to get out of sight, disorient his target."

Grant, Julie, and Fletcher were so caught up in her explanation that they never saw Morgan rise from her chair as Alex was talking. The *pop* they heard was their first indication.

Morgan had shoved Alex roughly into a chair and smacked her across the face.

"Do you know how *hard* we've worked to keep this place a secret!" Morgan shouted at Alex, her hands on the chair's armrests, leaning in. "To have found a place where we can live without worrying about being found? Did thoughts like these even cross your mind while in Drexel's custody, or did you ever manage to stop thinking about *yourself?*"

Alex glared at her as everyone watched.

"I didn't tell him about this place. I *did* tell him about you, Grant," she added with a fleeting glance at Julie, "and I would have told him more if he had asked me. I couldn't stop myself."

Grant studied her. "What, he used some kind of truth agent on you?"

She nodded.

Morgan was taken aback by this, and returned to her chair, sullen and dismayed. "I'm sorry."

"Wait a second," Julie broke in. "Just thought of something . . . Payton called your ring a Seal. *The* Seal. He said its 'time' was almost here."

Morgan turned to Julie, picking up on her train of thought. "And Marta told me that Grant would find out the truth soon. Then there is the prophecy on the stone tablet."

Grant finally caught on. "Whatever's happening to me—the Shift, the powers, the Forging, all of it—it's unfolding according to some kind of *timetable*."

"You know," Fletcher griped. "I had this figured out *weeks* ago, but does anyone ever listen to me?"

"So, the question then becomes . . ." Morgan began.

"What happens at the end of the timetable? And who made it to begin with?" Grant finished, throwing a quick glance at Alex. "We should talk to Marta about this."

"Oh, she's dead," Fletcher announced without import. "Marta never regained consciousness when the rest of us did after the recent . . . *incident*."

Grant gaped at Morgan. "But you told me *everyone* woke up after the Forging!"

"Marta was *very* old," Morgan said just as Fletcher was about to speak again. "She had a weak heart. We don't know if it was this 'Forging,' as you call it, that ended her life or not."

Grant digested this slowly. *Another one . . . Another one gone because of me . . .*

"Can we return to the matter of Drexel for a moment?" Morgan asked, partly because she meant it and partly to distract Grant from unpleasant feelings. "If Alex here didn't reveal our location to him, then who did?"

Everyone looked at Alex. She shrugged. "I *woulda* told him, while I was drugged, if I'd known. I've never been here before today. But he never asked me."

"Which means he likely knew already," Morgan reasoned. She turned. "Fletcher? Any intuition as to who our traitor is?"

He never hesitated. His eyes moved to Grant, staring for a long moment but as Grant was about to protest he looked past him and pointed: "Her."

They all turned, but Morgan said it before they could see who Fletcher was looking at.

"*Hannah*," she gasped.

Hannah had just run into the Common Room, slinging her blond locks over one shoulder and reacting in horror to the destruction and injuries she saw.

Grant stood, his features hardening. "Hello, beautiful."

Hannah froze at Grant's tone of voice. She gazed around, taking in the dozens of eyeballs all pointing in her direction. Something about the coldness of this greeting . . .

"Some-body's bust-ed," Alex sing-songed.

"How could you sell me out?" Grant asked, his face an unnerving, even calm.

Hannah's eyes went wide, her face flushed. "I didn't . . ." she blurted.

"How could you sell them out!" he shouted, pointing at the Loci.

Hannah stared at him blankly. "I, I didn't think—" she stammered.

"No, you've been doing a *lot* of thinking," Grant seethed. He was

317

fighting to keep his voice calm, not to shout again. As he spoke something new clicked. "All this time you've been spying on me, reporting back to Drexel about my actions. That's how he's been able to keep such close tabs on me. And you gave him the asylum. All of this misery and bloodshed is on *your* hands."

"No! I never meant—" Hannah started, tears forming in her eyes.

"But you *did!*" Grant bellowed. Small objects all around the room jumped in place as he shouted. "When you make someone trust you while lying to them, that's something you *mean* to do!" Grant's thoughts lingered on the conversation they'd had in the dinner hall of this very building, only days before.

The pool table upended itself and crashed against a wall.

"Grant, calm yourself," Morgan said.

Hannah spoke, her voice barely above a whisper. "My feelings for you—"

"When you sell out everyone who trusts you," Grant said coldly, "then no matter what the reason . . . it's premeditated. It's calculated." He took a dangerous step toward her. "It's *personal*."

Hannah glanced around at the anger in every face surrounding her, even from faces she didn't recognize.

A single tear appeared.

And then she moved.

"You're going to just let her *leave?*" Alex asked, not believing her eyes.

"She's not going *anywhere,*" Grant said in a determined voice, still watching Hannah where she stood.

"You might want to tell *her* that!" Alex said, eyes wide.

"Stop her!" Morgan shouted urgently.

Grant looked at Morgan quizzically, startled. Then he looked back at the Common Room door where Hannah had stood, and saw that it was closed. Hannah was nowhere in sight.

One second after his feet were in motion, he realized what she'd done—used her misdirection ability on him to escape.

Alex was hot on his heels as he opened the door, but he turned and put a hand out.

"I've got this. Stay with the others."

"But if you're alone, she can use her mojo to slip away from you," Alex protested.

Grant walked out the door. "She won't get the chance."

"Grant, wait!" Alex called.

He turned around in the hallway, angry now. Alex was looking all around.

"Where's your sister?" she said.

He looked.

Julie was gone.

Hannah was in a hard run, rounding the back of her car, when Julie crashed into her from behind, dragging her to the ground.

Julie had Hannah by the throat before Hannah figured out what was happening, and Hannah reflexively launched a defensive punch into Julie's face. Julie's head whipped around with the blow, but she didn't let go, a wildfire blazing in her eyes. Her whole body was shaking with anger.

"He *trusted* you!" she cried, hot tears forming, but she refused to let them fall. "He *cared* about you!"

Unable to deflect Julie's fury but not wanting to harm her, Hannah brought one knee up to her chin and kicked outward with her foot straight into Julie's chest. Julie flew backward, landing on her back a few feet behind Hannah's sleek black sports car.

Hannah jumped to her feet and got in the car.

She looked behind her and couldn't see Julie anywhere.

She's gone to get Grant. Go!

She put her key in the ignition.

Grant burst through the front door just as Hannah was starting her car.

"Stop!" he screamed, beating a path down the front steps.

Hannah put the car into reverse and hit the gas, as Grant came running toward her, waving his arms.

The back of the car lurched violently, and Hannah slammed on the brakes.

Grant stopped and knelt by the passenger's side of the car. Hannah stopped the car, a sickening weakness settling in her stomach. She got

319

out of the car and ran to the other side just in time to see Grant pulling Julie from beneath it.

Grant gently tugged on Julie's legs until he had her all the way out from under the car. She was lying in repose, frozen in the same position Hannah had last seen her in after kicking herself free. Except that her chest bore a black tire mark across it, and dirt and soot were all over her clothes.

Hannah took a step forward to see if Julie was breathing, but Grant gathered his sister up into his arms and turned sharply away from her.

Hannah couldn't seem to get her mouth to close. The inside of it went dry, and all of the moisture in her body now seemed to be spilling from her eyes.

"Grant, I . . ."

He turned slowly to face her, looking at her as if she were a thing.

A thing he no longer recognized.

Stumbling backward, she found herself back in the car. A few moments later, she was racing down the drive and out onto the black roadway, her mind filled with images of Julie's unconscious body and the hatred in Grant's eyes.

That look on his face . . .

It was all she could see.

47

"She's still comatose?" Daniel asked.

"Yeah," Grant said, rubbing his forehead. He held the phone with one hand, and stroked Julie's hand with another, as she slept. "She has some injuries to her vital organs. There was . . . internal bleeding."

"What's the prognosis?" asked Daniel's maddeningly clinical voice on the other end of the phone.

"She got out of her second surgery a little while ago," said Grant. He sounded weak, as if all of the strength had left his body. "All they can do now is keep her comfortable, and—" he huffed—"and hope she pulls out of it."

A breathy sob escaped Grant's lips, and Daniel remained silent, allowing him the moment.

Forty-eight hours had passed since Grant's confrontation with Payton and Drexel. Grant had not yet left Julie's side except during her surgeries, when he paced relentlessly in the waiting room. He wore a hooded sweatshirt, trying desperately to keep the nurses from seeing his face; the news still showed his photo every so often.

He had dozed occasionally since planting himself by her bed, but he would jerk himself awake after a few minutes.

Sometime during the last two days it had finally dawned on him that he needed to talk to someone. There were too many emotions and thoughts stomping through his mind, and he couldn't take it much more.

He was doing a good job of holding things in check when he was around the others. Morgan believed so strongly in him; whether he agreed with her or not, he couldn't bring himself to divulge to her the true depths of his doubts. Daniel might one day become a trusted friend, but it was much too early to bare his soul to the scientist yet. Alex he still felt like he barely knew, despite what had just happened. Julie had been taken from him.

And Hannah . . . Hannah had done the taking.

But she was gone now.

He barely cared where she was. And he didn't trust himself or what he might do to her if he ran into her right now.

Alex had arrived an hour ago to sit with him. It was early morning—though Grant had long since lost track of the time—and this was at least the third time she had visited in two days.

Daniel was giving Grant a wide berth. They kept in touch over the phone every few hours, and Grant had given him enough details for the doctor to piece together what had happened with Hannah. And Drexel.

"Grant, do you really think it was wise to let Drexel escape? I mean . . . I understand your desire to maintain Morgan's cover at the asylum, and we *don't* have any evidence to prosecute him, but—"

"No one *let* Drexel go."

"Right, but still, shouldn't we be looking—"

"Can we . . . another time?" Grant choked. "I can't . . . ."

Alex grabbed the phone out of Grant's hand.

"It's all good, Doc," she said. "Go count some molecules or something."

She hung up.

Alex dropped the phone into Grant's jacket pocket as he reached out and took Julie's limp hand in both of his. He squeezed it, wishing that the warmth and life of his body could enter hers as he gazed imploringly into her lifeless face.

"Wake up," he pleaded.

He could only weep. His throat constricted with the effort, and once more he thought of the vision of the snake, wrapping itself about his neck and squeezing . . .

"Please come back," he whispered. "I can't do this alone."

Dozing in and out of sleep for hours, Grant's thoughts wandered . . . Julie.

Her Parkinson's, which he'd discovered because it was in her medical records.

Marta.

The Forging.

The ring he wore . . . Why did Payton call it "the Seal"?

Payton . . .

Morgan . . .

The Loci and their unique talents . . .

The stone tablet . . .

Alex . . .

Her boss, the Keeper . . .

Hannah . . .

Daniel . . .

Drexel . . .

Harlan Evers . . .

His life before the Shift . . .

And his life now.

All the way back to that first day, stepping off the bus and seeing himself . . .

It couldn't be random, Grant was sure of it. There was something at work here, a plan—but he couldn't see it.

And according to Morgan, it was on some kind of schedule. *Tick, tick, tick . . . .*

Despite his best efforts, no matter where his thoughts began, they always circled back and ended on Hannah. Thoughts of her betrayal choked him. Why would she do this? It made no sense.

But it was done. Irreversible.

And if I need any reminders of that, all I have to do is sit by this bed.

Grant thought of Payton and Morgan and wondered if he might ever become as bitter a man as Payton was. No, he and Hannah had never gotten far enough along to have fallen in love.

Yeah, keep telling yourself that.

```
you can do this.
```

Daniel finished typing the words and looked at his watch. "6:04 P.M.," it read.

He nervously tapped his fingers on the keyboard, waiting. This was taking too long.

Come on. Say something.

```
       i can't, i'm sorry
```

```
  think it over
  please
```

```
      sorry
```

```
no don't leave
```

```
    [user logged off]
```

who was in the kitchen, but the sentiment was there all the same.

He had taken to using the desk chair as a makeshift wheelchair, since his had been destroyed by Payton. But Lisa had acquired a pair of crutches and was threatening to make him start using them any minute . . .

The sun was setting as Grant entered the apartment for the first time in three days. Daniel quickly logged off the chat room and switched off the monitor before Grant or Lisa noticed. Grant had made no effort to acknowledge his houseguests, and Daniel could see how red his eyes were and the lifeless sagging of his movements.

"Grant?" prompted Daniel gently.

"Huh?" Grant replied, barely coherent.

"How is she?" Lisa asked.

"Um . . ." he searched the floor as if trying to find the words. "No change. Did you get the uh . . . the picture of the tablet from Morgan?"

"Yeah, yeah," Daniel replied. "I spent a few hours hunched over it, but didn't seem to be getting anywhere so I was taking a break . . ."

Grant offered a barely perceptible nod. He changed jackets and retrieved some cash from the jar in the kitchen where they kept extra.

"Where are you going?" Lisa asked.

"Oh, I uh . . ." he mumbled, "I have to go home."

Lisa and Daniel looked at one another.

"Home?"

"My old home," he explained. "Where my dad and my sister lived."

"Right, of course, to find your father's safe," Daniel nodded. "Are you sure that can't wait, though? You need some rest."

Grant suddenly came to life. "No, what I need are some *answers!*"

"Grant, you're exhausted," Lisa said. "And scared."

"Don't tell me what I am!" he shot at her. "I've had it with all these secrets and games. I want to know what my parents have to do with any of this. I want to know who this Keeper person is that's playing chess with my life. I want to know why Hannah betrayed me. I want to know what this lousy thing *is*"—he held out his ring—"and why it *won't come off*! And I want to know *now!*"

A beeping sound startled all three of them in the silence that followed.

"It's the detector!" Daniel whispered, wild-eyed. "There's a shimmer in the building!"

"Can you tell where?" Grant asked.

Daniel grabbed his small device and studied it. "It's close."

"You two get in the bedroom—"

Before Grant could finish issuing orders, there was a knock at the door.

48

Grant put a finger over his lips, and walked to the door. He looked through the peephole.

"It's *him*, get down!" he whispered to Daniel and Lisa, looking frantically around for something he could use as a weapon. He spotted a broom leaning against the far corner in the kitchen.

Knock, knock.

Grant reached his arm toward the faraway broom. It twitched in place before finally leaping into the air and flying toward him. Daniel's detector immediately started beeping again, as Grant grabbed the broom out of the air and held it like a bat.

Blowing out a big breath, he placed one hand on the doorknob.

He opened it.

Payton stood on the other side, perfectly composed, hands clasped together in front.

Grant swung the broom hard and fast, a home run in the making. There was a blur of movement and then Payton was standing perfectly still again, in the same calm pose as before.

Half of the wooden broomstick lay on the floor at their feet; the other half was still in Grant's hands. Payton had drawn his weapon, sliced the broom, and sheathed the sword, all faster than any of them could see.

"If I wanted you dead, you would be," Payton said offhandedly. "Time is running out. And there are some things you should know."

"What could you have to say that I would want to hear?"

"My story," Payton replied.

"Not interested," Grant said.

"It's connected to your own."

Grant looked Payton up and down, but the other man's body language was impossible to read. This could easily have been a ruse; on the other hand, if Payton had wanted to attack, nothing Grant could muster would be likely to stop him.

And he hadn't attacked.

Grant glanced at Lisa and Daniel; Lisa was cowering on the floor behind the kitchen counter, while Daniel remained at the computer. Daniel shot him a "whatever you think" shrug, but Lisa looked as if she would kill the lot of them if Grant let Payton in.

"Very well." Grant stepped aside and Payton entered.

Lisa threw Grant a nasty look as she helped Daniel slide precariously to the living room in the desk chair. Grant kept a close eye on Payton, who took a seat opposite the sofa. Soon they were all settled in the living room, but Lisa was on the edge of her seat beside Daniel, seemingly ready to pounce should the intruder make a move toward him.

Payton broke the silence first. "I regret that it was necessary to damage your chair."

"Oh hey"—Daniel's expression soured—"if you *have* to destroy a guy's wheelchair, then, you know, I guess you just have to."

"Maybe you should say what you came here to say," Grant recommended.

"I came to give you this," Payton said, pulling a folded piece of paper out of his pocket. But instead of handing it to Grant, he extended it to Daniel.

Daniel took it. "What is it?" he asked, unfolding it.

"A key," replied Payton.

Daniel examined the paper, which was filled with symbols and alphanumeric letters.

"It's not a complete translation, but it's close." Payton said.

"This is the language from the stone tablet?" Daniel exclaimed.

Payton nodded, while Daniel immediately looked to Lisa. She answered his unspoken question by retrieving a printed copy of the stone tablet photo that Morgan had sent him.

"I'm sure Morgan has explained to you our history," Payton began, "and how it ended."

Grant nodded.

"That was nine years ago. After the cave-in in France, I was rescued and resuscitated. But it was not by luck or chance that my life was spared. The three men who found me had come looking for the same thing that Morgan and I were searching for—a fragment from the stone tablet.

"These men—they were kind to me, but eccentric, to say the least. They revived me, took me to the local hospital, but they never inquired about my identity or told me who *they* were. Not at first. They visited me several times in the hospital, and when I got out, they offered me a job. I had no intention of seeking out Morgan, so I took the job.

"Eventually, they told me that they knew of the significance of the ring on my finger. They explained to me that the rings are the keys to our mental powers, and they helped me figure out what my power was. One day I asked how they knew so much about me and about the rings. And on that day, they finally told me that they were members of a highly secretive order called the Secretum of Six."

He paused, leaned forward. "Words cannot adequately convey the power and authority this organization has at its disposal. They are like nothing else on this planet. So influential are they, so skilled in the arts of deception and camouflage, that even the world's governments know nothing of their existence. They are a small number of individuals who reside all over the world, though when they gather, it is at a central location. I've heard the word 'substation' more than once. They and those who preceded them have been watching and waiting for *millennia* for the coming of the rings and their wearers."

"Why? What are the rings? Where do they come from? Do you know?"

Payton shook his head. "The men of the Secretum call them the Rings of Dominion. The origin of the rings is the deepest of mysteries, but what I was taught is that sometime, somewhere, the Rings of Dominion were once worn and used by another group of people. The men who rescued me believed that the rings had been plucked out of some long-forgotten chapter of history and deposited here in the present. And now someone has put them to use again, using their mind-enhancing effects to create—"

"Heroes," Grant reluctantly said, leaning back in his chair. He let out a slow breath.

Payton nodded. "Perhaps. Perhaps not. You and *your* ring they have searched and waited for with the greatest consternation."

A secret order. Morgan mentioned a secret group that knew about the rings . . . said that Payton himself could be a member.

"Why?" Grant asked.

"Your ring is very, very special. It makes you similar to the rest of us, but *not* the same."

"Not the same how, exactly?"

"I don't know," Payton said. "But they called it the Seal of Dominion."

"Did you join this 'Secretum'?"

"I wasn't allowed. Ring-wearers may not join. As I carried out the work they assigned me, I picked up bits and pieces such as this. Eventually, I caught enough to understand why they were so interested in the stone tablet."

"Why?"

"They believed it foretold the time and circumstances surrounding the Bringer's coming. Everything they did was assigned a sense of urgency because of this looming event. Now that you're here, plans, devices, and strategies prepared centuries ago have been set into motion."

"And your sword? I've never seen anything like it. Where did it come from?"

"It was given to me by the men of the Secretum. One year to the day after I began working for them, they told me that they had been studying the ancient texts and had found a passage that referred to one ring-wearer who would die and be reborn, and then fulfill a specific role concerning the Seal and the one who wears it."

"You're supposed to kill me," Grant said.

Payton nodded. "It was all part of the prophecy. It is my destiny. It's the reason I'm here, and the reason I died and was revived. This I have been taught. They gave me the sword on that day. It's an ancient weapon, specifically fashioned to kill the Bringer—the wearer of the Seal.

"They sent me to study, to train, to learn every method of dispensing death known to man. But my assigned duty was a righteous one; they weren't creating a murderer. They wanted a *warrior*. They taught me about the Bringer's abilities and what you would be able to do. They taught me to strike quick, never to stop, to be relentless. Every day for over six years, it was drilled into my head that the wearer of the Seal *must* die, and that *I* would be the one to kill him."

"Then why *didn't* you?"

Payton broke eye contact for the first time and looked down. "I'm not certain. I am bound by a vow of honor and blood to end your life. And regardless of this prophecy business, I must fulfill that oath. But meeting you has caused me to question my purpose."

"Why would this Secretum want me dead?"

Payton shook his head. "It's not *you* they fear. It has never been about you. It's the Seal. They fear it mortally. Something about the Seal of Dominion is vastly different from all the other rings. Two years ago, they told me my training was complete and sent me out into the world to prove myself worthy. During my travels, I have spoken to others around the world who have experienced the Shift, and in recent weeks, I began hearing your name. Word is spreading about you. Those like us, those who know the truth about the rings, believe that you are here to save the world."

"You think maybe these men from the Secretum weren't being truthful with you? That they tricked you into coming after me? Is that why you're telling me all of this?"

"Doubt was planted, yes. This is the reason I have let you live. I've tried to reach the Secretum to confirm my suspicions, but they no longer answer me. It's possible they know that I have refused to fulfill my mission and have disavowed my actions."

Grant sat back in his chair, digesting this tale.

"*Grant!*" Daniel shouted.

"You figured out what the tablet says?"

Daniel looked up from his chair at the desk, his eyes wide with fear.

"Part of it. I've found what appears to be a key bit of the text."

Grant swallowed, listening closely.

"First of all, please keep in mind that the tablet is ancient. So some of these passages simply don't appear to have a direct English translation—"

"I'm with you, Doc. Just give me whatever you can."

"The tablet is called the 'Dominion Stone,' and in essence, it was created to tell of—rough translation here—a 'miracle-man' who would one day come, called the Bringer."

"I know this already," Grant replied impatiently. "This 'miracle-man' . . . What is he here for? What does he *do*?"

"Wait, there's something else. The tablet speaks of another figure of importance. By my best guess, this second person is the 'overseer of destruction.'"

"The Keeper," Grant said, though there was no need.

"Or . . . it could be the Thresher," Lisa offered. "The second person is not mentioned by name."

"How is he mentioned?"

"If I'm reading this correctly . . ." Daniel explained, "it says that on a day of reckoning, these two will clash to 'set the course of the future.'"

So there it was. It would be a fight.

"Um," Daniel spoke slowly, reluctantly, "it *also* says something to the effect of . . . 'no act of man can prevent the torment that day will herald.'"

49

Daniel gingerly sat up in bed, the darkness of night obscuring his vision. He rubbed at his eyes.

His "borrowed" hospital bed creaked slightly in its spot in the living room. He froze in place, listening for any evidence that his movement had been detected.

The apartment he shared with Lisa was dead silent; the only audible sound was her gentle breathing coming from the bedroom. The small condo had suited them well as a safe house during his recovery, but they couldn't stay here forever.

So now's as good a time as any, he decided.

Ever so carefully, Daniel strained in silence and threw his legs slowly over the side of the bed. His legs still wore the casts; it had only been a few weeks, but he was beyond ready for them to be removed. Constantly itching and unbearably hot, they often kept him awake at night. Still his broken ribs seemed to be mending nicely, and his wrist no longer caused him pain when he used it.

His hands reached out in the darkness and laid hold of the crutches. The rubber tips on the ends softened the noise as he hefted his weight up onto them and stood. Daniel froze again to listen, making sure Lisa hadn't heard him.

When he was satisfied that his movements were still unnoticed, he wobbled carefully to the front door, fumbled with the lock while trying to hold the crutches still with rigid elbows, and finally, cautiously, wrangled the door open.

Still Lisa remained peacefully unaware.

She would kill *me if she caught me trying this . . .*

On the other hand, she might just applaud me for learning how to use these blasted crutches.

He hobbled awkwardly out into the hall, careful to shut the door quietly behind him. Once out of the apartment, less stealth was required, and he took the elevator down to the ground floor. He shuffled out and looked around the lobby, only to realize that he'd never seen it before. They'd entered via the parking garage on the third floor when Grant had brought him here.

The lobby was larger than he expected, with a checkerboard pattern of large marble tiles on the floor, an ornate chandelier hanging from the ceiling, and a large collection of stainless steel mailboxes beside the stairwell door on his right. A set of glass double doors lay straight ahead, leading outside.

His crutches and teetering steps echoed loudly in the empty lobby until he got his hands on the front door. Double-checking that his keys were still in his front pocket, he pushed the release mechanism to open the main entrance and step out into fresh air for the first time in weeks.

He wasn't dressed for the night's unexpectedly cool temperature, but he tried to ignore it. He turned left onto a small concrete sidewalk that led to a set of electricity meters and panels attached to the front of the building and hidden by a row of tall bushes.

A young man sat on a skateboard there behind the brush, watching Daniel approach while shifting his eyes in all directions.

"You came," Daniel said with some effort, relieved.

"Yeah, and I was on time, too," the young man replied, sizing him up.

"Sorry," Daniel said, coming closer and lowering his voice. The kid couldn't have been more than fourteen. "I, uh, never caught your real name."

"Will," the boy said, looking around again. "Still don't know why we had to do this in person."

"Just needed to make sure," Daniel said, lowering his voice to a whisper now. "You understand what I'm asking you to do?"

The boy nodded in nervous, fast movements, but kept his expression even and cool.

"It's won't be easy," Daniel said. "And it will probably be painful."

"Just sign me up, man. I get it."

"Do you really?" Daniel said, edging closer. "I want you to be sure about that. You won't be the same after this is over."

Will looked Daniel in the eye. "I *told* you already. Just say when and where."

Daniel nodded slowly, sizing the kid up. *Okay, then.*

"Stay in contact with Sarah and the others," Daniel said, readjusting himself on his crutches. "Be reachable, and be ready to move. It'll happen fast."

Will nodded then hopped up onto his skateboard and rolled past Daniel and down the sidewalk.

Daniel watched him go in silence, sighing long and hard at his young friend and the innocence he had just thrown away.

Morning came, and Grant got up early to visit Julie before his big road trip to the old house.

Under different circumstances, it might have pained him to see his car in the condition he found it—the damage Payton had caused prevented him from putting the top up or using the windows. The passenger-side glass was entirely gone.

But then, today was not a normal day.

If such a thing existed anymore.

He needed to fill Morgan and the others in on all that Payton had told him last night, but he didn't want to put off this trip home any longer. It was a six-hour drive in normal traffic. Time to get it over with.

Grant revved the engine and spiraled downward to the exit. As he turned the final corner, a familiar tingle crossed the back of his neck . . .

A tingle that told him he was about to see someone he didn't want to see.

He drove up to the exit—which still sported a broken barrier from when he had crashed through it ahead of Payton—and suddenly he slammed on the brakes.

Hannah stood right in front of the car, blocking his way with her hands on the hood. The first day he'd met her at Inveo, she'd been so in-control. So strong. Confident. Now she looked like a teenager who'd run away from home. Her blond hair was matted down as if it hadn't been washed in days, her makeup had worn off long ago, and her clothes were filthy.

"Move or I'll move you," he shouted from the car. "I mean it."

"I need to talk to you," she said in a sad voice, "but I don't know what to say."

"Let me guess. You have information to share with me? Everyone I meet seems to have just the right information at just the right time."

Hannah looked down and shook her head. She slowly walked around to stand beside his car door. "I've only got one piece of information to offer you, big boy, and that's *why*."

"You know," he said, the car shaking slightly, "if I concentrated hard enough, I really think I could grind your bones into powder." He raised an arm in her direction.

"I don't believe you'd do that," she said softly, but took a step back all the same.

He looked into her eyes. "You've given me *so* many reasons to. Don't give me another."

She looked away, unable to maintain eye contact with him. "You won't let me explain myself?"

"Explain it to my sister," he growled, turning back to the steering wheel. The car shook violently.

Grant was about to drive off, but Hannah stepped closer, close enough to touch him. "Drexel tried to kill me," she said.

He paused, but wouldn't look at her.

"He blamed me for everything that happened. He was furious. I managed to get away, but he's still out there, and I think he's going to try and finish the job."

Grant's eyes swiveled to meet hers. "Come near me again, and he won't have to."

A squeal of tires and a cloud of blackened smoke punctuated his exit.

50

DANGER, the sign read in red block letters. *This structure is declared unsafe . . .*

He sighed. The grass and brush were severely overgrown to the point that it was difficult to see much of the house beyond. What he could see appeared to be suffering from heavy termite damage.

Condemned. They condemned my childhood home.

Grant made his way across the yard—feeling as though he needed a jungle knife to cut through the foliage—and approached the front door. Yellow tape was stretched across it twice, forming a large "X".

Grant took a step back, glanced over his shoulder to ensure no one was watching, and raised his arm. Focusing on the door, he shoved his hand forward, and the door was swallowed by the gloomy shadows of the house's interior.

He whipped out a flashlight and entered. The stench of rotted wood was overpowering. The interior of the house looked nothing like the vague images he retained of the few years he lived here as a child. The carpet was ragged and barely clinging to the floor. Many of the walls had holes that went all the way through. The kitchen was inaccessible, the wooden framework and ceiling over the room having buckled and collapsed inward.

He was almost glad Julie wasn't there to see it.

Making his way into the master bedroom, he found the attic door in the ceiling where he remembered it and pulled down on the small piece of cord that still dangled from it. A ladder that seemed sturdy enough, though it creaked with every careful step he took, folded down from the door.

In the musty, moth-infested attic, he had no real idea of where to begin looking for his father's safe.

Where do you hide something in a big, hollow, empty space?

At the far end of the room, his eyes landed on a small canoe, mounted from the ceiling via a set of rope pulleys.

In plain sight, maybe?

In early afternoon, Morgan walked out of the hidden basement and stopped in place.

Across the Common Room one of her residents—the teenage boy, Thomas, who had been held at gunpoint by Drexel—was in one corner, waving a sword through the air. A crowd was gathered around him, watching with interest.

"Better, but there's more power in your wrist than you realize," a familiar voice was saying. "Less elbow, more wrist. No, don't lead with your shoulder."

Morgan marched straight into the gathering.

"What are you *doing*!" she shouted. "We have no use for such things here." She snatched the sword out of Thomas' hand and tossed the sword at Payton's feet.

"You'd prefer a blanket to cower under? Your little fort here has already been invaded once. Drexel knows where you are. You really think he won't try again? If the others choose to fight, you won't be able to stand in the way."

"You have no authority in this place," she said with a forced calm, staring him down, unblinking.

"I knew you were a control freak, love," Payton replied, polishing the sword between folds of his shirt, "but I had no idea you considered yourself so lofty. If these people really are your 'friends,' then you owe them the right to choose their own fate."

"Get out," she said.

No one moved.

She turned to the others. "Not him! The rest of you! OUT!"

Everyone filed out except Payton and Morgan, who never took their eyes off of one another.

When the room was empty and the door closed, Morgan spoke again. "Let's get one thing straight. You said you've changed over the last nine years. Well, guess what? You're not the only one. So you've faced danger. So you've been brought back from the edge of death. So you've learned how to poke at things with a big piece of steel. You think that makes you special?

"You have *no idea* what most of these people have been through before they came here. I do. I know them. I know their stories, their fears, what makes them laugh, what makes them hurt. Because that's what I do. I take care of them." She stepped closer until she was inches from his face. "Don't you *ever* come in here and tell these people how to live their lives!"

Payton stared at her for a long moment, unperturbed. She was almost red in the face now. He still appeared unmoved.

"You're right, you *have* changed," he said slowly, not breaking eye contact.

Morgan let out a breath. She looked as though she wanted to slug him, but she merely clenched her fists.

"But not nearly enough."

If it was possible, her face became even redder.

"Your 'friends' were just telling me," he went on, "about how much they respect you. How they look up to you and rely on you. They seem to see you as some noble figure who's always collected and in control. That *persona* you project—it's so practiced and measured. But I see the truth below."

He walked around her as she stood unmoving. "You're holding it in," he said. "You keep it buried all neat and tidy, and you'd be mortified if they ever saw the *real* you. But it's making its way to the surface now. After all these years."

Her features remained red and angry, but took on the slightest hint of uncertainty.

"Feed that rage, love," Payton said, deadly serious. "You're going to need it. We all are."

He turned and began walking away, but Morgan remained rooted to her spot, breathing hard and fast.

"I won't become an animal. Violence solves nothing," Morgan said quietly.

He cast a glance over his shoulder. "You'd be surprised how many things it will solve."

The pulleys holding the canoe in place were rusted and didn't want to turn. Grant finally gave up and made it break loose with his mind. The old wooden boat shattered on the floor.

In the remains of what used to be the front section of the canoe lay a small, hard plastic, store-bought safe on its side, no more than a foot wide and tall. Grant hoisted it from the debris, found a secure place to sit and opened it.

He didn't toy with guessing the safe's combination. He merely focused his thoughts on the small front door and *lifted* it from its hinges. Inside were five Army file folders marked "Classified." Each had its own label. The first four, in turn, were "Frank Boyd," "Cynthia Boyd," "Julie Boyd," and "Collin Boyd."

His entire family.

Why would the Army keep top secret files on my family?

He flipped to the last file.

"The Secretum of Six."

Grant's heart fluttered. His father had known about the Secretum?

He began by opening his father's file. The first paper was an official commendation on his service record, signed by "Gen. Harlan Bernard Evers." Grant scanned the page. One paragraph jumped out at him:

```
Frank is the finest officer to ever serve under my
command, representing the best of what the United
States Army has to offer.  He has earned my full
confidence and absolute trust.  Major Boyd has
become the leading intelligence gatherer in our
entire department.  His experience has proven
vital to unraveling the mysteries of the Secretum.
```

So. Payton was wrong. The U.S. government *did* know of the Secretum, after all.

But what did Evers mean by "his experience"?

The next page was a photocopy of a large black-and-white photograph of his parents. Smiling both, his mother was sitting at a desk which his father was leaning over from the opposite side. It looked like the photographer had caught them in a candid moment, but they both turned to look into the lens and smile before the shutter was triggered.

Grant saw the indentations of handwriting through the paper; he turned it over to read what it said.

A scribbled note read, "Frank and Cynthia. X marks the spot."

X?

He flipped the page again and examined it closer. He gasped when he spotted it: a tiny "x" had been marked on the photo with a black pen; just above it, a miniature tattoo was visible on his father's left wrist. And . . . *There!* His mother had one too, in the same spot.

The tattoos looked remarkably like one of the symbols found on Grant's ring.

"Mom and Dad . . ." he breathed, unbelieving. "They knew all about the Secretum."

Grant leaned back, putting an arm behind him for support.

It couldn't be true.

He discarded the other folders for now and skipped to the one with "Collin Boyd" written on it.

The first document he came upon inside was a birth certificate.

A birth certificate for . . .

He shuddered.

The certificate was for "Grant Borrows."

There's a real Grant Borrows? I thought that name was just made up and given to me!

But this paper he held was no copy. It was an original; he could see the pen's indentations, though it bore no notary watermark.

He thumbed through the remainder of his file, the contents of which included photos from his early childhood, the results of his father's test on his mental acuity, and little else. No other birth certificate was enclosed.

Grant couldn't figure out what this meant. Why would his father have a birth certificate with "Grant Borrows" on it?

His thoughts started coming faster and faster, reeling back to past conversations, remembering things he had been told.

"So you're me, now," he heard his own voice saying to Collin that first day. *"Does that mean I'm you?"*

"It doesn't work that way," Collin had replied. *"I'm just a volunteer.*

I'm no one important. You're different."

Then the moment between moments where the hazy outline of his mother had spoken to him.

"Stay true to yourself. Nothing is as it seems," she said in that silky, dreamy voice.

And Harlan Evers had said before his death, *"If you go and find your father's files, you're going to learn things that will be hard to accept. Things about your parents* and *about yourself . . . Once this corner is turned, once you know this truth, there will be no going back."*

Finally, he thought of Morgan, quoting something that the old woman Marta had told her . . .

"She said you've always *been* who *you are now."*

And the truth dawned on him.

He didn't know how it was true, but he could feel in his bones that it was.

This couldn't be.

It just couldn't.

It was madness.

Grant could only shake his head.

"I wasn't changed *into* this person," he whispered. "Grant Borrows is the real name I was given at birth . . ."

51

"Bike won't start," Payton said to someone from the front hall. "Been knacked since I crashed it into Grant's car."

Terrific, Morgan thought from the Common Room. *He's stuck here. With us.*

A tremendous commotion came from the hall, where numerous residents seemed to be gathering near the front door. "Oh, lovely," came Payton's voice above the din.

Morgan followed his voice to find the front door open. Payton stood at the front of them, looking out over the threshold. Fletcher was next to him.

"What's going on?" she asked, forcing her way through the men and women who were already elbow-to-elbow, looking outside the door.

"You have a visitor," Payton said, not turning around. "The snitch."

Morgan's eyes drew into narrow slits when she finally made it to the front door.

Hannah stood just outside the door, leaning against the door post. She looked as if she barely had the energy to stand. She was filthy, her eyes were bloodshot, and—covered in sweat but not out of breath—she was probably running a fever.

Morgan had never seen the southern belle like this before.

"What do you want, Hannah?" asked Morgan.

"To warn you," Hannah said wearily, struggling to get the words out.

"About what?" Morgan replied, unimpressed.

"I'm not . . ." Hannah mumbled, trying to remain upright, "I . . . I don't *know*, exactly! Somethin's going to . . . I don't know *what*, but I overheard . . ."

"She's lying," Fletcher started to say, but broke off when Hannah's eyes rolled up into her head. She began to collapse . . .

In a flash, Payton had dropped his sword and she was resting in his arms. He was already holding her long before the sword ever hit the ground.

"Brilliant," he said, frowning, as he gazed down with disdain at Hannah, unconscious in his arms. He turned to face Morgan. "What am I supposed to do with *this*?"

"You'll think of something," Morgan replied. "But don't kill her. Well . . . wouldn't be the end of the world, but *try* not to kill her."

The Corvette pointed south, Grant sped toward L.A. on 395, letting the car almost drive itself. Traffic was light and so Grant's distracted thoughts didn't matter much. He was breathing fast, his blood pressure rising.

This . . . none of this . . .

His parents, members of the Secretum? The identity he'd known his entire life, a fabrication?

It *couldn't* be true.

He'd always assumed that those two words—*grant* and *borrow*— were someone's idea of a joke, given his current situation.

But no.

Rooting through some papers on the passenger seat, he found military discharge papers dated roughly one month before Julie's birthday. Grant began piecing it together . . .

Julie has no idea that the name she uses is not her *real name, either, because she's never been told differently. Once we were living at the orphanage, all of our official documents had our assumed names on them, so no one had reason to believe they weren't real.*

He turned to the file marked "The Secretum of Six" and opened it. This was the thickest file of all, full of handwritten notes, memos, and official Army documents.

One page was labeled "Official Enlistment Request Form." It had never been fully completed, but the names "Frank Boyd" and "Cynthia

Boyd" were scribbled hastily on top, followed by a brief, handwritten paragraph below:

The operatives listed above seek application to U.S. Army officer status. As former operatives for the Secretum of Six, their insider knowledge could help us decipher the mysterious organization's identity and intentions once and for all. Subjects created pseudonyms for themselves (listed above) to facilitate their escape from the Secretum, and have argued that their true names should be kept to prevent the Secretum from hearing of their defection. Subjects' extreme compliance with strenuous hours of debriefing indicate a willingness to submit to and work with U.S. authority. Applicants are highly recommended for fast-track approval.

That was it, then. His parents had been operatives for the Secretum but fled and joined the U.S. military. In exchange for giving the government every piece of information they knew about the Secretum, the Army made them officers.

There never *was* a Collin Boyd. It was only a pseudonym used to protect him from being found by the Secretum. He had perhaps three hours left before he reached the asylum and he knew one thought would dog him that whole time.

My whole life has been one lie built upon another . . .

And what if his father had never left? What if he was a double-agent? Grant couldn't bend his mind around the reasons the man would disappear. It made no sense.

Nothing made sense anymore.

Another hour and a half in the car only cleared up a few points. He had managed to read through a few more of correspondence and the pieces began slipping together. Grant's father must have learned of the Secretum's plans for the Bringer, joined Army Intelligence after defecting, earned their trust—no doubt along with plenty of enemies within the secret order—and spent his time researching the Bringer and how he would be identified.

345

What a cruel twist of fate that it turned out to be his own son.

Or was it really a twist? Daniel was always saying that there are no coincidences . . .

Grant turned back to the "Secretum of Six" file and rifled through it some more.

A detailed report written by his father stated:

> The Secretum of Six is an ancient religious order, dating back several millennia. Shrouded in the utmost secrecy, their beliefs are built upon a stone tablet they call the Dominion Stone. There are conflicting theories on where the Stone came from, but the Secretum claims it is the oldest existing object on earth. The predominant theory is that it was a marker, placed upon some kind of enclave built to protect the Rings of Dominion—a seal meant to lock the away the Rings until the time was right.
>
> It contains a prophecy, regarding an important figure who leverages an event that has not yet come to pass. We have been unable to determine what this future event is, but we know that all of the Secretum's activities are centered around it. Approximately six hundred years ago, enemies of the Secretum found a way to break the Stone into smaller fragments, and scattered the pieces around the globe. The Secretum seems to have been largely unaffected by losing it, as their scholars had studied and deciphered the writing on it several thousand years ago. Having the Dominion Stone back now would be merely an act of devotion.

A hand-written memo also in the file said,

> *The Secretum has money and resources that are vast, capable of wielding unimaginable levels of influence. Several major corporations report to them, including Paragenics Group.*

And Inveo Technologies, Grant guessed.

Secrets and lies. Speeding toward L.A., Grant felt his pulse hammer in his palms as he gripped the steering wheel. He knew answers to his questions were closeer than ever, but like a mirage shimmering in the mid-day sun on the highway, still of reach. Somebody, soon, would need to answer to him.

When Hannah finally awakened, Payton, joined by the uninvited Fletcher, began trying to pull more information from her. Even Payton's sword, however, failed to uncover little more than what she'd already offered.

"Something big is in the works," Payton said slowly, never taking his eyes off Hannah. "You don't know what it is, but you 'overheard' mention of it. That sum it up?"

Hannah nodded, and took another sip out of the glass she held with both hands. She looked like a caged animal, hoping to be rescued.

"Then tell me *who* you heard it from," Payton said slowly.

She looked down.

"Listen, young lady—" Fletcher began sternly, then stopped, as if realizing something. "It's obvious who she heard it from. Matthew Drexel."

"Drexel . . ." Payton uttered, a deadly gleam settling into his eyes. "I need to borrow a car."

"All right," Fletcher replied, suddenly curious. "Your motorcycle won't start at all?"

"No," Payton said absently. "It was making an odd sound."

Fletcher looked far away, the gears in his mind spinning rapidly. "What *kind* of sound?"

"Clacking of a loose screw, maybe."

Fletcher paused, then his eyes swiveled to Payton's. "Could you wait here just one moment?" He walked at a brisk pace out of the Common Room and toward the front door.

Morgan stood, alarmed by Fletcher's sudden exit.

"How much does he know about motorcycles?" Payton asked.

"Nothing I'm aware of," Morgan replied.

Fletcher ran back in at a dead sprint and pulled down on an old fire alarm attached to the wall.

"Everybody *out of the building*! Go out the back! Quickly!" he yelled.

For a moment, no one moved. They merely stared at him, startled.

"RUN!" he bellowed at the top of his lungs. "*NOW!!*"

In the Corvette, Grant abruptly gulped in a full breath of air and slammed back into his seat, as if he'd been punched in the stomach. All thoughts of his investigation were gone, replaced by an image that had intruded upon his mind. His eyes squeezed shut so tight, for a long second, the Corvette blasting ahead regardless.

When he opened his eyes again, he was pasty white, clammy, and an unchecked panic radiated from every pore of his body.

They were dying.

52

Lisa was growing increasingly tense.

Not only tense. She was angry at herself.

Bitter, even.

Daniel had stopped acting normal *days* ago, keeping secrets and telling half-truths. And he was always on that computer.

Something was up.

She'd tried to watch him closely but it'd led nowhere and finally she'd gone to her room, planning to keep tabs on him as best as she could. Maybe if she were out of sight, he might give up a clue. But nothing happened. And her eyes grew heavy.

She didn't know what woke her up that night, until she heard the whisper of the apartment door close.

Her heart racing in her chest, she dashed out into the living room—noticing the empty computer chair along the way—and looked one-eyed through the peephole in the front door.

Just in the far periphery of her sight, she saw Daniel hobbling onto the elevator.

She had to follow.

Heading into the hall and taking the second elevator, she pushed the button for the ground floor, assuming Daniel, in his condition, wouldn't be heading to the garage.

The elevator door opened onto an empty lobby. Through the glass front windows, she saw plenty of pedestrians and vehicles; the city was illuminated by multitudes of streetlamps and a flood of evening traffic.

But no Daniel. Yet he'd have to have headed outside.

She pushed through the lobby doors and stepped onto the sidewalk. The noise of the city rushed at her. It had been so quiet of late. One sound in particular caught her ear. A crash as if a trash can had been tipped over. It had come from the alley to the side of the building. She crept to the building's corner and peeked around.

Standing there on his crutches, about forty feet away, was Daniel, speaking forcefully to two very large, very . . . *capable*-looking men, who wore dark leather jackets and skull caps. Most startling of all was that Daniel appeared to be in no danger. Quite the contrary. The men were listening intently to what he was telling them . . . then staring intently at the thick bundles of money he'd placed in each of their hands.

What was going on?

Was he no better than Hannah? Was he something far worse?

No, that was nuts.

Lisa ducked behind a bush just as she spotted the three of them headed her way. She watched as the two bigger men turned and walked away from the building, while Daniel painstakingly hobbled his way back inside.

Devastated, she dragged herself inside and up the stairs to Grant's apartment instead of her own.

But Grant was still gone, and Daniel hadn't returned, either, apparently going back to their apartment one floor down. The apartment was empty.

The computer.

Daniel spent an awful lot of time on Grant's computer.

She crossed the room and sat down at the desk, flicked on the PC's monitor, and began digging through hidden system files for a keystroke log.

53

Payton's first thought when he began to come around was that something was burning in the oven.

And it might've been him.

He drunkenly thought back . . .

He had been talking to Fletcher, who panicked about something or other, and then . . .

And then came the blast so loud he'd thought the world itself might have exploded.

Payton finally opened his eyes to find himself surrounded by flames. The asylum was *roaring*, consumed in fire and heat. Horrified screams came from all directions. Unmoving bodies lay about, and smoke was pouring everywhere, running into his eyes and making it hard to breathe.

So much fire . . . It couldn't have spread this fast . . . Where did it come from?

He was vaguely aware that his head was thundering in pain. And something wet was running down his right arm. A *lot* of something wet.

But there was no time for that now . . .

"Morgan!" he shouted when he spotted her through the haze. She seemed to be having trouble waking up, jerking lazily there on the floor, up against the wall. Something had *blown* her clear across the room . . .

She had several nasty cuts and her shoulder didn't look quite right . . .

Payton quickly regained his bearings and stood to see what was happening.

Fletcher was helping people up, appearing to have taken only a few scratches from the blast . . .

Hannah was rising from the floor by the couch, looking all around, tears pouring from her eyes . . .

His eyes met hers from across the room. There was no gloating in her face. Only despair. She had known something was coming. And he wouldn't listen.

She turned and began helping others get up . . .

But some of them could not be roused.

In the distance, entire sections of the building collapsed, causing deafening rumbles.

How did this happen? It was too fast, much too fast . . .

Reflection would have to wait. Payton joined in the escape efforts as the building's girders groaned and creaked above him. The building wouldn't—*couldn't*—remain upright for very long. The survivors gathered and Hannah and Fletcher began leading them out of the Common Room, toward the facility's back door.

Payton got close enough to see that Morgan's shoulder was indeed out of its socket, as he'd suspected, but she appeared to be ignoring the pain.

If she even felt any.

She merely watched her people and her surroundings, all burning.

The asylum would be a total loss in a matter of minutes.

Morgan couldn't look away from her dream dying, no matter where she turned. He grabbed her by the arm and steered her after the others.

Several hallways were completely blocked off, and they were forced to find new routes more than once.

And as they ran, they encountered more residents. Burning and bleeding.

Crying.

Grieving.

Some of them were on fire even now, motionless on the ground.

But there was no time . . . no time to stop and help . . . no time to think . . .

They soon had gathered the remaining survivors into a pack, all racing toward a rear entrance, the front hallway having caved in from the blast that had undoubtedly come from something rigged to Payton's motorcycle.

Morgan stopped in the rear hallway to check another body on the ground, which was wrapped hideously around a free-standing pillar in the middle of the corridor. Whoever it was, they weren't moving.

Payton carried two survivors—one over each shoulder—but stopped next to her as the ceiling groaned again.

"She won't hold together long!" he yelled over the roar of the flames and the collapsing building. With that, he was gone, faster than she could see.

Others passed by as Morgan continued to check for signs of life.

Hannah hobbled by, half-walking, half-dragging another limping resident.

From high above them, a great, terrible crack reverberated, so loud it drowned out all else.

The post Morgan knelt by began to fracture and crumble . . .

"*MORGAN!*" Hannah shrieked.

Before Morgan could react, she felt herself being shoved, as a violent crash shook the foundations of the entire building.

She looked up to see that the entire pillar had come down. It had brought much of the ceiling and this part of the building down with it, but she was clear and unscathed. Wiping debris off her body, she sat up and gasped in horror.

Trapped under the largest remaining section of the pillar was Hannah.

Unmoving.

Grant drove his scratched, dented blue Corvette faster than he'd ever dared before, blazing a lightning trail down the evening highway. Traffic was building, the closer he got to L.A., but he zoomed around everyone in sight.

Flashing red-and-blue lights appeared in his rearview mirror, but he ignored them, seeing only what was in his mind's eye.

Seeing it *all*.

Grant flinched as various sections of the asylum collapsed. A few times, he felt the unique light in his soul dim as another ring-wearer fell. And another.

He could *feel* them. Falling. Fading away.

He was already too late, he was at least another hour away . . .

I wasn't there . . .

When they needed me, I wasn't there!

"Hannah!" Morgan yelled over the burning building and the ongoing crashes around them.

"Morgan," Hannah tried to shout, but it came out quietly. She was completely pinned under the cement pylon, unable to move even her arms. "Get out of here, go . . ."

"Payton! Fletcher! *SOMEBODY!!*" Morgan screamed. Her useless shoulder was no good, but she propped the other one up against the pillar and threw her entire body weight against it.

The pillar never budged, and the fire, which had spread up into the ceiling, leaped hungrily down onto the pillar.

"It's all right," Hannah said, smiling, as the fire crept toward her like lava rolling down a hillside.

Choking on the billowing smoke, Morgan reached out and took Hannah's hand.

Her pulse was fading . . .

"It's as it should be," Hannah said softly, trying to keep her eyes open. "I deserve this. You don't."

Morgan cried.

She could do nothing else.

Tears rained openly down Morgan's face as Hannah closed her eyes.

Whoever this woman had been, whatever she was responsible for . . . Morgan was alive because she had taken her place.

The building shook again, and Morgan knew she should be running away as fast as her feet could carry her.

But she clutched Hannah's hand even tighter.

Daniel made his way carefully upstairs to Grant's apartment as darkness fell over the city. Lisa had never come down for supper. He'd been on the phone for the last hour, making final preparations, so it hardly bothered him. But it was odd of her to disappear for so long.

He placed his key in the lock and swung the door open. Lisa sat at the computer, across the room.

"There you are," he said, hobbling inside, "Where have you been all—?"

"You want to tell to me what this is?" she said quietly.

He looked at her—*really* looked at her—for the first time. She had been reading something on the screen . . . A very familiar-looking screen . . .

She was calm as she looked upon him, but he could tell that she was serious.

Dead serious.

"You want to *explain* to me why you're making secret plans with people you meet in *chat rooms*? Or why you're holding clandestine meetings in dark alleys? Why money has changed hands between you and a couple of rhino-sized thugs?"

He closed his eyes and looked down. His shoulders sagged. "Look, I know how it—"

Lisa jumped up from her chair and traversed the room in a few quick paces. She crossed her arms, facing him with a grim, resolute face.

"Skip the excuses and explain, right now," she said. "Lie to me, and I'll break your crutches."

"*Payton!*" Morgan screamed again.

In a flash he was outside the building's exit, just down the hall— what remained of it—looking in.

"We need—help here!" she shouted back, coughing through the smoke.

He was about to spring into action when a figure casually walked out from a side hall to stand between them, facing Payton. The darkened figure was illuminated only by the dancing light of the flames that continued to grow. He wore a hat and overcoat.

Payton could make out none of the man's features; his mouth and nose were covered by a handkerchief.

"What's wrong?" the man said, and Payton could hear a smile in his voice. His eyes glimmered with a madness that was fitting of the chaos and destruction that surrounded him. "I should think a man like you would appreciate a little violence and mayhem."

"You did this?" Payton asked, carefully placing his hand on the hilt of his sword.

"Fun for a girl and a boy," the man replied, smiling again.

"What do you want?" Payton asked. "Who are you?"

"Who am I? What a strange question," the man sounded genuinely perplexed. "Especially at a time like this. Look around you. Don't you think your priorities are a little misplaced?"

The man threw off his trench coat to reveal a black jumpsuit covered in pockets. Guns and knives of all makes and sizes were tucked into those pockets, and his arms dangled loosely at his sides, ready to make use of his weapons.

Payton didn't respond to his question.

"Oh, very well," the man replied patiently, removing his hat and untying the handkerchief around his face. He threw them both aside.

Payton didn't recognize the man, but he had to fight the urge to look away in revulsion. The man's scalp was covered in hideous red scabs, and the skin on his face was disfigured—portions of it had melted.

"My name is Konrad," he said, whipping out pistols from hip holsters on each side. "As for what I *want*, well . . . Let's just say I've developed a fondness for the smell of burning flesh."

54

"Konrad," Payton repeated the man's name, while sharply drawing his sword. "The mercenary."

His first instinct had been to draw the sword using a burst of speed and jump quickly into action. But he could still hear Devlin's warnings about tipping your hand too early in a fight.

When you have the tactical advantage, maintain it for as long as possible.

Besides, he needed time to size the other man up.

"I know you," Payton said. "The Secretum sent you to attack Grant the day he underwent the Shift. Did you know you were there merely to test his instincts? The Secretum *knew* you had no hope of success. It is written in prophecy that *I* will be the one to kill him."

Konrad eyed him angrily. "You can keep your signs and portents. I couldn't care less. Borrows is *mine*, and if you want another shot at him, it'll be over my dead body."

As you wish.

Payton weighed his options. He could strike quickly now and end it, but his eyes drifted to Morgan. She knelt on the ground, not far behind Konrad, holding the hand of the traitor, Hannah. He couldn't see from where he stood if Hannah was alive or dead. Behind them all, a handful of survivors had gathered in the hallway, needing to escape the flames that continued to spread, but were now unable to reach this exit—the only remaining way out—because Konrad was blocking it.

And if what he had heard about this Konrad was true, the mercenary was resourceful and not to be underestimated. Even if he was mad from his injuries, he'd still survived them, and probably through sheer will.

"What does destroying this building get you?" Payton said, taking one step into the burning building. The sound of the rushing flames was so deafening he had to shout to be heard. The heavy thickness of the billowing, gray smoke seeped into his eyes and lungs. His throat protested the noxious fumes, but he forced himself not to cough. Not now.

"A blissful night's sleep," Konrad replied, leveling both pistols on Payton's position and releasing the safeties. He grinned a disgusting smile through his deformed, misshapen lips.

Payton didn't like the idea of fighting Konrad here, amidst this out-of-control hurricane of heat, smoke, and flames. Which no doubt had been Konrad's plan from the beginning. He had nothing to lose here—it wasn't like his burned body could get much worse. Payton, on the other hand, was surrounded by collateral damage waiting to happen.

This was a no-win situation.

After the last few days, Payton had no idea where his allegiances lay anymore, but he wasn't in the habit of allowing brutal death to come to the innocent.

The guilty, however, he executed without hesitation.

And no small amount of satisfaction.

"Don't suppose you'd care to tell me who hired you for *this* job?" Payton took another step forward, sword at the ready. Only six or seven paces now separated them. He had to time this just right . . .

"Doesn't matter now, you won't live long enough to meet him," Konrad replied, as if it were obvious. "In case you haven't caught on yet, you are not the adversary I was hoping to fight today." Konrad took a step forward as well.

"Well then," Payton whispered. "Keep hope alive."

He sprung.

A split-second later, he was rounding Konrad, but the mercenary raised the pistol in his right hand and pointed it at Payton's head, just as Payton grabbed Konrad in a headlock. The sword, still in Payton's other hand, instantly came around to slice into Konrad's throat.

Konrad fired.

But instead of a bullet, Payton felt some kind of liquid drenching his face and stinging his eyes.

A water gun?

He flinched, and pulled away, blinking hard.

That's not water . . .

"Thing is," he heard Konrad's voice say, "I know you, too, Mister *Thresher*. Read the full dossier. And I know exactly how to put the brakes on your hustle and bustle. Start with the eyes, and work your way down."

Payton could hear him smiling again.

But he could no longer see him, blinded by the gasoline Konrad had sprayed in his face. He wiped off as much as he could with his free hand, but the stench was overpowering, it had soaked into his hair and shirt . . .

And heat advanced on him from every direction. He staggered backward, grasping about with his free hand, unable to get his bearings. He was certain the flames swirling around him would lick his face any moment, igniting the gas.

"Look out!" Morgan screamed, just as a shot was fired.

At first, Payton stood still, believing that Konrad had missed.

Then he felt a searing pain in his left side, just above his waist.

Payton fell backward, onto his rear end. His strength seemed to be running out of his body along with the oozing blood.

He was dazed, his internal alarms allowing too much time to pass before his pain receptors triggered the growing heat on his right side. He choked, pulling backward quickly.

The wall is on fire . . .

All the walls are on fire, he realized.

What remained of the building would collapse soon, they were out of time, he couldn't see anything, and Konrad had killed him . . .

The exit finally appeared in sight, but Grant's focus remained elsewhere.

He watched.

He saw the column collapse, saw Hannah push Morgan out of the way.

Saw a shadowy figure appear out of the flames like some twisted, gnarled demon straight from Hell. But he couldn't see who it was.

It was then that he snapped back to reality and first noticed the flashing lights in his rear-view.

But instead of panicking, Grant barely gave the police a passing thought, focusing momentarily on the squad car's four wheels as he watched them in the mirror.

He closed his eyes for a single instant . . .

And the tires gave an ear-splitting *pop*, bursting into shreds of rubber. The police car dropped and began spitting sparks from all four wheel assemblies, digging grooves into the asphalt.

It was forced to stop.

Grant turned off onto the old service road that led to the asylum, still miles away.

No no no!!

I'll never make it in time . . .

"Payton!" Morgan screamed from somewhere behind him.

Payton's instincts kicked in as he felt a slight shift in the air to his left.

He brought his sword up super-fast, which was jarred by a heavy *clang*. He was an experienced enough fighter to recognize the weight and sound of the sound that impacted his blade—Konrad was using some kind of knife.

"I can't express to you how disappointing this is," Konrad's voice said from his left. The knife drew back and Payton forced himself to his feet, his free hand clutching his wounded side, from which blood continued to pour.

"First, Grant doesn't have the courtesy to show, and I can't *tell* you how much I was looking forward to seeing him again," Konrad continued, his voice circling Payton now, as Payton spun in place, struggling to keep up. "But the prospect of fighting the legendary swordmaster seemed like the next best thing. You *do* know you're a legend, don't you?"

Payton didn't respond, dizzy from trying to audibly keep track of Konrad's position.

Again he heard the whisper of Konrad moving, from behind this time. The mercenary thrust again with his knife, but Payton spun and blocked the blow. Without his vision, though, he wasn't able to match Konrad's movements perfectly. Konrad slashed at Payton's outstretched arm, cutting deep into his forearm.

"Grant bested me on his very first day. He was sloppy—not to mention ridiculously lucky—but he got the job done," Konrad went on, still circling Payton's position. Sometimes his voice was close, sometimes it was further away. "And yet here *you* are, trained to be unbeatable and I've crippled you with a child's toy."

Payton staggered left, felt flames all-too-close, and jerked back quickly.

Too quickly.

Sweat streamed off his forehead as he lurched backward, and Konrad kicked his feet out from under him. Payton went down onto his back, coughing and hacking through the smoke.

"So much for the great warrior," Konrad muttered from above him.

Payton's strength was all but gone as he heard the real gun's safety click into place.

"No!" Morgan screamed.

"Don't worry, sweetheart," Konrad said. "You're up next."

Payton was certain that somewhere nearby, he could hear whispering. It sounded like Hannah's voice, what was she doing . . .

His eyes had cleared just enough to make out Konrad's dark, blurry outline above him through the smoke and noise, and the outstretched arm that held the gun trained on him.

Payton could barely make out what looked like Morgan's shape, standing to Konrad's right with a piece of concrete from the fallen pillar . . . *He should be able to see her, why hasn't he noticed her standing right there . . .*

Hannah.

An unholy roar escaped Morgan's lips, and she slammed the concrete block as hard as she could into Konrad's head.

Konrad howled and stumbled forward. But he was on his feet again surprisingly fast, enraged and somehow oblivious to all pain. He punched Morgan sharp and hard in the face, and she flew back onto the ground. Konrad never stopped to see if she stayed down; instead, his momentum carried him back to stand above Payton again, and

Payton could now see red blood oozing out of a gash on the side of the mercenary's head.

"That's the thing about pain," Konrad said, grinning through his grotesque, blood-stained face. "Endure enough of it, and it doesn't even slow you down anymore."

Something inside Payton snapped. "Endure this."

Clenching the sword, he swung with abandon, arcing out sideways from where he lay, strong and fast.

Konrad howled like a rabid animal as his lower legs were separated from his feet at the ankles in one stunning stroke. The gun in his hand went off as he toppled down, but the shot was wide.

Payton had just enough strength left to prop himself on one arm beside Konrad and knock the gun out of his hand. Konrad was lost to the pain, screaming at the top of his lungs, unaware Payton was even there.

Through the thick smoke, Payton's eyes met with Morgan's, who had also propped herself up from where Konrad had sent her smashing to the floor. They both coughed violently through the smoke, but never wavered in their gaze.

And despite the years and circumstances that separated them, he could still read her like an open book. He knew she was thinking about how, even if only for a moment, she'd become the enraged animal she swore she'd never be. The sad resolve in her eyes told him that she didn't care anymore.

She knew exactly what was left for Payton to do now.

And she wasn't going to protest.

Payton flipped the sword around in his hand to hold it outstretched over Konrad's prostrate neck, and then swung it down sharply with every last bit of rage and strength he had left.

The adrenaline faded, loss of blood asserted itself, and he was lost in a sea of black.

55

The Corvette screeched to a halt at the end of the driveway, but he couldn't move.

Nothing remained.

Where the building once stood, was now blackened brick, burning doors and window frames, and orange fire burning out of control, pouring black smoke high into the sky. What remained of the building's walls were no more than fragments sticking up like shards of broken glass. A fifty-foot crater in the front yard was all that was left of Payton's motorcycle, and the entire front of the building had blown in from the blast, effectively destroying any chance of exit that way.

He knew many of the residents were still alive—he could feel it— just as he knew some of them were buried inside, unable to escape on their own. Some of them he only had faint impressions of. They were fading fast.

Grant exploded out of his car, running to find the few whose life he still felt, heading directly around to the back of the building.

There he found a congregated group of twenty or so survivors, all huddled together, crying, holding each other, choking and coughing on the flames and smoke. Tears smudged the soot on their faces in long streaks, and most of them never even noticed his arrival. They couldn't take their eyes off of the asylum.

Their refuge from a cruel world. Destroyed.

"*MORGAN!*" Grant screamed, rounding to the rear exit in a full sprint.

"In here!" he heard a faint cry.

He could see nothing through the smoke and flames, which were impossibly thick now. But he entered anyway.

How do I put this out?

Grant couldn't create water; he could only manipulate existing objects. Which gave him no advantage in this situation.

"Grant, quick!"

Morgan's voice.

"Where are you?" he yelled. He stumbled in the smoke, so thick it blocked out light, even the flickering of the flames.

"Here!" Morgan cried again, her voice closer this time.

He turned right and went forward several paces to find Morgan kneeling on the floor next to Hannah, who was still buried under the broken pillar.

"She's not breathing!" Morgan screamed hysterically, her face soaked with tears and sweat and soot.

"Back up, get back!" he yelled.

Morgan stood and took several steps backward.

Grant reached out with both hands, focusing his mind as hard as he could on the heavy pillar trapping Hannah.

But it wouldn't budge. It was too heavy . . .

"Come on . . ." he mumbled. *"Come on!"*

He forced himself to relax, going through the exercises Daniel had taught him. He closed his eyes and envisioned himself reaching out with two giant hands and picking up the column.

He opened his eyes to see the column floating a few feet over Hannah's body.

"Get her!" he roared.

Morgan flew in quickly and began hefting the younger woman out.

"I can't hold it!" he screamed.

Nearby, another part of the building came tumbling down in an unrestrained display of destructive power. A sharp blast of wind struck them both, and Grant stumbled off-balance for a moment.

He lost control of the pillar just as Morgan pulled Hannah to safety.

More screams penetrated the smoke and heat, from all directions.

"Help me!"

"Please!"

"Somebody!"

Grant turned to Morgan and pointed to the exit. "Get her out of here!"

"Payton—he's over there," Morgan bellowed, pointing. With that, she hoisted Hannah up over her shoulders in a manner Grant wouldn't have thought the older woman capable of, and swiftly made her way to the exit.

Grant turned to the direction she'd pointed and found Payton on the ground, bleeding badly from a wound in his side and another on his shoulder. A deep cut into his arm seemed to have stopped bleeding, but from the looks of it, he had already lost a great deal of blood.

Still, he had a faint pulse, so Grant followed Morgan's lead by heaving the big man over his shoulders and staggering through the smoke and flames.

Outside, he dropped Payton to the ground, where some of the others attended to him, including, Grant noticed, the boy Thomas.

Morgan knelt over Hannah, performing CPR. She turned and vomited up an ugly mess of black soot from somewhere deep inside her, but never stopped pumping up and down on Hannah's chest.

There was no time to get the rest of them out, they would die before he could reach them, the fire had spread to the whole building, going back in would be suicide . . .

The earth shook as another section of the building gave way and they all turned to look. A great gush of wind swept into Grant's face once again, and the feeling triggered an idea . . .

It had taken all the focus he had to levitate the pillar; this was a whole other level.

Still, it was the only idea he had, and there was no alternative.

"Morgan, get the others out of here!" he screamed.

She pulled up from breathing into Hannah's mouth to face him. "Where?! There's nowhere to—"

"Just take them out to the street or something!" he yelled, turning to the gathered crowd. "All of you! Get as far away from the building as you can!"

The group jumped into action as he tore off a section of his button-up shirt and tied it around his mouth. He ran recklessly back into the raging furnace. Fire leapt up to meet him as he jumped through what remained of the exit, but he ducked around it as best he could.

His shirt caught fire and he dropped to the ground and rolled. But he bumped into a wall, and there was no room left to roll. He stood and tore the shirt off, leaving only a white T-shirt underneath.

The screams continued, along with the cries for help.

He closed his eyes, envisioning each of them where they were. He estimated there had to be at least a dozen of them. Some were trapped under rubble. Others were free but blocked off by the collapsed building or flames on all sides. A few wouldn't live more than a few minutes. And none of them were accessible from his location.

"Everyone that can hear my voice!" he thundered. *"Get down on the floor as low as you can! But don't hold onto anything! Just lie still!"*

He gave them a moment to comply, watching those he could see in his mind's eye.

Grant made his way farther, deeper into the building. Eyes watering, lungs burning for oxygen, he knew he only had a matter of seconds.

When he could go no farther, when he felt his mind going hazy with lack of air, he stopped, let his arms hang at his sides, and looked around.

He was in the Common Room.

It'll have to do . . .

He closed his eyes and let out a breath. He needed more this time than he was able to safely control through concentration . . .

He needed the fear.

He thought of the building he was in and those that were about to lose their lives. Because he hadn't been there to help them. He thought of Hannah, almost certainly dead outside on the ground. And Payton, and Morgan . . . And he thought of how he might never get to speak to his sister again, hear her voice, feel her embrace . . .

The panic came, shooting through him in a savage wave of terror, and he bore down hard, opening his arms wide and flexing every muscle in his body . . .

A gargantuan rumble shook the foundations of the building, and suddenly every wall and the parts of the roof that still stood—all of which were engulfed in a sea of red-hot inferno—every piece of the building ripped free of its moorings and *flung* itself skyward, a cataclysm that tore the air.

For just a blink, Grant hesitated. Then he let panic stab his heart once again, unable to hold back a tremendous scream of emotional detonation. The pieces of the building still flying upward into the air, still in flames, exploded outward with a shockwave that toppled Grant to his knees.

Morgan and the others screamed, running to avoid the larger pieces of debris now falling from the sky like firebombs.

He'd done his best, but portions of the building flew everywhere, outward, into the surrounding woods, the street, the driveway. One barely missed Grant's car. They rained down in fire, but Grant had no strength left to run. He only hoped none would find him.

When the echoing blast faded, Grant opened his eyes again. The fire had vanished along with the building, and the smoke was beginning to dissipate as well, much of it swept away by the force of the blast.

He made a slow three-hundred-sixty degree turn, taking in every direction. He could see several survivors making their way carefully toward him, shell-shocked but alive. A few others he could feel alive but unable to move, flung aside by the clearing rubble or simply unconscious.

It was only when he stood that he saw the many charred bodies lying on the ground, cast about randomly like black feathers blown in the wind.

Some of them were burned beyond recognition.

A few he recognized, their faces frozen in horror, but hearts no longer beating.

So many he had failed. Failed them all.

Lisa sat back in her seat on the couch, and attempted to digest the story Daniel had just told her.

"You . . ." she sputtered, "Seriously?"

He nodded, watching her carefully.

"This . . ." she said, "I mean . . . It can't be *legal*."

"No," he replied, then added softly, "And, I could use your help."

Hands planted on hips, time seemed to stop as she glared daggers into him where he sat. "Have you *lost your mind?!*"

Daniel gave no answer.

"You. Want. My. Help?"

"No. I need your help," he said.

"I'm not your research assistant anymore!" she snarled, but besides the fire in her eyes, there was something else. Curiosity, perhaps. "What would I have to do?"

"I'll need a ride the night we do it, and I need a few supplies . . ."

Daniel could practically feel steam cascading off of her.

"How far are you willing to go with this?" Lisa asked, still looming above him.

He looked into her eyes with a hardened edge. "As far as it takes."

She said nothing for a long moment, then nodded. "I'll come. But I'm only coming to keep an eye on you."

56

Hours upon hours passed. The sun rose and set and rose again.

And Grant never stopped.

Never stopped lifting, moving, sifting through the wreckage. He left nothing unturned, refusing all help, sleep, or food.

More than once, Morgan or one of the others tried to get him to stop, slow down, take a break.

But Grant wouldn't hear them.

The police, fire department, and ambulances eventually arrived, but even they could not deter Grant or hold him back, as the medics quietly treated the wounded and the firemen doused the flames that had spread to the forest.

Even with all of the activity taking place, there was very little sound to be heard. A reverential hush consumed the entire property, save Grant's relentless searching. None of the survivors spoke; they merely watched. Everyone seemed immobilized by the fire, the death, and what Grant had done. And what he was still doing now.

Occasionally, he would emerge from the building carrying another body. He deposited them all at the edge of the blast crater, where Morgan waited to covertly remove the rings from their dead fingers. He had no idea if she planned to dispose of them or hide them, but either way he knew they'd be out of the picture in her hands.

The EMTs took it from there.

Grant, meanwhile, went back in. Every time.

Morgan was breathing oxygen through a mask hours later when she suddenly sprang up from her seat at the back of an ambulance and tore off the mask.

Before anyone could stop her, she ran past the medics and police and into the smoldering ruins. She passed Grant, who was still working like mad, using his powers to sift through what remained of the wrecked building.

Morgan never stopped running, winding her way through the building, searching for something . . .

"It's gone!" she shouted after a few minutes.

"What?" Grant turned in her direction.

She reappeared in front of him, defeated. "The stone tablet! It's gone!"

Grant glared at her sideways, returning to his work. "Who *cares*, Morgan! You've got the whole thing memorized, anyway! People are *dead* here—"

"Grant," she said softly, placing a hand on his arm. He stopped.

"It's the *reason* they're dead," she said.

He turned sharply to stare into her eyes. Eyes that were weighed down by immeasurable sorrow.

"The Keeper . . . he took it," Grant breathed heavily. "That's what this was about—he just wanted the Dominion Stone . . ."

She walked away, leaving him to his work.

Whoever you are . . . I'll kill you for this.

On and on Grant went, covered in grime and despair.

He never stopped once, angrily defying exhaustion its prize.

After almost thirty hours, many of the survivors had finally dispersed—some taken to the hospital by the medics, others gone off in search of homeless shelters or other places they might stay.

The sun was setting on the second night after the fire as Morgan and the few others who still remained watched Grant emerge from the wreckage like a specter for the last time.

It was done. He'd saved all that he could save and recovered what was left of those he couldn't.

Dirty, exhausted, and covered in grime, a dangerous expression darkened his features like a heavy storm cloud ready to strike.

All told, nineteen bodies had been recovered from the wreckage.
Nineteen.

Nineteen lights extinguished in his soul.

Grant was too spent to shed any tears for them. That might come
later. For now, the devastation around him had crept into his heart and
left no room for anything else. There were no words. No emotions. No
energy.

Grant walked slowly past Morgan and the others, as well as the
two ambulances that remained. Two EMTs came over and grabbed him
by the arms, meaning to finally drag him back to their equipment and
treat his smoke inhalation, but he angrily jerked loose and kept walking.

Morgan ran around in front of him, blocking his path. He noticed
for the first time that her arm and shoulder had been set in a sling.
Her hair and skin were dark and muddy, blood encrusted on her hands
and fingers. Her eyes were impossibly puffy, yet more tears poured out
now as she locked gazes with Grant.

But he never stopped walking or even slowed down. He simply
stepped around her. She reached out with her good arm and placed her
hand on his shoulder from behind. He paused only a moment before
dropping his head and shaking it slightly.

"Please don't," he whispered.

He kept walking until he reached his car.

Slowly the engine came to life and the car limped its way down the
lonely drive until it was out of sight.

No one spoke to Grant for the next forty-eight hours. They tried,
but he was unresponsive. He had returned to the apartment, walked
past Daniel and Lisa—who hushed instantly when he entered—without comment, and collapsed on his bed.

There he slept fitfully, stirring awake often. Hours upon hours, he
drifted in and out of asleep and awake states and all the subtle hues in
between.

Dreams came in spurts—violent, terrifying visions of roaring flames
and horrified screams. He awoke repeatedly with the putrid taste of
burning death in his mouth.

He went to the bathroom and washed his teeth several times,

trying to get rid of the taste of the heat and the smoke and the burning bodies. But it wouldn't leave.

All the while, every one of the Loci continued about their business—most of them in hiding or in the hospital, recovering from injuries—and all of them aware that the time of the prophecy was drawing ever closer.

Even Grant was aware of the passage of time and what it meant, but he was too drained, too emotionally decimated to do anything about it.

He wouldn't answer his phone, and he locked himself in his bedroom.

And without him, the others had no idea what to do.

Grant's first visitor since the tragedy came in the early evening, four days after the fire.

A gentle knock at the door barely captured his attention as he sat in the kitchen alone eating a bowl of cereal, staring into space.

He glanced at the door and kept eating.

Another knock. Louder this time.

"Go away, Morgan!" he said.

The door nearly caved in at the next knock. He stood up from his stool so fast he pushed it over and ran to the door.

Throwing it open wide, he shouted, "I said, *go away!*"

It wasn't Morgan.

"Hi," said the visitor.

It was Hannah.

Why hadn't he felt her arrival? He looked down; her ring was still on. But then, he'd stopped trying to feel her.

"You were hurt," he blurted. She looked better than she had the last few times he'd seen her. Shaken and battered, but not crushed.

"Cracked ribs," she said, placing a steadying hand across her torso, "and plenty o' scrapes and bruises. It's pretty hard to catch my breath. But thanks to you and Morgan, no permanent—"

"What do you want?"

She met his eyes, briefly. "Somethin' I can never have."

For a reason he couldn't define, Grant suddenly couldn't bring himself to look at her. He examined her shoes instead.

"Then . . . we have something in common," he said.

Hannah entered timidly, walking carefully around him, but refused to sit. She stood a few yards away, and she kept glancing at him nervously, but she was unable to keep her eyes upon him for very long.

Grant closed the door behind her and crossed his arms over his chest. He never offered her a chair.

Minutes passed in silence.

"Everyone kept telling me to slow down, to take time, think . . . *feel* . . ." Grant said quietly. "They finally got their wish. It feels like . . . I think I'm still on that street corner, standing at the bus stop. Watching myself walk down the street. I think maybe . . . I never left that spot."

Hannah looked down, unable to hold his eye.

"I know what you did for Morgan."

"It doesn't change anything," she stated the obvious.

He frowned, "No, it doesn't."

"I want to explain. I want to justify what I've done. But there ain't no happy ending to get to. Drexel hired me to spy on you, to find out everything I could. I never meant you any harm, personally. Do you remember that day we met, crawling through those air ducts at Inveo? I warned you then you shouldn't trust me."

Grant's thoughts and emotions were a million miles away.

"But you did. And instead of ditching you, like I should have—I felt something. Before I knew how or why . . . I found that I cared about you, deeply. I still do."

"Hannah," he interrupted, his voice a dry monotone, "I know what you came here for, so just say it and get it over with."

It wasn't an accusation. He was merely tired. He had no use for accusations now.

"I . . . didn't come to apologize," she replied.

He looked up at her for the first time.

"If I did, would it matter? What would it change?" she said, sadness filling her voice.

"I don't know," he replied. "Probably nothing."

"I did what I did, and there ain't an excuse big enough to undo it. . . . I'd probably be crying *now* if I was capable of any more tears, but after *everything*, and then the last few days . . . I feel like coffee beans that've been spilled all over the floor . . . Or no—which nursery rhyme was it? The one who couldn't be put together again?"

"Humpty Dumpty," he replied quietly.

"That's me," she said, nodding hopelessly. "Humpty Dumpty. No matter what I do, what I've done will always be there . . . A long, ugly list of demerits on my permanent record. And I can't ever reverse it."

Grant's demeanor suddenly changed, and he looked up, outside his window. His gaze was far away. "No," he said quietly. "You can't."

Despite her claim of being all out, tears spilled from her eyes.

"And maybe you're not supposed to," he said, emotion rising in his voice.

She got lost in his eyes, alone and confused.

"It's something my sister was trying to tell me . . . I didn't understand it *then*, but . . ." he said, shaking his head, then he took a single step closer to her. "We can't ever go back to the way things were after mistakes are made. There are always consequences . . ."

She examined his coffee table in great detail, afraid to look at him.

"But maybe it's not about what *you* do next," he continued, swallowing. "Maybe it's not up to *you* to fix what's broken."

More tears leaked out of her eyes, and she almost turned her body fully away from him now.

Something opened in Grant's heart—it had been stopped up by despair and grief—but now he found that his own eyes were moistening.

This was stupid. He had every reason to hate this woman.

It wasn't rational. It wasn't what any sane person would do.

But what Hannah needed right now was the very thing that Grant was craving more than life itself. And he hadn't realized it until now, seeing her in this state.

Since he couldn't give it to himself, he did the only thing he could do.

He offered it to Hannah.

He crossed the distance between them and grabbed her by the shoulders, forcing her to look into his face. And he embraced her.

Hannah was overcome. He could see the shock in her face. The question. She knew what she *deserved* and it wasn't this . . .

Her body went limp, breaking into sobs so violent that she shook uncontrollably, and she wasn't holding herself up by her own power . . .

No, Grant was doing that.

He was holding her tight. And he was shaking and sobbing as well.

"I'm sorry!" she wailed, head buried in his chest. *"Please*, Grant— I'm *so* sorry! I'm sorry I'm sorry I'm sorry . . ." She continued to blurt it out between heaving breaths until she had no more strength or words or breath.

When she finally stopped, he whispered in her ear.

"It's okay. It's all going to be okay now."

57

Very late that night and into the early morning hours, Matthew Drexel attended a scheduled rendezvous, made the drop, and then checked his watch as he struggled to get into the backseat of his car.

"Let's go," he growled at his driver. He was running late.

He rubbed his aching back as the driver took him to his next destination. He was still suffering from his run-in with Grant and Payton over a week ago, and he'd taken to using a cane to get around.

He knew the address of the meeting was among some warehouses on the outskirts of the city, so when his driver raised his eyebrows at the neighborhood, Drexel growled for him to keep his eyes on the road. This lead and the money it might offer were too good not to check out. Besides, he'd been in places far worse than this.

A dozen minutes later, his car pulled up next to a sagging old building and Drexel got out.

He was overcome by the desire not to stay in this place one minute longer than necessary. The building left him feeling . . . unsettled. But he couldn't put his finger on why.

Drexel approached the door and rapped his knuckles on it five times, as instructed.

The door opened to reveal a dark interior.

"Enter," a voice commanded.

"What is this?" Drexel said, put off by the lack of visibility inside the building.

He received no answer, and was about to turn around when something crashed into his head from behind. He lurched and wobbled, and fell to his knees, seeing stars.

"What the—!" he yelled.

Immediately two sets of hands were lifting him from under his arms and dragging him forward into the pitch-black interior.

They reached the center of the room, and the two who held him threw him forward, onto the ground. His eyes could see very little, but the room seemed like an abandoned warehouse with a shorter ceiling. Empty. He couldn't see far past the shadows before his face.

The shadows moved again and a fist landed square in his nose. He yelped and tried crawling away, but another set of hands grabbed his feet and dragged him back. And then what had to be no less than three men—*strong* men, to be able to take a big guy like him down—were everywhere at once, all over him, punching, kicking, bashing. A tooth was knocked loose. His legs screamed in agony as they were kicked again and again. Fists landed across his chest and stomach.

Minutes passed and then suddenly they stopped.

Then without a word, the three shadowy figures walked away, leaving him lying there.

A bright spotlight from somewhere above switched on and bathed him in light.

He spit blood out of his mouth to the side and squinted, peering out into the darkness.

"How does it feel?" a voice called out of the dark.

"Who are you!" Drexel demanded. "What is this?"

A figure approached out of the darkness, bearing down on him where he still lay on the floor.

But the figure wasn't walking. He was rolling in a wheelchair.

He came into view and Drexel recognized him.

"I want to tell you a story, Mr. Drexel," said Daniel, rolling his new wheelchair just out of Drexel's reach. A pistol rested in his lap.

"Cossick," Drexel said, piecing it together. "Do you have any idea what I'm going to—"

"It's a good story, full of blood, violence, and adult content. Right up your alley," Daniel said, cold and unwavering. "So *shut up* and listen."

Daniel's eyes pierced furiously into Drexel, but Drexel stubbornly held his gaze.

"Once upon a time," Daniel began, "there was a boy named Daniel. He was a happy little toddler until one day when he crawled up to an electrical outlet and stuck his finger inside. Afterward, the doctor told his parents that he was lucky to be alive. He took his first steps a few days later."

Drexel eyed the crippled man warily. He had no idea what this game was, but he didn't like where it was going.

"Daniel grew up and went to college. One morning on the way to class, his car was slammed into by an eighteen-wheeler. The car was smashed beyond repair, and the truck took heavy damage as well. But Daniel walked away from that accident with only a few cuts and scrapes. The police deemed it a fluke, 'one-in-a-million' they called it."

Daniel watched the man on the ground with contempt, everything inside him wanting to *spit* on this waste of human flesh.

"Three weeks ago, Daniel came down the stairs of this very building from his lab on the second floor and walked outside, where three thugs beat him within an inch of his life. It happened right out there—outside the very door you walked through just a few minutes ago."

A young brunette Drexel recognized as Cossick's assistant appeared from behind the wheelchair and raised up the footrests in front. Daniel very slowly and gingerly placed his legs—still in their casts—down onto the cold concrete floor. The brunette braced the chair from the back as he pulled himself up by his arms. Then she produced crutches.

Carefully, he took a few baby steps forward to face Drexel at arm's length, leaning heavily on his crutches. The brunette stayed behind the chair, watching him with a motherly concern that made Drexel want to wretch.

"You can knock me down as many times as you want. But I promise you, I will always—*always*—get back up."

"If you're going to kill me, just do it already so I don't have to listen to any—"

He stopped. And blinked.

They weren't alone in this enormous room. Over a dozen figures emerged from the shadows, forming a circle that surrounded him.

"Listen, we can just—"

"It's not a good feeling, is it?" Daniel asked, leisurely waving the gun about. "To be all alone. In the dark. Outnumbered. These are my new friends, by the way," he gestured wide to the circle. "All of *them* have stories, too. I bet you don't even remember Sarah here," he said, and a young woman stepped into the light. Daniel was right; Drexel didn't recognize her.

"But I'm sure you remember her mother, Joanna," Daniel said. "She was raped to death by a thug who broke into her home and stole a big-screen TV, a computer, and a few hundred dollars. The culprit was a 'friend' of yours, so you had Sarah's father framed for the crime."

Drexel wanted to back away from them all, but there was nowhere to go. They were everywhere.

"Or how about young Will," Daniel continued as a young boy slid into view atop a skateboard. "His older brother was one of your fellow officers. Yeah, I'm sure you remember him. He tried to take you down a few years ago, but he and his wife both died in a freak car accident. An *accident*!" Daniel repeated, underscoring his thoughts on that word.

"We could go on like this for hours. You've ruined so many lives . . . but you always got away with it. Those connections with the higher-ups pay off, don't they? When you get results."

"I just do what I'm told, that's all I've ever done."

"Nobody in the Los Angeles police—"

Drexel stopped him with a sour laugh. "The force?" He shook his head, watching Daniel's growing awareness. "Doctor, you need to think a little bigger."

Daniel was stunned. "All this time," Daniel said, aghast, "even before you met Grant or me . . ."

"We *all* answer to someone," Drexel said, a smile teasing the corners of his lips. "What? You're shocked and appalled that I was able to keep my true loyalties a secret?"

Drexel let out a single chuckle.

"You work for the Keeper."

"We *all* work for the Keeper, little man. Since minute one with you and your friends, we've been feeding into his plans. You're working for him *right now*, doing his dirty work, tying up a loose end that he won't have to contend with."

"Loose end. . . ?" Daniel said. He looked at Drexel differently. "What have you done?"

"Don't you read the newspapers?" Drexel grinned. "Your friends were involved and everything . . ."

"You were behind the arson at the asylum," Daniel gasped. He swallowed, realizing something else. "You hired Konrad! *You took the Dominion Stone!*"

"At *any* cost," he said. "Though the higher the better, I always find."

"Where is it?" Daniel asked. Drexel had turned his back to him. He could hear the hatred in Daniel's voice. That was good. He had him upset, thinking poorly.

"You're the Ph.D. Where do you *think?"*

"The Keeper," Daniel whispered.

He has the tablet.

Drexel suddenly moved, retrieving a gun from an ankle holster. This punk was in over his head. He spun quickly to face Daniel . . .

And Daniel shot him between the eyes.

Everyone froze as Drexel's body snapped backward and slammed into the ground.

Lisa's mouth was hanging open, but she couldn't move. It was almost as if by not moving, she could undo what had just happened.

Daniel still pointed the gun at Drexel's body, an inhuman expression on his face.

Lisa walked slowly forward for a closer look at Drexel's massive body, sprawled out on the floor. Blood poured slowly from the hole in his forehead. His eyes were still open. But he wasn't breathing.

"He's dead . . ." she despaired, turning to Daniel in disbelief. "You killed him!"

Daniel was locked in an emotion somewhere between shock, sickness, and satisfaction.

He'd really done it.

And he'd *meant* it.

Daniel brought his good hand up to cover his mouth as he searched an empty spot on the floor ahead. He didn't know whether to laugh or cry.

He felt like doing both.

58

Grant found a new vigor and sense of urgency the next morning, after sleeping deeply for the first time in weeks.

His first action was to track down Morgan and invite her and as many of the Loci as they could find to come to his apartment. Then he checked in with his sister at the hospital; she was showing increased brain activity, indicating deep dreams. The doctors said she could wake anytime. On his way back to the apartment, around mid-morning, he stopped at Daniel and Lisa's to ask them to come to the meeting as well. Lisa came to the door having just been roused from her bed by the doorbell. Apparently, she and Daniel had had some kind of very long night.

By early afternoon he was welcoming Hannah into his apartment for the meeting.

"Am I early?" she said, at his door.

"Not too bad," he smiled. "Morgan and the others should be here soon. I've offered to let as many of them stay here in the Wagner Building as we have space for. We need to talk things through and figure out where to go from here."

"You mean us?" she asked, alarmed.

"No, the *group*. As in, what's our next step. With the prophecy and everything."

"Oh. Right," she let out a breath and turned a pinkish shade of red. "Well, look at that, I made us both uncomfortable. Way to go, me." She laughed nervously.

He smiled, but said nothing.

"How's Payton?" she asked.

"Too stubborn to die, I believe is the way Morgan described it. He should be all right. He's coming to the meeting, in fact, against doctor's orders."

"*I* wouldn't want to be the one who tried to keep him away," she smiled.

They stared at each other for an awkward moment.

"Grant?" she asked, taking a seat next to him on the couch. "I was wondering something . . . about whether something *else* besides just me could ever be put back together . . ."

She didn't have to say any more; he knew exactly where she was going.

"I honestly don't know," he said. "Forgiveness is one thing, but with everything that's happening, I don't know if it's a good idea for us to . . ." He couldn't bring himself to say the rest.

"I understand," she nodded, looking away. "It's a shame, though. We never even had a first kiss."

He blushed.

"But you're right," she concluded, nervously standing up. "It's way too soon, *not* a good idea. I don't know what I was thinking . . ." she let out a nervous breath.

She walked away, but Grant followed, reaching to grab hold of her arm.

"I know *exactly* what you were thinking," he said, pulling her close. "Because it's all I can think about, too."

The world and all its sights and sounds and concerns and logic and reason faded to nothing, and it was simply *happening*.

Grant's heart pounded so loudly that blood rushed past his ears, but all he cared about was her lips on his and . . .

Before he got the smallest taste of her, the apartment door slammed shut.

They jumped apart, and twisted to face the door.

Alex stood there, her clothes hanging in tatters. She was breathing hard, unable to catch her breath.

She had a nasty black eye, she bled from a swollen lip, bruises covered what could be seen of her arms, and she stumbled toward them, limping, about to collapse.

"It's happening!" she gasped. "The end of everything . . ."

Grant caught her and lowered her to the ground.

She closed her eyes, but before unconsciousness swallowed her, she whispered:

"It's happening *now*."

One by one, Grant welcomed his friends into his apartment. Most he knew by name, a few he didn't.

Hannah and Alex were still there, of course, Hannah watching over Alex, who was resting uncomfortably on the couch. Hannah spent a while cleaning Alex's scrapes and bruises. They exchanged pained looks from time to time, and Alex winced frequently.

But neither spoke.

Half an hour later, Daniel and Lisa arrived. Daniel hobbled to Grant's bedroom, where the two men had a private discussion. Lisa sat uncomfortably in the living room watching the other two women, barely aware they were there.

Morgan and Fletcher arrived next, trailed by a small group of Loci. Morgan was still haggard and unrested, and her shoulder remained in the sling, but she'd cleaned herself up. When Grant emerged from his room—no longer smiling—her eyes were trained on him with intense interest. Daniel followed slowly. Fletcher was fidgety, his eyes darting about as he took in every detail of Grant's home.

Grant suddenly looked far away. Someone had just registered on his radar, entering the building. He'd been watching, waiting.

A few other Loci straggled in before Payton entered the room. He strode in scowling, as if nothing were wrong, though everyone else tensed sharply at the sight of him. The evidence of his recent fight was obvious: a long bandage could be seen sticking out from his sleeve, and though he tried to hide it, his good arm hugged his abdomen firmly where Konrad had shot him. There was a slight stagger to his gait.

Lisa turned angrily to Grant. "What's 'Sir Hacks-a-lot' doing here!"

The twenty or so present had gathered in a large circle in Grant's living room, but now many of them were on their feet.

"Payton is here at my invitation," Grant offered. "Everyone please relax. Like it or not, he's a part of this. And whatever's going on concerns us *all*."

"Here, I'll play nice," Payton said, as he unbuckled his sword from his belt and tossed it sideways to Fletcher who, disgusted, dropped it onto the coffee table with a loud clatter.

Grant waited until they were silent and watching him. When he had their attention, he began.

"Here's where we're at. Someone out there calling himself the 'Keeper' is using us. The rings were given to us intentionally, to turn us into something else. Something . . . superior."

"Someone's trying to make us into heroes," Fletcher said. It wasn't a question.

"Yeah," Grant replied, surprised. He had been planning to ease into that part of the conversation.

Fletcher nodded. "I suspected as much."

"Heroes," Morgan repeated slowly, straining to find a more comfortable position for her shoulder. "That's what this is all about? The Shift? The rings?"

"They're called the Rings of Dominion," Grant began. From there, he told them the highlights of Payton's story, about the Rings, the Secretum, and his ring, the Seal of Dominion. He revealed his trip to his childhood home, the truth of his identity, and his parents' membership in the Secretum. He finished by sharing the prophecy from the Dominion Stone that Daniel had translated.

No one spoke and significant glances were scarce as everyone present tried to accept the enormity of what had just been set out before them. Even Grant, who had spent some time with these facts already, found himself once again pondering it all.

Mostly, everyone stared at the coffee table in the center of the circle.

"I understand it's a lot to digest, but time is running out . . ." Grant said.

Morgan nodded, not looking up. "I get it, I'm just . . ."

Grant watched her face, which was showing a mixture of alarm and disbelief.

"This isn't what you were expecting," Grant offered.

Morgan looked up. "It's what I expected for *you*. I've known you were meant for something like this since the moment I met you.

But . . . you have to understand, Grant . . . the rest of us . . ."

"I know you're afraid," Grant said, "So am I."

"Fear is pointless," Fletcher announced. "My reservations about Grant notwithstanding, even I can no longer deny what's plainly before us. Everything that's happened to him—to *all* of us—it's been preordained. We've been cast in certain roles. We may have no choice but to perform them."

"No," Morgan was saying, shaking her head, breathing faster. "We'll find someplace new, a safe refuge where we can—"

"*Morgan*," Grant said forcefully, and everyone in the circle looked up sharply. "Lines are being drawn. Sides are being taken. Hiding, trying to keep the world at bay—it's not an option anymore.

"I know we've all been through some . . . painful experiences of late," he went on. "But there's a fight coming, and I think it's fair to say we all feel the weight of it, growing heavier. Dr. Cossick has new information to share with the group. But first, Alex has some news." He turned to her. "Maybe you should start by explaining what's happened to you."

"The Keeper happened to me. This," she glanced down at herself, "is my reprimand. I was a fool to think it could be kept from him."

"How did you escape?" Payton asked.

"He let me go on the condition that I would come straight here and tell you that the end has arrived. Whatever's coming that you all have to stop—it's coming now."

No one spoke.

"Once again," Fletcher piped up, breaking the silence, "it falls to me to point out the obvious. She's admitted that she is employed by the enemy. What proof do we have that she's a genuine double agent? Does *anyone* here really know anything about her at all?" he said, facing her.

Alex sighed, her face tilting down to examine her bare feet.

"Hate to admit it, Alex," Grant said, "but he's right. You told me that everyone has their own agenda, but you've never told me what yours is. I think we have to know."

She let out a very long breath and looked back up.

"Everything I told you about me was the truth. The Keeper really *did* hire me to keep tabs on you all. But that wasn't . . . the *whole* truth. It *is* my job to watch you, to keep up with your activities and report back on your progress," she said, stopping to take a sip. "What I didn't tell you . . . is that it was also my job to *select* each of you in the first place."

Murmurs filled the room as dark glances were exchanged.

"I was given a list to work from," she continued, "and assigned to seek out these people who were good candidates for the Shift."

"What criteria were used for creating this list?" Morgan asked.

"I don't know. But I *do* know that the information from my reports was the deciding factor on which of you were selected for the experiment. I'm sorry," she said, sad but resolute.

"Did you select me?" Grant asked.

"No," she replied. "You're special. You always have been. From what I gather, you were *always* earmarked for the experiments, but you were saved for last."

"So we're just 'experiments' to you? Trial runs so that *he* could be perfected?" Payton muttered bitterly, angling his head toward Grant. He locked cruel eyes on Alex. "I wonder what kind of person it takes to uproot and erase another's life?"

Alex's head unexpectedly turned to Payton in a flash. "I may have cleared you for the experiments, but the person you became after that was *your* doing. *Not* mine. And I *had* no choice in any of this; it was either take the job or take a nice long nap six feet under."

"I think it's safe to say," Grant spoke up, looking at everyone in the room individually, "that everyone in this room has regrets of some kind. We've all done things we'd like to take back." His eyes lingered on Daniel for a moment, before he turned back to Alex again. "But this is the moment of truth, Alex. And we need all of it."

She faced Morgan.

"You were the only one I never got to watch. Because, as you've always assumed, you were the first one to ever go through the Shift. And that's the truth. You *were* the first."

Alex looked down at her toes again and swallowed.

"I was the second."

"What?" Grant voiced what the entire room was thinking. "*You* were Shifted? But you're not wearing a ring."

"The Keeper was still in the early stages of his work back then. I had no idea then who he was or that he even existed, of course, I was just confused and afraid like all of you, but . . . there was an accident. I was just learning how to control my mental ability, and I was trying to help this guy. Unfortunately, he got some bad news and took it out on me; heated words were exchanged, and he . . . slapped me. And in a moment of anger, I used my mental power to . . . *damage* him."

"Damage him how?" Morgan asked.

"He's lived the last ten years of his life in a straitjacket, where he will probably remain until the day he dies. He would gladly hurt himself if he could. He's tried many times, over the years, or so I've heard. I was . . . absolutely horrified by what I'd done, and even more frightened because I couldn't *undo* it. I was just devastated. I never knew myself capable of such rage. And I was only a teenager . . .

"The Keeper found me, brought me to some kind of facility, and explained that I was his first failed experiment. I begged him to remove my ring, to take the power back. I told him I'd do anything he wanted if he would just take it away. I thought he was going to kill me, but he agreed. He used drugs to stop my heart long enough to pry the ring off my finger. And with that, my power was gone. But I was still living inside this new life that I didn't know or want. Like each of you, I couldn't go back to who I was before."

No one said anything as they all tried to absorb her tale.

"Being powerless to do anything about any of this . . . being forced to work for him all these years . . . I . . . It made me so . . . That's the reason I made contact with you, Grant, the day you were Shifted. It's been fourteen years, and I had nearly given up hope. But I knew you were different from all the others, and I thought you might be my last hope of escaping him."

"Who is he?" Grant asked.

"Grant, I've never seen him . . ."

"You just said you bargained with him to get your ring off."

"It was done by intermediaries, scientists, people who spoke for him and worked *with* him at this facility where they took me. I never even knew where I was, they blindfolded—"

"*What is his* name?" Grant shouted.

Alex flinched at his outburst before she collected herself.

"I would have told you already if I knew. I'm beginning to think he doesn't even *have* a real name."

Alex sat back in her seat, apparently finished.

Grant sighed. "All right. Thank you for telling the truth. Better late than never. Your turn, Doc," he said, but didn't stop watching Alex.

"The Keeper has the Dominion Stone," Daniel announced, generating a new swell of murmurs around the circle.

"So it's safe to assume that he knows everything we know," Grant said.

"It's safer to assume he knows *a whole lot more* than we know," said Fletcher.

"How did you come by this information, Doctor?" Morgan inquired.

"Matthew Drexel told me," he replied.

"You've *seen* him?" Morgan asked in a quiet voice. "Was it *him*—?"

Daniel nodded. "He hired Konrad to burn your building to the ground," he said, which drew another round of surprised expressions and mumbling. "But Drexel himself was acting under orders. He was working for the Keeper all along."

Grant fought the urge to curse.

Another manipulation.

This had to stop.

Now.

"Where is Drexel currently?" Payton snarled. It was plain to see that he was thinking exactly as Grant was.

"He's, um—"

"A dead issue," Lisa blurted out, lifeless eyes staring ahead into nothing.

"And we know for certain that Drexel was working for the Secretum? There's evidence of this?" Morgan asked.

"Oh, come on, Morgan," Grant said forcefully, before Daniel could answer. He rose from his chair with an exasperated expression. "Look at how Alex has been used for so long. He reeled Hannah in because she could get close to us. *You've* been a pawn in this thing for over a decade, with the tablet and Drexel and everything that happened at the asylum. Daniel nearly lost his *life* a few weeks ago. Payton was saved and trained at the hands of the Secretum. And then there's everything that's happened to me . . .

"Does *anyone* in this room seriously believe that they haven't been manipulated by the Keeper in one way or another? Everything that's happened to all of us points straight back to *him*. And personally . . . I'm sick of it."

Grant was pacing now, holding their full attention.

"I've just had enough, haven't you?" he asked them all. "Everything we're talking about comes back to this one issue: The Keeper has ruined all of our lives. He's killed innocent people. He's Shifted us, and given us bizarre abilities that none of us asked for. To what end, I can't imagine. He's manipulated our entire lives, pulled and prodded us, *changed* everything about who we are . . ."

He stopped pacing.

"And I don't know about you, but I'd like to show him the *depth* of his mistake."

Payton's eyes lit up, but everyone else looked at one another timidly.

"So it's like this. We can either sit back and wait for whatever's going to happen . . . or we can *end* the manipulations and stop all this before it happens. Right now."

"But how can it be stopped?" Hannah spoke up for the first time. "If it's predestined to be, then isn't it inevitable, no matter what we do?"

Grant was pensive, lost in thought.

No one spoke as his mind filled with thoughts at a frenetic pace, weighing options and making very fast decisions.

"What are you thinking, Grant?" asked Morgan.

His shoulders dropped. "I'm thinking I'm tired of running defense. I'm tired of just *taking* whatever is dished out at me. I'm thinking it's time we *end this*."

"How?" Morgan asked.

"Look around this room, all of you. In this one location, we have over a dozen individuals who can do things that no one else in the world can do. Haven't *any* of you wondered what might happen if we pooled those gifts and used them in a single, concerted effort?"

From their reactions, most of them hadn't.

"I know," he continued, "this is not what any of you want. But I refuse to believe that fate reigns supreme. I believe we might just be able to pull off the impossible."

Glances were exchanged once again, though many of them were filled with fear. Others, with a hardened resolve.

"I'm in," Payton said, his arms folded across his chest. "But the Keeper could be any Joe Bloggs on the street. How are we supposed to find him?"

"We don't have to. I think I've finally figured it out," Grant replied, turning his gaze to Hannah. "I just remembered. It was a secret place . . . underground."

Hannah nodded back to him, thinking the same thing.

"We're going to need detailed plans of that facility," Grant said, still gazing at Hannah.

"You'll have them," she replied, her features confident and set.

"Once we have those plans, Morgan, I want you to memorize every square inch of them. Put your head together with Fletcher and Daniel to formulate a strategy for getting us in."

Morgan nodded apprehensively, immediately catching on.

"Payton, you and I will be on point. Hannah, we'll need you to cover us with misdirection."

"I've got plenty of tricks left up my sleeve," she replied, smiling grimly.

Grant nodded. "It's not going to be as easy this time . . . Surely they've beefed up security since we were there."

When no one said anything for a few moments, Grant took the lead. "Let's get to work, then. Everyone without an assignment, you know your talents. Make yourselves useful. We go at sundown tomorrow."

59

"Lisa, you in position?" Daniel's voice echoed in her ear. He sounded nervous and it was nice that his concern was for her.

"Have I mentioned how much I hate this plan?" she whispered back in a helpless voice through her earpiece.

"Only in every way possible," Daniel replied. *"Just be careful."*

Lisa peered out through the windshield of the van, noting with growing fear that dusk was nearly over.

Which meant it was time.

She glanced at her watch. Almost seven o'clock.

The comm link was silent as she said nothing, running over the plan once again in her mind.

All the while, her eyes twitched to and fro across the landscape before her, her thoughts racing back to the events of two nights ago, when the man she loved had taken another's life in cold blood.

Well, that wasn't exactly right. Drexel had been about to fire at *him* . . .

Still, Daniel could have shot him in the arm or something.

But he didn't. *He* chose *exactly where to—*

"The others are ready," Morgan reported to both of them, also on the communications system.

"Let's get this over with," Lisa sighed.

"Fletcher, get ready for my signal," said Daniel.

Fletcher put his hands on the wheel of his van, which was identical to the one Lisa drove.

"I'm ready whenever," he said in a bored voice.

Grant held Hannah by both hands. They'd been interrupted before he could show her that he'd forgiven her and things had only gotten busier since then. Payton waited behind them, ready to spring into action. There'd been little point, despite the man's injuries, in trying to convince the swordsman to sit this out.

This was endgame.

"Hannah, we need you in place," Morgan said.

"You know what to do," Grant said to Hannah, mustering confidence. He'd surrendered to his feelings before and those he'd loved had disappeared or gotten hurt.

"I always know what to do when I'm with you," Hannah replied. Still confident, still calm.

He watched her—watched every square inch of her—with longing.

But there was nothing else to say. The silence between them said it all.

"It's time," Payton said from behind, still looking away.

Grant let go of her and turned to join Payton.

"Be careful," Hannah called out.

"You too," he spun his head.

But she was already gone.

"Please be careful," he whispered.

Did they have any chance of succeeding at this?

Was it crazy, what they were about to attempt?

No. The Keeper has to be stopped. No more manipulating.

He closed his eyes, remembering the sight of that enormous, round metal door underground . . .

"We're standing by," Grant heard Payton say into his comm link.

Grant's eyes were out of focus, staring into nothing. Payton glanced at him.

"Are you sure you're ready for this?" Payton whispered, covering his microphone.

Grant nodded vacantly.

"You *know* not everyone will survive," Payton said.

"Yeah," Grant replied, his voice already dead.

"Alex, are you in place?" they heard Daniel's voice say into their ears.

"Almost," Alex replied.

Grant snapped back to reality with something that had been tugging at the back of his mind since yesterday.

"Hey Alex?" Grant said. "You never said what your special ability was. When you had a ring of your own."

"I was empathic," she replied, whispering. *"I could feel other people's emotions. I could even zero-in on someone feeling a specific emotion and find them in a crowd."*

"But how would that drive a person insane?"

"I could implant *emotions, too.* Force *others to feel what I wanted them to feel."*

Grant didn't reply.

"This is harder than I thought," she said softly. Grant realized she was talking about the task at hand.

"Come on, Alex, it's time to go," said Daniel.

"Working on it. . . ." she replied.

"Can you do this, girl, or do you require help?" Payton grunted.

Grant frowned.

"I said I've got it," Alex replied. *"Call me 'girl' again and I'll choke you in your sleep."*

"Lisa, you're up," Daniel said.

In reply, Lisa punched the gas pedal, and her van roared to life. She ignored her instincts, which were telling her to slow down, and instead increased her speed, aiming straight at the barred gate ahead.

"On my mark . . ." Morgan said.

The gate drew closer, and she could see men pacing on either side of it in the distance.

"I think it's now!" Lisa cried, fingering a switch attached to a device in the empty seat beside her.

"Not yet," Morgan replied calmly, sounding distracted. She was no doubt keeping track of several things in her head—the speed of the van, the distance of the gate—in order to time this just right.

Lisa chose to trust her, but her heart was pounding so hard she thought she might pass out.

She was barreling forward at more than sixty miles an hour, and the gate was so close that she could read *Inveo Technologies—Security* written across the white metal arm in red.

"Now!" Morgan said.

Lisa flicked the switch and opened her door at the same time. The small device began to beep.

Five seconds . . . Not nearly enough time, what were they thinking!

She caught a fleeting glimpse of the guards ahead spotting the van for the first time as it devoured pavement on its way to meet them . . .

And then she was hurling herself out of the van and rolling on the grass beside the driveway. There was no time to stop, she picked herself up and ran for cover behind a brick wall on one side of the gate.

But before she reached it, an explosion ripped through the air behind her and toppled her.

Flames, smoke, and noise engulfed her. But she was in. Just as planned.

Fletcher floored the gas pedal on his van, racing toward another gate on the opposite side of the massive Inveo campus.

At Morgan's command, he bailed too, and a second explosion went off.

Grant and Payton scaled a tree right outside the Inveo property to a branch high among its limbs and watched the action on the ground inside. Right on cue, the two explosions went off one after the other. Guards poured from the various buildings and ran for the first gate when the second blast caught them by surprise.

Grant had to admit, his experience at Inveo two months ago had obviously made an impression. Their security force was at least three times the size it was when he was last here, and the black-clad men appeared much more efficient and better trained.

A few of the guards barked orders, and then several broke off from the main group and got into security cars, driving to the second gate. Others made for the two remaining gates, as a preemptive measure.

But the garage facility that he and Payton watched with interest was still occupied. Only now the guards they could see inside stood at attention, their weapons held at the ready. The security force was prepared for this. They wouldn't allow all of their men to be distracted so easily.

As expected, Grant thought.

But there was no time to lose. Police and firemen would be along soon.

"Alex, your turn," Daniel said.

Pandemonium reigned inside the Inveo complex.

The second shift was hard at work when the alarms started blaring and the warehouses and business towers were ordered to evacuate immediately.

Workers filed quickly out of the buildings, directed by guards telling them where to go and repeatedly shouting, "Please remain calm!"

"Coast is clear, Alex," Morgan whispered.

Alex took a deep breath and emerged from her hiding place by the garage bunker.

She steadied herself as she walked lazily in front of the large garage doors, all three of which were raised and open. Men stirred about inside, many gripping formidable weapons in their hands.

There was a moment's stunned silence as the men spotted her.

Alex wore nothing but a terrycloth robe. Her hair was sopping wet, and she was uncharacteristically wearing makeup—Hannah, who had cooked up this part of the plan, seemed to relish giving her a "much needed makeover." Hannah herself had desired this job, but she was needed elsewhere.

Alex peered at the nearest guard over dark sunglasses with a bored expression. An unlit cigarette dangled between two fingers, and her other hand rested in a side pocket.

"This area is restricted, ma'am," the stunned guard said, still taking her in, scrapes, bruises, Band-Aids, and all.

She noticed his look and glanced down at herself. *"Dreadful* golfing accident. I'd rather not dwell," she said, offering her best impression of Hannah's sultry accent and turning to look back at the chaos running rampant all around them.

"You're not allowed to be here," the guard said, nearly tripping over his own feet.

"Then perhaps you could be a *sweet thing*," Alex replied, massaging her neck with one hand, "and direct me to the executive jacuzzi. I could really use some . . . *downtime*."

"Umm . . ." the man stared at her bug-eyed, as several other guards gathered round, all of them sizing her up and down, many with smiles.

"All this excitement is making me *ever* so tense, boys," she said, smirking. The sunglasses had slid down to the tip of her nose now and she looked over them, even batting her eyes once.

"I'll take you there," one of the other guards said, grinning.

"Thanks, handsome," she said. She walked to him and lit her cigarette. "Hold this for a second, would you?"

She slid her sunglasses back up.

The guard held the fake cigarette in his hand just as it went off.

The entire group of guards shouted in pain and staggered backward, blinded by the brilliant light of a flash bomb.

Alex flung the robe aside to reveal a tank top and rolled-up jeans underneath. She pulled a small canister the size of a tube of lipstick from her pocket and sprayed it into the faces of the hunched-over guards. The gas worked quickly and soon each fell unconscious.

Pocketing the canister, Alex fingered her earpiece with her free hand.

"Grant, time to ring the bell," she said, unable to suppress a smile.

60

Hannah watched from her position as Grant and Payton jumped over the fence from their high perch in the tree. A nearby guard was turning in their direction but Hannah held her gaze on him until Grant and Payton were clear, ensuring he saw nothing but empty ground.

Hannah turned a full circle, keeping an eye on every direction. Three hundred yards away stood a guard tower from which a bright search light swept back and forth across the grounds. She could barely make out the tiny outline of the guard who stood behind the light, scanning for intruders.

You are going to be a problem, she thought.

She heard a female guard approaching her own position but deflected the woman as soon as she came into view. The guard walked close enough to touch Hannah yet never saw her.

"Hannah," Grant whispered.

She turned. At the corner of one of the taller buildings, a few hundred feet away, she spotted Grant and Payton crouching. Grant was watching her. A group of guards drove past them in a security car, and they ducked down as low as they could get. A separate guard paced across the front of the building, blocking their next move. As the patrol car passed them by, she sent an image into the marching guard's mind. Spotting a flickering flashlight at the other side of the building, he started and then ran toward the imaginary light.

Away from Grant and Payton.

They had their opening and bolted for the garage.

Then she spotted the search beam again from high above, and it was getting closer.

She turned back to the guard tower and focused her mind on the tiny speck of a guard she could see there.

It was a stretch at this distance, but Hannah sent a terrifying image into his brain, high atop the watchtower. Soon the searchlight's sweep ended. The guard disappeared, no doubt descending to the ground so he could escape the tornado he saw chewing up the property.

When he was far away from the tower, Hannah turned her attention back to Grant and Payton.

But they were gone, out of sight. She didn't see them at the garage bunker in the distance, either.

She bolted toward the last place she'd seen them . . .

Grant and Payton ran side-by-side for the garage without a word.

A pair of golf carts containing security guards stopped before them, blocking their path.

"Halt!" one of men shouted.

In a flash, the guard who had spoken was down, Payton standing over him with his sword pointed at the other men.

The security men split into two groups, some of them rounding on Payton, the others approaching Grant.

Grant gestured at one of the golf carts and it began driving by itself. It ran down one of the men who approached him.

Grant and Payton were now left with three opponents each.

Payton made easy work of his first, slicing and stabbing in non-lethal ways per an earlier appeal from Grant.

Grant knocked the first guard off his feet as the other two approached . . . A nightstick hanging from one of their belts caught Grant's attention and it flew free, whipping up to smack the guard in the nose.

Payton faced off with one of his two remaining guards, who was doing a surprisingly good job of blocking Payton's sword with his nightstick. Payton never saw the other guard whip around with a furious kick. The sword was knocked out of his hand and flew several yards away.

Blows to the head and the chest stunned him but he recovered quickly, tackling the two guards to the ground at the same time and laying atop them.

"Grant!" he shouted.

Grant was sparring hand-to-hand with his last guard as he saw Payton on the ground out of the corner of his eye. Grant threw a brutal back-handed punch to his attacker's face, disorienting him. Then he turned and searched the ground. He spotted the sword and it instantly leapt into the air and twirled end over end until it landed perfectly in Payton's outstretched hand. Payton had never bothered to look up.

Instead he smiled at the two men beneath him as the sword fell into his hand from above.

Grant was kicked hard in the back and went down. He spun as the guard pulled a Taser out of his belt.

Grant had just caught sight of the gun as the guard pulled the trigger.

Grant gasped, sweating heavily as the Taser's two metal darts shot toward him . . .

And then they stopped, frozen in mid-air, as his eyes were trained on them.

The guard tried to retract the darts, but there was a burst of movement and the wires connecting the darts to his Taser were sliced in two. The darts dropped to the ground.

"Cute toy," glowered Payton, who was suddenly standing in front of the guard. He knocked the man out with an open-handed thrust to the jaw.

"Thanks," Grant gasped, still trying to catch his breath.

"Save it," Payton said, pulling him to his feet. "This is taking too long."

They both ran once more for the garage bunker, which was close. Grant caught sight of other Loci at various points in the distance and heard Morgan instructing them on where to go, what to do . . .

Hannah ran in behind them as they approached the garage.

"I don't want you here for this," Grant shouted at Hannah. "It's too dangerous!"

She didn't acknowledge him, just kept walking, and he didn't have time to argue.

Grant led the way to the back corner of the building where he and

Hannah had emerged from after their last visit.

"Security cameras above on both sides," Morgan said in their ears.

The cameras on the ceiling flew from the walls at Grant's command and crashed to the ground with sparks.

It suddenly struck him that the stairwell in the floor may not even be there anymore. *It was only a backdoor entrance of some kind, they could have filled it in or covered it over.*

But no, there it was.

They descended the stairs quickly without speaking, Grant uprooting more of the cameras before they were caught on tape.

The trio arrived at the command room, and Grant and Payton made quick work of the three guards remaining there. Then they joined Hannah outside in the hall and ran to the small door opposite the stairwell.

Grant's heart jumped into his throat. He hadn't been nervous or anxious until this moment, but it just hit him out of nowhere.

This is really it . . .

They opened the door.

Waiting for them there was the massive, three-story-high round metal vault door, set into a small alcove that offered just enough room to swing the massive door open. He had forgotten about the dull humming that filled the room.

The control panel beside the door flickered, beckoning him. He pulled out the small electronic device that Daniel had given him and attached it to the panel.

"We're set, Doc," Grant said, fingering his earpiece.

"Stand by," Daniel replied into his ear.

Daniel set to work on overriding the door's controls remotely.

Minutes passed and glances were exchanged. Hannah repeatedly checked her watch.

"The police should be here by now," Payton grumbled.

"Daniel! What's the holdup?" Grant cried impatiently.

"I can't crack it!" Daniel said. "It's one of the most complex algorithms I've ever seen. This thing is unbelievable . . . It'd take *weeks* just to crank this thing through my laptop and get a real handle on it."

"Plan B, then," Payton said, eying Grant.

"Get back," Grant ordered.

The three of them backed out into the hallway, but Grant stood at the threshold, his eyes on the door.

He let out a deep breath and settled his shoulders.

"Calming breaths, Grant," Daniel's voice said in his ear. *"You can do this."*

"Then shut up and let me," Grant mumbled.

He breathed in and out, very slowly.

He envisioned the door opening in his mind.

Or rather, he *tried* to.

But it wouldn't budge.

Even in his thoughts, it was too heavy.

He bore down, straining hard, but it wouldn't move.

"I can't," he winced, bearing down. "It's too much, I can't get it . . ."

His eyes popped open. Someone's hand had grasped his.

Hannah stood there, smiling calmly.

"You're the Bringer," she said. "You can do *anything.*"

He held her hand tight as he closed his eyes again and concentrated once more on the massive metal door.

Sweat poured from Grant's brow, and finally a loud crack was heard as the seal was broken.

It groaned noisily as it slowly swiveled open to the left.

Grant blinked when he saw what was before him.

The vast open space of the underground facility he expected to see . . .

. . . was instead nothing more than a sheer wall of dirt and stone.

Nothing but a cross section of earth.

"What. . . ?" Hannah said beside him. "I don't get it."

"The Keeper lured you here, probably to test your abilities," Daniel mumbled.

Grant closed his eyes, and his face began turning red. "It's another setup," he said softly. "*He* planted it here for me to find. It was just another manipulation!"

"Grant . . ." Hannah began.

"*Another manipulation!*" he roared, and the door that towered above them slammed itself shut with a deafening *boom.*

"*Move!*" he barked, marching out into the hall.

He no longer cared about the security cameras or the guards or anything else.

This was too much.

They heard footsteps racing down the stairs, but Grant merely walked away from them, down to the other end of the hall. Then he turned and faced the stairs, hands at his sides.

Waiting.

Payton and Hannah hurried to get behind him, positioning themselves for the fight ahead.

Over a dozen armed men spilled out of the stairwell and into the hallway, aiming rifles and Tasers and other weapons at them, screaming, "Hands up!" and "Down on the ground!"

Grant's hands balled into fists at his side, he let out a primordial scream. Every one of the guards whipped violently backward away from him, crashing into the far wall, and then collapsing into heaps on the floor.

Grant started walking again, making for the stairs.

"Grant—!" Hannah called.

But he never acknowledged her. She and Payton were forced to run to keep up with him.

At the top of the stairs, he emerged into the large garage full of vehicles and unconscious guards.

Grant stepped to the middle of the room and froze there.

His face was completely red now, and his breathing was hard and thick. He closed his eyes.

Hannah had never seen such a venomous look on his face.

It was almost a . . . *bloodlust*. The thought came to her with a chill.

"Don't do this, Grant!" she cried.

"I strongly suggest," he breathed in a voice of homicidal calm, "you both run."

Payton grabbed her by the arm and pulled her toward the exit. "Come on!"

She screamed "Grant!" again as Payton wrenched her away.

Payton and Hannah had just cleared the building when the vehicles inside came to life and crashed through all four walls of the building, driving off in every direction. A pair of sedans moving their way forced the two of them to roll aside.

Cars, vans, and golf carts drove and drove until they crashed into whatever was in their path. Sometimes it was buildings. Sometimes it was trees or the outer fence. A few ran over security guards and kept going.

"Grant, stop!" Hannah screamed, rising to her feet.

But he wasn't finished.

An ear-splitting crack followed next, as if a fissure had opened up in the earth.

She and Payton were knocked backward to the ground once more by what could only be described as a visible *wave* of energy, rippling outward from the building, tearing through everything in its path. The garage was reduced to rubble instantly, and the wave moved outward in a widening circle. From the rumble beneath them, Hannah surmised that it had probably caved in the underground facility as well.

The wave lost energy as it expanded outward. The blast had enough power to tear down a few smaller buildings nearby, exploding them outward with the wave of the blast. Bricks and wood and cement made a terrible dissonance of sounds, coming from all directions. But the larger buildings in the distance merely trembled, without falling.

When the energy faded, Hannah and Payton looked up to see Grant sunk down to his knees, sobbing into his hands at the center of where the garage had stood.

Just as they reached him, his phone rang.

Grant angrily pulled it out and saw a text message waiting from an unknown source.

It read:

> you're finally
> ready

61

Weary and defeated, the group returned to the Wagner Building, dispersing silently, once inside, for empty apartments scattered throughout. Hannah and Alex helped Grant get back to his place. He was too tired and distraught to be trusted to make the trip alone.

They tried to steer him directly to his bed, but he went to the couch instead.

His body was worn, but his mind was alive, burning, swimming with thoughts.

It was a diversion, a manipulation, from him . . .

To get me "ready" . . .

Ready for what?

If we only knew what the prophecy means . . . If only I knew what's coming . . . Or who the Keeper really is . . .

Hannah and Alex left him alone to stew. They conferred quietly, gazing out the big picture window at the city's dark night below. But all three of them—and probably all of the others, wherever they were— were thinking exactly the same thing.

Whatever was destined to happen, whatever was "coming," it had to be soon.

And they couldn't stop it.

Grant jumped as his phone rang.

Again.

He saw that it was the same unidentified number that had sent him the text message. He answered it.

"Who is this?" he said, and Hannah and Alex turned to watch.

"Someone you know," a male voice answered.

"The Keeper?" Grant said, his breath catching in his throat. He was afraid to know the answer.

"Of course."

Tears formed around Grant's eyes.

That voice . . .

He knew that voice. Even now, he could remember the exact sound of it.

He would never forget it.

"Dad?"

"Son," came the calm reply.

"But . . . how are you even alive?"

"It's time for you to come find out," the voice replied.

"No, you tell me how any of this is possible," Grant said, eager to keep the conversation going. He glanced at his watch. "Everything, the rings, the Shift, what I can do . . ."

"Very well," the Keeper replied. "But after I have explained, you will come down to meet me. At once." It was neither a request nor a question. It was a prediction.

Come down to meet me . . .

Payton said something about a "substation" . . .

Of course! How could I be so stupid!

"Before the existence of the earth," the Keeper said, in a tone that indicated he was reciting a story he knew by memory, "a vast war was waged throughout the universe. It was war on a scale unparalleled throughout recorded history. The essence of evil dawned in the hearts of those who once knew only good. And they made a choice.

"They gave themselves over to that evil. Rebellion was sparked throughout the cosmos, and all that was pure was forever tainted by betrayal. The leader of this rebellion was caught, tried, and confined here, to the earth.

"Some believe that a man named Ezekiel recorded this leader's trial in a vague account:

'You were the seal of perfection,
Full of wisdom and perfect in beauty . . .

Every precious stone was your covering:
The sardius, topaz, and diamond,
Beryl, onyx, and jasper,
Sapphire, turquoise, and emerald with gold . . .'"

Grant's heart filled with dread. But he had little time to consider it as the Keeper continued . . .

"'You were the anointed cherub . . .
I established you . . .
You walked back and forth in the midst of fiery stones.
You were perfect in your ways from the day you were created,
Till iniquity was found in you . . .
You became filled with violence within . . .
Therefore I cast you as a profane thing
Out of the mountain of God.'"

The Keeper paused his soliloquy. "Is it becoming clear to you?"

Grant's blood was ice cold. "I, I'm not . . . I don't know . . ." was all he could manage, even though it was *painfully* clear.

"The leader of this rebellion—the one Ezekiel wrote about," the Keeper continued, "was the most beautiful of his kind. He was adorned with handsome garments and precious stones. But his pride was his undoing, and so he and all who followed him were cast down from the higher realm, and he and his servants were given *dominion* over all the earth. But all of his vestiges, raiment, and adornments were stripped from him. It is the *last* of these adornments—his most powerful insignia—that now rests upon your finger."

Grant couldn't breathe.

Couldn't think.

Couldn't believe.

"Dad . . . Are you telling me . . ." he gasped, "that this thing—this ring that *won't come off*—was worn by. . . ?"

"It was the seal placed upon him to signify his dominion and power. The Seal of Dominion."

Grant's stomach lurched.

"The rings worn by the others were salvaged from similar vestiges stripped of his followers," the Keeper ended his story. "Similar in make, yet wholly different in purpose."

"Why are you doing this?" Grant cried. "Why use these rings to turn us into some kind of . . . heroes?" Grant blurted out.

"My boy," the Keeper said, disappointed and reproachful, "don't be so *obtuse*. Have you heard nothing I've said? The Seal of Dominion is the highest emblem of absolute evil. Besides, what use would someone like *me* have for *heroes?*"

"What are you saying?" Grant asked, his voice low.

"Ask yourself how often you've been angry, confused, and frustrated since this began. How many times have you lost your temper? Why is your first instinct when threatened to snuff out your enemy's life sharp and efficient? You think this is a side-effect of your confusion? I gave you the instincts of a killer. A well-trained one. I gave you a body capable of using those instincts. And the Seal is feeding you the *will* to use them.

"Ask yourself why every one of you that underwent the Shift was one of society's outcasts. The lonely, the forgotten, the orphans. The ones no one would ever miss."

The world around Grant blurred and spun, and he didn't want to hear anymore. He thought he was going to throw up, but he couldn't stop listening.

"*Now* ask yourself why a man as powerful as me would seek to create heroes. Oh, my boy. *Soldiers*, yes. But heroes? Not even *close*."

Grant couldn't hold back the tears now. This was beyond anything he could've expected . . .

"But why me?" Grant shouted.

"I fashioned you to be the Bringer. And you *must* play your role, and face what is to come. There is no one else who can."

"And if I don't want to?" Grant asked, even though he didn't want to know the answer.

"I've already proven that I will go to any lengths to ensure that you're ready for what's coming. But the time for talk is over. Your destiny has come, and it's waiting for you. And I will do whatever it takes to ensure that you seize it."

"You're insane . . ." Grant sobbed. "You can't do this . . ."

"I can do *anything*, or haven't you learned that by now?" the Keeper replied malevolently.

"How could anyone be this—"

"Spare me the pontificating. Your mother served her purpose, and when the time came, she had the good grace to let go. Now it's your girlfriend's turn to do the same."

Time ran like molasses. Grant's face contorted in horror as the phone fell from his hands. Hannah turned to him, worried, from where she stood in front of the large picture window. He heard the shot ring out from far away.

And instinctually, he panicked.

A silver platter resting on a nearby shelf launched itself spinning into the air, passing between Hannah and the window . . .

But it was too late by a fraction of a second . . . The window shattered, and she fell.

"*NOOO!!!*" Grant screamed, running for her.

With Alex's help, he dragged her from the view of the window and whoever was out there shooting. Her eyes were closed . . .

No! No! No! No! No!

"Hannah!" he cried, brushing her hair back. "Wake up! Stay with me!"

Alex was contorted with shock and sorrow as she gazed back and forth between Grant and Hannah.

Hannah stirred as Grant cradled her in his arms, inspecting the wound. The bullet had struck her shoulder, but it looked like a clean hole, it wasn't that bad . . .

She's going to make it, she's okay . . .

He was looking into her eyes, smiling in relief when he realized *she* wasn't taking her eyes off of *him*.

And blood was everywhere, all over him, on Alex, the carpet . . .

Words she'd spoken once flashed through his mind.

"I have to be on a line-of-sight with whoever I'm doing it to for it to work . . . and I can only do it to one person at a time."

Grant looked at Alex. Her features were stricken.

Grief-stricken.

But still Grant saw only the flesh wound on Hannah's shoulder, as she gazed on him without blinking.

"It's all right, big boy, I'm going to be fine . . ." she whispered.

Pain swelled within him but he choked back the tears until he felt like his throat might explode.

But he held her tighter, rocking her slowly. Only his whimpers could be heard.

Hannah's pulse faded as Grant kissed her forehead, pushing her hair out of her face . . .

She fought to keep her eyes open, her voice fading. "Don't . . ." she said groggily. "Don't let them take . . . your soul . . ." she said, struggling to speak.

"Hannah—!"

She stopped breathing.

Her eyes fell closed.

And then Grant was finally able to see the truth. The wound wasn't in her shoulder.

It had torn open her neck.

She had bled to death in his arms in a matter of seconds.

Grant stopped breathing, too.

He couldn't take his eyes off her, couldn't blink, no words would come. Inside him, her light dimmed, dimmed, and then, with a sigh, vanished.

Grant pulled her tight with his eyes closed and rocked her back and forth, holding nothing back in his grief.

"Grant," Alex said quietly.

He didn't hear her, he only continued rocking and crying.

"Grant, she's gone."

She's really gone, he thought.

No!

I never got to tell her . . .

He let go of Hannah and looked up at Alex, his heart flattened in despair. Still he said nothing as he cried, his soul dark and empty without her.

Alex watched as Grant turned loose of Hannah's lifeless body. But he was no longer rocking back and forth. He was trembling. And as he did, a deep, powerful rumble shook the building to its foundations.

Perfect time for an earthquake, she thought at first. *Typical L.A.*

At least it *felt* like an earthquake.

But then she saw Grant's face. His skin had turned red, his eyes were open, looking all around through a haze of water, his cheeks were soaked, and veins appeared on his forehead as he trembled harder and harder in a blinding fury.

Grief and rage burned in his eyes. The building was shaking violently now, and Alex found that she couldn't get up off the ground, even as she watched Grant rise to his feet.

Everything in the apartment rattled as the tremors grew worse. Small objects took on a life of their own and flung themselves across the room. Furniture and appliances uprooted themselves, falling over. Dishes and picture frames whizzed by in all directions and shattered against the walls.

Alex put her arms up to protect herself from flying papers, books, plates, picture frames, and other objects swirling about the room in a wild hurricane of power.

She could barely see Grant anymore as he walked unharmed through the heart of the storm toward the apartment door.

The door threw itself open, crashing into the wall beside it, and Grant stalked onward.

"Grant!" Alex shouted above the din.

He spun around in a violent blaze, and the apartment seemed to turn with him. *"He killed her!"* he roared, his voice booming like a clap of thunder.

Alex saw madness in him, and she realized in horror that she was looking into the face of a stranger . . .

What was that?

Something in his eyes . . . .

No, now there was nothing.

"He is not going to get away with it!"

"Grant, *no!"* she screamed, grappling for words and trying not to hug the carpet as the terror around them built to an impossible crescendo. They held each other's gaze, but she couldn't mask her terror at what she was witnessing.

What would Julie say to him right now?

"Grant, if you do this . . ." she shouted, finding her voice, "you will lose *everything* in you that's *good!"*

His face was hard as granite as his next words came out through clenched teeth.

"I wasn't *made* to be good."

He turned and walked out, leaving her to stare in stunned silence at the spot where he'd been.

The door slammed itself shut behind him.

The deadbolt and chain locked themselves.

62

Los Angeles quaked.

Rippling waves shuddered the city to its core, and the upheaval grew ever worse. Bricks fell free from buildings, awnings crashed to sidewalks, ceilings caved in, and light posts and power lines were uprooted.

Electricity went out and night engulfed the city for miles.

Cars screeched and crashed into one another. Fire hydrants were shaken loose and overturned, water gushing high into the air. Pedestrians spilled out of businesses, residences, and other buildings in droves. Mothers and fathers picked up their children and tried to get as far away from the stampedes of the rioting city as possible. But they didn't know where to run.

And then everything changed.

It began with a single scream.

Then another. Others followed, lifting their gazes to the night sky, and the panicked cries spread like an outward-growing ripple in a pond. One after another after another joined in the chorus as all eyes turned upward.

The moon and stars were gone.

Fierce, pitch-black clouds billowed and churned uncontrollably through the sky as if a thousand volcanoes were erupting.

Bright orange hues danced behind the clouds and around their edges. The heavens themselves were sparking into a scorching holocaust of heat and flame behind the swelling storm.

All light was gone, darkness swallowing the city whole, broken only by hair-trigger flashes of angry orange light from above.

Terror struck every heart, and everyone inexplicably knew that *something*—something that would change the world forever—was coming.

It was coming now.

On the bottom floor of the Wagner Building, the elevator doors ripped apart and Grant emerged, trembling and cloaked in malice. His cyclone of rage surrounded him, whipping up dirt and dust and anything else in its path, and stretching wide enough to blow out the windows on the ground floor.

Outside, the world had gone mad.

But Grant had no interest in what was outside the building.

Hannah's blood still dripped from his clothes, the coppery smell flooding his nostrils and fueling his turmoil.

His thoughts returned again and again to the words of the Keeper . . .

After I have explained, you will come down to meet me . . .

He knew what it meant.

The Keeper was very near, and had been all along.

Grant turned before reaching the front door and entered the emergency stairwell. He descended to the basement, retracing his steps from the day he was first Shifted to the small mechanical room where he'd hid from Konrad.

The spartan room was exactly as he remembered it: musty, dim, and filled only with a pulsing hum, as if you could hear the building's heartbeat. The narrow, emergency "fire escape" door that led to the subway was to his right in the back.

But the furnace was symmetrical in design, and a similar space was open amid the pipes on the left side of the room. But there was no door there.

At the room's threshold, Grant's eyes went dark as they settled on the furnace.

The massive heating device *ripped* itself free from its moorings and exploded out into the hall. Grant himself was unscathed and unmoved.

The subway door gave way from the blast, and a hole appeared in the opposite wall.

The hole was roughly the size of a man, and Grant went through, stalking down the dark corridor beyond.

Sweat poured off of him, his breathing fast and hard. He came upon a small set of double doors that slid apart as he approached. A stark, stainless steel elevator car waited on the other side.

He entered.

Grant never bothered with the buttons on the panel. He merely thought *down.*

And down he went.

Like a falling bomb.

Waiting to explode on impact.

Alex made it to her feet as the miniature storm in Grant's apartment subsided.

Hannah's broken body held her attention, outstretched as she was on the floor. The girl was already pale, the blood having drained from her neck wound. Alex blinked back the tears and tried to think straight, tried to decide what she should do next.

Morgan. I should find Morgan.

A light from the broken picture window flashed in the corner of her eye.

Another tremor unbalanced her stance, but this one felt different.

It wasn't localized around the building—she could see the entire city shaking outside, high-rises swaying back and forth ever-so-slightly.

Peering down at the streets far below, she gasped at the massive swell of the crowd. Every person in the entire city seemed to be fleeing in all directions, running for their lives.

She looked up.

It was a sight no human had ever before laid eyes on. The sky roiled and crashed like waves at sea in a turbulent storm. Clouds darker than any black she had ever seen collided, swirled, stirred, sparked, and detonated.

Fire was devouring the night sky, and it was spreading . . .

Spreading *downward.*

It was *here.*

But Grant had gone mad.

And Hannah was dead.

A wild notion rushed through her thoughts, from out of nowhere.

She decided it was the best idea she'd ever had.

Payton needed to see it for himself.

Using the stairs, which buckled wildly beneath him, he made a treacherous journey to the bottom floor of the Wagner Building where, like many of the other Loci, he had taken up residence in the last few days.

He met Morgan halfway down, flanked by Fletcher. Daniel and Lisa were already in the lobby on the ground floor when the three of them staggered out of the stairwell. Not escaping their notice was the door that led to the stairs, which had been ripped off of its hinges, but they had no time to consider it.

Payton coolly met the eyes of the others—all of which were filled with fear—and then gazed again through the empty window frames.

No words were exchanged.

As a group, they filed through the front door and took in the full scope of the event before them.

They'd no sooner regrouped outside than a monstrous tendril of flame leaped out of the sky and bored into the earth. All five of them were knocked off their feet as an office complex two blocks down was hit by the massive fire bomb; glass, steel, and everything within the building sparked to flame as if it had been superheated in a single moment.

They rose to their feet again and watched an enormous plume of smoke rise from where the office building had stood. They doubted anyone had been inside at this hour of the night, but it was still a fearsome sight.

Payton's hand was instinctively on his sword. "We must do something before this gets worse," he cried urgently.

Morgan turned to him, resigned. "What would you suggest?"

Payton had no answer.

Lisa's face was more stricken and terrified than Daniel had ever seen it. He placed a hand on her shoulder, and she side-stepped into his grasp, until his entire arm was holding her.

"What is it?" Lisa whispered.

"Something bigger than anything that has ever been," Daniel replied quietly, repeating words he had once spoken to Grant.

"Alex was right," Morgan spoke up.

They all turned to her.

"It's the end of everything," she said.

Grant's fists were clenched tight as the elevator door slid open after a long ride to the bottom.

"Mr. Borrows. Right on time," a voice to his right said. It sounded busy, occupied, impatient.

Grant stepped out and found a short, balding man holding a clipboard and watching him through round, wire-rimmed glasses. He wore a scientist's white lab coat and a detached expression.

"If you'll just come with me, he's eager to get underway . . ." the little man said, turning to walk away.

Grant barely gave the man a fleeting glance.

Instead, his eyes swiveled all about, taking in the sight before him, just as the bald man was suddenly jerked away to the side, crashing into a distant wall.

Grant was inside an immense hollow that looked as if the dirt and rock underground had been scooped away. It was like being within an enormous crater that was upside down. The vast, circular space was over half a mile in diameter.

Directly in its center stood a gleaming silver cube of solid steel, offset by metal girders thatched across its surface. It rose over ten stories above him, not quite touching the top of the hollow. A set of double doors lay straight ahead. The whole area smelled unnaturally clean, like a hospital.

A contingent of guards in black jumpsuits guarded the entrance. They already had weapons trained on him as he approached. But Grant was moving unstoppably forward, a force of nature. The guards were knocked hard to the ground on either side, as if the Red Sea had parted before him.

The double doors before him were labeled in big letters:

SUBSTATION LAMBDA-ALPHA

The doors never opened.

Grant glanced at them, and both doors exploded outward in a tremendous blast. He deflected them with an instinctive thought, and the two doors parted, falling to either side of him.

All the while, he never stopped moving forward.

He never slowed down.

Alex ran out into the ground floor lobby, scanning everything for Grant's trail.

She caught sight of the stairwell door lying broken on the ground. She looked inside and pieced it together.

He hadn't gone out into the city.

He'd gone under it.

She raced down to the destroyed mechanical room, surveying the damage, grim evidence of Grant's outrage. A thin path led through the devastation, across the floor to the far wall.

Which meant there was no time to waste. Into the opening in the wall and to the waiting stainless steel elevator she ran . . .

Inside the tall underground structure, black-clad militia men advanced on Grant in droves as he continued his slow, steady progress through the building. Unarmed scientists in lab coats ran screaming from his presence.

Everyone who came within sight of him was lifted up off their feet and blown aside.

Walls, doors, windows, lights, even the floor tiles were all caught in the hurricane of Grant's approach, and he showed no signs of tiring.

Blood in his eyes and death in his heart, he moved steadily toward the heart of the building through a tall, wide main corridor made from the same pristine steel as the outside.

But he was oblivious to it all, the image of Hannah's bloodstained body consuming his vision.

He was equally oblivious to the shimmering glow coming from the ring on his finger. Brighter and brighter it glimmered, its radiance outshining the building's own lighting.

Still he continued on, destroying, uprooting, tearing apart.

Searching.

Where.

Are.

You?

Alex jogged out of the underground elevator and took in the unconscious bodies and destruction in the gigantic cavern.

She had to find him . . .

She had to *stop* him . . .

There was no one else left, she couldn't let him do this, not *now*, when he was so badly needed outside . . .

But she knew she was going to be too late.

"*Grant!*" she bellowed.

Alex was answered by distant shrieks from within the tall subterranean structure ahead.

She followed the screams.

Down the main corridor, all was dark save a glimmering, hazy light in the distance.

"*Show yourself!*" a thundering voice boomed.

It was Grant.

63

The small storm surged around Grant, whipping up a frenzy of wind, debris, and demolition.

The coals of hatred had taken hold of him and he was stoking them with every ounce of energy he had.

"*Come out!!*" he raged, adrenaline surging through every vein in his body.

"Stop him!" someone shouted from behind. He heard a large collection of footsteps approaching . . .

He lashed out with a swift, spinning backhand. He was too far away for the blow to connect, but three guards flew backward anyway, their heads cracking hard against the cold, steel walls. Weapons were unholstered, but a blink from Grant later, the guns were floating high in the air above the militiamen.

"I am getting very"—Grant said with a dangerous calm—"*impatient.*"

On his last word, a surge of energy released from him in a wave, and everything around him—the guards included—flew backward and crashed in a ferocious display.

"You have truly exceeded all my hopes," said a calm voice.

A very familiar voice.

The same voice he'd spoken to on the phone in his apartment.

Before Hannah had been . . .

Hannah . . .

Grant turned to see who stood before him.

A figure was there, cloaked in shadow, just over ten feet away. But it was clearly a man, wearing some kind of business suit.

"And now you are ready to face your destiny," the man said again, taking a step forward.

"Grant, *don't!*" someone shrieked from behind.

Grant turned to see Alex running to catch him.

"The world's gone mad, they need you—!" she was shouting.

Grant spun back around to face the man.

The light from Grant's ring poured upon his face and at long last, Grant saw—

All of the breath escaped from his body and he felt weak and sick. The fury around him stopped cold.

Alex skidded to a stop next to him, facing the other man, but Grant ignored her.

"No . . ." he whispered, shaking his head in disbelief.

Dressed in a crisp navy suit, the Keeper was an older gentleman. His hands were clasped in front of him, a pristine gold watch at his wrist, barely concealing a tattoo, like the ones Grant's parents had displayed in the old photograph he'd found. A neatly trimmed salt-and-pepper mustache adorned his upper lip. He was stiff and emotionless, studying Grant's every breath and gesture.

And he was utterly calm and unaffected by the chaos and destruction Grant had wrought.

"Grant. . . ?" Alex asked loudly, turning toward him but keeping her eyes trained on the Keeper.

Grant was frozen, absolutely unmoving. He stared at the other man with a mixed expression of rejection, shock, and betrayal.

Grant took in unsteady gulps of air and stared sorrowfully into the face of this man who had destroyed his life. The pieces were falling into place in his mind, one by one. The snake in his mind had begun winding around and around again, and now he knew its identity.

"You said he didn't have a real name, Alex," Grant said, anger rising. "You were wrong."

She looked at Grant. "What is it?"

"Maximilian," Grant replied.

He never took his eyes off the Keeper as he extended his left arm out in front of her.

The old bracelet on Grant's wrist peeked out from under his shirt sleeve. A sloppily-scrawled inscription was engraved by hand into the metal surface of the old shell casing. It read:

Max B. 1943

Grant's arm fell to his side as he looked into the other man's eyes. "He's my grandfather," Grant said.

Alex's jaw dropped, and she glanced back and forth between them. They plainly recognized each other, but they were also seeing each other for the first time in decades.

It was true, then.

Grant started breathing fast again.

"Where is my father?" he asked, barely able to find his voice.

"Long dead," the Keeper replied calmly.

"*You* killed him," Grant spat, the whirlwind around him surging. "Didn't you?"

"No," the Keeper replied without deceit. "The coward took his own life. To keep you from *me*."

"What?"

"When he found out what I believed about you—what I believed you would *become*—your father had your mental acuity tested to see if it was true. Or even possible. The results were precisely as I told him they would be. With your mother dead, he knew that alone, he would never be able to keep you from me forever. But he also knew that with him dead and gone, I couldn't take custody of you and your sister without exposing the Secretum. So he killed himself and cut me off. You and your sister were declared wards of the state. You know the rest."

Grant looked down, staggering backward a few uneasy steps. The fury around him built once more, objects and debris again swirling about the corridor . . .

"You're the reason . . ." he said, "that they're gone. The reason they're dead. The reason I had to grow up in that awful place . . ."

"Your father believed he was shielding you by taking his own life," the Keeper said, still perfectly calm. "The fool had no idea how far I was willing to go to ensure that you met your destiny. Outside of my influence, you grew up and chose for yourself a life of solitude—a life you were never meant to have. Steps had to be taken to correct this."

Grant shook his head through a cascade of tears, eyes locked on his grandfather. The insanity of it all . . . that someone could presume to predetermine the entire course of his life and manipulate it to that end . . .

"I'm going to kill you now," Grant said, barely audible among the cacophony. He balled his fists and bore down, closing his eyes.

The Keeper did not react. He merely watched in silence.

The ground trembled as Grant prepared to let out another primordial surge of energy . . .

But something struck his head from behind, and the havoc around him ended as everything faded to black.

"I think he's coming around, sir."

Grant tried to blink.

But something was covering his eyes.

He couldn't move.

And he was dizzy.

Very dizzy.

"Sorry about all this," said the Keeper, his voice oddly swirling all around Grant.

That's when Grant realized that he was strapped in a standing position to something upright that was *spinning* in place.

And the Keeper was his grandfather.

His grandfather! His father's father . . .

How was it possible?

All he remembered of this old man was a handful of visits as a young boy and old pictures he had seen once of his grandparents together. He'd never even heard from the old man after his parents died, and assumed him to be dead as well.

"What's going on? Why am I . . . going in circles?" Grant stammered.

"I know it's uncomfortable. It won't last any longer than necessary, I assure you," the old man said. "But you could destroy this entire structure with a single thought, if you laid eyes on it. Which is the precise reason for the blindfold. Your friend Hannah told you her abilities only worked on line-of-sight. She was partially right. *Awareness* is the real key. You could destroy an object behind you right now if you knew where it was."

Grant didn't reply, absorbing this.

His grandfather pressed on. "It's the same for all of you. Morgan can only remember facts that she's directly exposed to. Payton can only enact his super-burst of speed against opponents that he can *see*. Likewise, if you're disoriented, your powers are useless."

"I could still let out a blast of energy in all directions," Grant said, his jaw rigid, his teeth grinding.

"Of course you could," the Keeper replied. "But if you did, Alex would no doubt suffer the consequences as well."

"What did you do with her?" Grant asked in as much of a menacing tone as he could muster.

"She's here. She's fine. For the moment."

Alex watched.

Strapped to a stationary table of her own in the structure's colossal inner chamber, she watched as across the room, the table holding Grant slowly spun.

She couldn't move, couldn't speak. Tape covered her mouth.

Three armed guards surrounded her, watching her every move.

Which seemed like overkill.

After all, what could she do in this position?

Let's hope they're thinking that, too . . . she mused.

Meanwhile, she kept her eyes trained on Grant.

Waiting for an opportunity, an opening, to put her plan into motion . . .

"What is all this about?" Grant cried. "What have you done to me? *What do you want?*"

"I want to stack the deck in your favor. Rig the game so you win. I want *the Bringer*," the Keeper replied, as if it were obvious. "Events are unfolding very quickly, so time is short. But I'll try to explain as best I can. Let me begin at the beginning . . .

"As I told you on the phone, the Rings of Dominion—as well as the Dominion Stone itself—were hidden for millennia. Buried and sealed in a place shrouded in utmost secrecy, they were entombed. Sealed beneath the earth by the Secretum of Six. The Dominion Stone covered their hiding place."

"What *is* the Stone?" Grant asked as he continued to quietly spin.

"A marker, pointing to both the past and the future. They say it cannot be destroyed. But somehow, it was broken centuries ago by the enemies of the Secretum. Wars were fought for centuries for possession of the Stone and the rings—most especially *your* ring, the Seal of Dominion. Legend has it that the Seal was sought by dictators and rulers the world over, including the likes of Napoleon, Hitler, and Alexander. But thanks to the efforts of the Secretum, the Seal has been kept safe throughout history, and no one was permitted to wear it. Until *you.*"

"Was it the ring that caused the Shift?" Grant asked.

"No," the Keeper replied. "*I* caused the Shift. You see—or well, I suppose you don't at the moment, but if you could—I'm wearing a ring myself, a ring almost as special as yours. Not gold in color but silver, with a blue stone. And the talent it gives me is the transfer of consciousness from one living being to another."

"How can you be one of the Loci if I can't feel you?"

"There has always been a Keeper to lead the Secretum, and the Keeper has worn the ring I now wear since the Secretum was formed. They say that it was stolen—*taken*—from the opposite number of he who once owned *your* ring. The one this ring was taken from—'He alone knows the soul of man,'" the Keeper quoted knowingly. "And as the Secretum came to realize, if you can *see* a thing, then you can *change* it."

"Why do all this?" Grant said, trying not to shout. His rage was resurfacing in the form of impatience. "Why bother Shifting us, if it's not necessary for using the rings?"

"Now you're disappointing me," the Keeper said edgily. "There is only *one* practical application of this: *anonymity*. Think of it, Grant. You are the most powerful being on the planet, yet for all intents and purposes, *you do not exist.* Untrackable. Untraceable. A member of society, yet completely unknown by it. You're the perfect soldier. You can do *anything* by simply thinking it, and no one need ever know who you are."

Tears formed behind Grant's eyes once again, soaking into the cloth over his eyes.

"This body I'm wearing, these people you put us inside of . . . who were they before?"

"Husks. Vessels," the Keeper said with a hint of disgust. "Yours was a soldier who worked in covert ops, which is why you're able to fight so well. His instincts remain in you. But they were volunteers, all of them. For them, it was the highest calling."

"You've killed so many. You're responsible for *everything* that's happened to me, aren't you?"

"Of course."

"But why send Konrad and Drexel to try and kill me? How does that help you?"

"All part of the process. The apartment, the money, the car—it all came from me. Resources you needed to fulfill your role. If you hadn't been through everything you've gone through, if you hadn't learned, adapted, and grown with each new experience . . . if you hadn't *survived*, then you wouldn't have been worthy of your destiny. But I never doubted it."

Grant was reminded of something Daniel had told him the day they met.

"Where you see random occurrences, I see a purpose," Daniel had said.

Alex tensed.

Whatever else may have been happening here, this man was starting to get through to Grant. She could see it. She could practically feel the wheels turning in Grant's head.

And there was no time . . .

High above them, reality itself was rending at the seams, falling apart. Plunging the world into ruin.

Come on, Grant . . . make a move!

"So now you know the truth about how you were made. Above us is the *why*," the Keeper said simply. "Aboveground, the surface is crumbling. A cataclysm like nothing the earth has ever seen is taking place."

"You're just going to turn me loose to go fight it?" Grant asked incredulously, his temperature still rising.

"It's not quite that simple," the Keeper replied. "Destiny has come calling. But it's still up to you to answer."

Grant frowned.

"You must pass the final test. *Prove* to me that you are prepared to take this all the way. Right now, I have three armed men with semi-automatic weapons ready to fill Alex's body with holes—"

"Leave her alone!" Grant screamed.

"That choice is yours to make. They will obey *your* command. If you tell them to, they'll fire, and you'll be released to go perform your function. If you order her life spared, then countless others will lose their lives to the threat above. Prove to me that you're willing to pay any price to get the job done, and this will end."

Grant was trembling.

"I don't care if you *are* my grandfather, you're either very brave or very foolish to be making me angry," he said quietly.

"I have nothing to fear from you," the Keeper replied matter-of-factly. "You're powerless until *I* let you go. You can't even save Alex in your current state."

Grant gave a calm, easy laugh and his body relaxed.

On his finger he felt the warm glow of his ring begin to rise.

"I don't *have* to save her," Grant said. His blindfolded head slowly turned to point straight at Alex's location across the room, and stayed fixed on her position as he continued to rotate. "I can *feel* her."

The tape ripped itself off of Alex's mouth, and he heard her shout, though it seemed more in delight than pain.

"*Terror*," Alex said to the guards surrounding her, and Grant heard the men howl in fright and dropping to the floor.

Grant continued to whirl in place but he felt Alex next to him. And her ring.

"We removed your ring," the Keeper growled. "How could you possibly?"

"How quick the mighty forget," she said, rising from the table. " 'A ring can only be removed after its wearer dies,'" she recited.

"Hannah . . . *her* ring . . ." he whispered. He backed away.

"You may not have to *fear* your grandson, bubbles," she said, nodding at Grant. "But if you remember what *I* can do with one of these things"— she held up her ring—"then you should *fear me!*"

At the word *fear,* Grant heard the man topple, screaming and begging.

"By the way," Alex said, her voice closer now. "*I quit.*"

Grant heard her scuffling about him and then the sound of gears clicking into place. At once, his spinning slowed, then a few seconds later, stopped entirely. Alex pulled the cover from Grant's eyes and he forced himself to stand, despite his dizziness.

He looked up for the first time at the vast chamber they were in. Overflowing with scientific equipment and gear, as well as computer stations and huge monitors, the room was monstrous in size, stretching several stories high. Balconies overlooked their position from above. The Dominion Stone rested on an easel nearby, a bright spotlight illuminating it from overhead.

Grant approached his grandfather, who was still cowering on the floor, shivering.

Grant, too, was shaking. But not in fear.

Alex grabbed him by the arm. "We've got to go—"

They were knocked off of their feet by an explosion.

Alex lost her concentration and the Keeper sprang to his feet, fingering a remote device of some kind in his hand.

"That's more like it," he said, eyeing Grant. "I've been waiting for you to exert yourself."

A contingent of over fifty soldiers—all wearing gray jumpsuits with no insignia—entered the chamber, surrounding them on every side.

"Grant," Alex said, grabbing his arm again, "knock these guys out and let's just get out of here."

But Grant wouldn't budge, his eyes locked on his grandfather.

"Grant, forget him! Don't listen to anything he says!" she exclaimed.

"You really think I would *let* you escape?" the Keeper replied. "You think I wouldn't be *prepared?*"

His finger was still on the remote, even though the bomb it triggered had already gone off . . .

"Consider that first blast just a warm-up. His big brother is next, more than enough force to level this entire cavern and bring the building on the surface crashing down as well."

"You're willing to kill yourself over this? *Why?*" Grant asked between hard breaths.

"When I called you on the telephone earlier, I sealed my fate by defying the Secretum. I am no longer one of them; their purposes for you are not *mine*. *I* want to unleash your full potential. That's all I've ever wanted. The Secretum wants you under its thumb. They believed I was working toward that goal, but I wanted what was best for my blood and kin. To do that, your defenses had to be removed one-by-one through a carefully calculated game. I'm sorry for the pain the process has caused you, but it was the only way."

"And the Loci?" Grant panted. "Why did you do this to them?"

"Package deal. They're your army. Created to suit your specific needs, as the Bringer. The Forging has bonded you to them forever."

Grant looked around, into the eyes of the soldiers surrounding them. He was sure he could take all of them with a single thought, but didn't think he could stop his grandfather from pressing that trigger at the same time.

The Keeper rolled his eyes again, watching Grant. "My boy, if you had any *inkling* of what you were doing at all, you could have called the others here to help you by simply *thinking* it."

Grant met his grandfather's eyes with an even, triumphant glare.

"He did," a voice called from high above.

It was Payton.

The Keeper turned sharply to look up. His eyes danced at the sight of dozens of ring wearers encircling them on the balconies above.

All of their fingers were glowing.

64

"Payton," the Keeper said in recognition. "I had such high hopes for the Thresher."

"Anyone else *bored*?" Payton called out.

With that, he leapt over the edge of the balcony and landed neatly on the ground floor. If he ached from his recent battle with Konrad, he didn't show it. Sword in hand, he was off, slicing into guards on all sides in blurry swells of movement.

Grant used the distraction to force the bomb trigger out of his grandfather's hand and it sailed across the room.

The others above them followed Payton's lead, some jumping down as he did, others finding safer routes. All were met by the gray-clad guards, fists flying, guns blazing.

The guards outnumbered the Loci, but the battle was woefully one-sided. Payton zipped about, stabbing and parrying, taking down two or three at a time . . . Alex forced fear or embarrassment or misery into the hearts of everyone she looked upon . . . Morgan and Fletcher had put their heads together earlier and planted booby traps in connecting corridors, and now triggered them as some of the guards tried to flee . . . Even Daniel and Lisa were in the fight. They had stolen Taser guns from the Inveo plant the previous night and now used them on any nearby target.

Grant and his grandfather squared off in a solitary corner of the room. They began circling opposite one another, mirroring each other's moves.

Neither took his eyes off the other.

"What are you not telling me?" Grant bit out his words. "What is this *really* about? What's the big thing up top that 'only I can stop'?"

The Keeper's eyes flashed, briefly.

The building was rumbling again, keeping time with Grant's anger.

"It's you, isn't it?" Grant spat. "*You're* doing it. I kill you, and it all stops."

He wasn't asking.

The Keeper edged closer to Grant and then froze in place.

"No, my boy," he replied. "It's *you.*"

Grant froze, his mouth gaped open.

"The darkness," the Keeper said, "the storm raging in the skies above . . . it's the pain you feel. Your hatred for me. Your grief over Hannah. Your *blind rage!*"

Grant's head began shaking from side to side.

The Seal glowed, brighter and brighter . . .

"No . . ." he whispered weakly.

"What did you *think* this was about!" his grandfather roared, his countenance suddenly altering its cool exterior to reveal a venomous contempt. "You miserable little fool . . . it was *always* about *YOU!!*"

A mighty rumble shook the ground beneath them . . .

His ring glowed brighter . . .

But Grant was too stunned to move. His eyes were hazed over, lost, unfocused, looking far away at nothing.

This isn't happening . . .

It can't be true . . .

"The Bringer is a *force of destruction,*" the Keeper shouted. "The power of the atom . . . the energy of the sun . . . Crumbs on the table compared to what you're capable of. There is only one universal truth in this life: you are either *in* control, or you are *under* it. I've seen to it that *you* will take control of your own destiny and sweep through this world like nothing that has ever been. *You* will seize it and make it your own. *That* is your destiny, boy! It's the reason I saw to it that you were born. You will *take* dominion over this earth. Whether you want it or not!"

"But why?!" Grant cried. "*Why* did it have to be me?"

"History marches, son," the Keeper said, and he began side-stepping again, "and this is your moment in it. There is *nothing left* but for you to play the role that history has written for you—the Secretum has seen to that. It simply *is* what is."

"No," Grant tried to cry out with all that was in him, but only a whisper came to the surface. He was too lost, unmoving, staring straight ahead—almost catatonic.

He tried to focus his emotions, tried to concentrate on being calm, tried to quiet the storms within and without.

But all he could think of was Hannah and Julie and his father and his life that had been stolen and the innocent people above who were dying now and the blood that still soaked his clothes down to his skin.

"If only you could rein in those out-of-control emotions . . ." the Keeper taunted, circling him. "But you *can't*, can you? You've been pushed too far. You've lost *everything*! You've slipped over the edge and now you're falling. Farther and farther you go—do you feel it? There is *nothing* but grief and hate and pain. There's no one left for you to love."

A war raged inside Grant. As hard as he wanted to contain his emotions, all he could do was *feed* them. It was too much. The Keeper was right; he *had* gone over the edge and there was no coming back now.

Maybe he *should* just let go, it would feel so *good* . . .

The ring was glowing so brightly now, and it felt *right* . . .

"I have given you the ultimate power, my boy," the Keeper's voice intoned evenly. "You can change the world itself with a *thought*. You're in control. And I can only imagine what you must want to do to me at *this very moment* . . ."

Give in, Grant, he thought desperately.

Just give in.

Every blood vessel, every pore, every hair follicle on his body was screaming it.

Destroy him!

It will be so easy . . .

Grant was losing himself, he could feel it, and he didn't care . . .

Let the world turn to ash.

Nothing matters anymore, anyway.

"Do it!" the Keeper screamed maniacally. "Destroy this place! Take control and *bring the whirlwind!!*"

Grant bore down with all that was within him and beat it back.

"*No!*" he screamed and backhanded his grandfather so hard the old man flew across the room.

His knees buckled and he collapsed onto them.

Grant balled his fists and closed his eyes, straining to rein it in.

"Foolish child," the Keeper was saying. "Reluctance has *always* been your downfall. *Must* you take time to *think* about everything? That was your mother's fatal flaw as well, you know."

Time seemed to stop, and the struggle within Grant paused as he turned to the old man.

"My mother died giving birth to me. She died during labor."

A smile played at the edges of the Keeper's lips and he nodded. "*During* labor."

He got up off the floor and stepped closer to Grant.

"But not *from* labor," he said.

A titanic blast of energy exploded from Grant, shattering half the building.

The earth shook violently.

"*You murdered her!!*" Grant screamed.

The Seal shone so brightly now that the Keeper had to put a hand up to block it from his eyes, barely able to see through the glare.

But Grant could see the old man shrug indifferently as he struggled to remain upright. "She spit out the boy I needed," his grandfather said. "Her purpose was concluded. And she intended to keep you from me. I had no option."

The earth's rumbling grew stronger as Grant's face turned beet red.

Blood, hate, adrenaline, and rage surged through his entire being.

"I'll never forget the *sound* she let out," the Keeper shouted over the din, "as I put my gun into her chest and pulled the trigger. It was ear-splitting, like nothing I've ever heard! You gave your very first cry at that same moment, Grant. It was the sound of birth *and* death. And it changed the world."

Grant's fingernails dug grooves into his scalp, he wanted to yank out his hair by the fistful, this was just too much, he couldn't hold it in anymore, he was going to explode and deliver the world into the same madness that now consumed him . . .

"Come on, Grant," the Keeper said cloyingly. "*Become* the Bringer."

The building began to shake free of its foundations, crumbling all around. The great steel panels fell hard. Mortar, Sheetrock, and concrete crashing to the ground and shattering on impact.

It was a disaster zone.

"Everybody out!" Payton shouted.

"The Dominion Stone!" Morgan yelled, moving toward it.

"Leave it, there's no time!" Payton replied.

Alex stopped her efforts and turned to where she'd last seen Grant circling his grandfather. He was collapsed on the floor, head buried in his hands, and sobbing so loud she could hear it over the noise and destruction. The Keeper stood over him, speaking into his ear. And his ring was glowing brighter than the sun.

"*Grant!*" she screamed.

He didn't move.

The building was coming down, there was no time left.

She was barely aware of Payton grabbing her by the arm and pulling her toward the exit.

"No! Something's wrong—we have to help him!" she cried.

But it was no use, everyone was running, stampeding from the building. No one even heard her protests.

Only Grant and his grandfather remained inside as the outer walls of the building crashed down in a terrible cacophony. The destruction was working its way in, and Grant felt powerless to stop it.

This was who he was.

He was the Bringer.

Death and destruction were his reality, his purpose.

"No, Grant, you *know* who you are," a female voice said.

He looked up.

The room was gone, replaced by familiar swirling clouds of purple and pink. But he remained on the ground, and he could still feel the building quaking around him.

His mother approached and knelt before him.

"This is not your hour, Grant."

Yes, it is! he thought to her.

"No, baby," she said, watching him with utmost compassion. "Not this day."

His tears followed him to this place, even though he'd once thought that tears couldn't exist here.

Wherever "here" was.

They soaked his face, and he didn't care. *I want it to end!* he cried. *I can't keep going anymore! It's too much. He took you away from me, and I just want it to end!*

"I know," she said, smiling but sad. "One day you and I will get back the time that was stolen from us."

He sobbed.

"But not yet. Do you remember what I said to you?" she asked gently.

You said I had to be willing to sacrifice to reach the journey's end.

She nodded soothingly. "*Are* you?"

NO! he protested. *I can't go any farther!! NO MORE!!*

"You must," another voice said.

Grant looked up and gasped.

A second person stood before him amidst the clouds.

It was Julie.

Julie . . . are you dead?

"No. Don't you recognize this place? It's our safe house, where you and I meet in our dreams."

His sister was unlike he had ever seen her before.

She was radiant. Gone was the evidence of her illness, her injuries. She was still, at peace. She glowed with more than mere light. Her smile beamed down upon him, and he could *feel* it caressing his skin.

I don't have anything left! he cried. *I can't do this anymore, Julie, I can't!*

"That's a lie," Julie replied without accusation. "This flesh," she said, "is telling you to give up. It's telling you to let go. But *you are more.*"

I can't . . . This isn't . . . I . . .

"You promised me," she said gently.

He looked up at her.

"Never give up or give in," she said. "No surrendering to despair. I held up my end. And I want my brother there with me when I open my eyes."

But I'm not even me *anymore!* he exploded. *I don't know* who *I am!*

Julie took his hands and placed them over her heart.

"Listen to me," she said.

The clouds began to flash and fade, the underground complex peeking through. The rumbles and quakes grew worse still, and the entire building shuddered, ready to fall.

"*Listen*," she said again, and he focused on her calm, glowing face. "The face changes," she said slowly, with great seriousness. "The body breaks. And blood runs cold."

He looked up into her face, tears streaming out of him.

She leaned in closer to him and smiled, holding his eyes in gentle contact.

"But *who you are* . . ." she said, placing a hand over his chest, "is *indestructible*."

A gust of air escaped his lips as his chest collapsed, and he cried in tremendous heaves.

Julie squeezed his hand. Grant cried out and threw himself around her shoulders, holding her tight.

And he felt the warmth of her heart flowing through him.

The tears came down but they were different than before. Now they were strengthening him.

After a long squeeze, he let her go, and Julie backed up to stand beside his mother.

They both watched him, beaming with warm smiles.

Swimming in the warm feelings they flooded him with, Grant squared his shoulders.

He placed one hand on the cloudy ground beneath him.

And very slowly, he extended his legs.

The moment he was on his feet again, reality returned and he was inside the crumbling underground structure.

The ring on his finger—the Seal of Dominion—was glowing too brightly to look at. Its shimmering light filled up the entire chamber.

Still the Keeper stood there watching him, oblivious to the danger.

Grant took a deep breath and let it out slowly.

Peacefully.

He turned to face his grandfather.

And the earthquake immediately stopped.

Grant knew without seeing that the violence raging in the skies above, outside, had vanished also.

The Seal stopped glowing, as if someone had simply unplugged it.

But the underground structure was too far gone, and it continued its imminent collapse.

The Keeper's eyes grew big, disbelief written across his face. "What are you *doing*? Your hour is at hand! The prophecy—"

Grant didn't react. He only looked at the old man in pity.

"The Secretum wants to twist you and use you for their own purposes! But I made you master of your own fate! Will you so easily throw away the control I've given you?"

Grant spoke softly. "In all this time, has it never occurred to you that perhaps none of *us* are the ones in control?"

He turned away from him and walked to where the Dominion Stone stood on its easel. The spotlight that had shown upon it had long since fallen there in the dying building. But the tablet itself stood upright, stubbornly clinging to its easel.

He pushed the whole thing over.

"What are you *doing*?" the Keeper screamed.

"Making my choice," Grant replied simply.

The Keeper stared at Grant, thunderstruck yet making no move to stop him or even flee. "The Secretum is forever, boy! Even if I fall, another will take my place!"

Grant walked calmly away, though he could hear his grandfather's voice screaming, fading in the distance . . .

"You really think you can *resist* the Seal of Dominion?! Your destiny is written in stone! You may keep it at bay for a time, but the Seal is chaos, and it cannot be restrained!"

The structure finally collapsed and came to a rest behind Grant, his grandfather's echoes dying away, as he found his way back to the elevator.

Great billows of smoke chased him up the elevator shaft. He was forced to exit through the subway, as more quakes on the surface had collapsed much of the Wagner Building.

Ascending the subway stairs, he was greeted by blue skies and the light of a bright, beautiful, cloudless morning.

Cresting the top of the stairs and out onto the sidewalk, he found the others there waiting for him. But they weren't looking at him.

An enormous crowd had gathered, watching them. Quizzical expressions colored the spectators' faces. Every age, every race, every working class, every walk of life was represented among those who looked at the long line of men and women who had emerged from the collapsing building they stood before.

Grant, Alex, Morgan, Payton, Fletcher, Daniel, Lisa, and over a dozen others stood side-by-side in a row, stunned at the sight of the sea of people before them.

The world had just changed in plain view of everyone there. It would never be the same again.

No one spoke, as both sides of this strange spectacle looked at the other in consternation.

Grant's group certainly appeared the most bizarre, especially Grant himself. He was covered in soot and grime and blood, his clothes were torn, his hair was mussed, he looked as though he had drowned in sweat and tears.

He glanced down at the abominable object that rested on his finger and would never come off. His thoughts turned to his mother and his father. And to his sister, whom he knew would be awake soon.

And he thought of Hannah, as he looked back into the eyes of every person there. They seemed more interested in him than any of the others.

It was as if they were waiting. Watching, to see what he would do next.

From the corner of his eye he saw Alex surveying the crowd in front of them. She seemed like she expected it somehow. After a second, she turned to him, looked him in the face and, with a frown said, "You're not gonna *cry* again, are ya?"

Despite himself, despite everything, Grant grinned wide.

Then he laughed.

Out loud.

So hard his shoulders shook.

"Help me!"

Grant's head snapped up, scanning the crowd. The others did the same.

"Fear of falling," Alex said, squinting, looking about. "I feel it . . . over there!" She pointed past the crowd.

The entire crowd turned to look as Grant and the rest did, and saw a woman dangling from a metal fire escape ledge, three stories off the ground, just one block away.

Grant felt Alex's hand on his shoulder just then, but he didn't look at her.

There was no need.

No need for any more words.

He was tired, emotionally spent, every muscle in his body ached.

He had absolutely *nothing* left.

"Somebody please!" the woman screamed in the distance.

Grant set his jaw firmly in place.

Every person present watched and waited.

Waited for someone who would save the day.

"I can't reach!" the woman cried.

Grant let out a steadying breath.

He stepped forward.

"Hold on," he called out. "I'm coming."

EPILOGUE

Substation Omega Prime
The Secretum of Six
Ruling Council Inner Chamber

Far away and buried deep beneath the earth's surface, the ruling body of the Secretum of Six scanned the latest report. Glances were exchanged, notes written on paper.

"Substation L.A. is lost," one of them said, "as is the Dominion Stone."

"The Stone no longer matters," Devlin replied at the head of the table. Today his accent of choice was a hard, German inflection. "Its absence serves our end goal. Everything is falling precisely into place, as we've always known it would."

"Maximilian Borrows is dead," offered another.

"Also irrelevant," a woman spoke up. "Another will be chosen. What matters is that we have what we have awaited for so long. The Bringer has come."

Devlin smiled and intoned in his booming deep voice, "The prophecy of Dominion is fulfilled. The one we have prepared for and awaited for thousands of years walks among us. Everything is unfolding as we know it must. And do not forget, we still have a great advantage."

"What advantage?" the woman asked.

"The wheels turn all around him," Devlin replied. "Yet the Bringer does not see . . . does not *know* . . . what he will *bring*."

THE DOMINION TRILOGY
by Robin Parrish
continues . . .

BOOK II
Summer 2007

BOOK III
Summer 2008

ACKNOWLEDGMENTS

Thanks to ...

- My entire family for putting up with my insane work schedule. Special thanks to my wonderful, long-suffering wife Karen for enduring the "must write now" absences of your newlywed husband. We're in this together, babe. Now and forever.

- Ted Dekker for your friendship and all the great career advice.

- My friends Todd, Tina, John, Laura, Dylan, Mary P., Steve, and Mary S. for all the prayers and encouragement. Thanks for not letting me give up.

- All of the teachers, professors, and writing professionals who have, over the years, offered instruction and support.

- My editor David Long and his magic pencil.

- My brother Ross and his family, for always showing excitement and wanting to help.

- Mom, for demonstrating faith, expressing love, and always letting me chase my dreams.

- And my Father above, for proving to me time and again that everything is under your perfect control. You are so good to me.

Be the first *to know*

Want to be the first to know
what's new from
your favorite authors?

Want to know all about
exciting new writers?

Another New Voice in Suspense!

Jude Allman is hiding. Hiding from the world and hiding from God. Because when you come back from the dead three times, the world wants to know all about you, all the time. And it becomes clear that God may have something in mind for you, too.

When a terrible danger threatens those Jude loves the most, he realizes that his days of hiding are over. Does he have enough faith in God's faith in him to come out of his secure hiding place and risk truly living for the first time in years? Will it happen soon enough to save those he loves?